Every Crooked Nanny

Every Crooked Nanny

Mary Kay Andrews

HARPER

NEW YORK · LONDON · TORONTO · SYDNEY

HARPER

This book was originally published, with the author writing under the name Kathy Hogan Trocheck, as *Every Crooked Nanny* by HarperCollins in May 1992 and was reissued in mass market in 2004.

HarperCollins books may be purchased for educational, business, or sales promotional use. For information, please e-mail the Special Markets Department at SPsales@harpercollins.com.

FIRST HARPER PAPERBACK PUBLISHED 2013.

Library of Congress Cataloging-in-Publication Data is available upon request.

ISBN 978-0-06-219508-1

23 24 25 26 27 LBC 14 13 12 11 10

For my family with love,
especially Tom, Katie, and Andy,
and all the rest of the Hogans and Trochecks

A Note from Mary Kay Andrews

Dear Reader:

Twenty or so years ago, a character popped into my head and insisted I write her story. Julia Callahan Garrity was a feisty former Atlanta police detective turned private investigator turned owner of a cleaning business called the House Mouse. Callahan, her mom, Edna, and the House Mouse "girls" stuck around for eight installments. Over the years, I've aged (haven't we all?), but Callahan, being Callahan, has refused to follow suit. So when my publisher, HarperCollins, proposed re-issuing the Callahan mysteries in a new format, I agreed—up to a point. I may have aged twenty years and acquired a new pseudonym, a smart phone, and a Facebook page, but Callahan remains Callahan. She is still driving that beat-up pink van around circa-1990s Atlanta, fighting grime, and solving crimes—without the benefit of Google or a GPS. She is steadfastly "old school" and proud of it. I hope you'll enjoy meeting Callahan—or renewing an acquaintance with her and her friends—and that you'll enjoy these stories as they were originally written.

All my best,
Mary Kay Andrews

Acknowledgments

The author wishes to thank all those she bugged, questioned, nagged, verbally assaulted or otherwise contacted for assistance in writing this book. Any mistakes or missteps here are my own and not theirs. Those who gave legal advice include Elizabeth Belden, Warren Davis, Bill Hankins, Jerry McCumber, Leslie Fuller Secrest and Janet Ward. Major Timothy J. Buckley of the Marietta (Georgia) Police Department contributed Irish wit and valuable advice on police procedure. Richard Hansen, M.D., and Susan Hogan, R.N., gave medical advice. Other technical assistance was rendered by Paul Kelman of Central Atlanta Progress, Atlanta Pretrial Detention Center Director Tom Pocock, J.H. Matthews, security chief of downtown Rich's Department Store, Lynne Jackson, who explained the LDS lifestyle for me, and Thomas W. Trocheck, my resident engineer, development specialist and computer repairman. Thanks are due also to my literary agent, Sallie Gouverneur, who took on a neophyte despite her better judgement. I am grateful also to my former colleagues at the *Atlanta Journal-Constitution*, who advised, critiqued, and encouraged. A special thanks is due to a very special lady, Celestine Sibley, who opened the door and showed me the way.

Although some streets, locations, and neighborhoods referred to in this novel are authentic, the author has occasionally rearranged Atlanta geography to suit her own purposes. This is a work of fiction. The characters, incidents, and dialogue are the product of the author's imagination, and resemblance to actual events or persons, living or dead, is entirely coincidental.

Every Crooked Nanny

I

I KNEW IT WAS GOING TO BE a bad day when Neva Jean called that early in the morning.

"Callahan?" she said hesitantly.

"What is it now, Neva Jean?" She's one of the best housecleaners I have working for me, but you wouldn't believe the shit that happens in her personal life.

Neva Jean hesitated again. "No use lying. You'll find out anyway. Me and Swanelle were on our way to Valdosta Friday night when we got in a big fight. You know Swanelle's temper. Well, he got so mad at me he pulled into a Waffle House outside Macon, put me out of the truck, and took off and left me standing there. Me with nothin' but a bottle of Mountain Dew in one hand and the Danielle Steel paperback I was readin' in the other. Left me standing there in the middle of the parking lot wearing my house shoes."

I sighed, loudly. "Where are you now, Neva Jean? And how much money do you need to get back here right away? I've got you scheduled to work every day this week, and two of the other girls are already out sick."

There was extended throat-clearing at the other end of the phone. "I'm still in Macon, honey," she wailed. "Some of the girls working at the Waffle House have been taking turns putting me up, and they let me clean up there in return for meals, but my purse is in Swanelle's truck, and if I know him, he's gone off on a toot.

You reckon you could wire me bus fare back to Atlanta? You know I'm good for it."

I scrabbled on the kitchen table and found my checkbook. My balance had been lower, but not much. "Will twenty-five dollars do it, Neva Jean?"

"I reckon it'll have to," she said resignedly.

"Fine," I snapped. "Get somebody to give you a ride to Western Union, and I'll have Edna wire it to you. Make sure you're here by eight A.M. tomorrow. You've got the Mahaffeys and the Greenbergs, and you know they don't like anybody but you in their houses."

Just as I banged the phone down—hard—the front door slammed. Into my kitchen, which also serves as office and headquarters for the House Mouse, Atlanta Central Division, a cloud of cigarette smoke preceded a five-foot-two-inch woman in her early sixties. The blue hair was teased and tormented into an unnatural-looking winged creation I call her Hadassah do. It was Edna Mae Garrity, my live-in office manager and three-pack-a-day mother.

She set the morning paper down on the old oak kitchen table we share as a desk and sniffed the air.

"No coffee made?"

"I thought that was your job," I said, pointedly waving away the smoke she blew in my direction.

She deliberately shot a stream toward me, then turned toward the coffeepot. "You wanna tell me why you've got your panties in a wad so early on a Monday morning?"

I flipped open the daily appointment book and showed her a full day's worth of bookings penciled there in her own rounded, looping handwriting.

"We've got a full day's work, one big new client, and Jackie and Ruby are out sick. On top of that, Neva Jean just called; she's stuck in Macon with no money and can't possibly get back until tonight at the earliest."

Maybe I should explain here about the House Mouse. Jesus I hate that name. It's a cleaning service, actually. After I left the Atlanta Police Department last year, I had the hot idea of becoming a private detective. Lots of guys I know have done it after leaving the department. It seemed like a good idea at the time, but I overlooked one thing—my sex. Once I got my license, I found out fast that unless you're a man and latch on to one of those high-priced corporate-security consulting gigs, most private detective work is just nickel-and-dime skip-tracing and divorce work. Which I detest.

About then, Edna talked me into buying this cleaning service. Easy money, she'd said. She could get her longtime cleaning lady, Ruby, and some of Ruby's friends to come to work for us. And with all her contacts, neighbors, and friends, people she knew from the beauty parlor she'd managed for twenty years, we'd be in high cotton. She kicked in some money she'd been putting aside, and I took ten thousand out of my police pension fund and bought the business.

And since the stationery, brochures, and even the pink Chevy minivan that came with the deal all said HOUSE MOUSE, it was cheaper to keep the old name. Which I hate.

We operate out of my little bungalow in Candler Park, a nice tree-shaded neighborhood here in Atlanta. The business has grown steadily, I'll have to admit. I had no idea how many yuppies there were in this town who can't bring themselves to scrub their own toilets but who would gladly pay me or my girls $75 a half day to do it for them.

The downside is that every week some fresh disaster strikes. Either a heavy-duty vacuum cleaner burns out a motor, or one of the girls (most of whom are at least fifty) throws out her back, or some old biddy calls to complain we waxed her no-wax floor. Kind of makes you long for a nice clean Friday-night domestic knifing.

The disaster du jour on this particular Monday was three

clients who expected the House Mouse to show up this morning, and there I was with most of my mice out of commission.

Edna pulled the appointment book away from me and squinted at it through her bifocals. She's too vain to admit she needs glasses, so she makes do with these $4.99 K-mart specials. She tapped a pencil against her teeth, a sign of deep thought.

"OK, look, Jules," she said patiently. (She knows I hate to be called that.) "The Eshelmanns and the Browers can be switched to Wednesday. I'll call them and explain and offer to throw in a free window-washing for their trouble." (We usually charge $25 extra for windows.) "We can move Dr. Zimmerman too.

"But now these new people, the Beemishes, I hate to disappoint. Florence Foster recommended us to them. He's that big developer, you know, and their place over on Paces Ferry is huge. I quoted Mrs. Beemish one hundred seventy-five a week for the heavy cleaning, since they have a maid who does the light stuff, and she didn't bat an eyelash. If they like the House Mouse, they could set us up with a lot of those rich Northside clients, and then we could quit dicking around with these penny-ante fifty-dollar condo jobs."

I shot her a look for her dirty language, but she ignored it. Twenty years in a beauty parlor, and you pick up some amazing expressions. Anyway, even before my dad died and she went to work, Edna was never what you'd call a Southern Magnolia.

"Well, who do you suggest we get to do the Beemishes?" I asked.

She stared at me and sipped her coffee. "I'd go myself," she said, "but you know how my arthritis is. And they have stairs. Two flights. That's why I jacked the price up so high."

"I guess that leaves the head mouse."

"I guess it does," she agreed, pushing an appointment sheet across the table at me. "Here's our contract, with all the specifics on it and the address. Better take an antihistamine before you go; the place is thick with dust. And remember, this time vacuum the refrigerator vents and clean the tile grout in all the bathrooms.

The last time we sent you out you forgot to do it, and Ruby had to go out the next day to finish up."

I glared at her, but she was busily filling out the crossword puzzle in the paper and didn't look up. I grabbed the assignment sheet, and she lifted her head and swept her eyes over my torn T-shirt and jeans.

"You're not going to the Beemishes like that, I hope," she said. "The uniform service delivered some clean smocks and pants on Friday. And don't forget to put on a pair of white shoes. These rich people like to have the help dress like help."

2

_____

AS I PULLED ONTO Paces Ferry Road, I suddenly snapped out of the coma I usually fall into when I drive. Ten years as a cop in Atlanta, and in some parts of town I automatically go on autopilot. Buckhead was one of those places. I'd been a patrol officer in Zone 2 for four years, so the billowing white dogwoods, rolling green lawns, high wrought-iron fences, and Italianate mansions were ancient history to me. I sniffed the air for a whiff of my favorite spring scent, new-mown grass. Instead I got a lungful of eau de carbon monoxide. Glancing in the rearview mirror I saw black smoke roiling from the van's tailpipe.

Damn. I had no clue what was wrong. Since I'd bought the van along with the other House Mouse equipment three months ago—it was an '85—I'd already put $800 into it. Now the thing probably needed a ring job or some other faintly sexual-sounding and equally expensive repair. We'd need at least two or three decent new accounts to pay for that smoke.

The fence in front of the Beemishes' house was actually a pink stucco wall with an elaborate wrought-iron gate set into it. I pulled off the street and stopped at a contraption that looked like an old speaker from the Twilight Drive-In. A red button glowed and a static-broken voice said, "May I help you?"

I suppressed the urge to order a double Wendy's with chocolate shake, no fries. The gate swung open noiselessly. I noticed the wrought-iron curlicues actually formed interlocking _B_'s. In the corners, iron bumblebees hovered over dogwood blossoms. Nice.

As the van chugged down the driveway, I saw the smoke getting thicker, and now I heard a clunking noise coming from under the hood. Excellent. Now I could not only act like poor white trash, I could look the part.

It was a short but scenic trip to the front of the house. Spanish Revival from the '20s, I'd guess, with graceful balconies on the second story and a massive carved wooden front door. The drive circled around the front of the house, past a round rose garden in full bloom. A slim blond woman dressed in tennis whites was deep in discussion with an ancient black man in a straw pith helmet. I followed the drive around to the side, where a worn pickup truck was parked beside a vintage Cadillac. The help's cars, I guessed. A pink stucco garage held a white Mercedes station wagon with a vanity tag that read PEACH.

I pulled into a slot beside the pickup, shut off the ignition, and winced as the engine continued knocking.

The blonde rounded the corner, trailed by her gardener. She was like any other woman you might see bounding around the courts of the Piedmont Driving Club on a spring day. About five foot seven, the hair artfully teased and sprayed into the artificial wind-blown look uniformly adopted by that genus and species known in Atlanta as "Buckhead bitch." She was deeply tanned, her thin arms sprinkled with freckles. The shirt was white cotton, tucked neatly into a little white pleated skirt that reminded me of a high school cheerleader uniform. I'd bet she wore lace-trimmed spanky pants under it. The outfit was finished off with brand-new white Avias.

This had to be Mrs. Beemish's tennis outfit for gardening. In Buckhead, casual wear means tennis wear. The women have tennis outfits for shopping at the A&P, tennis outfits for driving carpool to Westminster Academy, the tony private school where they send their kids, even tennis outfits for tennis.

She stopped in front of me, put her hands on her hips, cocked her head, and let out a tinkling laugh.

I put out my hand. "Mrs. Beemish. I'm—"

She shook her head and laughed again. "Julia Garrity, what on earth are you doing working for a cleaning service? Is this some kind of undercover operation?"

OK, she knew me from before, obviously from college days, when I still used my first name instead of my more businesslike middle name, which I'd adopted in the training academy.

"Actually, no, I'm no longer with the police department," I said coldly. "I own the House Mouse. Look, do we know each other?"

She laughed that laugh again. It did have a familiar ring, come to think of it. Then she held out the hem of her short skirt and did a little pirouette. "Take a good look. Think fifteen years younger, forty pounds fatter, dishwater-brown hair, and the Tri Delt House at Georgia."

Christ on a crutch! "Oh, my God," I blurted out. "Lilah Rose Ledbetter! I never would have known you. Don't tell me you're Mrs. DuBose Beemish?"

She grabbed my hand and tucked it under her arm. "None other. Mama always said it was just as easy to fall in love with a rich man as with a poor one. So I shopped around until I met Bo at a Temptations concert at Chastain Park. We've been married eight years now. Wait until you see my two precious children!

"What about you, Julia, you never did get married, did you?" She didn't wait for an answer. Didn't need one obviously. The old Tri Delt hotline had probably already informed her of my long-term spinsterhood.

All this time, Lilah Rose was walking me around toward the front. Before going inside, she turned to the gardener, who was still trailing us.

"Cut about a dozen more of those Pink Perfections, Lester, then bring them around to the kitchen and put them in a bucket of warm water, OK? I want them to open up before the luncheon tomorrow."

She went through the front door of the house. The floors of the wide hallway were pale pink marble, the walls painted the same pale pink shade. A mammoth crystal chandelier hung overhead. On one wall a goldleaf console table was topped with a large Venetian glass mirror. The other wall was dotted with a collection of third-rate English landscape oils. (OK, I took art appreciation in college. I wasn't born a cleaning lady.)

We made a sharp right turn into a room that obviously served as the study. The walls were lined with pickled pine bookshelves loaded with the kind of leatherbound books interior designers buy by the inch instead of the title. There was a fireplace with a mantel of the same pickled wood and two huge overstuffed sofas covered with a black flowered chintz. The tables were littered with little snuffboxes, jade figurines, and silver picture frames. I hope Edna planned to charge the Beemishes extra for all the dusting we'd have to do.

Overhead was a huge brass chandelier, each candle arm topped with a tiny black lampshade. I could see the cobwebs from where I stood, and I didn't much like the idea of hauling a ladder in there to clean the damn things. This house was going to be a bitch. And even worse was the idea of cleaning toilets for a former sorority sister. Oh, she'd pay, all right.

Lilah Rose plunked down in one of the sofas and pointed to the one opposite. "Sit down, Julia. Let's catch up on old times before we get down to business, all right?"

Actually, I didn't have many fond memories of old times with Lilah Rose Ledbetter. I hadn't much liked her when she was homely back in college, and I liked her a damn sight less now that she was skinny, blond, and rich. She was part of a phase of my life that I found amusing and totally inexplicable: the sorority house, the rush parties, the whole thing. I'd joined because my favorite aunt had begged me to and insisted on paying for it. And, as Edna had pointed out, the Tri Delt house was a far nicer place to live and eat than anywhere she and Dad could have afforded. So I'd done the Greek thing for four years, and at the end I'd walked out of that life and into another one. That was all there was to it.

"Now, Julia," Lilah Rose was saying.

I interrupted. "It's Callahan now. Sounds more businesslike, and I like it better anyway."

"Sure, sugar," she said. "Anyway, I just remembered. I saw Noreen Deal at Junior League a couple months ago, and she said you'd left the police department to become a private investigator. So how on earth did you get into housecleaning from being a private eye?"

"I guess Noreen didn't hear I got out of security consulting." (Noreen Deal's mother is an old pal of Edna's.) "Earlier this year I had an opportunity to put some of my equity from the security business into this cleaning business. My accountant swears by diversification, you know."

OK, she didn't need to hear that my accountant was also my mother. And that I'd folded the private investigation business before it got me any deeper in the red than I already was.

Lilah Rose waved a hand. "Lord, don't I know about diversification! Bo has so many businesses I can't keep up with them all."

Before we could get any further into the girly-girl chitchat, a child's high-pitched scream erupted in the next room, followed by a wail, followed by the clatter of little feet headed our way. Suddenly two small children shot into the room and stationed themselves in front of Lilah Rose.

The older, a boy of about six, with sandy blond hair, pale blue eyes, and white-blond lashes, was dressed in one of those ridiculous short-all outfits. Long skinny legs stuck out from the shorts and ended in black cowboy boots. He was holding a wooden train engine in his hand and attempting to land a blow with it on the head of the other child, obviously his sister. She was about four, with the same eyes and hair, only her bob was topped by an enormous taffeta bow. She was dressed in a hand-smocked buttercup-yellow frock, with little white anklets and white kid shoes, with which she was delicately trying to kick her brother in the crotch.

"I'll kill you, you damn pest!" the boy shouted, clonking the girl over the head with the engine. The girl screamed in anger and pain and butted him in the stomach with her head. The two fell to the pastel dhurrie in a heap and started an all-out brawl.

Lilah Rose clapped her long acrylic-nailed hands together ineffectively. "Carter DuBose Beemish, stop that, you hear me? Meredith Ledbetter Beemish, get up right this instant!" The children, now engaged in trying to gouge each other's watery blue eyes out, ignored her.

"Stop it. Stop it right now," Lilah Rose shrieked, to no avail. Finally, she knelt down and slapped the boy's bare leg smartly with the palm of her hand. He screamed but quit trying to kill his sister and stood up.

"Mama," he said indignantly, "you know we don't hit. You hurt my feelings."

Tears welled up in Lilah Rose's eyes. "Oh, sugar, you're right. Mother is sorry, but she wanted you to stop hurting each other. Mother doesn't like her children to be angry at each other."

I fixed the children with a stare. Little beasts. I'd never had any children, probably wouldn't either, at this rate, but if these two had been mine, I'd have slapped them into the next county if they acted that way.

The little girl rose slowly and straightened her dress. "Mama," she wailed, though dry-eyed, "I'm feeling neglected and unhappy."

Lilah Rose gathered the children into her arms, stroking their mussed cornsilk hair. "Of course you are, sugar booger," she crooned. "Mother knows." She gave the children a final dose of effective parenting and a parting hug. "Scoot along now to Kristee, my loves. Mother wants to talk to this nice lady."

The boy blinked. "Kristee isn't here, Mama. We haven't seen her all morning."

His mother looked at the thin gold watch on her wrist. "Of course she's here, precious. She's probably out in the kitchen fixing you a snack."

The little girl stopped picking her nose and shook her head slowly. "No, she's not. She's not in the kitchen and she's not upstairs in her room and she's not out in the playhouse. Me and Carter looked. And her clothes are gone from her room. Mama, maybe Kristee ran away."

Lilah Rose sighed. "Excuse me, Callahan. Kristee is the children's nanny. She's Mormon, you know, from Utah. They are really so marvelous with children. She's supposed to take the children to a birthday party today. Let me just hunt her up and I'll be right down. Or, if you like, you could get started in the kitchen. Mrs. Garrity did say you do kitchens, right?"

I nodded and headed out the front door for the van, where I kept a rolling trolley full of cleaning supplies.

It took a few minutes to double-check the supplies and wrestle the vacuum cleaner out of the built-in rack in the side of the van and onto the bottom shelf of the trolley. I looked around past the garage and saw a door that looked to be the kitchen, so I headed that way.

Inside, Lilah Rose was talking into a white wall phone, in a voice that said she wasn't talking tennis dates. The freckles on her face stood out in relief, and the tan had turned a greenish shade.

"Yes, goddammit, I'm sure, Bo. I tell you she's not here. Her clothes are gone from her room. . . . No, the Mercedes is in the garage."

She stopped when she heard me enter and turned her back toward me. She lowered her voice, but I could still hear some of what she was saying.

"I think you better come home right away. Kristee's gone, and she didn't go empty-handed." There was a pause, and then her voice rose again. "I am not hysterical, I tell you, and I have no intention of taking a Valium. You just get home here and figure out what we're going to do about this!"

She slammed the phone down and began scrabbling around in a kitchen drawer. Finally her hand emerged, holding a pack of ultra-long menthol cigarettes and a silver filigree lighter. She lit up and sank down into a chair in the breakfast area.

I stood there frozen, not knowing whether to start cleaning or ask what was wrong.

"Goddamned Mormons. Supposed to be so damned dependable. Don't smoke, don't drink, don't fuck. Right? And we find the one fucking Mormon in Utah who does all of the above. She's probably halfway to fucking Salt Lake City by now."

I busied myself with a cleaning rag, spraying some Windex on the stainless-steel restaurant range.

After a few more minutes of ranting about jewelry and whatnot, Lilah Rose seemed to realize I was in the room again.

"I guess you've gathered we're in something of a crisis here, Callahan," she said slowly. "I'm just wondering if you couldn't help us out a little bit with this problem that's come up."

I stopped working on a grease spot on the back burner and pushed a hunk of hair out of my eyes. "I'm sorry, Lilah Rose," I said quickly. "House Mouse doesn't do child care. We don't have the insurance for it. We're strictly cleaning."

She laughed, but this time the tinkle was gone. "No, no, I don't mean with the children. I'll call a nanny agency here in town and get a temporary sent over today. What I need help with is more in the line of what you used to do, if you know what I mean."

I put the Windex back on the cart and sat down at the breakfast table. "Lilah Rose, maybe you better tell me what's going on."

3

___

THE LAST THING I NEEDED was to get back into the private detective business. No, House Mouse might be boring, but it was steady and safe, and if I could keep the equipment running and the girls healthy and out of jail, I looked to make a profit, albeit a small one, for my first year in business.

That said, we could really use some extra money. And my nosy gene wouldn't let me let it alone. Nosiness runs in my family, particularly among the women. My grandmother was a famous busybody in the small Florida town where she grew up, and Edna Mae—well, she managed the same beauty parlor for twenty years, and she didn't stay because the pay was so great. Beauty parlor gossip is generally high-octane stuff, and Edna Mae was hopelessly hooked. Although she supposedly works for me these days, she still subs on the books maybe one day a month at her friend Frank's place, the Salon de Beauté.

But back to Lilah Rose's problem, which I found absolutely irresistible. Lilah stubbed out her half-smoked cigarette in a small famille rose ashtray that sat on the glass-topped breakfast table and shakily lit another one.

"Well, as you've gathered, Kristee has taken a powder. Kristee may not even be her real name, I guess. But whatever her name is, the little bitch is a thief, a con artist, and a conniving little slut." She smiled a sad half smile. "It's not bad enough she was sleeping with my husband. When she left she took the family silver, some of my jewelry, the best pieces from Bo's coin collection, and God knows what else. The safe in Bo's office has been opened, but I have no idea what he keeps in there."

"Have you called the cops?"

"No-o-o," she said slowly, picking the pale pink polish off a fingernail. "Bo said to wait until he got home."

There was probably a good reason Bo Beemish didn't want the cops called in, especially if he was sleeping with this girl. I couldn't wait to hear the rest.

"Slow down," I said. I jumped up and went over to the cleaning cart and fetched my clipboard of blank contracts. I turned one over and started making notes, asking Lilah Rose to back up and repeat when it came to the important details.

"When did you last see her?"

Lilah sighed. "Let's see. I guess that'd be Friday—no, Thursday night. We were all at our place at Hilton Head over the weekend, and we got back so late last night I just assumed she was here, asleep."

"I'll need her full name, age, and where she's from," I said. "Also, tell me how you came to bring a Mormon girl from Salt Lake City to Atlanta, Georgia."

"Actually, she told us she was from a little town north of Salt Lake City. Toonigh, she said. I can only tell you what she told us. We checked her references, of course, and the agency highly recommended her, but a lot of good that did."

Her lips set in a tight line. "I should have known better than to get mixed up with somebody in a crazy religious sect. Big Mama, that's Bo's mother, she warned me, but I wouldn't listen.

"But honestly," she continued, "half the women in this neighborhood have hired these girls. Deanna Parish has had two girls who've kept her twins for the past three years. And the Eshelmanns and the Greenbergs have had Mormon nannies too."

"Did you hire Kristee from the same agency they used?"

"Well, no," she said, hesitating. "The agency they use requires that you pay for insurance and provide them with a car and give them two weeks' paid vacation a year. Plus they charge you a fifteen-hundred-dollar placement fee. Bo thought that was outrageous. But Polly Newman, that's the little Mormon girl who works for the Eshelmanns, she gave us the name of this agency back in Salt Lake City. She said it was new, and they weren't as expensive."

"So I called and talked to this woman who runs the place, Ardith something; I have her name in the file. She sounded really sweet. We talked for two hours about the kind of girl I was looking for.

"Two days later," Lilah Rose continued, "Ardith called me back. She said she had the perfect girl for us, Kristee Ewbanks. She sent us a snapshot. I'll have to say she's a cute little old blonde, with legs you'd kill for. So we talked to her on the phone, for about an hour, and we signed a contract and sent her a round-trip ticket to Atlanta. In September, she flew out and came to work for us."

"What can you tell me about her? What do you know about her family back home, previous employers, her friends here, things like that?"

Lilah ran her fingers through her short frostèd curls. "Well, some things I could tell you right off the bat, but for the rest, I'll have to get the folder I set up for her," she said. "It's in my desk in the study. I'll get it and be right back."

She ran out of the room, giving me a flash of her tanned thighs and—yes, lace-trimmed spanky pants.

In a minute, Lilah Rose was back, clutching a shiny hot-pink file folder. She sat down and leafed through half a dozen pieces of paper, plucked one out, and slid it across the table to me.

"Here's her contract," Lilah Rose said. "Bo had our attorney look it over, and he said it was all basic stuff."

The form itself was obviously a standard contract for services, the kind you can buy at any office supply or stationery store. At the top, someone had typed in NANNY FINDERS INC. and a Salt Lake City post office box with a telephone number. It specified that for a placement fee of $950, Nanny Finders would provide DuBose and Lilah Rose Beemish with a suitable household helper, namely Kristeena Ewbanks, age nineteen. Said nanny would be paid a weekly salary of $125, plus room and board, and would be given two days off a week.

The rest of the contract looked like boilerplate. The Beemishes had signed on one line, and the owner of the agency, one Ardith Cramer, had signed, as had Kristee Ewbanks.

By the time I finished reading the contract, I knew I was hooked. It would be criminally easy to track this kid down, even if she had taken off to Utah. I had an address for the employment agency, a snapshot of the girl, and probably a clear trail of silver, jewelry and coins, if she tried to sell anything. All I'd need to do would be to get one of my buddies at the police department to do a little computer time for me, and I should be home free. With a nice piece of change, especially if I upped my usual fee of $50 an hour to $65, plus expenses.

Besides, I told myself, I'd be doing a favor for an old sorority sister.

"What else have you got there?" I asked, handing back the contract.

Lilah gave me the entire folder. It wasn't much. There were two letters of reference, one from her high school principal, who said Kristee was a bright girl, dependable, of high moral fiber, and another from a woman for whom Kristee had babysat after school and during summers. There was a postcard from Kristee, with a picture of the seagull monument in Salt Lake City, telling the Beemishes how much she was looking forward to becoming a part of their family, and there was a travel agency voucher for a round-trip Delta airlines ticket between Salt Lake City and Atlanta.

"This is it?" I asked, looking up sharply. "No social security number, tax records, letters from the nanny agency? How about correspondence with her family? And where's the snapshot the agency sent you?"

Lilah Rose looked sheepish. "I gave the snapshot to the kids, so they would know what their new nanny looked like. To tell you the truth, I haven't seen it since. As for the other stuff, I never asked her for a social security number. She didn't want us to withhold taxes; she said the Mormons are against using taxes to buy weapons of war. And Bo said that was fine with him, he didn't need any more paperwork in his life."

A small buzzer went off in my head. I wasn't positive, but I felt pretty sure that the Mormons, whizzes at business matters, weren't the ones who refused to pay income taxes.

"Family?" I prodded.

It was clear that I was starting to get on Lilah's nerves. She picked at that pesky fingernail a few seconds before answering.

"She told us she was the baby of a big family—four brothers, all much older than she was. Said her mama had been dead four years, and last year her daddy up and married a girl who was only a couple years older than Kristee. The daddy and the stepmama were starting a new family, and Kristee didn't want to stick around."

"What about phone calls back home?"

She shook her head. "Not to her family, at least not as far as I know. But she did talk to that Ardith woman, I think, every once in a while. I could check the old phone bills, if that would help any."

I nodded. "What about friends? Did she socialize much in Atlanta? Do you know if she had a boyfriend?"

Here, Lilah perked up. "She had every Wednesday night off but she went out a lot of other nights too, because she said she had to go to youth group at the Mormon church. A stake, I think she used to call it. And I know for a fact she'd started dating somebody." Her face darkened. "Just between us, I was relieved when she said she had a boyfriend. I thought maybe she'd give up on Bo then. And I do think they stopped sleeping together, although I don't know if he was the reason why."

For the first time, I felt a pang for the new, rich Lilah Rose Beemish. I also wondered why she thought they had stopped sleeping together, but I refrained from asking. "Did she ever mention the boyfriend's name?"

Lilah scrunched up her face, deep in thought. "I think she said his name was Whit, or something like that, and he worked at some accounting firm here in town. She said she met him at church. But she had a girlfriend who works for another family in the neighborhood, Patti Jo Nemeyer. I'll get her phone number for you. She could probably tell you more about who Kristee's friends were."

Before I could pump her for any more information, a deep booming voice rang out from the front of the house. "Lilah Rose, where are you?"

Lilah Rose jumped out of her chair, stubbed out her cigarette, and quickly rinsed the ashtray in the sink. "Lord, there's Bo. Look, Julia, could you stay here for a few minutes, just till I explain what's going on to him? I don't know how he's going to feel about my hiring a private detective.

"And whatever you do, don't tell Bo I told you they were sleeping together, will you? He thinks I don't know, and I want him to go on thinking that way. I'll tell you one thing—I don't intend to let a nineteen-year-old nympho Mormon break up my marriage. At least, not yet."

She skittered out of the room before I could answer. I heard soft voices in the hall, then the sound of a door shutting.

Alone again, I looked around the kitchen. If I was going to get the cleaning finished before the Beemish kids reached puberty, I'd have to get started. I got a cleaning rag out of the supply cart. Even if Bo Beemish wouldn't agree to retain me to find the missing nanny, I'd still have the $175 that House Mouse planned to soak them for cleaning this mausoleum.

4

I WAS SITTING ON THE FLOOR, legs tucked under me Indian style, scraping away at some bright pink goo that appeared to be bubblegum stuck onto one of the lower kitchen cabinets, when I heard a deep male voice clearing itself. Without getting up, I swiveled around to face DuBose Beemish, who stood in the kitchen doorway, arms folded over his chest, surveying me as though I were part of the custom cabinetry.

How long he'd been watching me, I had no idea. Bo Beemish looked exactly as I'd imagined he would. Prematurely gray hair, lightly tanned face with red apple cheeks, icy blue eyes, deep cleft in his chin. He wore a nubby-weave silk sport coat, fashionably pleated khaki trousers, blue dress shirt open at the neck, with a necktie stuffed in his pants pocket. He wore no wedding ring. The large class ring on his left hand looked to be from Georgia Tech.

"You're the detective?" he said, in a voice that could only be called incredulous.

I scrambled to my feet, deposited my cleaning rag in a nearby bucket, and tried to regain my composure. The worst part of the cleaning business is having people treat you as though you were slave labor. I'd never gotten over the mixture of embarrassment and indignation I felt every time a client addressed me like a field hand.

Fuck you, buddy, I thought. You're the one in trouble here, not me. Out loud, my voice was cool, professional.

"I own the cleaning service your wife has contracted with for the heavy cleaning of your house. I'm also a former Atlanta police detective with ten years' experience. I have a master's degree from Georgia State University in criminology. I'd offer you my references, but as we've already seen from your experience with your missing nanny, references really don't mean all that much."

Beemish's eyes blazed for a moment; then he laughed. "Ain't that the goddamned truth," he drawled. "Well, come on back to the study and let's talk about what you're going to do to find this missing nanny." He walked over to a glass cabinet, reached in, pulled out a bottle of Johnnie Walker Red and a heavy cut-glass highball tumbler. "You drink Scotch?"

I shook my head. I'm a bourbon drinker myself, but I don't like to drink with people I don't know or with people I don't like. I didn't think I'd be drinking with DuBose Beemish.

I followed him back to the study, hurriedly smoothing my hair and wiping my hands on the seat of my jeans.

He seated himself behind the desk, poured himself two inches of Scotch, and took a long sip.

"Well." He sighed. "Lilah tells me she's filled you in on our little domestic crisis here. She also tells me she's tentatively agreed to hire you to see if you can't track down Miss Ewbanks."

"That's right. We haven't discussed terms or a contract or anything, though."

He smiled faintly. "Tell me, just what exactly do you propose to do for us? Should we sign a contract?"

I tried to hide my annoyance, but I think he got the picture. "I intend to do just what Lilah asked me to do: find the girl and, as far as possible, return your property to you. Whether or not you press charges will be entirely up to you, of course."

"Of course," he said, stirring the amber liquid with his index finger. "I was wondering how you intend to track her down without bringing in the police."

It was my turn to smile now. "Your wife has given me the file she assembled on Kristee. I'll start with the service that placed her. I'll also ask a friend to check the NCIC, that's the National Crime Information Center, to see if she has a prior history of criminal activity. I may eventually have to have someone out in Utah do some legwork for me, unless you want to authorize me to fly out there myself, but that wouldn't be something we'd need to decide immediately. I'll get in touch with the local church she attended, see if she told anyone she intended to leave town, and I'll talk to the people there who knew her. And of course I'll check local coin shops, once you give me a description of what's missing, to see if anything has turned up. I have a friend at a travel agency, who has friends at the airlines; I'll check to see if Kristee has flown anywhere. That's how I'll start. How I proceed from there I won't know until I get more of a feel for this girl."

I paused to catch my breath.

Beemish studied me for a moment more, and it appeared he had something else he wanted to ask, but after a second or two he apparently thought better of it.

"Fine," he said finally. "We'll need to talk money, naturally." A smile played about the corners of his upper lip. "What exactly does a private eye charge these days?"

I did some quick mental arithmetic. It had been a year since I'd last priced the other investigators in town, so I upped my hourly rate by 30 percent.

"I charge sixty-five dollars an hour, or a day rate of five hundred," I said. "Plus expenses for long distance calls, computer time if any, and, of course, mileage. I charge 30 cents a mile. If I have to contract out any work, I'll let you know ahead of time. I usually bill on a weekly cycle, and you'll receive a written report along with your first bill."

Beemish looked taken aback. "Five hundred a day!" he sputtered. "My God, that's more than I pay my bulldozer operator, and he owns his own equipment."

"Get your bulldozer operator to find the girl, then," I snapped. I hate discussing money, especially with someone who can clearly afford to pay whatever it takes to get a job done.

Lilah Rose slid in the door and quickly took up a position behind her husband's chair. "I think that's fine, Bo, don't you? I don't think I told you on the phone, honey, but your grandmother's amethyst ring is missing from my jewel case, and so are the diamond earrings you gave me for our fifth anniversary."

She addressed herself to me.

"A lot of the things she took were pretty ordinary, but that ring has been in Bo's family for at least a hundred years. It has a great deal of sentimental value, and of course the diamond earrings do too, plus the fact that they're about two carats. I don't even want to think about what Bo paid for them."

Her husband's face twisted into a scowl. "Goddammit, Callahan, I want that amethyst ring back. If my mother finds out it's gone, we'll never hear the end of it."

Just then the study door flew open and the two blond hellions burst in again.

"Daddy, Daddy," the little girl caroled, taking his hands in hers. "Kristee's gone, did you know? And she didn't even tell us good-bye."

Lilah moved to the children's side, quickly taking each child's hand in her own. "Daddy knows all about it," she told them. "Now give him a kiss, then let's hop upstairs and get ready for Jessie's party."

The two pecked their father quickly on his cheek and went running from the room.

Lilah Rose looked at me apologetically. "Callahan, we'll talk when I get back, I promise." She started to follow the children out of the room, then ducked back in. "You will be able to finish cleaning, won't you? I'm having a luncheon tomorrow, and there won't be time to get anybody else on such short notice."

"Yeah," I said, staring up at the cobwebby chandelier. "I should be able to get things under control in a few hours. Then I'll head for my office and start making phone calls about Kristee."

"Thanks ever so." She blew a kiss to her unsmiling husband and left the room.

I started to follow her, but Beemish leaned across the desk and put a hand on mine.

"Wait," he said, and then added a halfhearted "please." "There are some things I need to tell you about Kristee that I don't want Lilah Rose to hear."

5

I'VE ALWAYS HAD A LOUSY poker face. Edna tells me that when I was a snot-nosed kid, whenever she wanted to find out whether I'd committed some heinous offense, she had only to ask. I'd lie, of course, but she said the guilt was always written all over my face. I got away with very little. Which is why I try to keep fairly straight these days. It simplifies things.

So when Bo Beemish seemed ready to bare his soul to me, I was pretty sure I knew what he'd say. I squirmed a little on the sofa. Looked studiously at my hands, which were bleached out and pruney from the suds they'd been in earlier. Wondered if he knew I knew what I knew.

Fortunately, Beemish wasn't nearly as observant as my mother. Few people are.

He cleared his throat a couple of times, then picked up a pen and started doodling on a scratch pad. Without looking up, and in a fast, low voice I had to strain to hear, he began talking.

"This is absolutely confidential, Callahan. And I mean confidential." He glanced up, then ducked his head again.

"Besides the coins and the bonds Kristee took from the safe, she got some business records of mine. Highly sensitive business records.

"I'm in the middle of putting together a multimillion-dollar deal right now, the biggest deal I've ever packaged. If those records get out, the deal will be ruined, and so will I."

He looked at me now, and I could see real fear in those icy blues.

"You've got to find this girl, and find her quick. I mean it. If we have to pay to get her to hand over the records, I'm willing. There's much more riding on this thing than even Lilah Rose knows."

I blinked. "What kind of business records are they, Bo?" I had already decided that if he could call me by my first name, I could call him by his. "And how would Kristee know where they were or what they meant to you?"

"Just what are you insinuating?"

"I'm not insinuating anything," I said, in danger of losing my cool. "But the other things Kristee took are the kind of stuff a common burglar takes, stuff that can be converted to cash fairly easily. I need to understand what records she took and why so I can figure out what she might do with them. How she could get something out of them. If you don't want to tell me, fine. But I gotta tell you, that's gonna severely limit my ability to find this girl and get your property back. And another thing: my fee stays the same, whether I find the girl or not."

I knew that would get Beemish, tightwad that he was.

A nerve twitched below his right eye. He ran his tongue over his lips and beat a tattoo in the palm of his left hand with the pen.

"OK," he said. "I guess I'll have to trust you. Kristee knew about the deal because we had—uh, a relationship."

"A relationship," I repeated. "Are we talking employer-employee?"

"Not exactly. We were sleeping together."

I cocked one eyebrow in what I hoped was a surprised but non-judgmental expression.

"It was no big deal," he said. "It had nothing to do with Lilah or the kids or our marriage. It was strictly a little fling. Everybody does it. It was just that Kristee—my God, she was a sexy little thing! I'll tell you, they teach those Mormon girls stuff they don't teach Presbyterians. She was always running around the house in these little shorts, or showing up in the kitchen in some oversized T-shirt with nothing on underneath. She made it very clear she was attracted to me too. I was terrified Lilah would notice, so I told Kristee to straighten up. But she thought it was funny, sleeping with the boss right under Lilah's nose. She came on to me first, by the way. I swear.

"Anyway, she seemed real interested in my business. She said she wanted to go back to college. Maybe get a degree in business administration." He sighed. "I suppose I was flattered. Lilah's a good gal. She runs the house fairly well, she's a good mother and a terrific hostess. But she doesn't have the slightest interest in how I make all the money she loves to spend. I guess I talked pretty openly to Kristee about this deal I've got cooking. She acted like she was fascinated. She wanted to hear every tiny little detail. I never showed her any of the documents, but she knew where everything was in this study."

For the first time, he looked slightly embarrassed. "We—uh, spent a lot of time in here. It's the only room in the house with a lock on the door."

I looked down at the overstuffed chintz sofa I was sitting on. A mental image of the two of them—buck naked, flailing away—flashed through my mind. I gingerly scooted to the edge. Made a mental note to take some fabric cleaner to the cushions the first opportunity I got.

"Did she know the combination to the safe?"

"No, but it wouldn't have been hard for her to figure out. It's the months and days of my kids' birthdays, March twenty-fifth and fifteenth."

For all his business smarts, it was painfully clear to me that Bo Beemish was dumb as a stump when it came to everyday common sense.

"You gonna tell me what these records were? Are they bigger than a bread box? Smaller than a cash ledger?"

He shook his head. "I can't tell you everything. Not yet. I will tell you that they pertain to a parcel of land I'm developing up in Kensington Park. It's an eighty-seven-acre tract with twelve hundred feet on the Chattahoochee River. It'll be mixed use: houses, some small boutiques, an exercise club, and a couple of really nice restaurants. I'm gonna put up the best, most beautiful, million-dollar townhouses ever seen in Atlanta. L'Arrondissement, I'm calling it. Classy, huh? There are some problems with the project, though. And like the horse's ass I am, I told Kristee about some of them. With the documents she has, she could really hurt me."

"Blackmail?" I asked.

He nodded. "And worse."

"Can you at least tell me what these records look like?"

"They're in a brown accordion file marked with a label that says L'ARRONDISSEMENT. There are some deeds, some promissory notes, and a yellow legal pad with some memos. That's really all I can tell you."

"Swell," I said. "That's better than nothing."

I got up and headed for the study door. I still had a lot of cleaning to do before I finished the day, and I needed to get going. "Anything else you want to tell me before I start on the bathrooms?"

"That's it," he said. "Except for one thing."

"Yeah. What's that?"

"Don't forget to clean the tile grout in the sauna in the master bath," he said. "Goddamn maids never get all that black stuff out."

6

I DETACHED A SMALL TRAY of cleaning supplies from my trolley and went up the back stairs to the second floor. The upstairs *chez* Beemish was just as impressive as the downstairs. There was a thick-textured carpet the color of clotted English cream. I examined it and decided I could get away with just spot-cleaning the scattered stains. There was an expensive-looking Oriental wallpaper lining the walls and a long hallway punctuated with half a dozen doors.

I could hear voices coming from one, so I peeped in. The room was a pink-and-white fairy tale: canopy bed, white wicker rocker and dressing table, pink chintz ruffles everywhere. In the middle of it all, Lilah Rose was struggling to pull a fluffy party dress over the head of her daughter, who was struggling just as hard to keep it off. The skirmish must have been a protracted one because Lilah was speaking to her daughter through clenched teeth.

"Now, Meredith, you have to wear a dress to Jessie's party. All the other little girls will be in dresses. Don't you want to look pretty like your friends? Let's put on the nice dress Mama bought for the party."

"No, no, no, no," the child hollered, her face growing crimson. "I want my turtle shirt."

"Looks like a standoff," I offered.

Lilah Rose gave a start. "Jesus, Julia, I didn't know you were standing there. Is there something you need right now? As you can see, I'm having a little difficulty with Meredith. She's a very strong-willed little person, you know. Bo and I try hard not to stifle her self-expression."

Meredith jerked open a dresser drawer and began dumping the contents on the floor.

Lilah Rose turned her attention back to me. "Now what was it you needed?"

"Kristee's room. I'd like to look around, see if I can get any idea where she might have gone."

Lilah Rose plucked a folded pink and white seer-sucker sun-suit from the pile on the floor. "Here, sweetie. You love this." Her daughter scowled, but stepped into the romper and began fiddling with the shoulder straps.

"Oh, yes," Lilah said. "You won't find anything. She pretty well cleaned it out. But it's up that short half flight of stairs at the end of the hall. Bo built it as an exercise room for the family, but when we decided to have live-in help for the children, it made perfect sense to put her there. There's a stairway that goes directly down to the garage, so she could come and go in privacy." A wry smile crossed Lilah's face. "Of course, I don't guess it ever occurred to me the kinds of comings and goings the little slut would be involved in."

Meredith looked up at her mother with interest. "What's a slut, Mama?"

Lilah looked like she'd been smacked with a week-old mullet. "Nothin', honey. That's just a word grown-ups use sometimes. But little girls don't ever, ever say that word, do you hear? Not ever."

"No," Meredith agreed, nodding solemnly. "Never."

I left mother and daughter to their party preparations. As I started up the back stairs, I turned and saw the little girl hopping down the front stairs two at a time, all the while chanting, "Slut. Slut. Slut. Slut."

The maid's quarters were an abrupt change from the opulence of the rest of the house. For one thing, it was noticeably hotter up there. I'd have been willing to bet old Bo Beemish hadn't cared to install a zoned air conditioning unit to handle a room over the garage, doubtless the warmest room in the house.

I pushed the bedroom door open. The room looked like what new money thought a maid's room should look like. The windowless plasterboard walls had never been properly painted, and the burnt-orange carpet looked like a cheap industrial brand. Here and there, the room's occupant had made attempts to brighten the place up by hanging posters of bare-chested rock stars decked out in chains and tight black leather pants. There was a double bed, covered with an old aqua chenille bedspread. A nightstand beside the bed was made of that awful blond wood you see in 1950s-era motels. The stand held a gooseneck metal reading lamp and a few tattered paperback books.

Sharing space on the bed table was a new-looking white princess phone. There was a set of Atlanta telephone books underneath. I picked up the receiver and heard a dial tone.

I leafed through the paperbacks and the phone books, looking for handwritten notes. Nothing.

The only other furniture in the room was a matching blond dresser and a torn brown Naugahyde La-Z-Boy recliner. A small black and white television stood on an old milk crate. I pulled out each of the four drawers in the dresser. Empty, except for a forlorn-looking pair of pantyhose in the top drawer. I saw a scrap of black fabric and managed to tug it free from where it had caught at the back of the drawer. It wasn't much more than a snippet; actually, it was a tiny pair of black lace bikini panties. The label read VICTORIA'S SECRET.

I crossed over to the small closet. There were a lot of wire coat hangers and an empty plastic laundry basket, but no clothes or shoes, except for a worn pair of pink rubber flip-flops. They were at least three sizes smaller than my own size 9 gunboats.

Beside the closet, another door opened to a bathroom: white

tile, gold-and-white-flecked vinyl flooring, an institutional-looking sink, toilet, and plastic-walled shower stall. A limp towel hung from the single plastic bar. It was dry but obviously used. I pushed open the plastic shower door. A bottle of Pantene shampoo, the kind I'm too cheap to buy, stood on the floor. It was nearly full. So was the bottle of conditioner. I reached for the soap in the soap dish and sniffed. Attar of Roses. The Caswell-Massey imprint was hardly worn off. Little Kristee liked expensive things. She'd left about $20 worth of beauty products behind just in the shower stall. I wondered why she'd been in such a hurry. And how she'd afforded those nice things on a nanny's salary.

There was an overflowing trash basket on the floor. My scalp tingled pleasantly. One thing cops and cleaning ladies have in common: we pay attention to trash.

I took it into the bedroom and got a pair of rubber gloves from my cleaning supplies. I sat on the La-Z-Boy and started picking through the garbage.

It was the usual bathroom-variety stuff: a wadded-up plastic cleaner's bag, used strands of dental floss, Q-Tips, razor blades, lots of clumps of blond hair, dark at the roots, an empty tube of toothpaste.

There were also some things I hadn't expected to find, too. For one, there was a plastic birth control pill dispenser. It still had a week's worth of pills in it. The prescription label, from the pharmacy at the nearby A&P, read Nordette and was made out to Kristee Ewbanks. There was a doctor's name and phone number. I peeled the label off and tucked it in my smock pocket. I found a crumpled cigarette pack and two empty Diet Coke cans, both with fuchsia lipstick marks.

At the bottom of the basket I found a small crushed brown paper bag. Inside there was another empty cigarette pack, a worn-out tube of lipstick, some movie ticket stubs, a package of three rather furry-looking cherry LifeSavers, and some moldy white tablets that tasted like aspirin. This looked just like the detritus that layered the bottom of my own purse. Miss Kristee had recently cleaned out her pocketbook, I decided. Too bad she hadn't left it behind, with a detailed itinerary.

It never hurts to be optimistic, right?

I sat still for a moment and thought about what I'd found. Not much. But what I hadn't found was sort of interesting. There were books, but no religious tracts, not even a Bible. I'd thought these Mormons were supposed to be so devout. Maybe Kristee was a different kind of Mormon. I thought about the Coke cans. I wasn't sure, but I thought I recalled that Mormons regarded caffeine, in coffee, tea, or even cola, as taboo. The same with tobacco. I didn't know how they regarded their young maidens who slept with another woman's husband.

But I knew how to find out. The yellow pages had a listing for the information office of the Church of Jesus Christ of Latter-day Saints, their formal name. A booming male voice on the other end identified himself as Elder Jackson. In my sincerest voice I asked if he could send me some information about the Mormon church.

"Certainly," he boomed. "We'd be happy to welcome another Saint into the fold. If you'll give me your address, we'll send you a packet in today's mail." We exchanged pleasantries and I hung up.

As nice as it felt to sit in the chair, I hauled myself up and headed for the hall. I had a lot of grout to clean. There were some nasty crayon marks on that second-floor hallway wallpaper that I didn't like the looks of. And who knew what kinds of grunge lurked behind all those other closed doors. It was a veritable "Let's Make a Deal" of dirt. And all I had to do was choose a door.

7

BY THE TIME I FINISHED de-grunging the Beemish house and had made the drive home to Candler Park through rush-hour traffic, it was close to 7 P.M.

I was tired, dirty, and hungry. But no matter how tired or pissed off I am, the sight of my house always makes me smile. It's nothing special, really, just a dumpy little aqua-blue Craftsman-style frame house in a kind of dumpy neighborhood. The locals call Candler Park "an emerging in-town community."

By that I guess they mean it's the kind of neighborhood where gays and straights, blacks and whites, liberals and conservatives live cheek to jowl. The houses are modest working-class affairs, 1920s bungalows and a few very late, very plain Victorians. Lots of dogs, joggers, and economy cars bearing NO NUKES bumper stickers. Our business district is a funky crossroads called Little Five Points. We've got a vegetarian supermarket called Sevananda, three or four vintage clothing stores, a futon shop, a New Age gift shop, a feminist bookstore, and Atlanta's largest collection of honest-to-God spike-haired black-leather-clad punkers. Most of the business owners are unreconstructed hippies turned reluctant capitalists.

My house is maybe seven blocks away on a wide tree-shaded street called Oakdale. There's a wide porch across the front where Edna displays her giant mutant ferns, and we always plant bright pink geraniums in the front in the spring. When I bought it seven years ago, friends stuck a tacky pink plastic flamingo in the front planter. He's still there.

I recognized the beat-up olive-green Buick parked at the curb that night. Inside, the house was quiet. I walked through to the kitchen, yoo-hooing along the way. As I expected, they were sitting out back on the brick patio, yakking away. The screen door banged as I stepped out, and all three of them got quiet for a minute.

Edna had changed into a cotton sundress and was barefoot. As usual she had a lit cigarette in one hand and a big glass of iced tea in the other. Sitting at the table with her were two itty bitty black women. The larger of the two wore coke-bottle glasses perched on her nose, with her gray hair skinned back in a bun. The younger woman was shorter but rounder, and she wore a floppy straw hat. Between them, the two had a large pile of scraps of paper, and they were busy scratching the papers with a pencil.

"Look, Callahan," Edna greeted me. "Sister and Baby got back from their trip to Florida, and they brought me a bunch of blank lottery slips."

"It's Callahan," Baby hollered to her older sister. "Tell her how-do!"

Sister looked up and peered through the thick lenses. Behind the glass her bright brown eyes were filmed over by cataracts. "Don't you shout at me, you old biddy," she instructed her younger sister. "You're the one deaf as a doorknob. I knew who was there.

"Hi, baby," she cooed at me. "Bring your sweet self over here so I can hug on you."

I moved over closer, leaned down, and gave her a hug. Even if you were blind you could always pick out Sister Easterbrook in a crowd. She's the one who smells of Lily of the Valley. I don't know where she gets the stuff, but she always has a fresh bottle of it sitting on a crocheted doily on her dresser.

Sister and Baby Easterbrook are the oldest of our "girls." God knows just how old they are. They both live in a high-rise retirement home over on Ponce de Leon Avenue and clean a couple of houses a week for us, just to keep themselves in lottery tickets. We send them out together on jobs and always pay them in cash, so they don't lose their social security. Baby drives because her eyes are still fairly good, but she's nearly totally deaf, so she has to have Sister in the car to hear if an ambulance is coming or a train is approaching a crossing. Sister is legally blind. They get along just fine, but we usually try to send them to a house where the people aren't home, because once the clients see how old and fragile the sisters look, they usually want to set them in a chair and call the feds and report me for abuse of the elderly.

Baby patted a wrought-iron chair next to her. "Set here and tell us all about the new job Edna's so excited about. She's saying you're gonna get a hundred and seventy-five dollars. Can that be right?"

I poured myself a glass of iced tea from the pitcher on the table. "Looks like it might be more than that, now."

Edna sat up straight at that news. "How?"

I filled her in on the plight of my sorority sister and explained that I'd taken on one last investigative case because I couldn't resist the money.

"Hell, no," Edna exclaimed. "Besides, think of the kind of undercover work we could do if you got the detective agency going again. Nobody ever pays attention to the cleaning lady. Most of these people act like we're part of the woodwork. Why, we could collect evidence and do surveillance and all that stuff."

"That's right," chimed in Sister. "I seen them private eye shows on the television. Ooh, you should see the stuff me and Baby find in these fine people's houses. Liquor bottles and sex magazines and I don't know what all."

I held up my hand like a traffic cop. "No. We're not getting back into the detective business. This is a very simple one-shot assignment. No surveillance, no stake-out, no nosy cleaning ladies digging through dumpsters."

Edna waved her hand dismissively at me.

"I mean it, Edna," I said, giving her my best narrow-eyed look. "You are going to stay out of this, and the girls are going to stay out of this. My private investigator's license expires in another month. I'll find this girl, and that'll be the end of it."

Sister and Baby struggled to their feet. They must have been sitting there for a while, because they both had rolled their stockings down around their ankles. Both pecked Edna on the cheek. "Well, we're gonna get on home," Baby said. "I don't like to be in this neighborhood after dark."

I gave them both a quick hug and walked them to the front door. Inside, Edna had turned on the light in the kitchen and was rattling the pots and pans. "Soup and sandwich all right for dinner?" she called to me.

I walked into the kitchen and sat down at the table. "Just a quick sandwich, Ma," I told her. "I'm gonna make some phone calls on this Beemish thing, and then I'm gonna run over to the Yacht Club to see if any of the guys are hanging out there tonight. I need to get somebody to run something on the computer for me."

Before I'd left her house, Lilah had given me the names and numbers of some half-dozen friends who had hired Mormon girls to take care of their kids. I managed to talk to two or three girls, but none of them had ever met Kristee, they said.

I got lucky with Ashley Zucker. The woman she worked for answered the phone and put her on right away. "Did you know Kristee Ewbanks?" I asked.

There was a long pause. "Well, kinda."

"What was she like? Can you tell me?"

The girl on the other end of the line had to think about that for a minute. "Different. She was different from the other girls I've met here."

"Did she socialize with the other Mormon girls?"

Ashley giggled a little. "I don't think Kristee liked us. I called her three or four times to invite her to do stuff with us, but she always said she couldn't. She said Mrs. Beemish was real strict about her going out at night. But then Mrs. Beemish told Betsy, that's the lady I work for, that she didn't know where Kristee went every night. She thought she was going to church." Ashley giggled again. "Not even the LDS kids go to church every night."

I thought about this information for a minute. "Did you ever actually see her at church?"

"Just once. The elder introduced her as a new member. Later I saw her talking to this really cute guy. In fact, he was the cutest guy at our church."

"Do you know his name?" I asked.

"Only his first name, Whit. And one of the girls said he works for some accounting company."

I jotted down *Whit* and *accountant* on the yellow legal pad in front of me.

"OK, good. Do you happen to know if Kristee made friends with any of the other LDS girls?"

"Mmm," Ashley said. "Well, I heard she was sort of friendly with Patti Jo Nemeyer. She works for a family down the street from the Beemishes, but I just heard today that Patti Jo went back home to Utah this past weekend. Missed her family."

Patti Jo Nemeyer's name was already on my note pad. "Do you happen to know anything about the service that placed Kristee?" I asked.

"No," she said quickly. "And that's another funny thing. There are about five of those agencies around Salt Lake City. Most of us girls have talked to at least a couple of them. But only two of them place girls in Atlanta. The others send girls to Chicago and Philadelphia and Boston and New York. The girls I know here in Atlanta were placed by Mother's Finest or Nannies Unlimited. Kristee told me the name of her agency, but I'd never heard of them before."

Ashley gave me the phone number of Nannies Unlimited, the

agency that placed her. I thanked her for her time and hung up, called Nannies Unlimited, but all I got was an answering machine. I left a message and hung up.

Edna slid a plate in front of me. She'd fixed me a bacon, lettuce, and tomato on toasted whole wheat, my favorite sandwich. The tomatoes were gorgeous, thick and red. "Where'd you find these?" I said, lifting the bread to salt the sandwich.

"Sister and Baby got them down in Ruskin on their bus trip." She brought her own plate over to the table, and we ate in companionable silence. When I finished I took both empty plates and put them in the dishwasher.

In my bedroom I stripped off the hated smock and grimy jeans and slipped on a pair of white shorts and a big baggy T-shirt. I left off the bra, shoved my feet into a pair of sandals, and headed for the front door. "I'm going to the Yacht Club, Edna," I called to her. "I'll talk to you in the morning."

I thought about walking. The Euclid Avenue Yacht Club is only about half a mile from my house. But we've had a couple of rapes in the neighborhood, and although I can hold my own in a tight situation, I'd just as soon not have to deal with the hassle. So I fired up the van and circled the block around Euclid until a parking space came open.

It looked like a fairly slow night at the Yacht Club. I pushed open the door and looked around. The place is a narrow joint, about forty feet long by fifteen feet wide. The bar runs down the right side, and there are some homemade wooden booths on the left side. When the owners started the bar with their savings from the pension fund at Johnny's, another neighborhood bar, they furnished it with stuff their customers gave them. So they've got old sports jerseys, stuffed and mounted tarpons, and all kinds of junk hanging from the ceiling and the walls. The television set is always tuned to ESPN, and there is almost always somebody, like a newspaper reporter, an intern from Grady Memorial, or a cop, trying to talk the bartender into letting him use the phone behind the bar.

I scanned the room until I saw what I needed to see: a cop. Tonight it was a guy named Charles "Bucky" Deaver. Bucky is about my age and he is a big boy. Stands about six-foot-three and weighs about 240. He's the only grown-up I know still fighting acne. He has short brushy-cut blond hair and wears Buddy Holly black nerd glasses. He shops the vintage clothing stores in the neighborhood. This night he had on a short-sleeved chartreuse Ricky Ricardo bowling shirt with wide black lapels tucked into pleated baggy black-and-white checked trousers. His panama hat was pushed to the back of his head. In his left ear I could see a tiny gold earring. From where I stood it looked like a little piglet.

He was concentrating on a monster hamburger and didn't see me walk up until I slipped behind him and gave him a little goose.

He didn't even look up. "Callahan Garrity, you hot-blooded vixen. You never could keep your hands off me, could you?"

I grinned into the mirror over the back bar, slid onto the stool next to his, and helped myself to one of his onion rings.

"Got that right, Bucko. What's shakin'?"

He swallowed and shook his head. "Not a damn thing. Braves are losing. That new starter of theirs is getting the shit shelled out of him."

"What else is new?" I said, not bothering to cover my yawn.

Bucky and I go way back. We got to know each other years ago when a bunch of us were part of a special task force assigned to investigate a rash of murders of young black kids around Atlanta. We worked long hours and partied and drank—and sometimes slept—together. We got to be a pretty tight bunch. The unit was disbanded after we arrested a twenty-one-year-old record promoter for the killings. But most of us have kept in loose contact ever since.

From the other end of the counter, Tinkles, the bartender,

caught my eye. I nodded and he reached into the beer box and brought out an ice-caked green Heineken's bottle. He came down the bar and put the bottle and a frosted mug in front of me.

When the foam on my beer had settled and the Braves had safely lost the game, I was ready to talk business with Bucky.

"What's going on down at the shop, Bucky?"

"Guess you heard Fryberg got transferred over to vice," he said.

I nodded. "Somebody mentioned it to me. What do you hear from the other guys?"

My buddy didn't answer for a minute. He was occupied in trying to suck a white string of onion out of a large onion ring. That done, he inhaled the brown crust and delicately wiped his hands on the paper napkin in his lap.

"Shaloub went and got himself elected sheriff in that little hick town he moved to out in Forsyth County. You hear about that?"

I had. I hoped my face didn't turn pink at the mention of Eddie Shaloub's name. He was, you might say, a former gentleman caller. "Yeah. And I heard he left the sheriff's office last year to go into business for himself. He's selling those beepers, right?"

I actually knew exactly what Eddie Shaloub was doing these days. He'd called me several months earlier, ostensibly to sell me a beeper for the cleaning business. We'd had lunch at the Colonnade, one of those old-lady lunch places that has chicken salad and frozen fruit compote, and finished up at the motel next door. That's how it had been with Eddie and me for the past three years. It wasn't anything serious between us. I didn't think.

Bucky pushed aside the lettuce leaf on his plate, searching fruitlessly for another morsel of deep-fried food. That failing, he rolled the lettuce up like a cigarette and chomped down on it.

He chewed happily for a moment. "Yeah, beepers. Must be pulling down some bucks too. He invited me and a couple other guys out to play golf at this big-deal private country club up there last month. I tell ya, Callahan, I could get used to that kind of life."

We chatted aimlessly for a few more minutes, mostly about cop-shop politics and office gossip. Finally Bucky looked at his watch and laughed.

"OK, Callahan. We been shooting the shit here for forty-five minutes. You wanna tell me why you came looking for me tonight and what kind of favor you're needing?"

Honesty is one of Bucky's finer traits.

"You're right. I admit it," I said, signaling Tinkles to bring another round. "I do need a favor."

"Is this the kind of favor that could get my butt canned?"

"Only if you're dumb enough to get caught."

The niceties aside, I filled him in on what I needed. A check on the National Crime Information Center and the Georgia Crime Information Center, to see if Kristee Ewbanks had a record. I also gave him the description I had of Lilah's missing jewelry and the coins from her husband's collection. I knew Bucky could check the computerized records local pawn shops file with the cops every week. He wrote everything in tiny block letters on a bar napkin, folded it, and tucked it in the breast pocket of his bowling shirt.

"I don't guess these people have called in a report, have they?" he asked.

"Uh-uh. They're rich, Bucky. And the rich are not like you and me. They don't want any publicity or hassle. All they want is for me to find this chick and get her to hand over their stuff."

Bucky rolled his eyes. "Yeah, I know the type. OK. Now, is there anything else?"

I mentally scrolled down my TO DO list. "You might ask around quietly about this developer, DuBose Beemish. I think he's involved in something hinky."

"Hinky or kinky?" Bucky demanded, a wolfish grin spreading across his face.

"Both, probably. But I already know he screws around on his wife. I need to know now what he's done out of bed that someone might want to blackmail him over."

The wolfish grin faded fast. He leaned over until his face was inches from mine. The onion breath damn near killed me. "Look, Callahan. I don't know what you're getting yourself involved in here, but it sounds like a lot more than just tracking down a petty crook. I know you won't do what I tell you, but I'll say it anyway. You need to clean these people's house and tell them to go to the cops for the really dirty work. Seriously."

"Can't do it," I said lightly, hopping off the bar stool and digging in my pockets for some folding money. "I need these people's cash. Two of my girls have been out of work, and my van is making very expensive-sounding noises. Besides, this one is a cinch, Bucky. I can find this chick in my sleep, practically. As long as you help me out."

I pulled a ten and a five out of my pocket and placed them on the bar between us.

"Gotta go now, sweets," I told him. "Can you get that stuff tomorrow, do you think?"

He shook his head in mock disgust, but I knew he'd do it. I started to walk out, then had a thought.

"Hey, Buck, you still living in that rat hole over on North Highland?"

He tried to look offended. "If you mean my pied à terre, certainly. Why?"

"Leave the key up on the right corner of the door ledge day after tomorrow. I'll send one of my girls over to shovel the place out. Hell, if you leave her some clean sheets, she'll even make your bed for you. My treat."

"Outa sight," he said. "You got a deal."

8

I WAS READING MY HOROSCOPE in the *Atlanta Constitution* and enjoying the quiet. Edna had left early to pick up some cleaning supplies from the wholesale house. There was coffe in the pot, and outside the kitchen window I could see a blue jay angrily trying to defend the bird feeder from a squirrel. The window was smudged. Maybe I would clean it. Maybe not. It was only 8 A.M., after all. Too early for real work. Too early for our clients to start calling and wanting me to reschedule the rest of the week just so they could get their refrigerator defrosted immediately.

And it looked like a good day for us Leos. "Long-pending arrangements will result in financial windfall," the horoscope said. "Domestic situation should improve dramatically."

I was pondering what that could mean when I heard the sound of a heavy car door slamming. Actually, it sounded more like it came from a pickup truck. Coming up the driveway I heard the soft slapping sound of slippers against bare feet. I'd heard that sound before. "There goes my domestic situation," I said out loud.

I glanced toward the screen door. A tall woman with frizzy, bleached-blond hair tied in a ponytail stood on the other side of the door, smiling a lopsided kind of smile. She was missing a tooth in front, on the bottom. As usual, she had on dark glasses and smeared red lipstick that made her upper lip look unusually large. She was dressed in tight pink polyester shorts topped by a pale pink

House Mouse smock. The fishbelly-white legs, crisscrossed with varicose veins, ended in fuzzy pink house shoes.

"Come on in, Neva Jean," I said. "I see you got a ride home."

"Let me just tell Swanelle to go on," she said, and, turning, she waved giddily to the red truck in the driveway. "Woo-ooh, Swanelle, you can go on; Callahan's here. Don't forget to pick me up at five-thirty, now."

The truck backed out of the driveway, doing about forty mph. I listened with satisfaction as I heard the axle hit the bump at the bottom of the driveway.

Neva Jean stepped back inside, cha-chaed over to the refrigerator, and stood there with the door open, surveying the contents. Her lips formed a pout. "Now, who's been drinking my Mountain Dew? I put a six-pack in here last week and it's gone. Edna knows I like a Mountain Dew in the morning before I go to work."

I was back at the kitchen table by then, checking the daybook to see what Edna had planned for the girls.

"I don't know who drank your Mountain Dew, Neva Jean," I said evenly. "I myself wouldn't touch a drink that looks like carbonated antifreeze. Welcome back, by the way. I take it you and Swanelle made up?"

"You could say that," she said, winking broadly. "Took all night, too. Lord, I'm sore in places I didn't know I had."

I looked up from the book and tried to fix her with a serious stare. "Well, you tell that asshole husband of yours the next time he abandons you a hundred miles from home the night before you've got a full day's work lined up, he can kiss his wife's job good-bye."

I wasn't that mad, really. Neva Jean's always pulling stuff like this. This was the way you have to talk to someone like Neva Jean. "Like you talk to a mule," Edna had explained. "With a two-by-four upside the head."

Neva Jean sat down at the table opposite me, chastened, a little, and took a swig of the Nehi Orange she'd found in the fridge.

"You didn't cancel the Mahaffeys or the Greenbergs, did you? Mrs. Mahaffey especially wanted me to clean out her butler's pantry and scrub it down today. And the Greenbergs—if you miss a week there, the next time you go it's like a month's worth of cleaning. I swannee, those people don't even empty their own trash in between times."

"No, you're going to catch them both today," I said. "And after you're done with them, there's a condo in Inman Park. It's a new job. You can hit that on the way back from the Greenbergs. It's only five rooms."

I reached over to the pegboard on the wall in back of me and handed her a tagged door key with the address of the condo on it.

"They said they'd leave the check on the kitchen counter," I told her. "And you can tell Dottie Mahaffey that if she wants special cleaning like her pantry emptied and scrubbed, it's gonna be fifteen dollars extra. We're not running a charity here."

"Yeah, right," Neva Jean said, reaching for the horoscope page I'd been reading.

I snatched it out of her hands. "Neva Jean," I said, trying to sound stern. "I want that fifteen dollars extra *in a check*. You know, if you take tips from these people for extra work without reporting it, it's the same as stealing money right out of my purse."

Before she could answer that, we heard honking in the driveway and a loud backfire.

Edna was back from the wholesale house.

We hurried outside to help her unload the van. By the time we finished, two more of the girls, Jackie and Ruby, had pulled up to the curb and were gathered in the kitchen. They all wanted to hear about Neva Jean's exciting escapade in Macon, and the trashy details of how she and Swanelle had made up again. It was almost noon before I had everybody's schedule straightened out and had delivered Neva Jean to the Mahaffeys. Her car was in the shop, as usual. I put up with a lot from Neva Jean, but the woman can not only clean, she can lift heavy furniture.

When I got back home and walked into the kitchen, Edna was just hanging up the phone.

"Oh, Jules, the lady from that nanny agency in Utah just called," she said. "Here's the number. She said she'd only be in for a few more minutes."

"Save me some time here," I said. "What else did she say? I know you asked her about Kristee."

Edna was shameless when it came to meddling. "She about popped a rivet when I told her one of her holier-than-thou Mormon girls was out here stealing people blind and sleeping with everything in pants."

"You didn't really tell her Kristee was screwing her employer, did you?"

"Hell's bells, why not? It's true isn't it?"

I reached for the phone. "Remind me not to fill you in on any more confidential client matters," I told her.

Myra Murphy, the owner of Nannies Unlimited, answered the phone on the first ring. "Oh, yes, Miss Garrity," she said. "Your mother has been making some accusations about a person named Ewbanks. I want you to know she is *not* one of our girls. None of our girls has ever been involved in anything sordid like this. And I'd appreciate your making it known to the family that hired her that most Mormon nannies are fine, upstanding, responsible employees."

"No, no, Mrs. Murphy," I said, interrupting her. "I'm afraid you misunderstood my mother. She certainly wasn't suggesting that Kristee Ewbanks was one of your girls. I'm only calling you to see what you know about the agency that placed her."

"Well, thank goodness for that," she said. "No, the name your mother mentioned, and this Ardith Cramer: I never heard of them.

But I'll talk to my girls, and I'll call the other agencies around Salt Lake City and see what they know. Most of us started out working for the same agency seven or eight years ago, and we're very protective of our business. Our reputation is everything, as I'm sure you can understand."

"Of course," I said, trying to reassure her. "It would be wonderful if you could do some checking for me. I don't suppose the state of Utah has a regulatory agency that licenses nanny agencies, does it?"

The voice on the other end of the line lost its friendly tone. "Why, no," she said. "What would be the need of that? We're all Christian women here, trying to perform a service for upstanding families. I can assure you, we've never had any trouble of this kind from any of our girls."

"I'm sure," I said, trying not to let sarcasm creep into my voice. "It's just that I wondered how Ardith Cramer got into this business, and actually placed at least one girl, without any of you knowing anything about her."

"I wonder the same thing," Mrs. Murphy admitted. "Look, I've got to go out for a business appointment now, but I'll make some inquiries and call you back if I find out anything."

I thanked her and hung up. The phone rang again instantly.

"House Mouse."

The person on the other end exhaled slowly. "Good Lord, that's a silly-sounding name," she said. "What on earth possessed you to use it?"

"Actually, Lilah Rose, I bought the business with the name, and as our clients are used to it, I decided to hang on to it. Now, what can I do for you?"

"Have you found the slut yet?"

I looked at the kitchen clock. It runs twenty minutes fast, but Edna and I are the only ones who know that. It helps get the girls to their jobs on time.

"It hasn't been twenty-four hours yet," I pointed out. "Even Sam Spade takes longer than one day."

"Who?"

"Never mind. No, I haven't located Kristee yet. I was just on the phone to Utah before you called, trying to find out something about Nanny Finders and Ardith Cramer."

"Oh. That reminds me why I called," Lilah said. "I've got some information that might help. I looked through the telephone bills for the last couple of months, and there are some long distance numbers I don't recognize."

"Any with a Utah area code?"

"Well, no," Lilah said. "I thought that was odd, so I dug around until I found the number where we originally reached Nanny Finders. It had been disconnected, and the phone company wouldn't tell me when, or if they had a new number. It's funny, because Kristee distinctly told me she'd been in touch with Ardith Cramer. I think I once walked into her room when she was talking to her on the phone, come to think of it."

"Have you called the phone company to ask them about the long distance numbers you're not familiar with?"

"That's what we're paying you to do," she said. "Here, I'll read them to you."

She gave me the numbers and the dates they were called. One, with the area code of 803, I recognized as being in South Carolina. The other two numbers were from the 912 area, which could be anywhere in the southern half of Georgia.

"Have you thought of anything else that might help me find Kristee?"

"Yes," she said slowly, "I found a picture of her." Her voice wavered for a moment, and I almost thought she'd put down the phone. "I decided to look through Bo's dresser drawers. I found one, all right. It's of her, dressed in an orange thong bikini."

"Any idea where it was taken?"

"It's no place I recognize, but then, hopefully, Bo wouldn't have the balls to take her anywhere we'd be seen as a couple."

I thought about the sofa in her study, but I didn't volunteer anything.

"I'm looking at it right now," Lilah Rose said. "She's definitely sitting by a swimming pool; you can see a little bit of the water. It's probably a club or a hotel, because there are a lot of chairs and tables around. Oh, yes, and I'll bet it's in the south. You can see some pine trees and some azaleas in bloom."

"Very good, Lilah," I said, surprised at her observations. "I'll come over this afternoon and pick it up, if that's all right."

"Fine," Lilah said crisply. "Bo'll be home early, around five-thirty. Come a little earlier than that, and I'll give you the picture. Of course, I don't want him to know I've given it to you, so let's keep that between us. And another thing, Callahan. I hate to tell you this, but Bo is seriously thinking of calling in another private investigator. He told his attorney a little bit about what's going on here, and the attorney gave him the name of some man in Miami. Bo told me on the phone that he intends to call this man tomorrow unless you come up with something solid right away."

I managed not to swear until after I'd hung up the phone. I felt doomed. I had about four hours to come up with enough information to let the Beemishes know they were getting results for their money. I must have sat there in a funk for at least five minutes.

"All right," Edna said finally. "Tell me what the problem is with the Beemishes. They're bitching about your cleaning, aren't they."

"No," I said, shaking my head. "Lilah didn't even mention the house. No, the problem is that son of a bitch Bo Beemish. He wants to call in somebody else, some guy from Miami. I've got until five-thirty today to come up with some kind of concrete information about Kristee Ewbanks."

For once, Edna was quiet. She screwed her eyes shut as she took a long drag on her cigarette and then exhaled noisily through her nostrils. The eyes popped open.

"Fuck 'em," she said, pushing a yellow legal pad across the table at me. "Look, I know you don't want me getting involved in this, but it strikes me that we could get some serious detecting work done with two of us working on the case. You just write down on the pad who you want called and what you want asked. We'll divide it in half. I'll make calls on the house phone while you use the company phone in here. We can dig up something, I'm sure."

She stubbed out her half-smoked cigarette in the ashtray at her elbow and reached over and patted my hand—a rare gesture. "Come on, Jules, this money is too good to give up without at least trying."

Edna didn't know just how much we really did need the money. We stood to lose at least $2,000, maybe even more, if I lost the case. Normally, I wouldn't have been so panicked, but lately we'd had a run of unexpected expenses. In addition to the van, I'd just finished paying withholding taxes for my employees, and there was a nagging medical thing I didn't want Edna knowing about. We'd sunk most of our savings into the House Mouse. We definitely needed the Beemishes' money.

"All right," I said, trying to sound reluctant. "But just phone calls, you understand? No stakeouts, no wiretapping, no interrogating witnesses. Nothing. You hear me?"

She cupped a hand to her ear and bent forward. "What's that, dearie? I can't hear a thing you're saying. I'm just a deaf old bag with arthritis and a daughter with a severe attitude problem."

9

BY THE TIME I GOT TO the Beemishes, I was feeling fairly confident about my ability to retain the job. We'd gotten some impressive information in a fairly short amount of time. It didn't tell us where Kristee Ewbanks was, but it did give us an idea of how we might find her.

A black maid in a white uniform answered the Beemishes' door. She was in her twenties, very pretty, with long curving red fingernails. Her index fingernail on both hands was gold. Didn't look like she'd been doing any dust-busting.

She led me back to the study. The Beemishes were there already. Bo Beemish had draped his sport coat over the back of the desk chair and was sitting there scanning the stock pages of the *Wall Street Journal*. Lilah Rose had been talking to him in what sounded like a peeved voice, but she broke off when she saw me in the doorway. She had on one of those flowered-chintz Laura Ashley jumpsuits with the empire bustline and balloon legs. Her hair was pushed back with a matching headband. She looked about twelve.

Beemish put down the paper when I entered but didn't stand. Lilah motioned me to sit on the sofa beside her and asked the maid to get me a drink. I asked for Perrier, just to let them know I wasn't a total savage.

"So?" Beemish asked impatiently, once my drink arrived.

"Right," I said. "First off, your nanny's name wasn't really Kristeena Ewbanks. It was Kristeen Edwards. She wasn't nineteen, she was twenty-two."

"I knew it," Lilah Rose muttered to herself.

"And she wasn't from Toonigh, Utah, either," I added. "The only Edwards in Toonigh is an eighty-two-year-old bachelor who says he's the last of the line."

"Get on with it," Beemish commanded.

"She's from South Carolina: Estill, to be exact, although she's lived all over. I talked to an aunt back in Estill, who said, and I quote, 'That girl's been in trouble since the day she strapped on her first bra.'"

"I bet she has a criminal record too, doesn't she?" put in Lilah. "What's she wanted for?"

"Nothing, at the moment," I said. "Or at least as far as I can tell. Up to now, Kristee Edwards mainly dabbled in paperhanging."

"Huh?" Lilah said.

"Writing bad checks. She and a boyfriend traveled all over the country, writing bad checks. They also stole some credit cards and loaded them up, although Kristee was never charged with that. Anyway, the law caught up with them in Utah, about eighteen months ago. The boyfriend, who had a record, got sent to the state pen. Kristee was sentenced to a diversion center—that's a kind of halfway house where you live with a bunch of women in a communal setting, work at a job to make restitution to your victim, and receive some counseling. This diversion center was in Provo, in an old motel. Kristee struck up a friendship with a woman there named Ardith Cramer. She was a vocational counselor. I talked to the diversion center director on the phone this afternoon. According to her, this Ardith was very sincere but sort of confused about life. She was also apparently a lesbian. From what I can gather, Kristee conned Ardith into starting a relationship, although we suspect she isn't really lesbian. The director said Kristee tried to con everybody she came in contact with.

"Anyway, after Kristee finished her sentence about six months ago, Ardith quit her counseling job. She told the director that she and Kristee were going to move to Salt Lake City to make a new start. Maybe get jobs in a preschool, because Kristee was crazy about kids."

"She was good with ours," Bo murmured.

Lilah snorted but said nothing.

"The trail gets a little cold once they got to Salt Lake City," I said apologetically. "The way I've pieced it together, from talking to a woman in Salt Lake City who runs a legitimate nanny service, Kristee and Ardith were living in a little trailer park, and there was a nineteen-year-old girl who lived in the next lot over. This girl was LDS—Mormon. She'd just come back from a nanny stint in Texas. Apparently, she told Kristee all about how much fun she had and how nice these rich families were to work for. She also told her about the service she worked for, the one that placed her with the Texas family.

"Myra, the woman who owns her own agency, said the women apparently talked to a lot of other girls who were waiting to be placed by other agencies, including her own. Kristee tried to recruit the girls, but they were a little distrustful, because she obviously wasn't LDS, which the other agency owners are. But Kristee did offer the girls fifty dollars if they would refer her new agency, Nanny Finders, to someone who needed a nanny. I tracked down Polly Newman, the girl who used to work for the Eshelmanns; she's gone back home now, to get married. Polly said Kristee offered her a job, but when Polly told her she was going to Atlanta, Kristee asked her to try and find a placement there for her."

"I should have known better than to listen to that whey-faced little wimp, Polly," Lilah said, interrupting. "That takes care of us. But did they place any other girls?"

"At least one, maybe two," I said. "Polly told me that Ardith said they'd placed a girl in Savannah and another one somewhere near Charleston. I think that may explain those long distance calls you can't account for. Kristee was probably in touch with the other girls."

"Were they thieves and con artists too?" Bo asked.

I took a long sip of the Perrier, sucked on the lime for a moment, then slipped it tastefully back into my glass. "You could say that. I've only talked to the Sheehans; they're the family in Savannah. I called the long distance numbers you gave me, Lilah. The Charleston number doesn't answer. I'll keep trying, though. The girl the Sheehans hired, Beverly Mayes, was only there three weeks before she cleaned them out. In addition to the usual stuff, this girl stole some computer software her employer was developing. The Savannah police think Beverly Mayes headed for Atlanta, but they don't know much else."

"Jesus," Bo said, slapping his hands on the desk. "Those cops couldn't find their asses with both hands. So now where do we stand? It seems to me you could at least find this Ardith Cramer woman."

"At least," he'd said. I'd given them several solid leads that would eventually lead to Kristee, but it wasn't enough.

"Well, no," I admitted. "Ardith Cramer, unlike Kristee, doesn't have a criminal record. That makes her a little harder to trace. I can tell you that my associate"—Edna would love being called an associate—"found that Ardith has been gone from Salt Lake City at least six weeks. The phone was disconnected at that time, and the man who runs the trailer park where they were staying said he found some circulars and utility bills in the mailbox that were at least that old. I think Ardith is probably right here in Atlanta. If we could find her or Beverly, I think we'd find Kristee. They're probably busy trying to pawn your jewelry and coins and already planning their next scam."

"This is a city of two million people," Beemish pointed out. "She could be anywhere, right? And we still don't know where she is or what she's done with our property. You've done all right, I guess, giving us Kristee's real name and all. But in light of the fact that we now know we're dealing with a professional criminal, I think we're gonna have to change the game plan."

"Game plan?" I said weakly.

"That's right. I'm calling the signals here. I've discussed this situation with my attorney, and he and I have agreed it might be best to call in a more seasoned man for this job."

Beemish reached into the desk drawer and brought out an eelskin-covered loose-leaf check binder. "Of course, we'll pay you for the work you've already done. What is it, about two, three hundred dollars?"

For a second there, I felt my heart sink. Then I got pissed off, which was good. I do some of my best work pissed off.

"My day rate is five hundred dollars," I said. "Plus I've been on the telephone for the best part of the day. I have no idea what those charges will be. We can say an extra hundred for expenses, if you like, and then I'll refund the difference once I get my phone bill."

Beemish seemed relieved to be let off the hook that easily, and he smiled and started writing out a check.

"I understand completely your desire to get this matter wrapped up quickly," I said. "It's unfortunate, though, that I'll be leaving the case unfinished. My associate and I had developed quite an interesting plan to track Kristee. She has some contacts in the Mormon community here, and my former colleagues in the Atlanta Police Department have hinted they may know something about Beverly Mayes. . . ."

I stood up and placed the typewritten House Mouse report on the desktop—with quite a nice effect, I thought. I put my hand out for the check, and he dropped it into my palm.

"I'd be happy for you to share my report with your new investigator, of course, since you paid for it," I continued. I turned to Lilah Rose, who'd fallen strangely silent.

"Lilah, I'm assuming the House Mouse contract continues, is that correct?"

She nodded vigorously, then reached over and took the check out of my hand and tore it up. She dropped the little pieces on the rug. Her husband raised one sandy eyebrow at her but said nothing.

"Please sit down, Callahan," she said.

Her face was getting pink, and she reached in the pocket of her jumper and pulled out a cigarette and lit it. It wasn't until she'd inhaled and exhaled and flicked an ash in the ashtray, then quickly stubbed it out, that she spoke.

Her speech was slow, deliberate. "I guess it's time to cut the bullshit, as you'd say, honey," she said, gazing at her husband. "Bo, I want Callahan to stay on the case."

"No way," he said flatly. "She's an amateur, darling. I thought we discussed all that."

"We didn't discuss anything," she said. "You informed me that you'd hired somebody else, after I'd already given Callahan the job."

Beemish shook his head ruefully, crossed his arms over his chest, but said nothing. He regarded her as he did his children, with a sort of benign impatience.

"I know you were sleeping with her," Lilah said calmly. "I've known for a long time."

He pressed his hands to his face, covering his eyes. The smirk was gone. "Lilah, I swear—"

"Forget it," Lilah said. "I'm not interested in the details or in any of your excuses. And I'm not looking for a divorce either. But I *have* talked to JoAnne Rockmore about drawing up a new property settlement, just in case I change my mind." She glanced at me now, me, sitting there with my mouth hanging open. "You remember JoAnne, don't you? She was Tri Delt at Georgia a couple years ahead of us. Went to law school at Emory. She represented

Bootsie Duncan in her divorce from Channing last year. Bootsie just bought a health spa in Aspen, and she's had liposuction and got herself a real cute new behind and a new boyfriend."

Beemish's face was pale with anger. "Goddammit, Lilah Rose, this is not funny. I don't appreciate your pulling a stunt like this in front of a stranger."

I didn't much like it myself. In fact, I wished I could disappear.

Lilah Rose seemed to be enjoying herself. "Well, I can't say that I appreciated your fucking my children's nanny under my roof, sweetheart. It's really so low class. Besides, Callahan's not a stranger, she's a sister, right, Callahan?"

Tar baby, she don't say nothing.

Lilah went on, smoothly. "And I won't have you bringing some Miami thug around my home, talking to my children and scaring them and making a scene in front of all my friends and neighbors. Callahan has done a fine job. I really think she can find Kristee. And as far as anybody in the neighborhood is concerned, she's just a cleaning lady who asks a lot of questions."

Beemish raised his hands then, as if to surrender. "Fine. You wanna screw around and let that little bitch walk off with my mother's ring and your earrings and a hundred thousand in negotiable bonds, not to mention sensitive information about a business deal that could ruin me if it gets out. You wanna send a maid to find her, go ahead. But if the maid can't find her you won't need JoAnne Rockmore, because if we don't get those business records back, there ain't gonna be nothing for you to get in alimony."

He pushed his chair back from the desk, stood up, and stalked from the room.

"Do whatever you want," he said, not looking back. "You always do."

"Got that right," she shot back at him.

Lilah's face was impassive as she watched her husband leave.

"So, what's your next move?" she asked. "It better be a good one. I don't know how long I can hold this divorce threat over Bo's head. He always could read me like a book."

I glanced nervously at the door. "To tell you the truth, there are several things I need to check into. For one thing, I'd like to go back up to Kristee's room, if you don't mind, to make sure I haven't missed anything."

"Fine," she said. "Go on up. I'm going to go see if I can find a Valium. My nerves are shot to hell."

Upstairs, I walked slowly around Kristee's room. The dust smell seemed more pronounced than it had the day before, and the mattress sagged and the springs creaked when I sat on the bed. No wonder they'd chosen a sofa in the den for their trysts.

I reached under the pillow, then, hoping to find some clue I'd overlooked during my first search, maybe a motel key or an airline ticket voucher or something. There was nothing. I held the pillow up to my nose and breathed. It smelled of her, Kristee, her expensive shampoo mingled with the powdery scent of deodorant and something stronger, a perfume that might have been Opium. One of her blond hairs clung to the wrinkled pillowcase. I picked it up between my thumb and forefinger, then blew it to the floor.

On the bed beside me I placed the photograph that Lilah Rose had found. The girl in the picture was lying on a chaise lounge. One long bronze leg was stretched out, the other cocked suggestively. She was leaning toward the camera, smiling, lips parted slightly, letting the photographer take the full measure of the breasts that spilled from the orange bikini top.

Out of boredom more than anything else, I picked up the telephone, considered calling Edna to tell her to meet me somewhere for dinner. For the first time I noticed a small clear plastic tab that protruded from the bottom of the phone. I tugged at it, and it came loose. There was a neatly written short series of numbers, all preceded by an asterisk, a digit, and a single initial.

On a hunch, I punched the first number, 1, into the phone. "Domino's Pizza," a male voice said. "We deliver."

The second number, a 2, was followed by the letter W. I let it ring several times, but there was no answer. The third number, 3, had an A by it. I punched the number and listened as the numbers clicked off. It rang once and someone picked up and started talking.

It was a woman, frantic. "Kristee, where the hell have you been?" she demanded. "I've been worried sick."

10

THE BEST THING ABOUT THE RAIN that pounded the van as we inched our way along Cheshire Bridge Road was the fact that the noise of it drowned out the strange sounds coming from the muffler.

I hunched over the steering wheel trying to see, through the fogged-up windshield, the sign for the Cheshire Bridge Motor Hotel, where Ardith Cramer had finally admitted she was staying.

"Can you see what that sign says?" I asked Edna. "My side of the windshield is too blurry."

"Can't see the sign at all, much less what it says," she said cheerfully. Edna was next to useless as a navigator, even when she was wearing her bifocals. Right now she was too busy catching the colorful sights of Cheshire Bridge. Traffic was slow because of the heavy rain, so she was getting an eyeful. On the right was the Naughty Nitey Lingerie Modeling boutique. We could see two bored-looking women wearing black lace bustiers and garter belts sitting in the picture window. They were reading magazines. They didn't look exceptionally naughty to me. Next door was a Vietnamese pool hall. A knot of black-leather-clad toughs stood in the doorway, smoking tiny black cigars and drinking malt liquor from liter bottles. Halfway down the block we saw the Emporium, a gay biker bar that's been a Cheshire Bridge fixture since the '70s. A line of Harleys was parked outside. Edna's head swung back and forth as she took in the sights until I thought it would swivel right off her neck.

"Look at that, Ma," I said, pointing to a new strip bar across the street that had just opened in what used to be my favorite Mexican restaurant. A neon sign had been erected on the red-tile roof of the stucco building. It featured two green glowing breasts, with a red light twinkling on and off on each nipple.

"That I can read," she said, chuckling. "Titty City. Jesus, Mary, Joseph, and all the saints. I can't believe this is Atlanta."

"Welcome south, brother," I said.

We knocked on the door of Unit 1218 for about five minutes before we saw the dingy curtain part and heard a bolt sliding open. The woman who opened the door was short, with the wiry look of an athlete. There was a towel wrapped around her head, and she wore a faded T-shirt and a pair of old gym shorts. She was barefoot and there were wet footprints on the orange shag carpet.

"Just came back from a run," she said, not bothering to introduce herself. "I was in the shower and didn't hear you knocking."

I walked in and Edna followed. The woman looked surprised that there was someone with me, but she didn't mention it.

Edna sat herself by the desk, on the only chair in the room. I sat down on one twin bed, Ardith Cramer sat down on the other.

She busied herself toweling her short auburn hair. Her skin had the dull-red look of someone who's been out in the sun too much. The lips were thin, and her nose was slightly pointed. I could see large dark circles visible under the thick-lensed glasses she wore.

"What is it you want?" she said dully. "I told you on the phone, I haven't seen Kristee. I haven't talked to her since Friday. I told you that, didn't I?"

"Yes," I admitted, "you did."

"I think Beemish has done something to her. I know he's hurt her or something." She was repeating herself now, as she'd done on the phone, insisting that she hadn't seen Kristee but saying that she was sure something had happened to her.

"I told her to leave him alone," she said, staring absentmindedly at the soundless television screen bolted to the wall of the room. "Kristee told me she'd lucked into something big. It was gonna get us a lot of money. A lot of money."

"Did she say what it was?" I prompted.

She shook her head, shaking water droplets on the faded green bedspread. "Some deal Beemish was involved in. Kristee got some papers that proved it was crooked. She was gonna make him pay to get them back."

"Blackmail," I said.

She shrugged. "I told her to let it alone. She thought the whole thing was hilarious. She even talked about getting money from another guy involved in the deal. She wouldn't stop. I couldn't make her. I told her weeks ago that we should get out, but she wouldn't."

"Did Kristee tell you she was having an affair with Bo Beemish?" I asked bluntly.

Ardith blinked. "No. I don't believe you. Where do you get an idea like that? Kristee wasn't into men."

Edna snorted. I shot her a warning look, but it was too late. "I hate to have to tell you this, dearie, but I think your little girlfriend was into whatever could get her what she wanted. Men, women, guppies, gerbils: it really didn't matter, according to what we've heard."

"Who's she?" Ardith demanded angrily, motioning with her head toward Edna. "What the hell do you know about anything?"

"She's my associate," I said. "Now, are you sure you haven't talked to Kristee this week?"

"No," she said. "I haven't. I talked to her Friday, but when I called the house Saturday, there was no answer. I've been calling ever since, hoping she'd answer. I even took a cab over there Monday, but I didn't have the nerve to ring the doorbell, so I walked around outside the house and left."

"Where do you think she's gone?" I asked. "Didn't the two of you plan to meet up and split what she stole from the Beemishes?"

"I keep telling you, no," she repeated. "I don't know anything about any plan to steal anything. Kristee was the one working for them. I just work for the company that placed her."

"I don't believe you," Edna piped up. "Why don't you tell us where you and your girlfriend hid the stuff? Just give it all back, and I'll bet our client will forget all about this misunderstanding."

It had been a mistake, bringing my mother along on this interview, but I'd needed somebody to watch the back of the motel unit while I knocked on the front, in case Ardith decided to take off. As it turned out, I needn't have worried. There was no back door. So now Edna was in the room with us, doing her best bad-cop imitation. I could have strangled her.

"She's right about one thing," I told Ardith. "If you and Kristee make complete restitution, including the jewelry, and especially those missing business documents, our clients won't press charges."

"What charges?" Ardith said belligerently. "I don't know what you're talking about. What have I done to the Beemishes?"

"Well, there's conspiracy to defraud, theft by taking, and blackmail," I said. "Oh, yes, and since you arranged this little farce over the phone and by mail, we can add mail fraud and wire fraud. Those are federal charges, sweetie. I'm afraid you and Kristee won't be in any diversion center this time. Of course, once the cops pick up Beverly Mayes, there'll be even more charges."

"Why would the cops pick up Beverly?" Ardith asked warily. "She's a nanny, doing her job. She's not in any trouble."

"Cut the shit, Ardith," I said. "We know Beverly cleaned out the Sheehans in Savannah, and we know she's someplace in Atlanta. Is she staying with you?"

Ardith shook her head, unconvincingly. "Beverly is in Savan-nah."

"She's not in Savannah," I said, nearly shouting now. "Look, Ardith, I don't think you realize the seriousness of what's going on here. Beverly Mayes left Savannah last week after she stole some computer discs and a lot of other stuff belonging to the family she worked for. Kristee Ewbanks has more than a hundred thousand dollars' worth of the Beemishes' property, plus some important business documents. You're a party to all this, and the cops won't have a hard time proving it either."

Tears welled in Ardith's eyes. "You can't prove anything," she said bitterly. "Nothing. You say you want information from me? I'll give you information. Kristee's gone. And I think Bo Beemish killed her."

Just then I heard Edna start to groan, loudly. We both looked at her. She was clutching her stomach, bent nearly double.

"My diverticulitis," she gasped. "Can I use the bathroom?"

"It's in there," Ardith said, jerking her head to indicate an open doorway.

Edna rushed for the room, then slammed the door.

"She all right?"

"Probably. This happens sometimes," I said. "Look, can I use your phone to check my answering machine?"

"Yeah, but how about leaving me fifty cents? They even charge for local calls in this dump."

I took the phone off the nightstand, punched in my number, and beeped my beeper into it. While I was waiting for the tape to rewind I noticed a newspaper folded to the want ads. There were circles on the "help wanted" column.

Lilah Rose Beemish had called three times. Each time she phoned, she emphasized that she needed to see me at 10 A.M. at Rich's house tomorrow.

I hung up. Ardith went to the door and opened it. "Rain's

stopped," she announced. "I'm gonna go for another run. I can't stand being closed up in this room."

She started pulling on shoes and socks and went to the dresser and pulled out a headband, which she put on.

Edna was still in the bathroom. What in God's name was she doing? Finally I heard a flush and the sound of water running.

She unlocked the door and stepped daintily out of the bathroom, wiping her hands on the seat of her polyester slacks. "You're out of towels, did you know?" she said pleasantly.

"I know," Ardith said. She went back to the front door and opened it, then stepped aside to make it clear she was ready for us to leave.

I handed her one of my business cards. "If you hear from Kristee, tell her to call me. Tell her to make it soon, too, before the Beemishes call the cops."

"Right," she said through clenched teeth. "You can tell Bo Beemish if he's done something to Kristee I'll make him pay. Tell him that."

I nodded and stepped out into the warm spring night.

"She's lying," Edna said, as soon as we'd closed the car doors.

I was busy trying to make a turn onto Cheshire Bridge, so I didn't answer for a moment. "About what?"

"All of it," she said. "Kristee's been in that room—recently. And somebody else has been staying there too."

"How did you figure all this out?" I asked. "I don't suppose this has anything to do with your sudden bout of diverticulitis, does it?"

Edna patted her hair, tucking a blue-tinted lock behind her left ear. "Well, I needed an excuse to spend some time in the bathroom. Your great-aunt Opal had diverticulitis, and she used to live in the bathroom."

"So what'd you find?"

"Well, she may be staying there alone now, but she's definitely had company," Edna said. "She's got a box of groceries under the bathroom sink. There's a jar of peanut butter and a box of crackers about two thirds gone, and three kinds of cereal."

"So?" I said. "She's getting low on money, so she's eating in. Big deal."

"Do you know any adults who buy three different kinds of cereal for themselves?" she said.

"Did you find any long bleached-blond hairs in the shower drain?" I asked facetiously.

"Don't think I didn't check," Edna said. "There were just some short brown ones."

"What makes you think Kristee was there? She could have had other company, you know."

Edna got a smug look then, that smug look I hate. She squirmed around in her seat, finally pulling something out of her pants pocket. "Look at this," she said triumphantly.

I glanced at the small plastic bottle she held in her palm. "What is it?"

"A prescription pill bottle for Kristee Ewbanks," she said. "I found it in the bathroom and copped it. It was in a brown paper bag with some clothes and stuff that I bet belong to Kristee. This was the smallest thing in the bag. It was filled last week at the West Paces Ferry A&P pharmacy."

This time I didn't try to hide my annoyance. "What'd you take it for? If the cops come in on this thing, that could be evidence. You should have left it right where it was."

Edna didn't have an answer for that. So she sat quietly and sulked.

After ten minutes I couldn't stand it any more. "What's the prescription for?"

She held the bottle about an inch from her eyes and squinted. "I can't pronounce it. Wait, it's Pyridium. The bottle's still nearly full."

"Wonder what she was taking it for?"

"I know a way to find out in a hurry," Edna said. "Call your sister and ask. She'll know."

I made a face. Maureen and I were currently feuding over something her husband said to me a few weeks back. I called him on it and she stood up for him. Maureen is three years younger than me. She's a nurse at Grady Memorial Hospital, Atlanta's huge charity hospital. That's where she met Steve Kusic, the ambulance driver she ended up marrying. He's a lazy loudmouth slimedog, but you'll never get Maureen to see that. Since she married Steve, I've kept my distance. I can't stand the guy. Edna can't either, but she won't admit it.

"I could call Maureen. Or I could go to the library and look it up in a *Physician's Desk Reference*."

"Do what you want," Edna said. She clutched her big white plastic purse to her chest and pooched out her lower lip. Just like a goddamn baby, I thought.

Five minutes later I heard a sawing noise. Edna's head lolled over on her right shoulder. Her eyes were closed and her mouth was wide open. Her snoring nearly drowned out the chugging of the van's muffler.

11

THE PHONE IN MY BEDROOM was ringing as I stepped out of the shower.

I let it go a couple of times, hoping Edna would catch it, but she didn't.

So I padded out of the bathroom, leaving a trail of water on the carpet. "House Mouse."

"Oh, it's you," I heard my sister say.

"Yeah, it's me. This is my house, you know. You calling for Mom?"

Maureen let out a long audible sigh. "No, I can just tell you. Mom said you wanted to know something about Pyridium, right?"

I tried to keep the irritation out of my voice, but I'm sure my sister knew I didn't want to talk to her. "Well, I was gonna look it up for myself. But OK, what's the stuff for?"

"Bladder infection," Maureen said. "Fairly common in women. Why, do you have one?"

"No," I said. "I'm just checking out something for a client."

"So you're cleaning houses and prescribing medicine these days?"

"No," I said shortly. "But if somebody didn't take all their pills, would they still be OK?"

She laughed. "Obviously you've never had a bladder infection. You feel like you have to pee all the time, and then when you do, it's this godawful burning sensation. The Pyridium is just to help the pain. You also have to take antibiotics to kill the infection. What kind was your client taking?"

Edna hadn't seen any other pill bottles in Ardith's motel room. "I don't know," I told her. "Look, I'm standing here dripping wet. I'll talk to you later. Thanks for the help."

"Sure," she said shortly, and hung up without saying good-bye. "Bitch," I told the receiver.

The phone rang again just as I was trying to struggle into a pair of jeans. They were extra tight, so I had to lie flat on the bed and suck in my belly to get them zipped. I'd already made a resolution to buy myself a case of Ultra Slim-Fast.

"House Mouse," I said, trying to sit up straight without popping the snap of the jeans.

"Callahan, did you get my message about meeting me at Rich's this morning?" said the harried voice of Lilah Rose Beemish.

"Good morning, Lilah," I said. "Yes, I did get your message. I was just going to call to ask if we couldn't make it later in the day. I do have a business to run here, you know."

"Later won't work," she snapped. "I need you to meet me at the fur vault at the downtown Rich's when they open at ten A.M. That is, if you want to continue to work for us."

I could feel my chain being yanked, but there was nothing I could do about it. I needed the Beemishes' money. "What's this about anyway?"

"Oh, Bo's giving me fits about the jewelry and the other stuff Kristee took," she said. "He finally talked to our insurance man about filing a claim, and he said we have to file a police report."

"I thought you didn't want the police involved," I said.

"We don't. But Big Mama's gonna notice sooner or later about the amethyst ring and the silver and coins and stuff. So he decided to tell the police the house was burglarized."

"I don't think it's a good idea to lie to the cops, Lilah Rose," I said. "They're not stupid, you know."

"Now don't you start lecturing me too. Bo's been after me all morning. Besides, the house *was* burglarized. It's just that in this case we happen to know who the burglar was."

I decided to skip the lesson on the difference between breaking and entering and theft by taking.

"If you're filing a police report, why do you need me and why at Rich's fur vault?"

"Because I can't find my furs," she said. "And I'm not absolutely certain Kristee took them."

"Where else would they be?"

"Well, usually I have my maid take them to Rich's for storage as soon as fur season is over, sometime in March," Lilah said. "But Regina, that's my maid, quit right around that time, and I can't remember if she took them in, and I can't find a claim check. I called them yesterday, but they say they can't trace anything without a claim check. And I don't dare tell Bo I don't know where they are."

"What do you expect me to do at Rich's?" I said. "Search the store?"

"Exactly," she shot back. "See you there at ten. And for God's sake, please don't dress like a cleaning woman. Someone I know might see us."

I exhaled loudly and was rewarded by hearing my jeans pop open. Just as well. I wriggled out of them, kicked them under the bed, and walked into the closet in my underwear. Things didn't look good. My wardrobe tends to run to slacks and T-shirts these days. There were a few dresses, though. I picked out a navy blue linen thing that wasn't too bad, and looked around for a pair of shoes that weren't Nikes or Adidases. Found a pair of navy blue flats. I don't wear heels any more. Not since the days I worked vice squad and had to spend eight-hour shifts dressed in five-inch spikes as part of my hooker getup.

After I'd dressed I glanced quickly in the mirror and ran my fingers through my hair. It's short and curly, like a poodle's, my hair is. It used to be coal black, like my dad's was before he got sick. But I started going gray at sixteen, and now it's totally salt and pepper. "Stress highlights" is what Frank, Mom's hairdresser friend, calls my gray hair. "Old lady hair" is what Edna calls it. She's always after me to have Frank color it, mostly, I suspect, so people won't know she has a daughter old enough to go gray. I kind of like it, though, and I'm too lazy to keep going to a beauty shop to have somebody slather goo on my head every couple of months. Just as long as my skin stays good, I decided, I'd let my hair go stark white if it wanted to. I have good skin, everybody says. For twenty years I'd been lathering moisturizer on it morning and night, and now I could see the extra attention was paying off.

I grabbed a lipstick off my dresser and stuck it in my pocket. Since I started my own business, I make it a policy never to wear any more makeup than I can apply at a stoplight. I'll never make the cover of *Vogue*, but I get ten extra minutes of sleep every morning, and the sacrifice is worth it.

I was maybe ten minutes late getting to Rich's. I'd had to brief Edna on the day's business and then stop at the 7-Eleven to buy a pair of pantyhose, which I'd put on in the back of the van.

It was doorbuster day at Rich's, and the store was crowded with downtown office workers picking through the tables of sale merchandise that clogged the aisles on each floor. I could hear Lilah Rose's voice as I stepped off the escalator on fifth. Everybody in the store, I imagined, could hear that voice.

"Get the manager," she was insisting. "I want him here right now. You tell him Mrs. DuBose Beemish wants to see him."

As I approached the alcove where the fur salon was located, I could see Lilah Rose standing over a woman who was seated at a stylish white-and-gold French desk. A tasteful marble nameplate pronounced her Ms. Reynard. The woman's hair was white-blond, swept back in a chignon. Her skin was a ghoulish powder-white, with two bright red spots glowing on her cheeks. Her thin lips were a slash of matching fuchsia.

Ms. Reynard didn't look like a happy camper. "I've told you, Mrs. Beemish, the store has a policy against anybody entering the fur vault. It's for your own security, you know. I'm sorry you can't find your claim check, but if you'll wait until the computer comes back up, we can see if your furs were logged in. Maybe you'd like to do a little shopping and come back."

Lilah Rose reached in her purse (Fendi, it looked like), brought out a matching billfold, and flipped it open to the credit card selection. She plucked one out and threw it on the woman's desk. "Do you see that card?" she said, leaning down until her face was within inches of the saleswoman's. "That's a Prestige card. It means I spend more in this store than you make in a year. My husband goes dove-hunting with the chairman of the board of Rich's. Now, I want you to let me in that fur vault right now. Do you understand?"

I couldn't stand to hear any more of this harangue. "Excuse me," I said quietly. "Ms. Reynard, I think we can settle all this quietly. Is Horton Lundeen still head of store security here?"

"Yes, ma'am," she said.

"Fine," I said. "Why don't you call and ask him to meet Callahan Garrity at the fur vault? I think he might be willing to help us straighten out this little misunderstanding."

She started to say something but thought better of it. Pressing her lips into a thin line, she made the call.

Horton Lundeen hadn't changed much since the days when I'd known him as a desk sergeant at the Atlanta PD. His hair was in a gray flattop. He wore a cheap dark suit, a severely starched white dress shirt, and shiny black lace-up cop shoes. A National Rifle Association belt buckle the size of a dinner plate had pride of place on his flat belly. His face was scowling as he walked up, but he smiled, sort of, when he caught sight of me.

"Garrity," he said, pumping my hand vigorously. "You been shoplifting in my store?"

"No, chief." I laughed. "But my client here has a problem we were hoping you could help us with."

Lundeen and I stepped out of earshot of Lilah Rose, who was busy glaring at Ms. Reynard. I quickly filled him in on what I'd been doing since I'd left the force and told him why we needed to get into the fur vault.

"It's against the rules," he said flatly. "Insurance company insists."

I cocked my head to one side and fluttered my eyelashes in my most seductive manner. "Since when have you been a strictly by-the-book guy?"

"Fuckin' A," he agreed. "Let's go."

While we were negotiating the maze of elevators, long hallways, and locked doors that led to the actual fur vault, Lilah Rose ran down the list of what we were looking for.

"The most valuable one is the sable," she said. "Opera-length. Bo bought it for me after Carter was born. And then there's my old mink, full-length, with a shawl collar and push-up sleeves. And my fox stroller. I just wear it to run around town in. My name is sewn into the lining of all of them," she said, trying to be helpful.

"How much are these things worth altogether?" I asked, just out of curiosity.

She wrinkled her brow, mentally adding them up. "We'd have to check the insurance policy, of course, but I guess altogether we're talking in the neighborhood of thirty-five to forty thousand."

Some neighborhood, I thought.

Finally, we arrived at the end of a long dingy hallway. Horton knocked at a heavily scarred steel door with a peephole set into the middle. After a minute or so, a buzzer sounded and the latch clicked.

We walked through two more doors and then into the vault. It wasn't what I'd expected. It was huge, with long metal pipes hanging from chains crisscrossing the room in rows.

The place was wall-to-wall fur. My nose started to quiver involuntarily and my stomach felt a little queasy. I heard a small gasp of pleasure from Lilah Rose. I turned to glance at her. She was enchanted. "Look at all these beautiful things," she breathed.

There were furs in colors and styles I didn't know existed. There were mink stoles from the '50s, long raccoon coats that looked like refugees from the '20s, mink neckpieces that had ratlike little heads nipping at their own tails. There were fur bedspreads and zebra-skin rugs. There must have been thousands of them. Now, I'm no animal rights zany but all those dead animal skins hanging in that dimly lit chilly room made my flesh crawl.

"Is there a system as to how they're hung up?" I asked Lundeen.

"Ought to be," he allowed. "But I got no idea what it is."

"I guess we'll just browse," I said. I turned to ask Lilah where she wanted to start, but she was already moving down the rows, lovingly running her hands across each coat.

We must have walked like that for forty-five minutes, Lilah dreamily stroking each coat, me dragging reluctantly behind, eyeing the goods with distaste. My feet, even in flats, were starting to ache from the concrete floor, but Lilah, who wore crocodile pumps with three-inch heels, fairly floated along the rows.

"This could take all day," I said crossly.

"Mmm, you're right," she said. She plucked at the sleeve of a coat. "Don't you just love this old leopard cape? It's so Hollywood. I don't know when I've seen real leopard."

I looked at the hangtag on the sleeve. The thing had been in storage since 1965. "No wonder," I said. "Leopard's an endangered species. If you wore this out in public you'd probably be lynched."

Lilah sniffed indignantly. "I like it," she said, but she moved on.

At the end of the aisle a large aluminum box on wheels blocked our access.

"What's in here, chief?" I called out. "A live panther?"

Lilah Rose crinkled her nose in disgust. "Smells more like a dead skunk," she said. "Shouldn't somebody have cleaned these things before they brought them in here with other people's furs?"

Lundeen caught up with us and looked at the box. It had the remnants of various labels all over it and a series of numbers stenciled on the side. There was a large padlocked pull-down door.

"It's a merchandise hamper from one of our other stores," he said. "When furs don't sell by the end of the season, they send them over here to storage until we put them on end-of-year clearance." He squinted at the labels. "But I don't know why they'd leave the hamper here. Usually they unpack them, hang the furs, and take the hamper back down to the loading dock."

He reached around the back of his belt and drew out a ring of keys.

"Let's open this booger up and see what the deal is," he said, mostly to himself.

He fiddled with the padlock for a minute, then frowned. "This isn't one of our locks," he said. He reached back into his pocket and brought out a slim black file. We grinned at each other in recognition.

"You get a lot of call to use burglary tools at Rich's?" I asked.

"Be prepared," he said. "Boy Scout motto."

Within a few seconds he had popped the padlock and was rolling the door up.

Heaped in the bottom of the hamper were a pile of multicolored furs, a black sable on top.

"Oh, look," Lilah squealed delightedly, reaching to grab the sable.

As she pulled at the coat, the corner of a large plastic bag started to slide out of the hamper onto the floor.

I leaned down and moved the other two furs aside. The plastic was a heavy garment bag. Inside were the remains of what had probably been a very pretty, very clever blond woman.

Lilah wasn't paying any attention to me. She'd donned the sable and was doing a little pirouette. "My furs," she said. "We found my furs."

"And your nanny," I said.

12

AS HYSTERICS GO, Lilah Rose Beemish's were a very mild case. She'd found her nanny dead, at the bottom of a pile of her own fur coats. Emotionally, she was more attached to the furs, but I think what she saw of Kristee contributed to the upset.

Another woman might have passed out. I guess it was Lilah's good South Georgia roots. The Ledbetters, I think, were farmers. She'd probably helped out at more than one hog killing in her time.

She gasped and sniffed and boo-hooed a little, especially after seeing Kristee, which was only for seconds, because Horton whisked us out of that vault in a New York minute. The body appeared to be nude, and from the quick glimpse I got, it looked like she might have been strangled. There were raw marks around her neck, and her face was a gray-black. Thank God for the constant 40-degree temperature of that vault. Otherwise, we both would have been tossing our cookies on somebody's Blackgama.

Horton was a champ. He hustled us out of the vault and up into his tiny office, which was back in the bowels of the building, in double-time.

It wasn't long before the real cops showed up. Of course, it being Rich's, where half the cops in Atlanta picked up overtime or Christmas security work, there were no flashing sirens or yellow crime-scene tape being unfurled. No one wanted to create a nasty scene during a one-day doorbuster sale.

Instead, two detectives and three uniformed officers crammed themselves into Horton's office. From what they said, I gathered the crime scene crew was busy processing the fur vault.

The cops didn't tell us squat, of course. Dick Bohannon, a lieutenant who's been on the force for more than twenty years, was the homicide detective in charge. His partner was an athletic-looking black guy I didn't recognize. But Bohannon I knew. He's one of those men who have a belly with a life of its own. His was an amazing thing that jutted out over his slacks, leaving his belt buried somewhere under a shelf of flesh. He had nine or ten strands of graying brown hair, tortured into a complex series of hills and whorls, and a set of mutton-chop sideburns that made him look like a Mod Squad reject. He nodded curtly at me, then directed a stream of questions at Lilah Rose.

Lilah had tried straight off to call Bo, but his secretary said he'd gone out to inspect a piece of property, and there was no answer on his car phone. So she called the family's silk-stocking downtown law firm, and they instructed her not to answer any questions until a lawyer could get there.

While we waited, Bohannon whistled tunelessly to himself and leafed through a Rich's sale circular he'd picked up on his way into the store. "Looka here," he said, suddenly perking up. "Polyester Sansabelt slacks, nineteen ninety-nine. Say, Horty, you get a discount working here? They give one to part-time cops too?"

Horton nodded yes on both counts, so Bohannon carefully tore the ad out of the circular and stuffed it in his pocket. He noticed me watching him and gave me a friendly sneer. I know Bohannon better than I wish I did. I'd worked for him for a couple of months on the burglary squad the year before I left the force.

It wasn't that he was an exceptionally sexist pig. It was just that he was one of a long line of cops I'd worked for who had an attitude about women.

So I'd typed up reports, did a lot of filing, answered phone calls that the guys were too busy to deal with, slogged a lot of bad coffee, and listened to an endless stream of little-boy locker room talk. The following year, Bohannon had been transferred over to homicide, and when my own request for a transfer to homicide was turned down, I'd left. No big scene. No tantrums. Just a lot of failed expectations on my part.

"Well now, J. Callahan Garrity," Bohannon drawled. "I thought I'd heard on the grapevine that you'd gotten out of the detecting business." He pronounced it "bidniz." "In fact, didn't someone tell me you were working for a janitor company?"

I'd long since learned not to let Bohannon get under my skin.

"Actually, it's a cleaning service, Dick." I deliberately dropped the Lieutenant. "And I own it. Other people work for me. I've kept my private detective license, and I do some consulting work now and again. Mrs. Beemish here is an old friend from college days."

From the doorway, someone cleared his throat, in a genteel manner, of course, to announce his arrival.

I recognized Tucker Taliaferro at once. He wore a sedate dark suit, a red silk bow tie with matching suspenders, and highly polished hand-sewn loafers. His hair was beige, and a set of rimless spectacles sat on his thin nose.

He and Lilah Rose huddled for a minute or two, and then he pulled out a chair, which he primly dusted off with his silk pocket handkerchief before he sat down.

"Now, Lieutenant," he said, briskly. "Mrs. Beemish tells me she feels calm enough to explain what she knows about her former employee and her disappearance, although there's really not much she can tell you."

He spoke with that strange pseudo-Etonian accent that prep-school-educated Southerners love to affect.

Lundeen and I exchanged raised eyebrows across the room.

Lilah clutched her Fendi bag with both hands in her lap and crossed her legs in order to allow Bohannon maximum observation of her thighs, which I personally thought were a little too dimpled for a skirt cut six inches above the knee. Her tanned face screwed itself up into a distraught little frown as she related how her family had been duped by Kristee and her business partner.

"She was lesbian, you know," Lilah whispered in shocked tones. "Of course my husband and I had no idea the girl was like that."

"Things had been going along fairly well, up until now," Lilah went on. "Bo and I and the children left Atlanta Friday to go to our place in Hilton Head, so I couldn't tell you what she did over the weekend."

"When did you leave town Friday?" Bohannon asked. "Did the girl tell you anything about her plans for the weekend? Did you talk to her at all on the phone while you were gone?"

"We left around six P.M.," Lilah said. "Bo had a late meeting. Kristee said she wanted to go see a movie with a girlfriend, and they were going to have a special program Sunday at her church." She laughed harshly. "Her church? Fat chance. Turns out she wasn't Mormon at all. We didn't talk to her at all over the weekend. In fact, we never saw her again after Friday."

"And you and your husband can both establish your where-abouts for the entire weekend? " Bohannon said, casually.

Taliaferro looked startled. "Why do you ask? Do you suspect my clients of having something to do with this mess?"

Bohannon favored him with an indulgent smile. "We suspect everybody the girl knew of having something to do with it, until we prove otherwise. I was just wondering if the Beemishes saw anyone in Hilton Head who can verify that they were there. No big deal."

The lawyer nodded warily at Lilah Rose.

"Well, we got in late Friday night, so I don't know who might have seen us. Saturday morning we played mixed doubles with some friends, Gloria and Tom Waring. We had brunch with several other couples, and in the afternoon the children and I were on the beach for most of the day."

"And your husband?"

Lilah looked annoyed. "He was in the house on the phone. He has a very important deal in development right now, and there are details only he can attend to. He'd come out for a few minutes and bring me a drink, or help the children with their sand castles, but then he'd go back in to wait on another call. The children and I came in around four-thirty, and they had naps while I showered and fixed my hair. Around six-thirty the babysitter arrived, and Bo and I went to dinner at Le Château. I guess André, the maître d', would remember we were there. We were home by nine P.M."

"And you both stayed there until Sunday?"

"*Late* Sunday," Lilah Rose snapped. "Saturday night, Bo dropped the babysitter off and then he met a business associate for a drink at his hotel."

"And what time did he get in?" Bohannon asked.

Lilah tugged her skirt down toward the direction of her knees. All these questions were clearly boring her. "I'd imagine it was around midnight," she said. "I dozed off, and although I heard him come to bed, I didn't check the time."

"But he was there in the morning?" Bohannon suggested. "And on Sunday?"

Lilah Rose recrossed her legs and jiggled her right foot, letting the heel of her high-heeled pump dangle from her foot. "We slept in late," she said. Her face flushed a bit under her tan. "I might as well tell you. My husband and I had a little tiff Sunday morning. I was angry that he'd spent so little time with the children the day before. It was supposed to be a family weekend, you see. I was really angry. So I left the condo, got in my car, and drove to Beaufort."

Bohannon smiled indulgently. "And what did you do while you were in Beaufort? Did you see anyone?"

Lilah faltered for a minute. "Let's see. I guess I just wandered around town, did some window shopping, and ate lunch. And, well, I guess I had too much wine with lunch, because on the drive back to Hilton Head I got so drowsy I had to pull off the road and take a nap. When I woke up, it was late afternoon. I'd left the house without my watch, but I guess I got back to the condo around four or so."

Taliaferro winced at Lilah's words but kept silent.

"A nap," Bohannon repeated. "You took a nap. Where did you say you ate in Beaufort? Did you see anyone who'd remember you?"

Lilah's foot jiggled again. "I doubt anyone would remember me. I don't believe I know anyone in Beaufort. The restaurant was one of those near the waterfront. I remember it was packed. The Blue Crab, I think it was called. The waitress was so busy she barely paid attention to me."

"Got a credit card receipt?" Bohannon asked.

"No," she said. "I paid cash."

"So no one else can account for your whereabouts for—what, six hours on Sunday?"

Taliaferro interrupted. "Mrs. Beemish has accounted for her whereabouts," he said curtly. "Surely that should do."

"We'll see," Bohannon said. "But you're sure you never saw Kristee Ewbanks again after Friday," he repeated. "Not even Sunday night, when you got in, or Monday morning?"

"Never," Lilah said. "It was late Sunday when we got home, and the children and I slept in on Monday. I never saw her again until just now." And tears welled up in her big blue eyes.

If Bohannon noticed the tears, he wasn't letting on. "And you say the girl stole from you? What kind of things?"

"Yes," Lilah said. "She was a trashy little thief. That's why we were here today, to see if my furs were in storage or if she'd taken them along with the jewelry and the bonds and the silver coins. I have a list at home, if you'd like to send someone over to get it."

Bohannon glanced at the calendar on Horton's desk, which he'd commandeered. "So the decedent disappeared, along with silver coins and jewels, sometime between Friday evening and Monday

morning, when you noticed she was gone, along with a considerable worth of valuables. This is Wednesday. And you're just now
getting ready to file a police report?"

Lilah Rose colored prettily. "We hated to make trouble for the
poor girl," she said. "And we didn't file a missing person report,
because she's an adult. We figured she might have run off with that
boyfriend of hers. But our insurance agent just insisted we file the
theft report."

"Boyfriend?" Bohannon said. "Didn't you say she was a lesbian?" He pronounced it "les-bee-un," with considerable spin on
the last syllable.

"I suppose you could say she liked it both ways," Lilah Rose
said, smirking. "His name was Whit. The last name was an Atlanta
street, I remember. Somewhere over near Piedmont Hospital." She
wrinkled her brow, trying to remember, then brightened. "Collier. That's it. Whit Collier. He's a Mormon boy she met through
church, or so she told us. In fact, he called and left a message on
our answering machine for her."

This was news to me. "He did?" I said. "Why didn't you mention it?"

Lilah Rose did not like being questioned by two people at once.
"You didn't give me a chance, Julia," she said, by way of reproval.
"Anyway, he just called and asked Kristee to call him back. That
was all. No time or date."

Bohannon asked a few more questions, but it quickly became
clear that Lilah Rose was tiring of this whole ordeal. In the beginning she enjoyed being the center of attention. She probably
regarded the whole thing as little more than an amusing anecdote
she could share with the girls at her next charity luncheon. Now,
though, things were getting tedious.

She dabbed at her eyes with a tissue and glanced meaningfully
at the wafer-thin gold watch on her wrist.

Taliaferro caught her signal. "Look, Lieutenant," he said,

"there's not very much more Mrs. Beemish can tell you about this thing. However, Ms. Garrity has been investigating this case for the past two days, and I'm sure she can tell you more about this girl than my client can. She can certainly tell you how to reach this Ardith Cramer. Of course, if you have more questions later, Mrs. Beemish would be happy to accommodate your needs."

With that, Taliaferro gracefully helped Lilah Rose from her chair, took her arm in his, and waltzed her out of the room.

"I'll be contacting your husband," Bohannon called to Lilah, but she didn't turn around. "And we'll check the Blue Crab, in case anybody does remember you."

13

BOHANNON PESTERED ME WITH questions for another thirty minutes after Lilah floated out. I told him what I'd found out about Kristee's background and how to reach the aunt in South Carolina Edna had talked to.

I also told him where he could find Ardith Cramer. He'd have found her on his own, quick enough, but I still hated ratting her out like that.

On the way out of Rich's, I fought my way through to the stocking counter and bought myself half a dozen pairs of their store-brand pantyhose. It might seem like a callous thing to do after finding a body and all, but it *was* a doorbuster sale. The stockings were $1.29 a pair, marked down from $2.95. I even bought Edna two pairs of the steel-belted-radial control-top stockings she likes to wear.

Driving home, I ran over Lilah's account of the Beemish family weekend in Hilton Head. I wondered if the hot business deal Bo was working on had any connection with the papers Kristee had stolen from him. It was a "sensitive" matter, Beemish had said.

So sensitive he might kill to get the papers back?

Edna was on the phone when I walked into the kitchen. I rattled the Rich's bag at her, but she waved it away and kept talking.

"Yes, ma'am," she said, affecting her most syrupy southern accent. "Oh, yey-yuss. All our workers are bonded and fully insured and all of them have completed our training course in Contemporary Methods in Environmentally Conscious Household Management. That's right, we here at House Mouse are deeply concerned about the earth's precious ozone layer, and we use absolutely no aerosol cleaners."

She jotted down an address on the worksheet in front of her. "Fine. . . . Yes. Tuesdays, then. . . . Right. Seventy dollars for the whole house, and the check is payable to House Mouse. . . . Fine. 'Bye now."

She hung up and beamed at me. "New client. That woman Neva Jean cleaned in Inman Park referred her. She's looking for an environmentally correct service, and I told her she'd come to the right place."

"You told her an amazing crock of shit," I said, fetching a cold Diet Coke from the fridge. "A, we're not bonded. B, we're not insured. C, you upped our rates by twenty bucks, and D, we've never given the girls a training course in their life."

Edna didn't look up from the new client form she was busily filling out. "A, this ying-yang is so dumb she'll never check to see if we're bonded and insured. B, I told her we'd use only non-ozone-threatening cleaning products, which cost extra to buy. C, our new rate for Environmentally Correct Cleaning is seventy dollars. I'm thinking of taking out an ad. I see this as the wave of the future."

She had me there. My sixty-two-year-old mother is an honest-to-God visionary. And here I'd thought all this time she was just a pathological liar.

I poured the Coke over some ice and sat at the table. "Well, I guess we can stop looking for Kristee now."

"Where'd they find the body?"

I almost spat out a mouthful of Diet Coke. "How'd you know?" I asked.

She pulled an envelope out of the neck of her blouse and handed it to me. It was still warm.

"A delivery service dropped it by about fifteen minutes ago," Edna said.

I started to open the envelope and noticed that it appeared to have been preopened.

"There's a check for three thousand dollars in there," Edna said. "From Bo Beemish. If that's what private detectives make these days, Jules, we're in the wrong business."

A note was stapled to the check. "Should I bother to read this?" I asked.

"Go ahead," Edna said. "It's not as though I read all your mail, you know."

The note was short.

> *Thank you for your efforts. Enclosed is your fee for services rendered, plus a bonus to show Lilah's and my appreciation for your discretion.*
> *Best wishes.*

"Looks like we've been kissed off," Edna observed. "Now tell me about the body. Who found her and where?"

I rattled the Rich's bag again and pointed to myself.

"You found her in a Rich's bag?"

"No, Ma. Well, actually, she was inside a plastic fur storage bag from Rich's, so I guess you're partially right. We found her in the fur vault while we were looking for Lilah's furs. She'd been strangled, and Lilah's furs were dumped on top of her. The body was locked in this sort of rolling merchandise hamper. Looks like she'd been there a couple of days, too."

Edna dug around the papers on the table until she found her pack of cigarettes. She lit one, inhaled, and held it up appreciatively.

"Wonder if Lilah will get Rich's to pay for having her coats cleaned again? In the old days, when Dick Rich was running the store, they would have bought her a new coat. Beemish did it, of course," she said. "That's why he gave you that check. He's buying you off. What do you say we go to New Orleans and have brunch at the Commander's Palace? Want to?"

"You think Bo Beemish really believes he can buy me off a murder for three thousand bucks? Ma, you gotta quit watching so much television. He *is* trying to buy me off, but it's to get me to forget this crooked business deal he's into, not Kristee's murder. And no, we're not gonna use his money for a trip to New Orleans. We'll give back the extra thousand, and with the rest we'll have the van worked on and pay some bills."

"Killjoy," Edna muttered. The phone rang before she could offer any counter arguments. I beat her to the punch and picked it up.

"Callahan, did you get Bo's little note?" a voice said.

"Hello, Lilah," I said. Edna's hand snaked out then and reached for the check, but I snatched it away from her and tucked it into my own bra. Two could play this game.

"Why, yes, I did get the note. But I'm afraid you're due a refund, because Bo made it out for a thousand dollars more than he owes us."

She giggled. "Oh, Bo never makes mistakes when it comes to money. He just wanted to let you know how much we appreciate your help in getting this whole mess cleared up. You know, when the police went to that Ardith woman's motel, they found Big Mama's ring hidden in a box of groceries under the bathroom sink. Bo says after she's in jail a few days she's sure to tell the police where she put the rest of our things."

"Jail?" I said incredulously. "Are you telling me that the police arrested Ardith Cramer? What's she charged with?"

"Murder, of course," Lilah said in the same tone of voice I'd heard her use with her children. "And robbery, too, I guess, for stealing our stuff."

Her voice dropped then.

"God, I hope she decides to do the smart thing and confess right away to killing Kristee. I suppose if they had a murder trial, we'd have to testify or something, wouldn't we? How incredibly lurid."

"Yes, I imagine there would be a trial," I said wearily. "Especially since Kristee was probably killed at your house, and her body was discovered under a pile of your furs."

"Don't remind me," Lilah Rose wailed. "Can you imagine anything more disgusting? I'll never wear those furs again. In fact, I'm calling the chairman of the board of Rich's right now to tell him I expect them to pay for replacing them. Can you believe their security is so lax that anyone could just waltz in there and dump a body on my furs? Have you ever heard anything so perverted? I tell you, Callahan, things haven't been the same at Rich's since that chain came in."

"Say, Lilah," I said, when she finally calmed down about fine old southern institutions being ruined by Yankee carpetbagger hooligans. "You do still want House Mouse to continue cleaning, don't you?"

There was a dead silence from the other end of the line. "Well, now," Lilah said. "Sugar, that was another thing I wanted to talk to you about. One of my neighbors has this marvelous Jamaican cleaning lady. And her niece just came over here, and she desperately wanted a job, and I thought, Well, it would be a Christian gesture. And actually, she's going to come five days a week and care for the children, so of course I couldn't justify having a cleaning service *and* Drucilla, now, could I? And I've already given your business cards to the girls on my tennis team, and they swore they'd call you. I knew you wouldn't mind. You don't, do you, sugar?"

I'd felt the brush-off coming from the first time she called me sugar. And actually I didn't mind that much. It really pissed me off to think of me or my girls cleaning Lilah Rose Ledbetter Beemish's pink marble bidet.

"Not at all, Lilah," I said. "I understand perfectly. But we did have a contract, you know."

"Oh," she said in a tiny voice. "I'd forgotten. But we can just tear that up, right?"

I looked up at Edna. She was shaking her head no and rubbing her thumb and forefinger together in the international gesture for "Get the money."

"Normally, I'd do it in a minute, Lilah Rose," I said. "But my business manager is a real bear about these things. Usually she insists that a client who wants to break a contract pay for at least half the term of the contract."

Edna nodded happily and pointed to the envelope stuffed in my bosom.

"Tell you what, Lilah," I said. "How about if I just keep Bo's check to pay for the rest of the contract?"

"Oh, fine," Lilah said, sounding relieved. "Callahan, now that this nasty thing's over, let's have lunch at the Driving Club, all right? I'll call you."

"That'd be nice," I said perfunctorily, knowing she'd never make good on the invitation. "Oh, and one more thing. Tell Bo for me that I don't consider myself bought off, will you?"

"Of course not," she snapped. The dial tone beeped in my ear.

"Toodles," I said.

14

FINDING WHIT COLLIER that afternoon turned out to be embarrassingly easy. Even Neva Jean could have done it. Well, maybe.

All I had to do was call Orran Underwood, a CPA my sister Maureen used to date before she lost her sense and married the moron ambulance driver.

Maureen's throwing over Orran for an ambulance driver broke Edna's heart. In my family, an accountant is right up there with a plumber or an electrician or a pharmacist in terms of occupational desirability. Edna had fond dreams of Orran's marrying into the family and doing our taxes every year for free and finding thousands of dollars of tax loopholes. As for me, well, Orran was on the short side, and to say his hairline was receding would be charitable. Still, he had a great sense of humor and there was an ineffable sexiness about him. If he hadn't been Maureen's old boyfriend and thus sloppy seconds, I might have gone after him myself.

"Orran? Julia Garrity," I said.

"Julia," he boomed. "What's up? Did that beautiful sister of yours get divorced? Does she ever mention me?"

"Forget her, Orran," I said. "She got fat since she got married. She took up bowling. She goes square dancing, for Christ's sake."

"Stop."

"It's true," I insisted. "Her and the ambulance driver wear matching Western shirts and bolo ties. With the names embroidered over the pockets. You're better off single, believe me. Look, here's why I'm calling. I need you to tell me how to find a CPA."

"Look for a guy with a plastic pocket protector and a holster for his calculator," Orran said, giggling at his own joke.

"Yeah, right," I said. "But I really need to track this guy down. All I know about him is his name and the fact that he works for an accounting firm in town. Oh, yeah, he's also a Mormon."

Orran pondered that for a minute.

"OK, here's what you do. Call the state licensing board, it's here in Atlanta, and ask for his address. They should have all that info, I think. Or try the Metropolitan Atlanta Accounting Association. If neither of those ways work, call me back and we'll think of something else. Accountants generally aren't hard to find."

"Thanks, Orran, you're a peach." I made lip-smacking noises into the phone to emphasize his peachiness.

"Yeah," he said. "I know. Listen, just how fat is Maureen? Is she, like, gross?"

"Think over two hundred pounds," I lied. "Circus fat. Shamu, they call her down at Grady."

We hung up after I made up some more stuff about Maureen. Actually, she's not fat at all. She's the skinniest person in our family. But it makes me feel good to fantasize about her as a fat lady, and it seemed to cheer up Orran.

Unfortunately, the state licensing board telephone was manned by one of those career civil service types whose attitude is that they own everything in the computer and the only way they'll give it up is at gunpoint. The woman, who identified herself as Ms. Darnell, sounded like she slept in her pantyhose. You know the kind.

I had better luck with the local accounting association. I simply assumed my snottiest tone of voice and identified myself as Cynthia Darnell of the state licensing board and said we needed an updated address for Whit Collier. The young girl at the association was properly cowed. She found the information immediately and even gave me a home phone number for Collier. Success.

Whit Collier worked for a small private accounting firm near the square in downtown Decatur, a pretty little town just east of Atlanta.

Since I had bad news I decided to go see him in person rather than call. Besides, I'd never seen a real Mormon in the flesh before, unless you count Dale Murphy, who used to play for the Atlanta Braves.

The offices of Kilton, Boore and Fuller were in a tidy nut-brown two-story house on a shady side street in Decatur. I parked the van in a gravel lot behind the house and went around to the front door.

A young harried-looking receptionist was sitting at a horseshoe-shaped desk in what had once been the front parlor of the house. Her voice seemed to echo in the wood-floored room. She was talking on one phone line and two other lines were buzzing. She barely looked up as the door closed behind me.

I held up a fat manila envelope I'd brought along as a prop. It actually contained the owner's manual for the van. "I just need to drop these forms off to Mr. Collier," I whispered to the girl.

She nodded distractedly.

"Is his office back that way?" I asked, pointing to a central hallway that seemed to bisect the house.

She shook her head no and pointed upward, toward the second floor, then turned her attention back to the buzzing phones.

I climbed the uncarpeted stairs slowly. It had already been a long day. At the head of the stairs I saw another hallway with two doors opening off it. One room had the door ajar. Another secretary was inside, running off copies on a Xerox machine. The door across the hallway was open a crack.

I pushed it open without knocking. The room was small and crowded with unpacked cardboard cartons.

Whit Collier was almost hidden behind a stack of thick file

folders. His fingers ran nimbly over a calculator and his eyes were glued to the open file on his desk.

"Knock, knock," I said tentatively.

He didn't look up. "One minute. Let me just finish this column."

The minute gave me time to appreciate the benefits of all that clean healthy living the Mormons supposedly swear by.

I was surprised by how young Collier looked, no more than twenty-six or so, I'd bet. He had a headful of thick hair, a burnished reddish-blond color cut a shade closer than was the vogue. I couldn't see what color his eyes were, but his lashes were pale red-blond and he had the freckles that seem to go with that shade of hair.

His suit jacket was hung across his chair back and he was working with his shirt sleeves rolled up. He had strong-looking broad shoulders and the look of someone who worked out a lot.

He finally finished tapping on the calculator, scribbled something on a paper in the file, and looked up. He seemed surprised to see me.

"I'm sorry," he said, rising hurriedly from the chair. "I thought you were Carol, one of the secretaries. Can I help you?"

"Callahan Garrity," I said, sticking out a hand and offering one of my House Mouse business cards. He grasped my hand, shook it firmly, and stuck my card in his breast pocket.

"Have a seat," he said, gesturing toward an armchair facing the desk. Seated behind his desk, he looked at me expectantly. The eyes, by the way, were blue. Sky blue, if you're into Crayola colors. He reached in a desk drawer, got out a new folder, and reached for a blank form from a stack on the corner of the desktop. His pen poised over the paper and he looked at me again. "Miss Garrity, are you here for individual tax preparation, or will we be doing corporate work for you?" he asked.

"Oh, no," I said quickly. "I'm sorry. I'm not here about taxes at all. I'm a private investigator. I've been working for Mr. and Mrs. DuBose Beemish. Were you aware that your friend Kristee Ewbanks was missing?"

He put the pen down squarely on the open file folder. "Missing? Why would you think Kristee is missing?"

I studied his face, but I honestly couldn't read much in it. "She hadn't been seen for four days. And when she left the Beemishes, a good deal of their valuables vanished at the same time. What makes you think she's not missing, Mr. Collier?"

He blushed violently. "I'm not sure that's something I need to discuss with you," he said in a low, even tone. "It's a private matter."

"Not any more," I said quickly. "Kristee's dead."

He stared at me for a moment, then buried his face in his hands. His voice was muffled. "No," he said. "I don't believe you."

"I'm sorry. But it's true. Her body was found this morning. The police think she was murdered."

"Where?" he said, looking up. "Utah?"

"Utah? No. She was found here in Atlanta. In the fur vault at Rich's."

Collier flung his arms into the air then and rolled his eyes up toward the ceiling until all I could see was the whites. Then he squeezed his eyes shut tight and I heard strangled-sounding noises that seemed to come from somewhere deep inside his chest. Next came a torrent of thin, reedy-sounding syllables. It sounded like half singing, half sobbing in a make-believe language. This went on for a minute or two, but it seemed more like an hour. I sat riveted to the chair, not knowing if I should attempt CPR or try to slap him out of it. After a few seconds, it dawned on me that he was speaking in tongues. You don't see a lot of that at Sacred Heart, the parish church where I was raised, but I'd seen a television program once where they spoke in tongues. This seemed to be a similar dialect.

The speaking stopped as suddenly as it had started. Collier's chin dropped down on his chest; then his head shot back erect and his eyes popped open again.

"Who did this to Kristee?" he demanded, as calmly as though he hadn't just been possessed of the spirit.

I hesitated a moment.

"I have no idea," I said finally. "The police are handling the murder investigation. I was hired by the Beemishes to find Kristee and recover their property. But as of a few hours ago, I'm no longer working for them."

"Then why are you here?"

The question startled me. I guess I'd just followed up on what I knew out of instinct. Old habits die hard. But Collier was right. My job was done. I had no bona fide reason to be here. So I made one up.

"I thought you should know about your girlfriend's death before the police called," I said. "Just a courtesy, that's all."

He sighed and massaged his temples wearily. "All right. Thank you. It would have been . . . hard, hearing about Kristee from the police."

I got up to leave then, but my curiosity got the better of me.

"Mr. Collier, you don't have to tell me anything, obviously. Still, I was wondering. Would you mind telling me why you said Kristee wasn't missing? What made you think she was in Utah?"

A small tear trickled down his cheek. He brushed it away impatiently. "She told me she was going back West," he said. "That sodomite, Beemish . . ." He seemed to struggle with his emotions. "He'd forced himself on Kristee. Forced her to have—relations with him. She was ashamed. Humiliated. And terrified it might happen again. So she waited until they went out of town last weekend, to their beach place. She had a prepaid return-trip ticket, and she told me she was going to use it to go back home. She wanted to do temple work, work for the church. I encouraged her to go. A city like Atlanta is no place for an innocent young girl to live without protection."

Innocent wasn't a word I'd heard in connection with Kristee Ewbanks so far, but Whit Collier was obviously grieved about the news of the girl's death, so I didn't push the matter. Much.

"When did you see her last?" I asked.

"Sunday. Afternoon some time. I had some home visits to make—for the church, you know. So I didn't see her until late in the afternoon, and then only for a few minutes. I went by the house and we talked. She was packing. Her plane was going to leave around seven P.M. That was the last time I saw her."

Since Collier was in a talkative mood, I decided to keep asking questions. "Did you know anything at all about Kristee's background? Her real background?"

He seemed to bristle then. "I knew she'd made some mistakes. She was very young. But we talked about it. She'd had a hard life, losing her mother like she did. She was eager to make a fresh start."

"Did you know she wasn't really a Mormon?" I pressed.

The smile was a sad one. "You know about that, I see. Yes, I knew too. We met at a ward dance, you know? At first she tried to pass herself off as LDS. But it didn't take long for me to guess. It didn't matter though. We'd been reading Scripture together, and Kristee had become fascinated with church teachings. She was a very quick student. We talked about going up to Palmyra, New York, to the spot where Joseph Smith found the golden tablets. And of course she wanted to go back to Utah to be baptized a Saint there, in the Temple. I encouraged her, naturally."

"Naturally." I edged toward the door, unsure of what I'd hoped to accomplish by visiting Collier, or how I could talk myself out of the room. "Well," I said hesitantly. "I'm sorry to have brought you such sad news. But I'll leave you to your work. Thank you for seeing me."

I was out the hall and headed for the stairs when he caught up with me.

"Wait," he said softly, placing a hand on my shoulder. He pressed a pamphlet in my hand. "I'd like you to have this," he said earnestly. "I'm sure it will answer many questions you might have about our church."

"Right," I said, looking at it. "Thanks."

The pamphlet was pale blue, with a Bible school drawing of Jesus with outstretched hands. *Come and See* the title said. *The Church of Jesus Christ of Latter-day Saints.*

He turned and was gone, back to his office. I lit out of there fast. I guess it was the Bible tract that spooked me. I can remember, as a child, hiding behind the door while Edna or my dad tried to shoo away the Jehovah's Witnesses or Mormons who came to our door to proselytize. Daddy would politely explain that we were Catholics and believed we'd already found Salvation, thank you very much. But I remember one time Edna told a sour-faced woman in an ankle-length dress that she'd knocked on the door of a whole houseful of tree-hugging, naked, dancing druids, and would she like some wolfsbane punch? Maybe I remembered that sourfaced woman. I think I halfway expected a whole band of Mormons to appear and drag this backslid Catholic straight to the baptismal font in the Temple. I was history in a hurry.

15

THE ONLY GOOD REASON I had for snooping around Bo Beemish's fancy new development was nosiness, pure and simple. Besides, if I ever hit the big time, Edna and I might want to live on the Chattahoochee River in a two-million-dollar Georgian Revival mansion.

Anyway, it was a nice day for a drive. I called WDB Enterprises—that's the name of Beemish's development company—to find out exactly where L'Arrondissement was. His secretary was hesitant to tell me until I identified myself as a real estate broker with a client who was CEO of a Japanese electronics company. Then she was more forthcoming with directions.

It was in the far north corner of Fulton County. "But there's really nothing much to see yet," she said. "And we don't have our construction fences up yet. We'd prefer that brokers wait until we have our sales office on the premises, with our marketing director there to explain the plan to you."

I persisted, in a nice way, until she reluctantly gave me directions.

I decided to stop by the Fulton County courthouse on my way, to check the deed information. They have a Northside annex, where you can look up that stuff without making a trip clear downtown to Atlanta, where there's never anyplace to park anyway.

I found the deed book without too much trouble. Beemish, it seemed, had bought up several pieces of property on the river about three years ago. From the stamps on the deeds, it looked like he'd paid a couple million dollars for the whole parcel, with the mortgage secured by SouthStates Fidelity of Charlotte, North Carolina.

A trip to the planning office revealed that Beemish had tried, unsuccessfully, to have the land rezoned from agricultural to planned unit development right after he'd bought it. The records showed the rezoning request had been denied, on the recommendation of the county's zoning review board. But a handwritten note attached to the file folder said the property in question had been annexed into the city of Kensington Park the previous September.

I looked up at a clerk who was standing behind the counter in the development office. "Excuse me," I said, showing him the file folder. "I'm sort of confused about this file here. Does it mean this tract of land isn't in the county anymore?"

The clerk, a thin young man with a straggly mustache, glanced down at the file and smiled condescendingly. "It's still in the county physically, of course. But this shows the property was annexed into the city of Kensington Park seven months ago. I'm surprised you didn't read about it in the newspaper. The county made a big stink about losing that land, but Kensington Park made them an offer they couldn't refuse: sewer lines, garbage pickup, regular police patrols. So the owners petitioned the city to annex them in, and the city did."

"Isn't that unusual, for a small town to take away a big chunk of riverfront land from the county?"

He smirked. "You really are out of it. Happens all the time. Look at Roswell and Marietta," he said, naming two of the wealthier bedroom suburbs on the outskirts of Atlanta. "They ate up valuable chunks of land in Fulton and Cobb counties, but there was nothing the counties could do to stop them."

I still didn't get the annexation deal. "Why would the property owners want to be annexed? Doesn't that mean they're taxed double?"

Just then a cute little blonde walked into the office and up to the counter with a stack of file folders. The clerk's expression brightened. "Hey, Vicki." He shot me a look. "Anything else you need here?"

"Just one more thing. How does a piece of property get annexed?"

He gave a huge sigh of exasperation. "Easy. The property owners petition the city to take them in. If enough owners ask, the city just does it. OK?"

"OK," I mumbled, taking a last look at the file folder. "How do I find out who requested the annexation?"

"Talk to somebody in the Kensington Park City Clerk's office," he said, moving down the counter to help the fair Vicki.

I had to dig in the glove box of the van to find my metro area map book. I had a vague idea of where Kensington Park was, but I preferred not to circle the city on Interstate 285 looking like the Lost Dutchman.

Once I got my bearings I had no trouble finding the town. You just take Interstate 75 north to Georgia 400 and get off at the first exit where you see cows grazing instead of a Taco Bell.

Kensington Park was one of those small towns that predate the city of Atlanta by a couple of decades. It had started out as the home to Kensington Mills, a yarn-spinning plant that had supplied material for Confederate soldiers' uniforms. The original plant had been burned by Yankee soldiers, but years after the war another mill had been rebuilt on the same site. The mill had provided steady jobs for townspeople until the late 1970s, when American textile mill-owners discovered it was cheaper to hire Sri Lankans than it was Kensington Parkers.

These days Kensington Park was a ritzy bedroom community, home to executives who worked in downtown Atlanta or in one of the new glass office towers that were springing up at the edges of the city.

The old yellow brick mill still dominated Kensington Park. Someone had the bright idea to buy up the old hulk for back taxes and turn it into a new city hall. Only, in typical government-ese, it was now called a Municipal Services Facility.

I parked around back and followed a brick walkway around to the heavy glass front door. CITY OF KENSINGTON PARK: MAYOR CORINNE H. OVERMEIER was lettered on the door in an arc of gold leaf.

Inside, I followed a linoleum-floored hallway until I found a door marked CITY CLERK.

A plump woman in her fifties was seated at a large wooden desk, engaged in deep conversation with a much younger woman. The younger woman had brown hair cut in one of those outdated Farrah Fawcett dos, while the older woman's gray head was bent over the pages of a catalog.

"Now this cake-taker, that's a special this month, Darlene. And if you buy it, you're gonna get a deviled egg dish and the stacking salt and peppers for three dollars more. Do you want that in the paprika or the harvest gold?"

Darlene looked up at me guiltily and pushed the catalog away. "Let me think about it, Wilona, and I'll tell you at lunch." She smiled quickly at me and headed for the door.

Wilona tucked the Tupperware catalog under a glass candy jar on her desk. "And what can I do for you today?" she twittered. "Register to vote?"

I smiled back pleasantly. Always smile at secretaries and clerks. "Actually, I'm not eligible to vote, because I'm not a resident. But I am looking for some information about the annexation of some property called L'Arrondissement. Could you help me with that?"

"Oh, the old Harper property," she said. "I can't seem to get my tongue around the fancy name that developer put on it. What is it, anyway? French?"

"Yeah, it's French. I think it means something like police station. I can't pronounce it too well myself, to tell you the truth."

I was now oozing affability. I could feel it. Wilona seemed like a woman who knew the answers to questions I hadn't thought of yet. If I could be pals with her, who knows what I might find out?

"Well, what is it you need to know?" she asked. "I'm the city clerk, have been for twenty-five years. If there's anything gone on in Kensington Park I don't know about, it most likely ain't happened."

I edged down into the chair by her desk that had been vacated by Darlene.

"Wilona," I said. "I'll be honest with you. I'm a private detective. I'm working on a case that shouldn't have anything to do with Kensington Park, but here I am anyway. I need to find out some stuff about the Harper property."

She'd clasped her hands together on her desk, her head tilted while she listened. "A private detective? No. A little old gal like you?"

I nodded. "Used to be a cop with the City of Atlanta. But I quit that a couple years ago and started my own business."

Wilona shook her headful of gray pincurls vigorously. "Lord, I know what you mean about Atlanta." Her voice lowered to a whisper. "It's all niggers running the show now, they say. Said there's not a white person working down at City Hall, or the police station neither. I heard they got niggers sittin' up in the mayor's office and white folks working as janitors. Beats all."

I tried not to wince at her use of the n-word. You still run into that, even in Atlanta, the city that was supposed to be too busy to hate. I never have gotten used to it, though.

"Why, our own chief of police, Miles Norman, used to be in the police department down there. Took early retirement and come out here to get away from the darkies. And of course Mr. Shaloub, our mayor pro tem, I believe he used to be an Atlanta policeman too, before he moved out here and started selling them phone beepers."

"Mr. Shaloub?" I said, startled. "Is that Eddie Shaloub?"

She laughed a tinkly, knowing laugh. "Lord, yes, none other. I bet you knew him pretty good back at the Atlanta police department, didn't you? No good denying it to me. I never knew a man had such a way with women. Cut up? Lord, he comes in here and cuts the fool. Those snappin' black eyes of his don't miss nothing."

"He's vice mayor, did you say? How long has he been on the City Council?"

Wilona did some quick figuring in her head. "Let's see. This is his second term he's starting. I'd guess he's been on the council for three years now."

Now that she mentioned it, I suddenly recalled my conversation with Bucky Deaver. He'd said something about Shaloub being in politics, but either I hadn't heard or he hadn't said where.

"Yes, I know Mr. Shaloub," I said, throwing her a knowing wink. "But about the Harper property," I continued. "How did it happen to be annexed by the city?"

She wrinkled her forehead, considering the matter. "I suppose somebody in the city decided it would be nice to have the taxes from that land. But I don't know, really. I can tell you that the developer, Mr. Beemish, was very enthusiastic about being annexed. He come out here to all the council meetings, took everybody out to lunch at that fancy country club he built over in Gwinnett County, and talked up how he was going to build such a nice community with big fancy houses and a shopping center with a restaurant that serves wine. I think he bought some other small lots around the Harper property. In fact, he had to, in order to be contiguous with the city."

"Contiguous? Could you explain that to me? I'm not a lawyer."

She patted my arm in a conspirational way. "Neither am I, honey. All contiguous means is that his property touches the city limits. State law requires that his property touch our city limits before we can bring him in."

"And the Harper property didn't?"

"No, ma'am. There was a little bitty old strip of land between it and our city limits. Belonged to old Inez Rainwater. She lives out there in an old mobile home with a couple of nanny goats out in the yard. She's a nasty old bat and crazy as a loon. Has been since her youngest boy got kilt in a loggin' truck accident on the Roswell Highway. After that, she got nutty as a fruitcake. Come to town wearin' nothin' but a cotton slip on hot summer days, till Chief Norman put a stop to it by threatenin' to arrest her for indecent exposure."

All this town history was a bit overwhelming. "Wait a minute," I said. "You're losing me here, Wilona. How did Beemish get annexed into the city if his land wasn't contiguous? And how did he get the land rezoned after the country turned him down?"

She eyed me like a schoolteacher eyes the class idiot.

"Bought the Rainwater property. Didn't I tell you that?"

"Maybe I missed it," I said lamely.

"Paid an awful price for that land, too," she said smugly. "I checked the doc stamps on the closing papers. Give the old lady close to eighty thousand dollars for not even two acres of land."

"Is that too much?"

In answer, she got up and walked stiff-legged to one of the gray metal file cabinets that banked the wall in the rear of the office. She yanked open a drawer, thumbed through some cards until she found the one she wanted, and pulled up the card in back to mark her place.

She sank into the chair with a grimace of pain, but thrust the card at me. It had plat-book pages and lot numbers and what appeared to be a legal description of a piece of property. In a corner was typed an appraisal amount: $38,000.

"Does this mean the Rainwater property was only worth thirty-eight thousand?"

Wilona rewarded me with a smile. "That's right. And Mr. Beemish gave Miss Inez more than twice that. Even promised her she could leave the mobile home right there where it's at until they start clearing for lots."

I was surprised to hear of Bo Beemish's generosity. He hadn't struck me as the Eagle Scout type. "Mr. Beemish's secretary told me on the phone today that they had started clearing the lots. Would Miss Inez still be living out there?"

She shot me a reproving look. "I wouldn't know where Miss Inez is," she said primly. "I've got city bidness here. I don't go out tromping the woods spying on nutty old ladies."

Wilona struggled to her feet again, more slowly this time, and walked over to the open file cabinet to replace the card she'd shown me.

"Wait," I said. "What about the rezoning? Why did the city decide to give him the rezoning if the county had already refused? Their zoning board recommended denying the rezoning."

She kept her back to me. "Fulton County don't know all there is to know about everything," she said. "Niggers run everything down there, don't want white folks gettin' anything *they* can't have. Mr. Beemish is goin' to build some right nice houses out there, and those folks want a Kensington Park address. We're gonna run our sewer line out there, and then we're gonna sit back and collect all those nice taxes."

She turned around and stared at me. Hard. It looked like maybe we wouldn't be pals after all.

"Why'd you say you cared about all this anyway?"

She had me there. Why did I care?

"Uh, thanks for the help, Wilona," I said. "And if you see Mr. Shaloub, tell him Callahan Garrity was by and said hey."

"If I see him," she muttered, and turned away again.

16

BEING AS I WAS in the neighborhood and all, I decided to drop by L'Arrondissement.

I followed the directions Beemish's secretary gave me, making only three wrong turns, which is about average for me.

At what turned out to be my last wrong turn I saw an old country store and gas station. At one time there had been dozens of stores like it around rural north Fulton County. Now, though, with all the expensive country club subdivisions and strip shopping centers, it looked like something out of a time warp. It was a crumbling old white-brick building with one of those faded DRINK COCA-COLA signs painted on the side. There was one rusting gas pump outside. The price for gas was 49 cents a gallon. I guess it hadn't pumped much unleaded supreme.

I pulled up, got out, and pushed open the screen door, admiring the warped metal Sunbeam Bread sign on the bottom. Inside the store it was dark and cool. But the shelves were more than half empty and some of them were being dismantled. It was lunchtime and I suddenly realized how hungry I was, so I decided to treat myself to a car picnic. I yanked open the lid of an old chest-type Coke cooler. But instead of finding icy bottles of sodas like I'd hoped, I was greeted by a chorus of chirps. There was a metal screen cage full of crickets sitting in the box. Alongside it were stacks of small plastic tubs. An earthy smell rose up. Night crawlers. If I'd only brought along a cane pole, I could have done a little fishing. I shut the lid, glanced around, and saw the real drink cooler, a modern glass-windowed affair. The majority of the drinks seemed to be malt liquor, beer, or wine coolers. But if I drank a beer in the middle of the day, in the suddenly intense spring heat, I'd end up napping instead of snooping. Regretfully, I settled on a tall bottle of NeHi Orange.

From a rack nearby I grabbed a bag of Ranch-style Doritos, and from the bread shelf I picked up the biggest, gooeyest-looking honey bun I could find. Given the look of the other merchandise in the store, there was no telling how old the thing was. I could have finished my shopping with a Slim Jim, but you have to practice self-control sometimes.

The cashier, the only other soul in the store, was a fat teenage boy perched on a stack of beer cases behind the cash register. A set of earphones rested in a nest of dirty red hair, and his head bobbed occasionally to some secret beat. Probably Twisted Sister.

I had to wave the honey bun under his nose to get his attention.

He put the magazine down reluctantly. "That it?"

"Yeah," I said, peeling some one-dollar bills out of my pants pockets. "Do you happen to know if a new subdivision called L'Arrondissement is around here?"

He sighed loudly and slipped off the earphones. "You talkin' to me?"

I repeated the question.

"That's Mr. Beemish's project?"

"You know Bo Beemish?" I let the surprise show in my voice.

"He owns this store," the kid said. "Bought it off my old man a couple months ago. You come by here next week, this dump'll be gone. Nothing but a pile of boards and bricks and shit. Mr. Beemish says he's gonna put in a dry cleaner and a 7-Eleven and a video rental store. Promised my old man he'd give me a job too."

"How nice," I murmured. The last country store in north Fulton County and Bo Beemish was going to bulldoze it. What a visionary.

"So how far away is the subdivision?" I asked. "Am I close?"

"You better not go messin' around over there," the kid warned, looking up at me. Some ripe-looking zits nested in the pale peach fuzz on his upper lip. "They got private security over there all the time. With guns. Those sum-bitches will run your ass off if they catch you messin' around."

I gave the kid what I hoped was a superior smile. "I'm a real estate broker. I've got a client who's interested in building a house there," I said sweetly. "I'm sure the security officers only bother underage hoodlums who go tearing around on dirt bikes, throwing beer cans right and left."

"I never seen no real estate lady in a pink van like that piece of shit you're drivin'," the kid said. "Real estate people come around here all the time, but they drive Caddies and Mercedes-Benzes and BMWs. I'm tellin' you, lady. They'll run your ass off. See if they don't."

"My BMW's in the shop," I said through clenched teeth. "That van belongs to my cleaning lady."

I held my hand out for my change, but instead he let it fall onto the counter. "Sorry." He smirked.

As I was pulling out of the gravel lot I noticed a small sign pointing down the narrow two-lane county road that ran beside the store. L'ARRONDISSEMENT, it said. I looked over at the doorway to the store. The kid was leaning against the doorjamb, watching me with undisguised curiosity. He saw me looking at him and casually flipped me a bird.

Disguised as a high-class real estate agent, I restrained myself from doing the same. "The little shit," I muttered. I drove a few miles down the road, following the same little signs. Here and there along the way I saw a crumbling rock chimney and an outcropping of bushes marking the foundation of an old home, long gone. In one old yard a flame-orange azalea bloomed, oblivious to the kudzu vines trying to strangle it out of existence. There were even a handful of little houses, wood-framed, mostly, with peeling paint and a battered car or two in the dirt-swept front yards. Blue jeans and underwear hung on a washline, signaling that there were still working folk living out here, fighting off the creeping prosperity that had taken over this part of the county.

Mostly, though, the houses were abandoned. Every quarter mile or so I saw signs. RIVERFRONT ACREAGE FOR SALE they said, and COMING SOON, RIVERWOOD ACRES, and things like that.

Finally, I spied a larger sign on the right-hand side of the road. A raw red gash showed where a new road had been cut back through the swath of greenery that lined both sides of the little road.

I slowed down. An ornate sign set in a massive gray river-rock wall announced in curving script that I had reached L'Arrondissement. *An exclusive shopping and living community. Thirty-five fine estate homes starting at $800,000. WDB Enterprises, Developer.*

At the entrance to the project, work had begun on what looked like a small stucco kiosk. The security shack, I guessed. Wire tornado fencing had been strung on metal poles along the road, probably to act as a temporary gate, until Beemish could build a six-foot-high wall to keep out the riffraff.

I pulled into the road. A marker showed that I was driving on Lilah Lane. How sweet. A little farther along I noticed signs tacked up on tall pine trees that lined the street. Each tree was wrapped with an orange ribbon. I guess that meant they wouldn't be cut down. Or would be. It was hard to tell which. POSTED: NO TRESPASSING, the signs read. PRIVATE DRIVE. NO TURNAROUND, NO EXIT, they announced.

The street was caked with mud and tire tracks. As I rolled slowly forward I saw up ahead where the clearing had started. Half a dozen pieces of heavy equipment were parked there. Two-story-tall pine trees and mounds of underbrush had been bulldozed aside and stacked in a pile. There was a small mobile home, which was obviously the construction trailer, and a couple of pickup trucks parked beside it, but I didn't see any human activity. It was twelve-thirty; I hoped all the construction workers were on their lunch break. My plan, such as it was, was to look around, to see what kind of "problems" Kristee Ewbanks might have been black-mailing Bo Beemish over. If stopped, I'd simply tell anybody who asked that I was a real estate broker scouting out potential homesites for a client.

I cruised slowly down the road, admiring the scenery. In a few places, the road broke where the developer obviously planned to put in lateral streets. Ancient-looking oak trees dotted the land-scape, interspersed with an occasional dogwood, magnolia, or sweet gum. I even saw a couple of towering old pecan trees. God, this was a gorgeous spot. No wonder Bo Beemish had such big plans for it. Land with these kinds of hardwoods, level, with river frontage, had all but disappeared from this part of Atlanta.

The road curved back through the underbrush for maybe half a mile. Close to the side of the street, red clay showed where the vegetation had been scraped away. It looked like a scar. Finally, the street ended in a wide cul-de-sac. I pulled in, parked the van, and got out.

Lot clearing hadn't reached the back part of the property yet. I could hear blue jays and mockingbirds high up in the branches of the trees, and squirrels scampered around in the mat of fallen leaves. I stood still for a minute and stretched. The sun shining down on my head felt good. Off in the distance I could hear a faint trickling noise.

I headed through the underbrush toward where the water seemed to be, carefully trying to step over rotted logs that might harbor snakes. I don't do reptiles. I was also looking out for poison ivy. That stuff tears me up.

A couple of hundred yards in, I could feel the air grow cooler and moister. The bigger trees dropped off to scrub, then to noth-ing but tall grass. After walking only a few feet, I could feel my sneakers squishing in wet mud. The land curved gently down toward the riverbank. Maybe five feet away, I could see the green-brown waters of the Chattahoochee River swirling past in a swath about forty feet wide.

I walked down the bank a short way to get a better look at the river frontage and was so busy admiring the view I almost stumbled over an outcropping of rock.

Looking down I saw I'd stumbled across the construction workers' dining room. Fire had blackened an area inside a ring of rocks. Beer cans, Gatorade bottles, fast-food wrappers, even an old cooler had been stacked in a garbage heap about three feet high. There were charred pieces of two-by-fours. Flies buzzed about. I wrinkled my nose in disgust. The workers had picked the prettiest part of the property for a trash dump.

Angrily, I kicked a heap of trash and cursed when my sneaker-clad toe struck something hard.

I looked down and kicked aside a half-burned clump of paper bags. I could see a smooth-worn gray stone poking out of the ground. I kicked at the trash some more, clearing away enough to see some kind of carving on the rock.

I knelt down and gingerly pushed aside some more trash, wishing for my rubber gloves that were back in the van with the rest of my cleaning gear. The rock—it looked like granite—had been partially buried. I dug away some of the damp dirt until I could see what looked like a carved lily flower. There were numbers too, something that looked like part of a date, maybe 1923, but it was hard to be sure because the rock had been broken and the numbers were worn nearly smooth.

I was so busy digging in the dirt I didn't even hear the crunch of leaves underfoot. Didn't hear the whir of a quiet motor.

What I did hear was a sudden loud pumping noise, followed by a huge *boom*. I even saw a little plume of sawdust and bark exploding from the trunk of a pine tree not five feet from where I stood.

After my feet touched the ground again, I whirled toward where the shot seemed to come from. A candy-apple-red golf cart was moving quickly along a path carved through the woods, a path I hadn't noticed before. There were two men in the cart. The driver wore a blue work shirt. The passenger didn't wear a shirt. He did have a shotgun, however. He was standing up in the cart, pointing it at me, grinning evilly.

Blind anger welled up from within me. "What the hell are you doing, you asshole?" I screamed. "You could have killed me!"

In answer, the man with the gun lifted it, aimed, and fired again. This time a Styrofoam Big Mac container at my feet exploded into about a million nonbiodegradable pieces.

I didn't wait for any further communication from the golf cart. I took off running, parallel to the river, where a screen of underbrush promised to give me a little cover and them a somewhat bumpy ride. Branches tore at my jeans, scratching my face and ripping at my arms. This time I wasn't watching for poison ivy or poison snakes. I glanced behind, to see if the cart was following me. It wasn't. The men had stopped at the trash dump and had gotten out to see what I was looking at.

I ran a short way up the river, then angled back through the woods toward where I hoped the cul-de-sac was. Through the trees I could see the pink paint of the van. I stopped and crouched behind a fallen oak tree to see if anyone was guarding it. There was no one around. I tried to catch my breath, but my chest felt like it would explode. My thighs were shaking uncontrollably. I thought I might pee in my pants, I was that scared.

I looked over my shoulder in the direction I'd come from. There was no whirring sound, no flash of red golf cart bearing two homicidal rednecks, which was enough to get me out from behind that oak tree and over the hundred yards between me and the van in less than twenty seconds.

With my right hand I turned the key in the ignition while my left hand was locking the driver's side door. As I was backing the van up, I heard that whirring noise again. In the rearview mirror I saw the golf cart emerge from the path that I'd overlooked before. When he was about sixty yards away, the guy with the shotgun raised himself to a standing position in the cart and pointed the gun at me again. I gunned the motor of the van, then heard it. He was screaming a rebel yell.

I didn't take the time to see what Johnny Reb would do next. I backed the van out, threw it in first, and spun out of there. The van lurched forward and, miraculously, didn't stall out. I heard the shotgun go off again, somewhere to my left this time.

The scenery was pretty much a blur on the way out. I did see a bunch of men standing around the heavy equipment, but I didn't stop to wave howdy.

In fact, I didn't slow down until I had to merge onto Georgia 400. It's stupid, I know, but I kept glancing in the rearview mirror the whole way home, half expecting to see a red golf cart tooling down the interstate. Every time I saw a glimpse of red, I urged the van a little faster. I did maybe 50 miles an hour the whole way home, a new land speed record for the Chevy. And I didn't slow down until I pulled into our driveway back in Candler Park.

17

THE HOUSE WAS QUIET, EMPTY. It was Edna's day to work late at the beauty shop. After I sucked down the last beer in the refrigerator, in one gulp, standing at the kitchen sink, I stopped being scared and got on with the business of being pissed off.

Jesus Christ, I'd nearly had my head shot off by those rednecks in the golf cart. And for what? Trespassing?

I toyed with the idea of calling Beemish and threatening to sue but quickly decided against it.

Why in hell had those morons shot at me? What was going on in that subdivision that was worth maiming or murdering over? I hadn't had enough time to see if Beemish had established a marijuana farm, and the guys who'd shot at me didn't look like illegal aliens, so I could rule out at least two kinds of criminal enterprise. The only thing I'd seen at L'Arrondissement was land. Beautiful land, yes, but Beemish had paid a lot of money for it and he obviously stood to make a lot more once the project was finished.

What had Kristee been blackmailing Beemish over? Had it been something so serious he'd been willing to kill her to keep it quiet? The only thing out of the ordinary I'd seen at L'Arrondissement was that trash heap. And as far as I knew, messiness hadn't yet been declared illegal in Georgia.

Instead of calling the Kensington Park cops to report a murder attempt, I called Bucky Deaver and got him to give me Eddie Shaloub's work number.

"Callahan," Shaloub greeted me. "I've been thinking about calling you for a week now."

I looked down at the goose bumps that still covered my arms. "A girl senses these things, Eddie."

"You ready to buy some beepers for that cleaning business of yours? I'll make you a deal you can't refuse."

Shaloub was always doing business. Always. Even when he was on the force he always had some minor scam going, selling life insurance policies, buying and selling run-down rental properties.

"You never stop, do you, Shaloub?" I said. "I don't need any beepers just yet. But I promise, when I'm ready, I'll call you. OK?"

Shaloub's nasty little chuckle was as oily as ever. "As I recall, Callahan, you usually do call when you're ready. And say, Callahan," he continued, "since you called, would you mind telling me what you were doing trespassing on private property out in Kensington Park earlier today?"

"You gonna have me arrested?"

"I'm not, but WDB Enterprises might."

"How'd you know why I was calling?"

"I didn't," Shaloub said. "One of their security people called our police department to report scaring off a trespasser suspected of trying to vandalize some of their heavy equipment. They gave a description of a woman with dark curly hair and a pink Chevy van. The license plate was registered to an outfit called House Mouse. Sound familiar?"

"What?" I sputtered. "I never got near their equipment. And I vandalized nothing. You know me better than that. Did those fuckheads happen to report that one of them tried to blow my head off with a shotgun?"

"I take it they missed," he said calmly.

"Damn straight," I said. "This is rich, Shaloub. I call you up to complain about being shot at and you end up threatening to have me arrested. How'd you find out about this so fast, anyway?"

"Old habits die hard. I've got a police scanner on my desk. Anyway, I'm chairman of the public safety committee, so it's part of my job as city councilman."

"Since it's part of your job," I suggested, "why don't you have one of Kensington Park's finest go out to L'Arrondissement and charge the slob who shot at me with assault with a deadly weapon? He's easy to find. Look for a fat turd about six feet tall with long black hair in a ponytail. Last time I saw him he wasn't wearing a shirt and he was toting a twelve-gauge Remington pump action. I want his ass arrested."

"Just calm down, Garrity, OK? You were a cop once; you know how this works. You want this guy arrested, you come out here and swear out a warrant against him. But to be frank, I doubt Chief Norman is gonna arrest this guy. For God's sake, Callahan. You were on clearly posted private property. Witnesses saw you poking around out there. They've had several thousand dollars' worth of thefts and vandalism out there in the past two months. Day before yesterday, somebody poured sugar into the gas tank of their motor grader. Tires have been slashed, temporary power lines cut, and that construction trailer out there was broken into two weeks ago. Somebody trashed the place and stole an answering machine, a fax machine, and a typewriter. If one of our patrol officers had caught you out there, they would have arrested you on the spot. Count yourself lucky they only shot at you this time."

Now I knew where I stood with my old flame Eddie Shaloub. Nowhere. "I'm surprised you haven't asked me what I was doing out there," I said coldly.

"I don't need to," he shot back. "Beemish called me a little while ago to ask if I knew who you were. He says he paid you for your services in this nanny business, but you persist in believing he had something to do with her death, even though the police have arrested her girlfriend and charged her with the murder."

"Did Beemish tell you he was screwing this girl?" I asked. "Did he tell you she was blackmailing him over something going on out in that subdivision?"

"Mr. Beemish hasn't confided to me what his relationship with the girl was, but from what I hear she was screwing everyone in sight. As for blackmail, I don't know anything about that either. But I've been all over that project with the rest of our council members, and I can assure you nothing funny is going on there. If there was, I'd know about it."

Shaloub was lying. I knew it and he knew it and he knew I knew it.

"Well, fine, Eddie," I said. "I don't guess there's anything further for us to discuss today. Thank you for your time."

"Wait," he burst out. "Don't hang up yet. Listen to me, Callahan. Stay away from that project. Bo Beemish has millions invested out there, and his insurance people are getting antsy about the thefts and vandalism. I happen to know he's hired more security people, and our Kensington Park officers are stepping up patrols too. The next time, that fat guy's aim could be much better."

After I hung up I remembered I'd never gotten to eat my little picnic. I didn't have the energy to go out to the van to fetch my goodies, and besides, somehow warm orange soda and a stale honey bun didn't appeal to me anymore.

I took a long hot shower and washed my hair which was festooned with bits of twigs and leaves left over from my race through the woods. The soap and shampoo stung all the little scratches and cuts I'd suffered in my retreat from the golfers, but it felt good to be clean. Afterward, I changed into a pair of shorts and a clean T-shirt. I padded into the kitchen and looked around for something to eat. The bourbon bottle under the sink was still half full, so I poured myself a Wild Turkey on the rocks. Sustained rooting around in the refrigerator yielded a hunk of sharp cheddar cheese, which I grated over some taco chips I found in the pantry. Over that, I ladled some extra hot salsa, and for a green vegetable I garnished the thing with some jalapeño peppers. Zapped it in the microwave for a minute and there was my lunch. Bachelorette's delight.

There were a bunch of messages on the answering machine, mostly from clients leaving instructions about extra stuff they wanted done or from people who wanted to change cleaning days. I made some notes for Edna. Dealing with the public was her job.

The most interesting message was from Ardith Cramer.

Her sullen voice I recalled from the motel was gone. She sounded panicky, and I could hear shouting, singing, and swearing in the background.

"Miss Garrity," she said. "It's Ardith Cramer. I'm in the Atlanta jail. I've been assigned a public defender. His name is Prahab, Dinesh Prahab. He came to see me today. I told him I didn't kill Kristee. I don't think he believes me. But he thinks I should talk to you, to see if you know anything that could help me. I'm sure Bo Beemish had something to do with this. Could you come see me? Please? I'll leave your name at the front desk. Please? I've got to go now."

The tape ran out. Shit. My nice little missing person case had turned into a big messy homicide.

I'd been paid off by the Beemishes, so that should have been that. It wasn't, of course. Ardith Cramer was just too damned handy as a suspect. That didn't mean she didn't do it. In the real world, sometimes the most obvious person really is guilty. But this time, things were a little too neat.

I replayed the tape because I hadn't caught the name of Ardith's attorney. Then I got out the white pages of the Atlanta phone book and looked up the number for the Fulton County public defender's office.

I got put on hold twice before Prahab finally came on the line. Although I was expecting someone who spoke the pidgin Eng-

lish of a 7-Eleven clerk, Dinesh Prahab spoke perfect English, albeit with a pronounced southern accent.

He didn't sound happy to be discussing his newest client. "Yeah,
I saw Ms. Cramer," he said, emphasizing the "miz." "Naturally she
insists she's innocent. All my clients are innocent. She told me
you'd been looking into this Ewbanks woman's disappearance. Is
that correct?"

"I was," I said, "until she turned up in the fur vault at Rich's.
Look, have you talked to anyone in the DA's office about this case
yet?"

"What's your interest?" he asked. "I thought my client said you
were working for the family that employed the dead woman."

"I don't really have an interest," I snapped. "But your client
called and left a message on my machine, begging me to help her.
You don't want to talk to me, fine. I've got other stuff to do. I've got
a business I'm trying to run here, and it's not a detective business.
My former clients, the Beemishes, have terminated my services.
And frankly, I'm not in a financial position to do any pro bono
investigative work for you."

"All right," he said, "you've made your point. I'm sorry. Anything you could tell me about this case would be helpful. I didn't
mean to be rude, but I had a long day in court today, and if my case
load gets any heavier, I'm gonna have to start sleeping in the office.
And frankly, from what I could get out of Ardith Cramer today,
this isn't going to be an easy case to defend. Would it be possible
for us to get together and talk? This evening maybe?"

I looked at the clock on the microwave. It was almost 4 P.M. I
still had the House Mouse payroll to do, plus I was in no mood to
go out this evening. Still, I *had* called him.

"Whereabouts do you live?" I asked.

"Virginia-Highland," he said, naming a trendy nearby yuppie
nesting ground. "How about you?"

"Candler Park. You know the Euclid Avenue Yacht Club?"

"Is that the biker bar at Little Five Points?"

"It's not a biker bar," I said. "You wanna meet me there around eight?"

"Sounds good. Hey, how will I know you?"

I looked down at my T-shirt. I didn't intend to change clothes for this guy. I was wearing one of my favorites, my Andy Griffith Show Rerun Watchers Club shirt.

"I've got short dark curly hair and Barney Fife on my chest," I said. "What do you look like?"

"I'm sure I'll be the only Pakistani in the place," he drawled. "Look for a guy with a turban and a snake in a basket."

18

DINESH PRAHAB WASN'T WEARING a turban. He also didn't have a gold hoop earring. Some disappointment.

The guy sitting in the booth nearest the door had dark hair that had gone to salt and pepper. He was maybe forty. With his dark mustache, he looked like a swarthy Burt Reynolds if you squinted your eyes a little. He wore a starched white dress shirt with the shirttail out over a new-looking pair of blue jeans. A frothy drink sat on the table in front of him.

I slid into the seat opposite him. He was making notes in a little leather-bound notebook, and he didn't look up.

"Hello," I said tentatively. "Are you Dinesh?"

He flipped the notebook shut and dropped it into the briefcase that lay open on the seat beside him. He looked up and stared at my chest for a minute.

It took me a moment to realize he was checking for Barney Fife.

"I'm Dinesh," he said, extending a hand to shake mine. "Thank you for coming, Miss Garrity. I'm having a whiskey sour. May I order one for you?"

So that's what the thing with the fruit hanging off it was. I hadn't seen an honest-to-God whiskey sour since college days. When I was nineteen, a whiskey sour was the drink of choice for junior sophisticates.

"Please call me Callahan. I didn't know those guys could make a whiskey sour," I said, pointing my head toward Tinkles and Don behind the bar. "I'll just have a beer, if it's all the same to you."

He got up and went to the bar to fetch my drink. He looked a lot shorter standing up, maybe only five-foot-four. Tinkles peered over Prahab's head and raised his eyebrows a couple of times at me. I gave a fair approximation of fluttering my eyelashes seductively.

Prahab returned with a frosted glass of beer and set it squarely on a coaster. Come to think of it, I hadn't known the Yacht Club had coasters either.

"Now," he said, settling himself in the booth. "What can you tell me about Ms. Cramer and this murder investigation?"

So much for small talk.

"I can't tell you as much as I'd like," I admitted.

I filled him in on what Edna and I had discovered about the bogus nanny-placement agency and the burglary ring.

"Amazing," he said, sipping on his drink. "Ms. Cramer strikes me as a fairly intelligent woman. Did you know she has almost enough college credits to earn a master's degree in social work? I called the college she attended. How on earth did someone like her get mixed up in fraud, theft, and murder?"

"It's been my experience that you don't earn college credit for common sense," I said. "Call it love. Ardith Cramer fell in love with the wrong person. From what I've heard, Kristee Ewbanks was a perfect little sociopath. She conned everybody she came in contact with, including, unfortunately, your client."

Dinesh wrinkled his nose in disgust, patting a folded linen handkerchief at his lips. "Lesbians," he said. "Yes. They can get pretty violent at times."

I leaned across the table until my face was inches from his. "Have you defended a lot of lesbians?"

"No," he said. "But I've heard cops tell stories, and my colleagues in the PD's office—"

"What?" I interrupted. "What have you heard? And how do you know I'm not a lesbian?"

He took a closer look. With my short, unruly hair, my faded T-shirt and jeans, I probably looked pretty butch.

"Are you?"

I leaned back in the booth. "No. But I don't think you should go making assumptions about your client and any violent propensities she might have. I met her, you know. She struck me as someone with a chip on her shoulder, but I doubt she's the kind of woman who strangles her lover and stashes her in a department store fur vault."

"I hope she's not," Prahab said calmly. "Despite what you think about my sexual prejudices, I really would like to help Ms. Cramer. But I think I will need your help."

"Fine. What do you need to know?"

He reached into his briefcase and brought the notebook out again. He also slipped on a pair of wire-rimmed glasses, thus destroying any last vestige of Burt Reynolds.

"To start with: Beverly Mayes, the nanny Ardith placed with a family in Savannah. Do you know where she might be?"

"No," I said regretfully. "My associate and I haven't been able to trace her whereabouts. We thought she might have been staying at the motel with Ardith. Did she deny that?"

"Ms. Cramer says Beverly stayed in her room for two days only. One morning she woke up and Beverly was gone. She took what little money Ardith had left and disappeared. Apparently, Beverly was someone Kristee knew before Ardith. Ardith says it was Kristee who recruited Beverly for the scheme. She claims only to have met her two or three times before Beverly left for her job with the Savannah family."

"What about that family? Maybe they have some idea where Beverly might have gone?"

He shook his head. "The family won't talk to me. And there's not enough money in my budget to go down to Savannah and try to depose them. I think Beverly is a dead end."

"Shit," I said. "Since she knew Kristee from before, she might even be a suspect. All right. What kind of physical evidence do the cops have against Ardith?"

He glanced down at the notebook. "You probably know about the ring that belonged to the Beemishes. The police found it wrapped in tissue paper and hidden under the bathroom sink. Ardith claims Kristee gave it to her to keep. She was going to try to pawn it to pay for the motel room and airplane tickets. After Kristee disappeared, Ardith was afraid to do anything with it. She sold blood at one of those sleazy blood banks to buy food."

"What else?"

"Well, the motel clerk told the police he saw a woman fitting Kristee's description drive up to the motel around six P.M. Sunday. He remembered the car because not too many Mercedes-Benzes pull into that lot. He says Kristee got out, knocked on the door of the unit where Ardith was staying, and went in."

"Did he see Kristee leave again? And did he say he saw Ardith answer the door?"

"No to both questions. The desk clerk said the next time he looked outside, around eight P.M., the car was gone."

"Anything else?"

Prahab smiled sadly. "Unfortunately, there is more. Someone in the unit next to Ms. Cramer's called the desk around six-fifteen to complain about noise. The caller said two women next door were shouting and swearing and screaming and crying and smashing stuff. The clerk says he called the room. Ms. Cramer answered the phone, and he warned her he would call the cops if they didn't quiet down. She apologized and hung up."

"Wonderful," I said. "How does Ardith explain that?"

"She admits she and Kristee had an argument. She says she was furious when Kristee showed up with the bonds and jewelry from the Beemishes. The plan was for her to stick around a little longer. Then when Kristee told her she'd been blackmailing

Beemish and having an affair with him, Ardith says she lost it. They had a rip-roaring fight. But she says the only thing smashed was a water glass Kristee threw at her. Ardith says she eventually calmed down after Kristee swore she had broken off with Beemish because she was afraid of him. Kristee even told her she was going to go back to the house, pack her things, and leave that night. The plan was for the two of them to leave town the next morning, go to Miami, and try to sell the bonds and jewelry and coins. From there, Kristee wanted to go to the Cayman Islands."

"When does she say Kristee left?"

He consulted the notebook again. "Around seven-thirty. They ate dinner and Kristee left. She was going to go back to the Beemishes', get her stuff, drop off the Mercedes, and take a cab back. But Ardith says she didn't come back that night. The next day, when Ardith called the house, Mrs. Beemish answered the phone, so Ardith hung up. She thought Kristee had double-crossed her and left town without her."

"Sounds like something Kristee would do," I said. "Did anybody in the restaurant where they ate see Kristee and Ardith together that night?"

"They didn't go to a restaurant," Prahab said. "Kristee got on the phone and ordered take-out Chinese food to be delivered. And Ardith says she doesn't know the name of the place Kristee ordered from."

"Maybe we can track it down," I offered. "If a delivery boy saw Kristee alive that night, that might mean something."

"Afraid not," Prahab said. "I checked the phone book. There are at least four dozen Chinese restaurants that deliver in that area. I had my investigator call some of the places to check it out. She called four or five places but got nowhere."

"This isn't looking too good, is it?"

Prahab picked the orange slice off the plastic spear anchoring it to the side of his glass. He nibbled systematically at the wedge, finally placing the cleaned rind in the ashtray on the table.

"No, it's not," he said. "That's why I suggested Ardith call you. I asked around the office about you. I hear you were with the Atlanta police for a few years."

"But never in homicide," I reminded him. "I was a uniformed officer, and then I worked in property crimes. After I got my private investigator's license, I worked the usual stuff, divorces, skiptracing. I've never really worked a homicide before."

"I have," he said shortly. "But as I'm sure you know, our office budget for investigation is almost nil. We just don't have the resources. Ms. Cramer insists that Bo Beemish is responsible for Kristee Ewbanks's murder. I have no idea how we could prove something like that. He is, from what I've learned, a powerful prominent person."

"But Ardith could be telling the truth," I pointed out. "Look. Ardith told you that Kristee said she was blackmailing Beemish. And she was afraid of him. Beemish himself told me Kristee had stolen some papers concerning one of his business deals. And just today, when I went out to the new subdivision he's building, two guys chased me in a golf cart and tried to blow my head off with a shotgun."

He looked shocked. "Did you report that to the police?"

"I tried," I said. "They seem to think I was trespassing."

"Tell me something," Prahab said. "If what you say is true, why haven't the police questioned Beemish?"

I took a long sip of my beer, which was getting warm. I hate warm beer.

"According to his wife, Lilah Rose, Bo was in Hilton Head with her all that weekend," I said. "They didn't return until late Sunday. I'm going to check it out, but they both have alibis."

Prahab pulled the maraschino cherry off the plastic spear and popped it into his mouth. He chewed silently for a moment. "So much for that theory."

"Maybe not," I said. "Maybe Lilah Rose was lying. She told

the cops some story about spending the day in Beaufort alone, but she could just as easily have gone to Atlanta and killed Kristee. Or maybe Bo came back to Atlanta early Sunday night, surprised Kristee at the house, throttled her, and killed her. Maybe he packed her up in his wife's fur coat and stashed her in the fur vault at Rich's the next day."

He looked at me dubiously. "You really think we can prove any of that?"

I looked right back at him. "What's this *we* shit, Kemo Sabe? I haven't agreed to investigate this thing for free."

"I know," he said. "Look. I think I'm going to suggest to Ms. Cramer that she plead guilty. There are no aggravating circumstances. It was probably just a lover's quarrel. If we plead out, the DA will drop the other charges. She'll get life, do maybe seven years at the women's prison at Hardwick. There are worse deals."

"You're trying to guilt-trip me, aren't you?" I asked. "You think I'll help you because she's a woman, and she's getting railroaded by the establishment, and I'm a sucker for that kind of shit."

He shrugged. Then he picked up my nearly empty glass, which I'd placed on the table, and moved it back to the coaster. He took his handkerchief out and carefully buffed the water ring my glass had left on the tabletop.

"Go see her," he said. "Maybe she'll tell you something new."

19

I'D MADE THE DOCTOR'S appointment for 8 A.M. With a little luck and a lot of stealth, I'd be up and out of the house before Edna could ask too many questions.

I don't remember much of that morning, just that it was again unusually hot for a spring day. Finding out the results of a mammogram seemed like serious business, so I'd worn a dress. Black. The disc jockeys on the morning drive show said it could get up to 90 degrees that day. Then they started started making stupid dead-Elvis jokes. When the hilarity got too inane I shut off the radio with such force the knob came off in my hand.

Rich Drescher's office was in a pale pink neoclassic temple. Maybe the architect thought an ob-gyn's office should reflect a woman's sensibilities. Personally, I thought the building looked pretty silly.

The receptionist was chatting with one of the nurses when I walked into the waiting room. They fell silent when they saw me. The thought occurred to me that they were discussing the Callahan Garrity case. It was paranoia, of course, but finding a lump in your right breast will make you paranoid.

After she called my name, the nurse walked me right past the examining rooms and into Rich's private office. I couldn't decide whether that was a bad sign, either.

Rich smiled up at me like he always does. "How 'bout them Dawgs?" he said, referring to the Georgia Bulldogs. He's corny, but as gynecologists go, he's the best. Drescher and I go way back. We even dated a few times in high school before he fell in love with Jana Spears. She was a tall serious type who was president of the National Honor Society. They got married in secret their senior year of high school; then, somehow, both of them worked their way through college and med school. Jana was what Rich liked to call a pecker checker. She did research on sexually transmitted diseases for the Centers for Disease Control, which is headquartered in Atlanta.

I collapsed into the wing chair facing his desk and accepted the mug of hot coffee he handed me. It had a color drawing of the uterus, ovaries, and fallopian tubes on the side.

"Tell me," I commanded.

A month ago, in the shower, I'd been shaving my underarms when I encountered a bump in my right breast that I hadn't remembered being there before. At first, I'd thought it was an ingrown hair or something. It was the size of a small pearl when I found it. Two weeks later it was a bigger pearl. That's when I'd called Rich in a panic. My grandmother died of cancer when Edna was a teenager. Edna had had a radical mastectomy before she was forty. My own breasts weren't State Fair winners or anything, but I'd grown attached to them.

The idea of cancer scared me shitless. It had taken all my courage to go in for the mammogram. Once the test was done, part of me didn't want to know the results. That's why I hadn't returned the nurse's phone calls until Rich had tracked me down and threatened to throttle me.

His usual smile was a little lopsided that morning. "We found a suspicious mass in the right breast," he said. "You wanna see the picture?" He opened the folder lying on the desk in front of him and slid out an X-ray.

My mouth was so dry I could barely speak. I held my hands tightly in my lap. Forced myself to breathe. In. Out. In. Out. "Just tell me," I croaked.

"It's not that bad," Rich said. "The mass looks like nothing much. Probably just a silly little old fibroadenoma."

I shook my head to signal my ignorance.

"It's probably a noncancerous breast lump," he said. "Kinda like a hemorrhoid on your boob." Rich had always had a way with words. "But with your family history, we like to be extra careful with these things."

My tongue seemed especially sluggish that morning. Carefully, I formed the words. "Will you have to remove the breast?"

"Relax," Rich said. "Really. All we're going to do is take a look at the tissue. We've got two options here. We can do either a needle biopsy or an excisional biopsy. Either way it's day surgery. With the needle biopsy, we give you a little Valium to relax you, then we numb the area with a little Xylocaine. The needle draws out some tissue, and we send it to the lab to see how it looks. What I'd recommend though, again because of your family history, is an excisional biopsy."

Almost unconsciously, I felt myself start to calm down a little. Rich Drescher has that effect. With his frizzy blond hair and brown puppy-dog eyes, he looks like an oversized lap dog. In high school we'd called him Drescher the Undresser.

"Tell me about this other thing. What did you call it?"

"An excisional biopsy," Rich said. "We'll check you into the hospital early in the morning. Give you a sedative, then take you to the operating room. I'll make a small incision, take out a slice of tissue, and send it down to the pathology lab. We'll get the results back while you're still on the table. Then, if the force is with us, we'll staple your boob back together and send you home."

"And if the forces aren't with us?"

He held the X-ray up and scanned it closely. "No shit, Callahan. I really have a feeling this is just a fibrous mass. Women your age get them all the time."

I let the crack about "women your age" pass.

"If there are some abnormal cells, we'll go to plan B."

"Is that a mastectomy?" I forced myself to say the hated word. A vision of myself floated through my mind. Me at the beach, wearing one of those flowered swim dresses like my Great-aunt Edith used to wear. Or me, strapped into a special bra fitted with a giant plastic breast in one cup. The prospect of losing a breast suddenly seemed equal to losing an arm or a leg.

Rich was talking again, but I was having a hard time concentrating. I kept thinking about Edna, losing a breast before she'd even gone through menopause.

He was saying something about precancerous cells and calling in a specialist.

"Lonette Jefferson is the best breast surgeon in town," I heard him say. "We were residents at Grady together, and she's on staff at the new Women's SurgiCenter. If we do find something, I'll refer you to her. She might recommend a simple lumpectomy, followed up with radiation and chemotherapy, or in an extreme case a mastectomy, either partial or radical.

"Lonette is the conservative type," Rich assured me. "She's not going to go cutting on you unless it's absolutely necessary."

He pulled a desk calendar toward him. "So. Let's get this baby booked. I'll have one of the girls call the SurgiCenter to check for a room. They can probably schedule us right away. How's Monday morning look for you?"

I'd been daydreaming again. "What? You're not talking about doing this thing *this* Monday, are you?"

"Callahan," he said, waving a pencil at me. The pencil's eraser looked like a birth control pill dispenser. "You've been ducking this long enough. My nurse called you three times before you'd agree to come in and get your test results. You can't run from this, you dumb-ass. Let's get the surgery scheduled right away. Jana and I kind of like having you around. Hell, since your girls started cleaning the house, we actually have time to spend with each other.

That Jackie of yours even put all our medical journals in chronological order. What about this same time, eight A.M. Monday, assuming I can get the room booked?"

I could feel my neck getting all prickly again, and the in-out breathing wasn't working too well either. Rich was moving way too fast.

"No, really, Rich. I'm not hiding. I've got something important going on. I'm doing some investigative work on a murder case. My client is in the Atlanta jail. I can't get operated on Monday. Let me see if I can make some headway with this case, and I'll call you sometime next week. All right?"

He folded his arms across his chest. "I know you, Garrity. You're a world-class procrastinator. If I don't hear from you by Monday, nine A.M., I'm calling you at home personally. If you don't answer the phone I'm coming out to the house to find you. And if you try to hide, I'll go to your mother and tell her why I'm looking for you. Edna will know how serious this is, even if you don't."

"That's not funny, Rich," I said. "Don't even joke about telling Edna. You know how she is; she's totally hyper on the subject of cancer. I don't want her dragged into this. It's none of her business, and you've got no right telling her about it."

"You're right," he said calmly. "Totally against professional ethics. But I'll do it if it means you'll have this lump looked at."

He scribbled something on a prescription pad and handed it to me.

"That's Dr. Jefferson's office number. The lump is probably nothing. But cancer isn't anything to mess around with. You might want to call Lonette and ask for a consultation. I'll let her know she may hear from you."

I got out of the chair and headed for the door. My whole body felt numb.

"Nine A.M. Monday, Callahan," Rich repeated. "Call me and tell me a time next week when we can schedule your biopsy. Or I'm goin' gunning for you."

20

IT WASN'T UNTIL I looked up and saw the giant neon Bluebird Truck Stop sign that I realized I had headed for the Atlanta jail.

When you think about it, it's sort of funny: a gigantic bluebird of happiness perched atop a truckstop, looking down on a jail. Actually, it's not really the jail at all. It's the Atlanta Pre-Trial Detention Center. Aside from the bluebird, you know you're getting close when you start seeing all the bail bondsman offices.

I sat in the van for a few moments after I pulled into a pay parking lot. What the hell was I hoping to accomplish by seeing Ardith Cramer again?

Her own lawyer wasn't convinced of her innocence. And even if she hadn't killed Kristee Ewbanks, Ardith was still guilty of helping Kristee pull off the nanny scam. The Beemishes hadn't been blameless victims, but they *were* victims. Their home had been ransacked, they'd been blackmailed, and their children had been put in the care of a remorseless little criminal. I wondered if Lilah Rose and Bo knew how lucky they were that their *real* valuables hadn't been harmed.

The sun was beating down hard on the windshield of the van now, and I could see the attendant in the cashier's shack staring at me to see if I was going to pay up. "Shit or get off the pot, Garrity," I heard myself say out loud.

What the hell. I'd driven to the jail in a kind of fog after leaving the doctor's office. If my subconscious wanted me to go see Ardith

Cramer, that's what I'd do. I had promised Rich Drescher I'd go in for surgery next week. All right. That would be my deadline. If I couldn't find a way to get Ardith off the hook for Kristee's murder by then, I'd drop fighting crime and go back to battling waxy yellow buildup.

If the city's planners had wanted to pick the most depressing setting in Atlanta for a jail, they'd done a good job. At least half the businesses around the jail were empty or boarded up. There were pay parking lots and vacant lots, many with concertina wire stretched across to keep the homeless from congregating there. The only going concerns seemed to cater to either the hopeless or the helpless. As I walked toward the jail I passed a labor pool. A knot of empty-eyed men loitered on the doorstep. I kept my eyes pointed ahead, felt them staring, ignored the comments. Across the street was a gray brick single-room-occupancy hotel, so long a part of the scene its sign no longer had a name: just ROOMS BY DAY OR WEEK. At the corner there was a confectionary, a place to cash checks without identification, to buy a pack of smokes, a bag of chips, maybe a bottle of cheap wine or beer. Directly across the street was a grimy little café. The only cars in the postage-stamp-sized parking lot in front were two Atlanta Police cruisers. Coffee-break time.

The sidewalks here were crumbling; weeds grew up through the cracks. I felt sweat beading on my nose and my back.

Ahead of me, the jail loomed large, like an up-ended red brick shoebox. Completed in the early '80s, city officials had admitted the day after the jail opened that it was already obsolete. I'd read in the newspaper that this year the jail had already processed 78,000 prisoners. It had been built to process 30,000 annually. Somebody was always suing the city to try to force them to provide better health care and security for the prisoners; the city was always blaming the state for not giving it enough money to run the place.

As usual, there was construction going on outside. Piles of

sand, bricks, and lumber blocked the narrow sidewalk leading to the door. Workers sawed and hammered desultorily in the mid-morning heat.

Once I'd picked my way through the mess to the entrance and pushed open the door, I was plunged into semidarkness. Half the light fixtures in the lobby weren't working. Here and there people lounged, dozing on the scarred wooden benches that lined the west wall of the lobby.

I hadn't been to the jail in at least two years, but I swear these were the same people who'd been waiting here on my last visit.

At the glass-walled information desk a detention officer checked to see whether my name was on the list of people approved for contact visits with prisoners. She nodded silently as her finger found my name on the computer printout and buzzed me into the holding area.

A few seconds later another buzzer sounded, and I pushed open the door leading into the holding and visiting area.

Nothing had changed here. The concrete block walls were still beige and blue. The smell was the same, a combination of urine, blood, vomit, stale smoke, and Pine-Sol. The same white-uniformed trustee pushed the same mop down the twenty-five-foot-long hallway. Narrow metal doors lined both sides of the corridor. Each was punctuated with a small, six-inch-square window. Faces were pressed up to the windows, mostly black faces. These were the isolation cells for prisoners with AIDS. The violent ones wore blue cotton prison jumpsuits, the sick ones wore bright orange.

The men's holding cell was on the right. Designed to hold a dozen prisoners at the most, this morning it held maybe twice as many. They were splayed out on mattresses on the floor, squatting on the floor against the wall, standing in line waiting to use the pay phone bolted to the cell wall.

At the end of the corridor the hall veered right into a room broken up with small cubicles, each with a four-foot-high dividing wall. I sat down in a metal chair to wait for my client. Ten minutes passed. Finally a female jailer brought Ardith into the cubicle and told her to sit.

At first I wondered whether they'd brought down the right prisoner. This woman seemed to have shrunk. The hair I remembered as reddish-brown was dark brown and matted to her head. A navy blue jail smock and slacks hung limply from her body. The ruddy skin tone had faded to a sallow yellow, her nose was swollen and red, and her lip had been cut. She shuffled in wearing jail-issue paper booties.

The jailer, a short stocky black woman with orange-blond hair, handed me a document to sign, swearing that I wasn't bringing in any explosives or contraband. Then she left.

Ardith made a halfhearted attempt to smile. At least I thought it was a smile. It was hard to tell with someone who had a perpetually sullen look on her face. I could tell the effort was costing her.

"You OK?"

She nodded. "A lot of women up here seem to think I need a new girlfriend. After I got my nose busted trying to persuade them otherwise, they put me in isolation. It's better, really. No cigarette smoke and no whores bothering me. My lawyer promised to bring me something to read. Thanks for coming, by the way. My calling you was his idea."

"It's all right." I looked at her closely to see if a few days in jail had changed her attitude toward me. I couldn't tell. "What made you decide you needed help?"

She shrugged. "Does it matter? Kristee's dead. Beverly ripped me off. I'm broke. I don't know a soul in this town. My lawyer said there's not much he can do for me. So I called you. So help me."

When she put it so graciously, how could I refuse?

"Look," I said, tilting my head to try to get her to look me in the eye. "Look at me, dammit. It matters to me. If I do help you I won't be getting paid anything. When I work for free, which I really can't afford to do, I like to know why. So far, all I've been able to get out of you is a bunch of lies. Now I want you to quit jerking me around and tell me what the deal is here."

She stared at her hands, which were folded in her lap. The nails had been bitten short, and her stubby fingers were covered with little scratches. She gingerly ran one finger along the swollen ridge of her nose.

"If you help me get out of here, there's a chance I could pay you something," she said. Her voice was so low I wasn't sure I understood her correctly.

"Pay me with what? You've got a court-appointed lawyer, you've been staying in a nineteen-dollar-a-day motel, for which you owe a week in back rent, and I happen to know you've been living on saltines and peanut butter."

"I've got a way."

I rose out of the chair so fast and hard it fell over backward with a loud crash. Ardith looked up at me in shock.

"I'm outta here, Ardith. You obviously aren't ready to cooperate. And I don't have time to screw around with somebody who won't help herself. Have a nice life."

I picked the chair up and set it back on its legs. I was halfway down the corridor, walking fast, when I heard her calling out.

"Ms. Garrity. Come back. Please."

Don't ask me why. I went back. She was scrunched into a ball in her chair, a pathetic little rodent hiding from a mean hungry cat.

"What?" I demanded.

"I want you to help me because I didn't kill Kristee," she said woodenly.

"You've already told me that," I said. "Tell me something new."

Her eyes finally met mine. "I talked to somebody last night who offered to help me."

"Who?"

"My former father-in-law. He's rich, I guess."

I looked at her dumbly. "Ex father-in-law? You were married? Didn't you tell me you're gay? And I thought you told me you didn't know anybody in Atlanta."

She made another stab at smiling. It was an improvement over the scowl. "Yeah, I was married. It was a long time ago. Even dykes get married sometimes, you know. And I was telling you the truth. I don't really know my ex's father."

I sat back down in the chair. "Why don't you tell me about it."

She took a deep breath. "I was nineteen. I met him in college, at the University of New Mexico. I was from a hick town in Colorado; he was from Atlanta. I'd never seen a black guy who wasn't a janitor or a garbage man. He was there on a baseball scholarship. He seemed exotic, I guess. We dated. I was young and dumb and so naïve. God. I was too stupid to be real. The first time we screwed I got pregnant. That's the truth. My parents had a fit when they heard. They never even met Geoffrey. We got married, but we both knew as soon as it was legal that it wouldn't work. We broke up before the baby was born, but we didn't get divorced until a year later."

She seemed removed from the story she was telling, as though she was reciting a long-forgotten fairy tale. I wanted to hear how it ended. Somehow I knew it wasn't happy-ever-after.

"What happened to your husband? And the baby?"

She shrugged. "Geoffrey lost his baseball scholarship and dropped out of school. He came back east after we split up. I kept the baby for a while. But it was too hard, trying to go to class and work and take care of him too. And I didn't have any help. Finally, my mother-in-law flew out to see us. She saw the dump we were living in and offered to take Demetrius. It was OK by me. I hardly ever saw him anyway. This way, he'd be living with a family, a black family. He'd get what he needed, and I'd get what I needed."

"Which was what?"

"Enough money to finish school. All I had to do was agree to let Mr. and Mrs. Driggers adopt him."

I'd heard that name before. "Driggers? The people who own Driggers Ford and Driggers Toyota? Wendell Driggers is a real big shot in Atlanta."

"I guess," she said. "Geoffrey always had plenty of money while he was in school. When he lost his scholarship and we got married, his parents got pissed off and quit supporting him."

"What happened to your husband?"

She laughed. "Sounds funny to think about having a husband. It was so long ago, I'd forgotten I was ever married. I heard he played some minor league ball around Georgia. He got hurt, though, and moved back home with his folks. Then he joined the army. He was stationed in Germany for a while, but Mr. Driggers said last night that they don't know where he is now. They seem to think he was mixed up in drugs or something over there."

"And the baby?"

"He'd be about seventeen now, I guess. Mr. Driggers said he's OK. He wouldn't tell me too much about him. I think he's afraid I'll want to see him or something."

"You don't want to?"

She was staring at her hands again. "No. What's the point?"

I couldn't answer that one.

She looked up finally, met my eyes with hers. "This is all ancient history. I called Wendell Driggers last night and told him I was in a jam. He almost hung up the phone. Then he said he'd help me. But he said I couldn't see the boy. I said fine."

Ardith reached into the pocket of her smock and pulled out a torn piece of newspaper with a phone number scrawled on the margin.

"That's Mr. Driggers's office number. He said to have someone call him, and he'll talk to you about making my bail. Don't call their house, though. He doesn't want his wife to know I'm in town. Maybe you could give that to my lawyer?"

I nodded in agreement. "Now. Why don't you tell me more

about what happened after you got to Atlanta? And no more lies. Or I really will walk this time."

I wouldn't say Ardith spilled her guts after that. She was still distrustful, still reticent about admitting all the details of their scam. What surprised me most was the way she talked about Kristee Ewbanks.

"We had something," she insisted, leaning close to me for the first time since we'd started talking. "I took psychology in college. I dealt with criminals in the diversion center. It was my job. But Kristee was different from those other women. She didn't need a man to make her life work. And she was smart. Too smart, as it turned out. She was ambitious too. For herself, for us."

I didn't say anything. Just kept listening.

"We never planned to keep the nanny business going for long," Ardith was saying. "We could have made a lot of money off it, if we had wanted to. But it was just a way to get some capital. That's what Kristee called it: operating capital. We were going to go to the Cayman Islands after we left Atlanta. You don't need a passport to get in there, you know. We were going to start a bed-and-breakfast on Grand Cayman Island." She laughed bitterly. "A nice fantasy, huh? Too bad Kristee had to fuck it up by getting herself killed."

I glanced at my watch. Visiting time was nearly over, and I still had a lot of things I needed to know.

"Do you have any idea what might have happened to the rest of the stuff Kristee took from the Beemishes?" I asked. "The police still haven't found anything else, the bonds or the coins or silver, and certainly not the business records Bo Beemish told me were missing. Could Kristee have stashed it someplace else? Maybe planning to leave town without you?"

"I've thought of that," Ardith admitted. "Sunday night, when she didn't come back and nobody answered the phone at the Beemishes, I figured she'd gone off without me. I have no idea where she might have hidden the other stuff. The only thing she gave me was the ring." Her eyes narrowed. "Hey, why don't you ask her boyfriend where the stuff is? Maybe he helped her hide it himself."

"Collier?" I said. "I doubt it, Ardith. I went to see him. He's the genuine thing, a real Mormon. When I told him Kristee was dead the other day he nutted up on me, starting talking in tongues and crying."

Ardith's face looked blank. "Who the hell is Collier? I was talking about Bo Beemish. I never heard Kristee mention anyone named Collier."

Oops. "What can I tell you, Ardith? Kristee was apparently playing the field. As part of her Mormon gig she went to a Church of Latter-day Saints on Ponce de Leon and got herself an honest-to-God Mormon boyfriend."

She sighed. "I should have known. I bet he was tall and blond and athletic, right? Kristee had a thing for muscles."

"That about describes Whit Collier," I said. "If it's any comfort, she apparently made up some elaborate scenario for him. Even after he figured out she wasn't really Mormon, she had him believing that she was a likely convert and Bo Beemish was a big bad wolf who had taken advantage of her. He told me he saw Kristee Sunday night, and she was packing her bags to fly back to Utah. She was going back there to read Scripture and get right with God so the two of them could be married in the Temple."

"What?" Ardith said. She started to giggle. It was the first sign I'd gotten that she had a sense of humor. "That's great. Kristee as a faithful Mormon maiden. What an actress that girl was!"

"What do you suppose she was up to with Collier?" I asked.

"Kristee liked to mess with men's minds," Ardith said. "It was a game for her, that's all. Does this guy have any money, do you know? Maybe she was running a scam on him, too."

I'd considered that possibility myself. "I don't know if he has any money," I admitted. "But I can check that out. And while I'm at it, I'll check to see where he was Sunday night. I think he told me he was out doing the Lord's work."

Ardith shook her head ruefully. "I wouldn't spend too much time worrying about some big dumb Mormon boy," she said. "Find out where Bo Beemish really was that night. I know that bastard had something to do with killing Kristee. He or his friend must have done it."

"Which friend?" I asked quickly.

"Some guy," she said. "Kristee never mentioned his name. Sunday night, when she was bragging about blackmailing Beemish, she said she had something against Beemish's business associate too. That's what she called him, I think, a business associate. It was somebody involved in that real estate deal of his."

Ardith's eyes suddenly misted over and a tear rolled down her cheek. She let it fall.

"I still can't believe any of this is real. When she was taunting me with her affair with Beemish that night, I halfway thought she was making it all up. That's how Kristee was. She'd start telling you something, something that was true, and before long she'd mixed in a lot of lies. Little stupid lies. She was so good at lying. I don't think she knew herself what was the truth and what was invention."

She wiped at her eye with the sleeve of her smock and winced when the fabric brushed her swollen nose.

I reached out and grabbed Ardith by the shoulder. She stared at my hand but didn't push it away.

"Ardith, listen to me. This could be important. What did Kristee say about this business associate? He could be the one who killed her. Or he might know whether Beemish did it."

She sniffed loudly. "Wait. I'm trying to remember. I think she said Beemish and his friend had taken her to the Hilton for a weekend. Could that be right?"

"The Hilton? Why would he take her to the Hilton for a whole weekend?" I wondered aloud. "No. I'll bet it was Hilton Head Island. That's a resort island off the coast of South Carolina. Beemish has a place there. Is that where you mean?"

"Yeah," Ardith said. "If it has a beach, that's the place. Kristee adored the beach. That was one reason we were going to the Caymans. She read somewhere that the beaches there have sand like powdered sugar."

"What else did she say about that weekend? Did she say anything about Beemish's friend? Like his name?"

"No," Ardith said. "I told you, this was all a game to her. She did hint that she'd slept with both of them. I thought she was saying that to make me jealous. She said if Beemish found out he'd kill her and the friend. She thought the situation was hilarious. And the friend must have had money too. Kristee said he'd be glad to give her a nice present to keep quiet about the deal at—what's the name of that subdivision? Some French name?"

"L'Arrondissement," I said.

The jailer came back then. She tapped Ardith on the shoulder. "Let's go home. Visiting hour is over."

Ardith got up from the chair. Her shoulders returned to the slumping position. She seemed inches shorter than when I'd seen her in the motel.

"Call Mr. Driggers," she urged me. "He promised to help."

"I will," I promised. I watched her shuffle out. Her paper booties made a rustling noise as they slid across the tile.

———

I COULD HEAR THEIR VOICES before I pushed open the back door. All the House Mouses were crowded into the kitchen, seated at the table, except Neva Jean, who stood in front of the open refrigerator door with a fried chicken drumstick in one hand and a Mountain Dew in the other.

"Was that the last drumstick?" I asked, knowing the answer already.

"Mm-hmmph," she said, chewing hard to get rid of the answer.

"That was goin' to be my lunch. I've been thinking about that piece of chicken all morning," I said mournfully.

"It was delicious," Neva Jean offered. "Your mama can fry chicken like no white woman I ever knew."

Edna was trying to talk on the phone amid all the commotion, but the din from the girls' chattering made it hard for her to hear. Finally she put her palm over the receiver and held it straight up in the air. "Shut up," she hissed. "I'm trying to conduct business here."

The chatter subsided to loud whispering.

"What's going on?" I asked, dragging a step stool out from behind the kitchen door. "Who called a staff meeting?"

The conversation trailed off to nothing, and the women were strangely silent, with the exception of Sister, who was trying to make herself heard to Baby, seated beside her at the table.

"When Miz Jeanine told me she didn't want us to clean today

I 'bout fell out," she hollered. "You know we been doing Miz Jeanine's condo since she sold the big house on Tuxedo five years ago. What you reckon she's so mad at us 'bout?"

Baby reached over and slapped a withered finger up to her sister's open lips. "Quiet down, Sister. Can't you see Callahan's here now?"

Sister's milky eyes squinched up tight. "Hey there, sugar," she said, turning toward Neva Jean, who was now lapping up a dish of coleslaw that had also been earmarked for my lunch. "We been waitin' for you to get here."

"No, ma'am, Miss Easterbrook," Neva Jean said. "This here's Neva Jean. That's Callahan sitting over there by the stove."

Edna hung the phone up then, with a huge pained sigh. She picked up a lit cigarette from the saucer of a coffee cup, took a deep drag, and exhaled. "And where the hell have you been? I've been calling all over town this morning trying to track you down."

I put on my most innocent face. "Oh. Didn't I tell you I was going to the Atlanta jail to interview Ardith Cramer? What's going on here? Why are all the girls sitting around our house scarfing down my lunch?"

"What's going on here is a disaster," Edna said. "At eight o'clock this morning the phone started to ring. It hasn't stopped since. All our Buckhead clients are canceling. This one's going out of town. That one has hired live-in help. This one is mad because somebody forgot to dust the friggin' étagerè last week."

She got up from her seat at the table and stalked over toward the stove, thrusting the appointment book at me.

"Look at that," she said, jabbing her finger at the scratch-throughs. "It's a conspiracy, I tell you."

I peered closely at the book. I couldn't read much of Edna's writing anyway, but I certainly couldn't see anything that looked like a conspiracy in our appointment book. "What kind of conspiracy? Who'd want to conspire against a rinky-dink outfit like the House Mouse?"

"I don't think, I know," Edna said, fairly spitting the words out. "It's that little bleached-blond Buckhead princess sorority sister of yours. I just got off the phone with Florence Foster. She says Lilah Rose Beemish called her this morning and chewed her out for referring us to her. Florence said Lilah Rose is claiming some valuable antique snuffboxes went missing after we cleaned over there Monday. Lilah Rose told Florence she was calling everyone she knows who uses us to tell them what kind of cleaning service we're running here."

So that was how the Beemishes were going to deal with me.

"Well, Florence didn't cancel, did she? I thought she was an old friend of yours from the beauty shop."

"Hell, no, she didn't cancel," Edna said. "I told her you personally cleaned the Beemishes' house. She knows how disgustingly honest you are. And not only that, I told Florence that Bo Beemish was a crooked snake who thought a whole pile of new money gave him the right to run the world. She said she never did like Lilah Rose, but since Lilah's on her symphony benefit committee, she's been trying to introduce her around."

I hooked my feet under the bottom rung of the step stool and ran a finger down the day's bookings. The situation looked serious. Neva Jean had two big jobs booked for the day; both were crossed out. The Easterbrooks' steady Friday appointment, old Mrs. Trahern, had also been scratched through. Altogether, two thirds of the day's jobs had been canceled. Obviously Bo Beemish knew I had been out touring L'Arrondissement. This was his way of putting pressure on me to butt out.

"What do you intend to do about this mess?" Edna and the other girls looked expectantly toward me.

I handed the book back to Edna. I was damned if I'd let the Beemishes run me out of business. "We're going to take care of business, is what we're going to do. First we'll try a little good cop/bad cop.

"Girls," I said. "I want all of you to call back your clients who canceled. You tell 'em Edna wants to give their standing cleaning appointment to a new client. Tell 'em you wanted to double-check with 'em before you let Edna give away their spot. And remind 'em if they give up their day and want to rehire us later, Edna's gonna charge 'em the rate for new clients, which is twenty dollars a day more. And tell them you've got to know right away, because Edna's really pissed about their canceling."

"Ooh-whee, I love it. I love it." Jackie tittered. "That snotty Mrs. Whelchell gonna have a conniption when I tell her. She had to wait six months to get my Friday spot, and she said her husband already raises hell about how much we charge. I hope she does drop us. She don't even let me watch my soaps while I'm ironing."

Edna looked doubtful. "Where are we going to get new clients to take the place of these ones Lilah Rose Beemish is scaring off? Just tell me that, Miss Smartie Pants."

"Marketing, Edna, marketing," I said. "I'm appointing you marketing director as of this moment. First, you call back Florence Foster and tell her we're waxing her kitchen floor for free this week. Just a little way to say thank you to our loyal clients. And also tell her that any time she refers a new client who signs on with us that we'll knock ten dollars off her bill that week."

She nodded appreciatively. "What else?"

"Call up all our other regulars who didn't cancel and offer them the same deal. Tell them what days and times we have open and act like you're letting them in on the best thing since sliced bread. Tell them about your environmentally sensitive cleaning deal, too."

Neva Jean was already dialing the phone, trying to get back with her two biggest clients.

"One more thing, girls," I said.

I got up from the stool and stood in the middle of the kitchen floor, so they could see I was in my authority mode. I did a slow

360, my hands on my hips, giving each one of them my most soul-searching stare.

"I've got an idea that some of y'all may be cleaning houses off the book," I said. "I know it goes on in this business: an apartment here, a condo there, you take a referral that should go to the House Mouse and do it nights, weekends, or your off days, using House Mouse supplies and equipment, and you keep the money yourselves. You call it moonlighting. I call it thieving.

"Now, Edna and I have put every penny of our savings into this business, and we can't afford to lose our investment. We've treated y'all like family since we started the House Mouse. Gave you loans to bail your boyfriends out of jail." Jackie stared intently at the spotless white sneakers that were her trademark. "Wired you money when you were stranded, penniless, out of town." Neva Jean had the grace to blush. "Picked up your blood pressure medicine at the drugstore and brought it to you when you were sick in bed." Ruby beamed her thanks; I was sure Ruby was the only one who wasn't moonlighting. "And we have even," I said, raising my voice, to make sure the proper persons could hear me, "paid certain people in cash, thus defrauding the United States government and putting ourselves in peril of being arrested, so that certain people wouldn't lose their social security benefits or get kicked out of their senior citizens' high rise."

Baby and Sister looked at each other, rolling their eyes up in their heads so all I could see was the red-rimmed whites.

I took the appointment book and slammed it, open, on the kitchen table. Placed a pencil beside it.

"We're gonna call this amnesty day. Edna and I are going to leave the room now. While we're gone, we hope some people will decide to get right with God and put their off-the-book business *on* the book. If one of you should decide to do this, be sure and write down the day and time and the client's name and phone number. If you've been giving them a cheaper rate than we charge, call them right now and tell them you're turning legitimate and they'll have to pay our going rates. Throw in a refrigerator cleaning or a free day of laundry if you have to, to sweeten the pot."

When I'd finished my speech I turned on my heel and marched defiantly out of the room. Edna followed.

"That was some pretty tough talk in there," she said, sitting on the couch and pulling an ashtray toward her. "How'd you know they were all moonlighting? I never would have suspected the Easterbrooks." She lit up another cigarette, inhaled, and exhaled. I could tell she was regarding me with newfound respect. Edna thinks I'm a cream puff.

"That was one of the things the dingbat who sold us the franchise warned me about," I admitted. "She said they all do it if they can get away with it. It's kinda like union featherbedding. Up until now, we could afford it. We can't any more. As for Baby and Sister, I've always known they had a touch of larceny in their souls. They never leave this house that they don't stuff a packet of Sweet'n Low in their purses."

"I'm going to watch that," Edna promised. "But if all the girls come across, and we can drum up some new business to replace the people we've lost, I think we'll be all right. That bitch Lilah Rose may have done us a favor."

"Maybe," I said. "I've got a feeling we haven't heard the last of the Beemishes. Especially not if I manage to get Ardith Cramer off the hook for Kristee's murder. There's something rotten going on out at that subdivision of his, and I intend to find out what it is."

Edna had to hear all the details of the jail interview then, and she made me slow down as I tried to rush through the details. She also made me repeat the good parts, like how Kristee had apparently slept with both Bo Beemish *and* his business associate on the trip to Hilton Head.

"I love it!" She cackled, her head nearly obscured by the haze of blue smoke hanging about her blue hair like a halo. "This is better than *General Hospital* and *Days of Our Lives* combined. Lesbian love triangles, mixed marriages, crooked real estate deals, a phony nanny scam, and a body in the fur vault."

I hadn't had time to give it much thought, but this investigation *had* taken some rather strange turns.

"Don't forget the Mormon boyfriend who speaks in tongues," I threw in.

"Mormons," Edna said, snapping her fingers. "That reminds me. Two of them boys showed up at the front door this morning, wanting to gospelize and proselytize."

"What boys?" I asked.

"The ones in the white shirts and black pants and little skinny ties. The ones that ride bicycles and come to your door in pairs wanting to come in and talk to you about the good news."

Suddenly I remembered having called the Latter-day Saints church and asked for information about Mormonism. "Uh, those were probably missionaries. They might have come because I called up and asked some questions about the Mormon religion," I told her. "But I never told them they could come to our door."

"Well, they came," Edna said. "Bugged the shit out of me, wanting to know what religion I was and did I believe Jesus Christ was Lord and Savior and wasn't I a widow?"

"Why'd they want to know about your marital status?"

"They told me if I converted to their church, then they could baptize your daddy and the two of us could be married forever in heaven."

"Did you tell them Daddy's been dead fifteen years?"

"Yes, ma'am. And they told me they baptize dead people all the time. Said they could baptize your granddaddy and grandmama and everybody else in the family too."

I'd have paid anything to have listened to my mother's conversation with those missionaries. "How'd you finally get rid of them?"

"I told them twenty-five years of marriage on earth to the same man was more than enough for me, and when I got to heaven, *if* I did, I was looking forward to playing the field."

"That's when they left?"

"No, they wanted to sit here and read me some Scripture from some little zippered-up thing they called the Book of Mormon. They left after Neva Jean came in and started telling what-all she and Swanelle did last night after renting a video called *Beat Me, Hurt Me, Make Me Dirty*. I guess Mormons got rules against having sex in the flatbed of a pickup. Those two boys' faces got kinda red, and they started squirming like they had ants in their pants. When Neva Jean got to the part about what she and Swanelle did with the Karo syrup, they took off out of here like bats out of torment."

"Good for you, Ma," I said. "Hey, after you get the booking situation under control here, I've got some investigative work for you to do."

Her face lit up as though she'd won the $50 pot at the Sacred Heart Tuesday-night Bingo game.

I gave her the phone number for Whit Collier's church and told her to make up a story to get them to tell her what he'd been doing Sunday night. I also asked her to call the Georgia Secretary of State's office to see if Bo Beemish had any business partners registered in his corporate filings. "Also, call Bucky Deaver at the cop shop. The number's in my Rolodex. Ask him how he liked the cleaning job Jackie did for him and tell him I need one more favor. Ask him to run Whit Collier's name through the NCIC to see if he has any kind of record. While he's at it, get him to check Beemish too.

"If you get done with all that, you might take a drive out to Kensington Park. The city clerk out there is named Wilona, and she thinks I'm too nosy for my own good. See if you can get a look at the minutes for the council meeting for the hearing where the city approved annexation of something called the Harper property. It should be public record. Make sure and write down who voted which way on that, and on anything else that pertains to L'Arrondissement."

"What about you?" Edna asked. "What kind of trouble are you gonna be getting into while I'm playing telephone tag?"

"I'm not quite sure yet," I admitted. "I think I'll go looking for an honest bureaucrat."

DINESH PRAHAB WAS IN A RUSH. "I can't talk to you now, Ms. Garrity," he said. "I'm due before Judge Bolden in five minutes, and if I'm late again she's going to cite me for contempt. Can I call you back later this afternoon?"

"This will only take a second," I assured him. "I talked to Ardith Cramer earlier today. As it turns out, there is someone in Atlanta who may be willing to help her make bail. I'd suggest you call Wendell Driggers at his office."

"The Ford dealer?" Prahab said in disbelief. " 'Drive a little to save a lot with Driggers'? How could someone like Ardith Cramer know him?"

"It's an interesting story. Call him and you'll find out all about it. Gotta run now. 'Bye."

I thumbed idly through my address book. The pages were crammed with scribbled phone numbers and notes about who did what. I knew a guy who cut sun roofs in cars, a plumber who worked Sundays and holidays, a clerk in the De Kalb County coroner's office, and a professor at Georgia Tech by the name of Joo who could find anything in any computer anywhere. I knew the travel agent who makes all Ted Turner's travel arrangements and an FBI agent who'd read the bureau's original unexpurgated file on Dr. Martin Luther King, Jr. But I didn't know anybody who knew anything about crooked real estate developers.

All I really had was a strong hunch that whatever Beemish was doing with his riverfront land was probably illegal, and that it probably involved the "business associate" that Kristee had mentioned to Ardith. Most local governments adopted stringent regulations in the 1970s designed to protect the corridor of the Chattahoochee River, one of the last wild rivers in the Southeast to run through a large urban area, from rampant development. But for some small towns, like Kensington Park, zoning was considered just another set of rules invented by Yankee planners. Kensington Park held to the theory that what a developer did with his property was his own damn business. There was an umbrella planning agency, the Atlanta Regional Commission, that had some kind of regulatory authority over the river corridor, but I was unclear exactly what it did.

Before the renegade rednecks had run me off from L'Arrondissement I remembered seeing a sign tacked to a tree: RESIDENTIAL MARKETING BY BUCKINGHAM BROKERS, INC.—MARLINDA YOUNG, REALTOR.

I called Buckingham and asked for Ms. Young, identifying myself as someone interested in building a home at L'Arrondissement.

"Yes?" A silken voice came on the line. "This is Marlinda. How can I help you?" When I explained that my husband and I were interested in one of the one-acre riverfront lots, Marlinda's voice grew husky, warm, excited. She would have been great on one of those 900 sex phone lines.

"Why don't you and your husband come to our office for tea today?" she breathed. "I can show you the schedule of lot prices and tell you about the fabulous builders who will be participating in our community."

"Oh, I'm not worried about the lot prices," I assured her. "D.W.—that's my husband—D.W. and I have already seen the lot we want. But D.W.'s afraid there might not be room for the swimming pool, being that close to the river and all. D.W. says I can build whatever kind of house I want, as long as he has his pool. He swims laps. Do you know what the regulations say about pools so close to the river?"

Her chuckle was throaty, intimate. "I'm sure the city of Kensington Park won't give us any trouble about your little old pool," she said. "They've promised to give us any variances we need."

"But D.W. says you have to get approval from the state or somebody," I insisted. "Who could tell me for sure?"

Marlinda was tiring of my annoying little questions. "Just a moment, please, and I'll check with my office manager," she finally agreed.

Five minutes passed. When Marlinda came back on the line she didn't sound quite as sexy. "My office manager tells me he's sure there will be no problem, but to be safe you could call the Atlanta Regional Commission and they could explain the permit procedure," she said smoothly. "Now, if you'll just give me your name and tell me what time to expect you and your husband?"

I hung up quickly. Now that she mentioned it, I remembered reading about a several-years-long running battle the ARC had had with a homeowner who'd built an elaborate dock and boathouse and extended it out into the river. The ARC had been trying for years to make him tear it down.

It took fifteen or twenty minutes to cut through the maze of receptionists, secretaries, and political flunkies to get to a person with any real knowledge at the ARC.

A kindly secretary named Jennifer finally took pity on me and told me I needed to speak to a Mr. Andrew McAuliffe.

"He's not here right now, though," she said.

When I told her how important it was that I reach him, she hesitated.

"Well, it's one o'clock, and it's Friday, and he doesn't have anything scheduled for the afternoon. On a nice day like this, he likes to trout-fish on his lunch hour. If you drive up to the river landing at Settles Bridge Road and see a green Jeep Wagoneer parked there, that's Mac. Walk down the dirt road to the riverbank. If you see a sexy-looking guy with gray hair and a gray beard with a black Lab, that's Mac. But for God's sake don't tell him I told you how to find him. He'll have my hide."

Out in the garage I rummaged around among the lawn tools and coolers and broken sprinkler heads until I found a wadded-up hunk of gray-green rubber. Dad's old waders. Finding the rest of his fishing equipment was trickier. Just as I was about to give up, I glanced up and saw some poles laid across the roof rafters. I grabbed four or five. The lines had rotted and the reels looked rusty, but I managed to find one bait-casting rod I thought would work. Pushed way to the back of the workbench, I spied an old red metal tackle box.

I threw the whole mess in the back of the van and took off. It was one of those gorgeous spring days that always make me wonder why everybody in the world doesn't move to Atlanta. The sky was a gentle blue and the sun was a benediction. Up until now, the early spring weather had been cool, so cool that the dogwood blossoms clung to the branches. The azaleas were making a show too, blazing white and pink and crimson in every yard I passed. The Braves were playing a rare afternoon home game down at the stadium, and their new young pitcher had a no-hitter going in the fourth inning. On the drive out to the river I left the windows of the van down and let the wind have its way with me. This was why I'd quit my day job. I had to restrain myself from breaking into a chorus of "Dixie": you know, "old times there are not forgotten" and all that stuff.

At the Settles Bridge lot the green Jeep was parked where Jennifer said it would be. And the beaten path to the riverbank was easy to spot. I unloaded my gear and headed off. Sure enough, about two hundred yards down I saw a black Lab frisking about with a tennis ball. A few feet away, standing in waist-deep water, was a lone fisherman. He wore a tattered khaki hat on his head, so I couldn't see his hair, but he did have a gray beard.

McAuliffe didn't see me; he was concentrating on flicking his line back and forth, back and forth, toward a small pool on the other side of the stream.

I unrolled my own waders and peered into the legs to check for spiders, rats, or other unwelcome visitors. Seeing none, I took off my sneakers and got into them. Rigging my line was more of a problem. The only lure left intact in the rusted-out jumble of Dad's old tackle box was a ridiculous four-and-a-half-inch red-and-white balsa-wood minnow. One of us kids had given it to him for Father's Day years ago, and though he'd joked about how it even scared off an ugly old alligator gar, he'd named the lure Elmo and proudly tucked it into the tackle box.

Elmo in hand, I waded into the river and was shocked to find quite quickly that the icy water was rushing into my waders. I looked down. The rubber had cracked in places, causing dozens of tiny pin-sized holes to create a colander effect. I gritted my teeth and gently cast Elmo out.

Not too bad, I thought. He plopped into the water with a loud splash. McAuliffe looked over at me and frowned. He stepped a couple of feet downriver and started casting again. I decided to show off my prowess with the rod, slowly playing the tip back and forth with the popping wrist motion Dad had taught me. Amazingly, there were no bites.

I cast Elmo out again. This time, he landed with another splash, inches away from where McAuliffe was flicking his fly rod. He looked over at me with real annoyance. "Go away."

Jennifer was right. McAuliffe was kind of sexy, if you went in for weatherbeaten, outdoorsy types. He probably ate granola for breakfast and slept under red flannel sheets.

"But I like fishing here," I said.

"That hunk of junk you're fishing with is scaring off the trout," he groused. "Haven't you got a spinner or a nice quiet Rapala you could use?"

"Afraid not. This was the only usable lure I could find."

He glared at me. My lips were starting to turn blue and I could feel my teeth chattering. I was soaked up to my waist, and my feet and legs were totally numb. "I'm done fishing anyway," I said brightly. "You must have gotten them all."

With relief I slogged toward the bank. I sat down on a fallen pine log and peeled the waders off, pouring about a gallon of water out of each leg. I yanked my socks off, wrung them out, and laid them beside the waders. I found a large flat rock nearby and stretched out to try and dry off.

The sun glittered off the surface of the river like a sea of silver sequins, and I had to cover my eyes to avoid the glare. I guess I started to drowse off, until I felt someone breathing in my face. I opened my eyes slowly and looked into the friendly brown eyes of the Lab. He dropped the tennis ball at my side and gave a short bark. I tossed the ball a few feet away and he bounded off after it. I drowsed off, but woke when I heard another bark. It was my new friend. This time I threw the tennis ball as hard as I could, into a thicket of underbrush about fifty feet down the bank. "That ought to keep you busy," I muttered.

When I woke up again, the dog was back and so was McAuliffe. He'd sat down on a nearby rock to remove his waders. I sat up and stretched my legs. The jeans were nearly dry, but they felt stiff and tight. McAuliffe gave me a cursory smile and concentrated on placing flies back in his tackle box. A stringer with three silvery rainbow trout lay in the grass, and the dog sniffed them nosily, wagging his tail in approval.

"Looks like you had some luck," I said.

He glanced at the fish with a shrug. "Not really enough to mess with," he said. "Don't know why I kept them."

I decided to blow my fisherwoman cover. I don't think I'd fooled him anyway. "You're Andrew McAuliffe, aren't you?"

"You the woman who called my office looking for me?"

"How'd you know?"

"Jennifer got to feeling guilty that she'd sicced you on me," he said. "She called me on the car phone, and I just happened to be getting Rufus's ball out of the truck when it rang. She warned me some woman wanted some information about L'Arrondissement."

"That was me," I admitted.

Before he could ask, I filled him in on the murder case I was working and explained why I was interested in Bo Beemish and L'Arrondissement.

"I think there's something crooked going on over there, and I think the dead girl, Kristee Ewbanks, knew about it and was blackmailing him over it," I told McAuliffe. "I think that could be why she was killed."

McAuliffe snapped his tackle box shut and reached for the dog, scratching him between the ears. "Don't you think it's kind of far-fetched to think even somebody like Bo Beemish would kill someone over a real estate deal?"

"You know Beemish?"

He nodded his head. "I know him. He was one of the first to build townhouses on Lenox Road in a neighborhood that had always been single-family homes. Talk around Fulton County was that he bought himself a couple councilmen to push the rezoning through."

"That's just what I think he did in Kensington Park," I said.

"Can you prove it?"

"Not by myself," I said. "I was hoping maybe you could help me figure out what's going on at L'Arrondissement."

McAuliffe snorted. "Lady, I'm no detective. What makes you think I'd know whether Beemish is doing something illegal?"

"It's a long shot," I told him. "But I was guessing maybe he's building too close to the river or something. I know Fulton County wouldn't give him the zoning he wanted, so he got annexed into a town that would give him carte blanche."

"It's called zoning shopping," he said. "I walked that property the last time it was up for rezoning, before Beemish bought it and the surrounding parcels. I thought then that the land was in the floodplain, and I think the same thing now."

"Great," I said. "Do you have any reports or anything that would reflect that?"

"It never got that far. The previous owner lost his financing shortly after that and withdrew the rezoning request."

"So Beemish applied to Fulton County for rezoning, they denied his application, and he took the deal to Kensington Park," I continued. "Does the ARC have any jurisdiction to find out how Beemish got them to do that?"

"We're not an investigative agency. We don't have subpoena power or anything like that. But I can tell you from what I know about how things get done in Atlanta that some money or big favors changed hands over L'Arrondissement. It's an old story. What the ARC does have jurisdiction over is the Chattahoochee River Corridor. And L'Arrondissement is in it. I'm scheduled to begin a river review of the project next week."

"How long does that take?"

"A month or two," he said. "But until we issue our report, Beemish can't do any work out there. Then the city council has to comment on our report, and it has to go through a series of public hearings."

"Guess again," I said. "I told you I was over there yesterday. He's already started cutting roads and clearing lots. But he's not accepting any visitors just yet. I almost got my head blown off by two of his security guards, and when I complained about it, one of the Kensington Park city councilmen, a former friend of mine, told me I was trespassing and it served me right."

McAuliffe nodded his head in recognition. "It's the old blow-and-go strategy. Beemish has big money tied up in that land, and he can't afford any delays. So he told his contractors to fuck the regulations and start clearing. He figures by the time we catch up with him the lots will be sold, the roads in, and houses halfway up. He's betting we won't make him tear down houses and reforest lots. It's a good bet, too. And if we did take him to court and the court gave him a fine—what, ten thousand? Big deal. He's already written it into his development costs."

"They really do things that way?" I asked.

"Look around you," McAuliffe said. "Houses built right on the edge of the river. That's illegal. Tennis courts cantilevered out over the river. Same thing. Hell, there's a guy who built a glass office tower not five miles from here. The county denied him zoning, so he sued in federal court and won. He gets to sit in his penthouse office and watch storm water pour off his parking lot into the river. The asshole is polluting the river he paid a premium price to look at."

"What's wrong with a little rain?" I asked.

He shook his head at my ignorance. "If it were only rainwater it wouldn't hurt anything. But water draining off paved surfaces picks up oil and gas from cars parked there, and it drains soil off too. It all ends up in the river. And it ain't good for the trout and it ain't good for your drinking water, which the city of Atlanta gets from the river, as you know."

"Is that what's wrong with Beemish's development?"

"I don't really know until I get out there. I've looked at the preliminary plans. He's got a shopping center planned for the front part of the property. That's a lot of parking spaces, more than our river corridor plan permits. And then there's the floodplain. The first time we get a really bad rainstorm the river is going to rise, and a lot of those big fancy mansions are going to end up with more riverfront than they bargained for. And that's not even mentioning the fact that he's building higher density than any county in Atlanta would permit."

"What's density?"

"Houses per acre," McAuliffe said patiently.

I checked my socks. They weren't dry yet. I put my sneakers on and laced them up slowly, enjoying the late-afternoon sun on my back.

"It sounds as if nothing Beemish is doing out there is that big a secret to people like you," I said. "There must be something else. Something he paid somebody to help him hide. That must be why they're making such a big deal about security. They're hiding something else."

"Like what?" he said. His eyes were an odd gray-green color.

I smiled winningly. "That's why I put on these leaky waders and came out here to corner you on the river. I've been out to L'Arrondissement. All I saw was a big trash pile. I need somebody who knows about this stuff to take a look around."

"So hire an engineer," he said. He stood, picked up his fly rod and tackle box, and whistled for the Lab. "Come on, Rufus, let's go home." He started up the dirt path without looking back at me.

I grabbed my own gear and raced after him. "With what? I've told you, my client doesn't have any money, and neither do I. My best shot at helping her prove her innocence is by finding out who did kill Kristee Ewbanks. She was blackmailing Bo Beemish. I know that much. Now I need to find out why."

McAuliffe didn't slow down until he reached the Jeep. He unlocked the tailgate and carefully stashed his gear. Rufus leapt into the back and hopped over the seats, landing in the front passenger seat.

"Look, Callahan," McAuliffe said, turning to face me. "I can't help you. It's not my job. In sixty days, I'm going to file my report with the ARC. It'll probably say something like 'This project is not consistent with plans for the river corridor as set out in the Metropolitan River Protection Act.' I'll file it, the city will appeal it to the state, they'll kick it around for a year or two, and in the meantime Beemish will either finish the project and make millions or sell to another developer who'll start the whole process all over again."

"Screw the process, then," I said heatedly. "You say this shit happens all the time. I say it sucks. But this time there's a murder involved. I've got a client sitting in the Atlanta jail getting beat up every night by whores and crackheads. They stole her running shoes. I could maybe get her out, *maybe*, if I could get just one bureaucrat to go out on a limb and prove he gives a flying fuck about something besides the process."

He slammed the tailgate shut, opened the driver's door and slid into the seat. "I'm not a bureaucrat," he said evenly.

"So what are you?"

"I'm an engineer," he said. "Shit. All right. I'll regret this, I know. But if you really want to go over there and look around, we'll do it. Sunday morning, early, when no construction crews might show up to make a little overtime. There's a little store near there, or at least there was the last time I was out that way. Meet me in the parking lot at eight A.M."

He eyed the House Mouse van parked beside his jeep.

"That your car? I thought you told me you were a private investigator."

"It's a long story," I said. "I'll tell you about it Sunday."

23

EDNA HAD A POT going on each eye of the stove and something rising golden brown in the oven. She hummed an off-key version of "Sentimental Journey," and I couldn't swear, but it looked like she was doing a solo Lindy as she stirred a bubbling pot of black-eyed peas. The kitchen smelled like Sunday dinner and it was only Friday night, which usually is pizza night at Chez Garrity.

"You're in a good mood," I said as I sat toweling my hair dry. Some women go shopping when they're happy. Some women sip champagne. When Edna's happy she cooks. Which explains why I'm always twenty pounds overweight. "What are we having?"

"Black-eyed peas that Ruby put up from her garden last summer. Corn I froze from old Mr. Byerly's garden. Fresh green beans from the De Kalb Farmer's Market, the sliced tomatoes the Easterbrooks brought us from Florida. Biscuits with Ruby's homemade fig preserves. And banana pudding with vanilla wafers." She frowned. "It's not much. And I don't know how those green beans will be; they looked a little wilted. I was gonna do a ham, but they wanted a dollar fifty-nine a pound at the A&P. I'm not paying that for pig meat."

"All this just for us?" I was immediately suspicious. "Who did you invite to dinner? If it's Maureen and Steve I'm going out."

She poured me a tall glass of iced tea and squeezed a wedge of lemon into it. "What are you talking about? This is just some odds and ends I had in the freezer. I'd be ashamed to fix this for company."

That's Edna for you. She'll knock herself out fixing a huge dinner with fried chicken and pot roast, five kinds of vegetables, two kinds of hot breads, a chocolate cake, and a sour-cream pound cake; then she'll spend the whole dinner apologizing for "just dibs and dabs." She doesn't fool me.

"What are we celebrating?"

My mother took a long drink of her own tea. "Well, for starters, we're not out of business. Half the cancellations had a sudden change of heart after the girls called them back, and we also picked up enough new jobs that Jackie's cousin LaSonya is going to come to work, just part-time for now. And you were right about the moonlighting. Every single one of those girls, except Ruby, had off-the-book jobs. It looks like most of them are going to come on the books."

"Fantastic," I said. "I should have given you that promotion long ago. Handle this job right, and you might make V.P. for Public Relations next week."

"Shut up," she said happily. "I haven't told you everything yet. I called that Mormon church about Whit Collier. The woman on the phone acted real funny when I asked about him. She said they didn't give out information about members. But then she said if I wanted to talk about 'Brother Collier' I'd have to talk to the ward president."

"Did you?"

"Sort of."

"What's that mean?"

"The woman put me on hold for a long time. I could hear voices talking back and forth in the background. Then a man came on. 'Brother Collier is a member in good standing of this church,' he said. 'He has been spoken to about past transgressions, and we will say no more about it.' Then he hangs up."

"What the hell do you suppose that means?"

"I haven't a clue," Edna said. "Now let's eat before it gets cold."

During dinner we gossiped about the girls, and Edna filled me in on my brother's current marital woes. Kevin was separated from his wife, Peggy, and Edna was clearly on Peggy's side. "I told your brother if the two of them split up not to bother coming home to me," she said, dousing her tomato with a dollop of homemade mayonnaise. "That Kevin is just cheap. I don't know how a child I raised could be such a tightwad. He's even drinking generic beer these days. Generic."

After thirty minutes of filling my face, I had to push myself away from the table. "My God, Edna, that was good," I told her. "If the House Mouse goes bankrupt, you could always open a restaurant."

"Don't think I haven't thought of that," she shot back. "I got a name and everything. Edna's Eats."

I started clearing the table, but she waved me to sit back down. "You haven't asked me about the rest of my mission," she said expectantly.

"I've been waiting for your report," I said.

"I checked the Secretary of State's office. WDB Enterprises' officers are W. DuBose Beemish, Lilah Rose Beemish, and Lenore Carter Beemish."

"Lenore must be his mother," I offered.

"Agent of record is a lawyer named Tucker Taliaferro," she added.

"Hmm. That's the lawyer who showed up to represent Lilah Rose when the cops were questioning us at Rich's," I said. "Good work. What else have you got?"

"I took a drive out to Kensington Park," she said. "I don't know why you and that nice city clerk didn't get along."

"Just because she's a racist old bag who's suspicious of anybody asking a few honest questions, I guess. I take it you were more successful?"

"We are dear friends," she assured me. "I told her I was with the North Fulton branch of Women for Better Government, and she hauled out a bound copy of council meeting minutes for the last year. She even gave me an empty desk to work at and a cup of Mocha Mint Delight. We had an International Coffee moment. I gave her my sour-cream pound cake recipe. She gave me a recipe for a hideous orange Jell-O salad I wouldn't feed a cat."

She got up and opened a kitchen drawer and brought out a small spiral-bound notebook, then sat down and donned her bifocals.

"My notes," she said. "You'll need these for our file. Let's see, on July seventh, Councilman Shaloub made a motion that the city act to annex the old Harper property. There was some discussion about the heavy cost of extending services that far from the city limits, especially sewer and water lines, but the motion passed three to two, with Mayor Corinne Overmeier breaking the tie. Voting for it were Vice Mayor Shaloub and Edwin Strong. Voting against were Calvin Rainwater and Miriam Butler."

"Did you say Rainwater?" I asked.

Edna glanced over the rim of her bifocals. "Yes. Wilona is a terrible gossip. She gave me the rundown of everybody on the council. Corinne Overmeier is divorced; she's in real estate sales with Buckingham Brokers."

"That makes sense," I said. "The mayor votes for Beemish's annexation deal, and he rewards her by giving her company the contract to market houses in L'Arrondissement."

"Edwin Strong manages the Wal-Mart over at the mall. Ruth thinks he wears a toupee. Calvin Rainwater is a Kensington Park fireman. And, yes, his great-aunt is crazy Miss Inez, whose property Beemish bought. You'd think he'd be for the annexation since it gave his loony aunt some money, but no. Miriam Butler is a housewife, vice president of the Kensington Park Jaycettes, and active in the Democratic party."

Edna gave me a long disapproving look.

"And we know who Eddie Shaloub is. He's that character you used to date. He's got a telephone-pager business now."

"I know," I said.

"Well, I never did like him when you were dating," she said. "And what I found today proves I was right about him."

"What?"

"Just about every motion that had anything to do with the Harper property was introduced either by Shaloub or Corinne Overmeier," Edna said.

"So? Maybe he's in favor of progress."

"What he's in favor of is lining his own pockets," Edna said. "Wilona let it slip that Shaloub has already bought a lot at L'Arrondissement, and he's gonna build some swanky house there. I don't know what kind of money those telephone pagers sell for, but it's hard for me to believe that somebody who was an Atlanta cop not too long ago is making that kind of money. I know you certainly aren't rolling in the dough."

"Come to think of it," I admitted, "the last time I saw Bucky Deaver he mentioned that Eddie invited him and some other guys to play golf at his country club up there. Those clubs charge as much as fifty thousand for initiation fees and ten thousand a year for dues. That's some heavy money."

"I know where he got it, too," Edna insisted. "After I got done looking at the council minutes I got Wilona to tell me the name of Shaloub's business. Phone-Home, it's called. Cute, huh? When I got back here I called the Secretary of State's office to see who his corporate officers are. Miles Norman, the Kensington Park Chief of Police, is his corporate secretary, but his agent of record is Tucker Taliaferro."

"Bo Beemish's lawyer." She smirked. "Are we starting to see a pattern here?"

I was starting to feel sick to my stomach. Shaloub's elastic interpretation of ethics had always been a joke around the cop shop, but I'd never thought of him as someone who'd sell his vote for cash on the barrelhead. The idea made my flesh crawl.

"Oh, Jesus, Ma," I said. "You're right. And that country club

Eddie belongs to. Wilona told me Beemish took the council members to lunch at his fancy club in Gwinnett County. I bet that's the one Eddie belongs to. And I'll bet he didn't pay the full membership price either."

Edna paged through her notes, looking for details she'd overlooked. "Corinne Overmeier certainly sold her vote too," she pointed out. "And this Wal-Mart guy probably didn't vote for the annexation out of the goodness of his heart."

"Favors," I said. "It's the name of the game when it comes to developers and politicians, from what I hear. But I've got a feeling Eddie is more deeply involved with Beemish than those other two. He called me right after those goons shot at me. At the time he told me he knew about it because he has a police scanner on his desk, and they called the cops. What a laugh."

A small yellow envelope was sticking out of the edge of Edna's notebook.

"What's that?" I asked, plucking it out.

She looked at it like she hadn't seen it before. "Oh. Oh, yes. A cop was sticking it in the mailbox as I pulled in the driveway this afternoon. I stuck it in here and didn't even look at it because I was in a hurry to get in the house and get to the bathroom after all those International Moments."

I ripped the envelope open. It was a citation from the city. For operating a business in a residential neighborhood. There was a $500 fine and a demand to cease operations immediately.

"Look at this," I said, handing the notice to her. "Who could have ratted on us?"

We get along fine with all our neighbors. Most of them are working people like us, who mind their own business. Old Mr. Byerly next door swaps us vegetables from his garden for a once-a-month house cleaning, and Erik and James, a gay middle-aged couple who live across the street, are close friends. We keep their dog when they go on buying trips for their antique business.

"First the cancellations and now this," Edna moaned. We exchanged stares. "You get the feeling somebody is trying to put us out of business?" she asked.

"Don't worry about it," I told her. "We'll get this straightened out. Now, anything else you forgot to mention to me? Anybody wanna haul us in for jaywalking or throw us in the pokey for tearing the tags off our pillows?"

She smiled wanly. "Bucky Deaver wants you to meet him at the Yacht Club. Tonight, at eight-thirty," she said. "He sounds nice. Is he married?"

24

AFTER THE DISHES WERE CLEARED I sat at the kitchen table and made notes to myself about the Ewbanks murder. I was determined to find out who Beemish's business associate was. If Beemish really had been in Hilton Head when Kristee was strangled, the associate could have been the murderer.

Right now, Eddie Shaloub was looking like a prime candidate for that role. It was a long shot, but the other council member—what was his name, Edwin Strong?—could also have been the unnamed associate. Hell, given Kristee's history, Corinne Overmeier was even a possibility.

I needed to find out just how watertight Beemish's alibi for Sunday night was. Lilah's too. That story of hers about driving to Beaufort and falling asleep on the way back sounded a little too cute. But how would I find out what Shaloub and the other council members had been doing that night? And to be on the safe side, I meant to check out Whit Collier too.

By the time I looked at the kitchen clock and saw it said eight-thirty, I'd covered a yellow legal pad with a series of names, questions, circles, arrows, and diagrams. What it all meant I couldn't say. At the bottom of the page I'd sketched a woman's torso, sort of a crude Venus, with only one breast. Funny what the subconscious will do. I scratched through the sketch hastily, grabbed my purse, and headed out the back door.

Edna had gone out right after dinner. She and her best friend,

Agnes, had tickets to see Robert Goulet at the Fox Theater in *Camelot*. Those two never missed any musical starring an over-the-hill movie star. I'd have been willing to bet they'd seen more of Mickey Rooney, Howard Keel, and Mitzi Gaynor in the past few years than they had of their grandchildren.

I'd parked the van at the curb that afternoon because Neva Jean had left her car in my spot in the driveway. Now my windshield bore a bouquet of paper scraps tucked under the wipers. There were three tickets. One for blocking a driveway, which was bullshit. I was maybe three inches in front of Mr. Byerly's, but he never drove at night anyway. The other tickets were valid, on technicalities. My emission control sticker had expired a week ago. And, yes, I apparently had broken a rear taillight, possibly while fleeing L'Arrondissement the previous day.

I tucked the tickets in my purse and pulled the van as far up in the driveway as it would go. Then I started the hike to the Yacht Club. The van was just too damned conspicuous. Anywhere I went in it I was likely to be stopped and ticketed or harassed.

Actually, the cool night air felt good on my face. I'd gotten a little sunburn on my nose and cheeks during my nap at the river that afternoon. I have the kind of skin that burns if I stand too near a toaster. I walked fast and made it to the Yacht Club in ten minutes. I could see people inside pressed up against the windows, and a handful of guys were standing in the doorway, sipping beers.

I pushed through the crowd toward the bar. I had spotted Bucky's spiked blond hair from the doorway. Tonight he was wearing what looked like a white gas station attendant's jumpsuit, unzipped to show a healthy amount of chest hair. *Lamar* was embroidered in script over his left breast pocket. He was perched on a stool, both arms draped around the neck of a cute young thing. She was dressed in an abbreviated black tank top and a micro-miniskirt. She wore purple and orange eyeshadow and her platinum-colored hair cascaded from the top of her head in an off-center ponytail; she looked like a heavy-metal Pebbles Flintstone.

Bucky was busy whispering into her ear, so he didn't notice my approach. I tapped him on the shoulder. "Buford," I whined in an accentuated southern-white-trash accent, "Junior and Bubba want to know when their daddy's coming home again."

The blonde gave him a disgusted look, disentangled herself from his clutch, and motored to the back of the room where the young studs were gathered around the dart board.

"You again," Bucky muttered. I hopped onto the stool Pebbles had just vacated.

"You were the one who asked to meet me," I told him. "Besides, she was much too young for a man of your vast maturity and experience."

Don brought me a Heineken and Bucky a Rolling Rock. We shot the breeze for a few minutes. When Don moved away to wait on some other customers, Bucky shook his head and sighed.

"Garrity, what in the hell have you got yourself mixed up in?"

I took a deep breath. "Word's out, huh?"

"You know?"

"An Atlanta cop stuck a citation on our door today for running a business in a residential neighborhood. There were three tickets on the windshield of my van when I came out of the house tonight. This morning, a slew of our regular customers called up and canceled. Did I also mention I was shot at the other day? Yes. It does not take a two-by-four upside the head to persuade me that someone is out to get me. I figure Bo Beemish and his wife are directly responsible for my being shot at and having my customers drop out. For the sudden interest Atlanta's finest has taken in my law-abidingness, I see the fine hand of Eddie Shaloub."

Bucky hunched himself over his Rolling Rock and took a long swig. "Shaloub didn't call me personally," he said slowly. "He knows you and me are tight. But a couple of new guys just happened to mention to me that they'd heard you were after Eddie's hide because of his sudden—uh, disinterest in you."

"And they believed that crock?" I said, keeping my tone conversational despite my rising anger. "It always comes down to that, doesn't it?"

"Waddya mean?"

"I mean that just because I slept with Shaloub a few times in the past, everybody who knows that wants to believe I'm some cock-crazed slut who'd ruin a good man just because he dumped me."

Bucky looked morosely down at his beer. "Aw, come on, Callahan, I never thought that about you."

"Not seriously," I said. "You know me better. But you wondered about it, didn't you?"

He nodded his head. "OK, you got me there. But I wouldn't be sitting here if I wasn't an old friend, would I?"

I thumped him on the shoulder, leaned over, and gave him a quick kiss.

"You're true blue, Bucky. Now why'd you want to meet tonight? Did you have time to run that name Edna gave you through the NCIC?"

"That's what I need to talk to you about, Callahan. I can't be doing this anymore. You understand? They've got new rules. My captain gets a computer printout of all activity on the computer. He knows who's checking what. I can't make up any more stories about this shit to cover my butt, ya know? There's limits, Callahan."

"I know," I said sadly. "I won't ask again. Promise. But did you run Collier?"

"Nothing," Bucky said. "Zip. The guy's clean. He's from some burg called Beechy Creek, Arizona. Got a valid Georgia driver's license and O-positive blood."

He pushed a piece of paper toward me. Written on it were Collier's name, current address, social security number, and phone number.

"Now I wanna tell you something, Garrity. And I want you to listen. Drop this thing you're working on."

I started to protest, but he put the hamlike palm of his hand across my mouth to shush me.

"I mean it," he said. "I talked to Tyrone Singletary, Bohannon's partner. He gave me a peek at the Ewbanks file. He's got a strong case. Your client was the dead girl's spurned lover. They had a fight. Witnesses will say there was a racket coming from the motel room. The Ewbanks girl was strangled, but she put up a struggle. There were traces of your client's flesh under the dead girl's fingernails. They've got color photographs of the scratches on your client's hands, and jewelry stolen from the dead girl's employer was found in her motel room."

I leaned closer to Bucky to avoid being overheard. "Does Bohannon's file explain how Ardith managed to get Kristee's body out of the motel room without being seen? Does it explain how Ardith, who is two inches shorter than Kristee, got that body over to Rich's fur vault? How would someone new to Atlanta know to put a body there?"

He shook his head sadly. "No good. Ardith had applied for a job at the downtown Rich's three days before Kristee was killed. Did she tell you that? Bohannon's got all her employment records. She'd worked as a stock clerk at some Salt Lake City department store called ZCMI; it's the equivalent of Rich's. She'd know all about the good places in a store to hide a body. Face it, Callahan, they've got the goods."

"I know it looks that way, Bucky," I said stubbornly. "But honest to god, this woman did not do it. She was conned into this Mormon nanny scam by Kristee. I'm telling you: Bo Beemish paid off Shaloub to help him get his property annexed into Kensington Park, and with two other council members, Shaloub greased the skids to get the deal OK'd all down the line, even though Beemish is building houses in the floodplain and doing all kinds of other illegal shit. Look at how Eddie's living. How do you suppose he can afford dues at the country club he belongs to? This is reality, Bucky. And think about this. Bribing a public official, and taking a bribe if you're an elected official, is a federal offense.

"Kristee Ewbanks knew about the whole deal. She'd stolen a bunch of business documents out of Beemish's safe and was blackmailing him. And Kristee told Ardith she was also going to put the screws to Beemish's partner in the deal. That has to be Shaloub."

Bucky ran his fingers through his hair, spiking it even higher. "Can you prove any of this, Callahan?"

I tasted my beer. It had gotten warm, so I pushed it away and motioned to Don to bring me another. He slid a cold one in front of me. I took a long gulp and felt the cold brew sting as it went down. "I'm working on it," I told him. "But good help is hard to find."

We shot the breeze for a while and I let him beat me at darts before I decided to call it a night.

"Do me one last favor, Bucky," I said. "If you hear any more guys at the cop shop talking about my wanton lust for Shaloub, you tell them that's a joke. You tell them I told you Shaloub was, and you can quote me, 'sad in the sack.'"

Bucky guffawed despite himself.

"Tell 'em I stopped dating him because I was looking for something a little higher in the food chain. Yah. Tell them I said I don't do miniatures."

I winked broadly at him and slid off the bar stool. Tucked a five and a one under my unfinished beer and headed home. I'd suddenly lost my taste for witty banter. I was sick to death of the whole scene.

It was only ten-thirty or so, and Little Five Points was just starting to jump. People were still shopping at the Junkman's Daughter, a funky vintage clothing boutique, and there was a line waiting to get into the trendy new Jamaican eatery. I could hear strains of wild clashing sounds coming from the Point, a Little Five Points pub that was a venue for cutting-edge rock bands. That night's featured attraction was a new group, Stiff Kitty. It was unseasonably warm for late April, so there were crowds of neo-hippies, skinheads, punkers, and other counterculture flotsam and jetsam. Cars cruised up and down Moreland and Euclid, looking in vain for an empty parking space.

I'd only walked another block when I realized how still the street had gotten. But I had company. Three black-clad skinheads trailed along about ten yards behind me. I'd vaguely noticed them lounging near the doorway as I left the Yacht Club but had overlooked them as part of the usual scenery.

I quickened my pace a little, but they did the same, matching me step for step. I glanced back. Two of them were young men, their heads shaven clean except for a pelt of jet-black hair cut Mohawk style down the center of their gleaming white skulls. They wore black T-shirts with the sleeves ripped off, tight black jeans, and black boots. Their clothing was crisscrossed with a web of metal-studded black leather straps and ominous-looking chains. The female member of the party was dressed in the same color, except her face was powdered a ghostly white, her lips a slash of greenish black. They couldn't have been more than eighteen, but the boys were big, over six feet, it seemed to me, and they were solidly muscled.

In walking faster I'd left the business district behind. Now I was on a quiet residential street, a mixed bag of two- and three-story brick apartment houses and small bungalows. The only lights seemed to come from the blue flicker of television screens behind locked and barred windows.

Home was less than two blocks away. I tucked my purse under the crook of my elbow, football style, in case my followers were purse snatchers, and broke into a trot, hoping to convince them to quit the chase. In a second one of them was at my side, throwing an arm across my throat to stop me. His friend came up behind me, grabbed my hair, and yanked my head back hard. I started to scream. The first one slapped me hard across the face. My head buzzed and I felt something warm trickle from my nose.

"Not a fuckin' sound, bitch," one of them hissed at me. I heard a series of high-pitched giggles coming from the girl. She stepped up, pushing her face so close into mine I could see the ravages of acne under the rice powder. She spat in my eye and followed up with a series of short, hard slaps that brought tears to my eyes. "Bitch cop," she said shrilly. "We got something to tell you."

The tallest of the three grasped my arms and locked them behind my back. I'd had self-defense training in the police academy, but I guess my reflexes had slowed considerably since leaving the force. I struggled briefly to escape, but the bigger one only twisted my arms tighter, nearly wrenching them out of their sockets. The other two stood behind me, so I was unable to kick out at them.

The shorter boy jerked my hair again. "Leave it alone, bitch," he said, "or next time we come to your house and have a talk with your old lady."

The girl giggled happily. "An old lady. Yah. Let's do an old lady." She slapped me again, on the right side of the face. I heard a ringing in my ears. The next thing I knew, they'd dragged me off the sidewalk and into the gravel parking lot of a darkened, abandoned apartment building.

They shoved me to the ground and took turns kicking at me. The girl, who wore stiletto-heeled black boots, took deliberate aim and stomped me hard on each breast. I did scream then, a loud, ungodly animal sound that I couldn't believe was coming from my body. A dog started barking somewhere nearby, and I heard a door opening from the house across the street. Suddenly porch lights up and down the street were snapping on.

"Let's split," one of the boys hissed. But before they did, each of my attackers kicked me again, savagely but quickly, in the side and the stomach.

They ran off into the darkness.

I lay there for some minutes, my knees drawn up to my chest, rocking back and forth in the dirt, like a mother soothing a fretful infant, only the crying was coming from me.

25

IT WAS MORNING, and the sunlight streaming through the bedroom windows hurt my eyes. Edna was pounding on my door.

"Julia," she bellowed, "go to the door. The goddamn Mormons are back again."

"I'm asleep, Ma," I whimpered.

"You're not asleep. You're hung over from staying out at that bar and drinking all night," she said. "You called these little pricks, now you go deal with them."

I heard her walk back toward the kitchen. And I heard the doorbell ringing.

I shot upright, but the pain from my chest and ribs nearly kicked me back flat. God, I'd forgotten how much I hurt. The pain was so intense it was nauseating. But the doorbell kept ringing. I eased out of bed and managed to get into a bathrobe and slippers without throwing up. The clothes I'd worn last night were in a heap on the floor. Last night I'd been so tired and shell-shocked, I'd stripped down and crawled into bed in my underwear.

The mirror over my dresser showed that my injuries looked more alarming in daylight. There were two black quarter-shaped bruises on each of my breasts, and a handful of black wedge-shaped bruises on my chest, shoulders, and upper arms where the skinheads had kicked me. By standing on tiptoe I could see more bruises on my ribs, lower back, and butt. I felt sore all over. My face was the worst, though. My forehead and chin were scratched and scraped from where I'd rolled on the gravel trying to fend off the blows. My left nostril was cut and crusted with dried blood, and a purplish black streak decorated the right side of my face. "Looks like you were shot at and missed, shit at and hit," I told my reflection.

I ran my fingers through my hair in a futile attempt to pretty up for company, but the damned doorbell drove me to distraction. I shuffled stiff-legged to the front door and looked out the window.

Two earnest young men, teenagers really, had planted themselves in front of the door. They wore neatly pressed white shirts, thin dark ties, and black trousers. Each had a leather-bound case under his arm. One was tall and skinny, with wet-combed reddish hair. His friend was short, slightly plump, and blond. Their bicycles were lined up side by side on the walkway.

I considered turning the sprinklers on them, but decided to use tact instead. I'm famous for my tact. "Go away," I said helpfully. "We're Catholics. We drink wine in church and worship graven images."

The boys exchanged glances. But the redhead was made of sterner stuff. "We understand someone here is interested in learning more about the Book of Mormon," he said. "We're here to talk about Salvation, not religion."

I opened the door a few inches and stepped out onto the porch. I figured giving them the full view of my battered face and body might scare them away.

But I underestimated the fervor of the young. The redhead looked at me with interest, like a science project on bread mold. "We're sorry to call on you so soon after your hospital stay," he started.

I laughed despite myself. It made my nose bleed a little. "Look, boys," I said. "We had some missionaries here yesterday. They pretty much answered all the questions we have about the LDS church. So thank you for stopping by."

The blond summoned up the courage to unzip the leather case he carried. He thrust a couple of religious tracts at me, then turned to go. *Come and See* said the top pamphlet. It was the same one Whit Collier had given me in his office. "Excuse me," I said, as they headed for their bikes. They stopped and looked back at me expectantly, hoping they'd brought a wanderer into the fold.

"Do, uh, Mormons ever speak in tongues?" I asked.

The missionaries exchanged puzzled glances. They'd clearly been coached to answer all kinds of questions and challenges, but I don't think they'd heard this one before.

"Well, ma'am," said the blond. "Sometimes an LDS member might speak in biblical phrases unfamiliar to Gentiles. But in the mainstream church of LDS, no, ma'am, I don't believe most of us do that, under normal conditions."

"Wait right here a moment, please," I told them. With difficulty, I made my way to my bedroom, dug in my purse, and found the scrap of paper Bucky'd given me the night before. Outside, the boys were astride their bikes, handy-like, in case they needed to make an emergency escape.

"By the way," I said casually, "where did you fellows say you were from?"

"Bountiful, Utah," said one.

"Arizona," said the other.

"Would you know anything about a place called Beechy Creek, Arizona?"

They exchanged shocked glances. The blond started to speak up, but the one with glasses interrupted. "No, ma'am," he said. "Never heard of it." He jerked his head imperceptibly and started pedaling down the walk. The blond shrugged and followed.

I slipped the paper in the pocket of my robe and shut the front door. And locked it, recent occurrences in mind. I could smell bacon frying in the kitchen, and Edna was humming. Suddenly I was starved. "Hungrier than a bitch wolf with twelve suckling pups," as Neva Jean might have said. But the memory of my appearance propelled me back to my room.

I stood under the shower, as hot as I could stand it, for a long time. After I blew my hair dry, I got out my old makeup bag, the one I used for heavy-duty dates. Hoped the stuff hadn't passed its expiration date. I smeared some beige base over my face, gently working it over the bruises and scrapes, and added a coating of the kind of concealer intended to cover up under-eye dark circles. I followed that with a layer of beige powder and some blusher. Porcelain Rose. The warpaint took the rawness off my injuries, but not even a layer of spackle would have covered them altogether.

I found an old boyfriend's striped rugby shirt in the closet, put it on and buttoned all the buttons, and slipped into my loosest pair of jeans.

In the kitchen, Edna was draining bacon on a platter covered with paper towels. "Stir the grits, would you?" she said, not looking up from her chore. I did as I was told, adding more salt, since she wasn't looking. I poured myself a cup of coffee and sat down at the kitchen table, burying my head behind the front page of the morning *Constitution*.

She pushed a plate, covered with bacon, scrambled eggs, toast, and a mound of grits, swimming in a pool of butter, under my paper. Cholesterol city. That's what I love about the South. I had to put the paper down to eat.

Edna chewed quietly for a while, turning the pages of the paper as it lay flat on the table. She cleared her throat. "You get in a bar fight last night?"

I looked up sheepishly. "I feel so stupid about it, I hated to tell you. I was walking home from the Yacht Club. It was late. Two punks must have been following me. They were babies, really.

Probably just wanted money for a Happy Meal. They jumped me and tried to grab my purse, and for some idiotic reason I decided to fight them off."

A look of horror crossed her face. "Babies didn't do that to you, Julia Callahan Garrity. You could have been killed. Do you know how many rapes there have been in Candler Park already this spring? And me captain of the Neighborhood Watch. Why didn't you just give them the money?"

I shrugged. It hurt. "It doesn't hurt, Ma. I guess I got mad. It's not big thing. Somebody's dog barked and they ran away. And I kept my purse."

She reached over and touched the bruise on my cheek, then ran her fingers over the scrapes. "Did you wash your face with antiseptic?" she demanded.

"I used a whole bottle of Bactine," I said dutifully.

She pulled the telephone toward her, dialing rapidly.

"Don't call the cops," I said, alarmed. "It won't do any good."

"I'm calling your sister Maureen," she said. "And I don't want to hear a word out of you."

"Uh huh. . . . OK. . . . Yes. . . . Yes, she did. . . . Scrapes and bruises, it looks like. . . . All right." I sat helplessly back in my chair, as my mother discussed my injuries with my sister the nurse, as though I were a stray dog hit by a car.

She hung up the phone with a look of satisfaction. "Maureen's coming right over to look at you," she said. "And she's bringing a tetanus shot just in case you got any dirt in those scrapes."

Before I could protest, the phone rang. I beat her to it on the second ring and she glared at me.

"House Mouse."

There was a confused pause at the other end of the line. "I beg your pardon?" a man's voice said. It was Dinesh Prahab.

"House Mouse is the name of my cleaning service," I explained. "You know, the business that allows me to take on pro-bono cases?"

"Oh, yes," he said, coughing politely. "Ms. Garrity, I'm sorry to call on a Saturday, but it's something of an emergency. I spoke with Wendell Driggers last night, and he has made arrangements to put up bail for our client."

"Your client," I corrected him.

"Whatever. But as a condition of his assistance, he wants to see you."

"Why?"

"He didn't say," Prahab said. "I assume he wants to ask you for more details about the case. All I know is that he'd like you to go out to his home at ten o'clock this morning."

I craned my neck to see the wall clock. It was right at nine. "Impossible," I snapped. "Who does this guy think he is? I'm not dressed. And did I mention that I was mugged last night?"

"Mugged?" he said with genuine alarm. "I hope you weren't hurt. Do you think it has something to do with the Ewbanks murder?"

I glanced over at Edna, who was pretending to work the crossword puzzle.

"Ah, yes," I said carefully. "Yes. That's what I think."

"My God," Prahab said. "I had no idea. You must tell me all about what happened later. Right now I must go. I'm meeting some people for brunch."

He gave me Wendell Driggers's address, which was in Cascade Heights, an area west of town long favored by Atlanta's black elite.

"Where are you going?" Edna asked me, as I headed for my room to change. "Your sister will be here any minute to give you your tetanus shot."

"Tell her to use it on herself," I called over my shoulder. "Sleeping with Kusic, she's bound to have picked up cooties."

It was another picture-book spring morning. People walked their dogs, jogged, and puttered in their front yards. In Cascade Heights, the yardmen were doing the hard work. As I cruised

Cascade Drive, I recognized the homes of the president of the city's largest black-owned bank, the chairman of the board of a huge Atlanta-based insurance company, and the new chief of staff at Grady Memorial Hospital. The new-money buppies—black urban professionals—were building subdivisions on smaller lots in the area, but Atlanta's finest, oldest black families clung tenaciously to their hillside mansions.

High on a hill, at the end of a winding driveway, I saw an imposing white frame mansion with green shutters. Massive Greek columns marched across the front porch, and a burly young man rode a riding mower back and forth across the spreading green lawns. A small sign at the foot of the drive said EVELYNWOOD. PRIVATE RESIDENCE.

By downshifting to first and stomping on the accelerator as hard as I could, I managed to power the van up the steep driveway. At the top of the hill I followed the drive around to a large garage.

If the sign hadn't told me, I'd have known by the lineup outside the garage that I had the right house. Parked in a row were a sporty white Mustang, a sedate gray Taurus sedan, and a long, gleaming navy blue Lincoln Continental.

A powerfully built black man played a hose over the hood of the Lincoln. He looked to be in his early sixties. He was wearing one of those expensive silky warm-up suits you'd never dare to wear for actual sweating, and what looked like hand-sewn black loafers on his sockless feet. He had a broad forehead, deep-set eyes, and a fringe of tightly curled gray hair.

The van continued to knock for a full minute after I cut the engine and hopped out. Wendell Driggers shot a squirt of water on the van's dusty hood. "Chevy," he said, as though uttering a profanity. "Oughta come see me about one of our new Aerostars. Fine vehicle. Not like this piece of crap."

I stuck out my hand. "Callahan Garrity, Mr. Driggers. How do you do?"

"Let's go inside," he said. "Can't hear over the lawn mower."

He opened a door in the garage and led me into the kitchen. Although Evelynwood was an old house, dating probably to around the 1920s, the kitchen looked like the galley of the Starship *Enterprise*. The appliances were all black glass and polished chrome, the countertops a gleaming gray granite. The chrome downlights hanging over the work counter looked like futuristic hubcaps.

He led me over to a black glass-topped table and motioned me to sit down in a black leather pilot's chair.

"Grapefruit juice?" he asked, pouring himself a glass from a beaker on the counter.

The chair was hard, reminding me of my bruises. "No, thanks," I said.

Driggers seated himself at the table and studied me for a moment. "How much do I owe you?" he said abruptly.

"Excuse me?"

He pulled a checkbook out of the pocket of his warm-up suit. "What is your fee for investigating this murder case?" he said patiently. "How much time do you have in it already, and how much more work do you think you'll need to prove Ardith innocent?"

I figured up in my head the hours I'd spent on the case, not counting any of the work I'd done for the Beemishes but starting with my meeting in jail with Ardith. I told him what it amounted to.

"About proving her innocent, though, I can't tell you that," I said. "It's . . . complicated."

"Do you believe she is innocent?" he asked.

"I do," I shot back. "What about you?"

He sipped his juice. "I'm not familiar with the particulars of this case. Nor do I want to be. I don't really care about any of that. But I don't want my grandson's mother standing trial for murder in this town. I won't have it coming out in the news. My wife couldn't stand the scandal."

I'd seen photographs of Evelyn Driggers in the society pages of the newspaper. She was one of the few black women in town who moved easily through both Atlanta's black and white social circles. Her love of exotic footwear had earned her the nickname of Bootsie.

"Can I ask you something?"

He looked up from his checkbook. "Yes?"

"Does your grandson know anything at all about his mother? Has he seen Ardith? Does he knew she's here in Atlanta?"

Driggers set the pen down on the open checkbook.

"Let me tell you about my grandson," he said coldly. "We were never consulted about that marriage. My son didn't even tell us we were grandparents until Demetrius was a week old. And then they split up. My wife flew out there to Arizona when the baby was only fourteen months old. He and his mother were living in a trailer. No hot water, nothing but a hot plate to cook on. Ardith was so busy working and going to school she had no time for the baby. When Bootsie got there, he had a cold and his ears were so infected the doctor said he'd have permanent hearing loss. That girl was no kind of mother. She was only too glad when Bootsie offered to bring him home to us in Atlanta. We gave her some money to get her a decent place and to finish school. She gave us Demetrius."

"Gave him to you?" I said, raising an eyebrow.

"We legally adopted him," Driggers said. "My son, his daddy, hasn't been around in years. We don't know where he is now. And, yes, Demetrius knows his mother is white. If you see him, there's no denying it. He thinks she lives out west somewhere. That's all he knows, and he's never asked us about her in all the years since we explained it to him. If you do your job right, he won't know she's in Atlanta.

"That boy is everything to us," Driggers said proudly. "He's on the dean's list at Westminster Academy," he said, naming the city's top private school. "He's on the soccer team and the debate team and is president of his class. Colleges call every week. I want him to study law at Princeton. His grandmama wants him to stay home in Atlanta and study medicine at Morehouse."

He leaned across the table. "We're not gonna let this fool white girl screw things up for Demetrius like she did his daddy. You think she's innocent. Fine. Prove it. I told her lawyer to call my attorney. I know the magistrate judge. We'll get her out of jail. But there's just one thing. Ardith Cramer is not to come anywhere near my boy. She is not to call him and she is not to see him."

He ripped the check out of the checkbook, then, and handed it to me. It was enough money to get a valve job on the van. Hell, it was enough money to trade in the van on a new Ford Aerostar. One with an air conditioner and a CD player.

As usual, I couldn't let things alone. "Don't you think you should let Demetrius meet his mother?" I asked. "Don't you think Ardith deserves to at least see him?"

Driggers stood up, walked to the sink, rinsed out his juice glass, and set it in a chrome rack to dry. He turned to face me. His face was calm, but his voice was angry.

"She doesn't want to see him," he said. "Told me so herself, first thing, when she called me from the jail. Said she couldn't even remember what he looked like.

"Can you imagine that?" he asked, his voice incredulous. "A mama not remembering what her only baby boy looks like? I'll never forget what he looked like. He was the prettiest thing I'd ever seen. Light-skinned, the color of café au lait, like you get in New Orleans. Had freckles like his daddy did, long curly black lashes, and silky red-brown hair. Me and Bootsie played with him like a little play toy. You never saw such fools in love with a baby." He shook his head in disbelief. "Ardith doesn't deserve to see my boy. She knows it too."

We heard a car roar up the driveway, then, and the sound of doors slamming. Driggers frowned. "They're home early. You better go on now."

Before he could say anything else, the kitchen door opened and a smiling woman with short-cropped white hair bounced in, her hand affectionately ruffling the hair of a teenage boy. They were laughing about some shared joke, but they stopped when they saw the stranger standing in their kitchen.

Demetrius Driggers was still beautiful. He was tall and slender, long-legged in his baggy soccer shorts. His hair was damp, a mass of ringlets, and his eyes were a surprising shade of green.

"Bootsie, this is Miss Garrity," Driggers said to his wife, as he propelled me by the shoulder to the door his wife had just entered. "She's trying to sell me a new security system for the house."

"That's nice," I heard her say.

Driggers gave me a gentle shove out the door and into the garage. "Call me at the office when you get that price worked up," he said. "We'll see if we can't dicker a little on it."

26

FOR SOME REASON, Wendell Driggers's check didn't make me feel much better than Bo Beemish's had. I kept seeing images in my head of that beautiful teenager, Demetrius Driggers, with a price tag hanging from his hand. And me with a sales receipt.

When I got to the interview area at the jail, Ardith was waiting for me. She'd washed her hair, and there were no fresh battle scars. I pushed a paper bag across the table to her.

"What's this?" she said warily.

"Open it."

Wordlessly, she pulled out a pair of running shoes, socks, a hairbrush, some deodorant, shampoo, and a crossword puzzle book. "Thanks," she said.

"The shoes are generic," I said. "The store I went to doesn't carry New Balance. And I didn't know what size you wore, so I bought eights. I hope they'll fit."

"I'm a seven," she said. "They'll do."

Ardith hadn't been a barrel of laughs during my other encounters with her, but today she seemed spacier than ever.

"Did Dinesh tell you the news?" I said excitedly. "Wendell Driggers knows the judge in your case. They're gonna set bond at a hundred thousand dollars, and Dinesh thinks he can have you out of here by sometime Monday."

"Great," she said. "That's good news."

"What the hell is bugging you, Ardith?" I exploded. "I tell you we're gonna get you out of jail in two days, and you react as though I told you Dan Quayle was coming to town. I don't expect you to pin a medal on me or anything, but a little enthusiasm might be a nice change. Do you have some problem you want to tell me about?"

She fiddled with the running shoes, making a big thing of running the laces through the eyelets. "No," she said. "You've been decent to try to get me out of this jam. I guess I'm just tired. You don't get much sleep in jail. Half the women howl all night."

"What else?" I asked.

She looked up at me, her face paler than I'd remembered. There were dark circles under her eyes, and her cheekbones seemed pronounced. She'd lost weight already.

"It's hard for me to get excited, you know? I get out of jail Monday, but I'm still charged with murder, and they're still going to go after me for the nanny thing. I don't expect you or the cops to understand this, but Kristee and I really did have a relationship. I cared about her. Now she's dead. What have I got to look forward to? I've got no one in this town. No place to stay, no job, no money. I'll have to stay in Atlanta until the trial. And they'll still probably find me guilty and send me to prison. Dinesh warned me about that himself. As far as I can tell, the only thing that's about to change for me is my address."

I hadn't considered things from her viewpoint. What *did* she have to be thrilled about?

"Look," I said, "I told you I think we can prove you're innocent, and I meant it. I've got some decent leads now, and I'm working hard to follow them up. Your father-in-law paid my fee this morning, plus some extra money. I think it was meant as a bribe to keep you away from Demetrius."

She bit her lip at the mention of her son. I plowed ahead.

"There's enough money here to pay your back rent at the motel, plus at least another week's rent. After that, you'll need to find someplace cheaper, and of course you'll need to find work. If you're interested, you can clean houses for me. It ain't brain surgery, but it's honest work, and the pay is fair. We can look into it. Now I need some more information."

She took off the paper jail slippers she'd been wearing, folded them, and stuffed them in the paper bag with the toiletries I'd brought. Then she sat up and squared her shoulders. "What else do you want to know?"

"I've finally seen the police reports," I told her. "There's some bad news. They found traces of your skin under Kristee's fingernails. And they've got Polaroids of those scratches on your hands, taken when they booked you. The district attorney's going to say those are defensive wounds, that Kristee scratched you while you were strangling her. And they've also got something about a gash on her left index finger. What do you know about that?"

Ardith held out her hands to show me the now-faint scratch marks. "I told you we had a fight in the motel room. Kristee went wild, scratching and kicking me. The cut on her finger, I don't know about. She threw a glass at me and it broke, but I picked up the broken glass, not her. I didn't see any cuts on her hands when she was at the motel."

"Fair enough," I said, taking notes. "Now what's this about your being in Rich's the Friday before Kristee was killed? Why didn't you mention that? Or the fact that you'd worked for department stores out west?"

She shrugged. "I didn't think it was important. Sure, I applied for a job at Rich's that day. I also put in applications at Macy's and Sears. Do the cops have that in their report? I worked in retail sales years ago when I was in college, and later in graduate school. I was running out of money. You didn't expect me to get a job at a diversion center here, did you?

"Besides," she added, "I'll bet the Beemishes knew their way around Rich's. And Kristee was found with Mrs. Beemish's furs. Maybe she killed Kristee and took the body up there."

"No," I said. "It won't work. The Beemishes were in Hilton Head that weekend. They weren't at Rich's applying for a job that Friday. You were. You'd know how merchandise moves in and out of a department store. And it's important that I know you were in the store because the cops will think you were setting up a way to get the body in the fur vault."

"But I wasn't," she said stubbornly.

"I know that," I told her, "but the cops don't. I'm going to take a closer look at the Beemishes' whereabouts that weekend. And I've got a good idea who that business associate was, the one Kristee talked about. Did she ever mention the name Eddie Shaloub? He's one of the city councilmen in Kensington Park, the town where Beemish is building his new project. I don't think it will be too hard to prove he went to Hilton Head for the weekend with the two of them."

"No," she said quickly. "Beemish was the only person she mentioned by name."

I snapped the notebook shut. "That's it, then. Except for one more thing. I saw your son this morning."

Her face didn't change expression.

"Don't you want to know how he was?"

She shook her head violently. "I promised Mr. Driggers I wouldn't call him or try to see him. I won't go back on my word."

"You don't want to see him?" I said, unable to hide my anger. "You've got a beautiful seventeen-year-old son who you haven't seen in years, and you couldn't care less. You sold him to those people, and now you're letting them pay you off again to stay away from him."

She held the paper bag tightly in her hands, turning it over and over. She stuck her chin out defiantly. "It's none of your business," she said heatedly. "You don't know anything about me or that kid."

I got up to leave then. "You're right," I told her. "I don't. See you Monday."

Maybe as soon as I saw the extent of my injuries that morning, I'd made up my mind to pay a visit to the people who'd paid for them.

Midafternoon, now, and the sky was beginning to cloud over. It seemed like a good time to find Lilah Rose at home, in between tennis and shopping and kiddie birthday parties.

The iron gates at the entrance to the Beemish estate were open and two men in white painter's clothes worked desultorily, touching up the trim. I zipped past and up the drive. Since I was no longer employed by the Beemishes, I parked by the front door, alongside a cute red Miata convertible, a big Volvo wagon with two baby seats in the back, and a brand-new Range-Rover. I rang the doorbell and was greeted by the same Jamaican maid who'd answered the door on my last visit. Today her nails were painted silver.

She looked at me with alarm. It must have been my bruised face, because I'd changed into a skirt and blouse for my meeting with Wendell Driggers.

"I hope I'm not too late for the committee meeting," I told her breathlessly, pushing past her and into the entryway.

I was mad and moving fast down the hall, but I did notice with some malice that the place looked—well, cruddy. There were fresh handprints on the walls, and I spied a discarded peanut butter and jelly sandwich remnant under a marble-topped table in the hallway. As I strode past the living room I saw toys and books scattered everywhere.

Tinkling laughter came from the direction of the study, so I kept going. I poked my head in the doorway. Lilah Rose and three other women sat on the sofas, heads together in deep discussion. "For party favors we'll get Tiffany's to donate some of those darling silver caviar spoons," a petite brunette was saying.

I cleared my throat and the women looked up at me with pleasant if blank expressions. All but Lilah Rose, who looked like she'd spotted a dog turd in the pitcher of mimosas she was pouring.

She put the pitcher down and stood up. "What do you want?"

I put on my best party manners and scooched over beside the two women on the nearer sofa.

"Why, Lilah Rose," I exclaimed. "Is that any way to greet an old sorority sister?"

The committee members looked at me with newfound interest. "We were Tri Delts together at Georgia," I said cheerily. "Of course, that was way before Lilah Rose married new money. Nowadays she only puts out for clothes or jewelry or furs. But in college, Lilah was quite the party girl. She gave it away like matchbooks. Lilah, honey," I drawled, "tell the girls here about how you single-handedly gang-banged the entire KA house on Robert E. Lee's birthday."

I thought I heard one of the women, a tall frosted blonde, suppress a titter. Lilah Rose's face was contorted in a most unladylike way.

"Get out," she hissed. "I'll have you arrested for trespassing. I'll have your business license revoked. I'll call the police."

"You do that, honey," I drawled. "But first I want to show y'all some of my souvenirs."

As I started to unbutton my blouse, the other women stirred themselves into action.

"Lilah," said the brunette, hastily air-kissing her hostess near her cheek. "I've got to run. The kids will be home from ballet practice." She literally ran for the door, followed closely by the other two women, who made similar excuses.

"Wait," I said, rising from the sofa. "Don't you want to see my bruises?"

Lilah followed the women to the front door, murmuring abject apologies. I distinctly heard her say something about "former cleaning lady, unbalanced, just released from drug rehab." The front door slammed shut, and I heard her little Pappagallo flats clicking furiously down the marble hall floor. She burst into the room in a fury.

"What the hell do you think you're doing?" she screeched. "You've humiliated me in front of my committee for the Garden of Eden Ball, just because my friends decided to stop doing business with you. Are you out of your mind?"

I pulled my blouse open and pointed to my chest, which was streaked black and purple. "This isn't about cleaning, you sniveling bitch. You see these bruises? See the cuts on my face? Your husband, the big he-man developer, paid some skinheads to beat me up last night. They could have killed me."

Her mouth dropped open, but only for a second. "Bo wouldn't do that," she said flatly. "You're making this up. I'll bet one of your cop boyfriends did this to you. Bo fired you and you're trying to get back at him, but it won't work. And don't think we don't know you've been working for that nasty bull dyke who killed our nanny."

I buttoned my blouse slowly, for the effect. "I *am* working for Ardith Cramer," I said. "You've got that much right. But I've got news for you, Lilah Rose. Your husband is in this up to his neck, and I intend to prove it."

She flipped her hair out of her eye, reached in her pocket for a cigarette, and lit it. "Grow up," she said, trying to sound bored with the whole discussion. "So he slept with the little slut. That doesn't mean he killed her. Bo was with me in Hilton Head that weekend. We have witnesses to prove it. I'm not even upset that he slept with her. In fact, we're going to Saint Bart's next week, sort of a second honeymoon."

I had to laugh at this glimpse of her little fantasy world. "Can you prove he was in bed with you all night last Sunday, Lilah? Can you prove he didn't charter a plane back to Atlanta for a cozy little rendezvous with Kristee? You know he took her to your condo in Hilton Head for the weekend back in March, don't you.

He and Eddie Shaloub had a cute little ménage à trois, right there in your condo. You know that's where the picture you found was taken, right by your own pool."

The color drained from her face. "I don't believe any of this. The police have arrested the person who killed Kristee. Now you'd better get out of my home or I'll have you arrested too."

"Speaking of arrests," I said, "I think Bohannon is going to want to talk to you again about the time you allegedly spent in Beaufort."

"What do you mean?" she said quickly.

"Just this. I called the Blue Crab this morning. The health department shut them down a month ago. Some problem with their live holding tank for the crabs. There's no way you ate lunch there that day."

"It was another seafood restaurant, then," she said. "Bo and I eat at the Blue Crab so often, I guess I said that by mistake. It was probably the Beaufort House where I ate."

I shook my head slowly. "Nice try, but I don't think so. I don't even think you were in Beaufort that day. But don't worry, I'll find out where you really were."

"God damn you," she said through gritted teeth. "You don't know anything. I tell you, I had nothing to do with Kristee's murder. Nothing. Do you hear me, you bitch? And if you keep up this talk, I'll have my lawyer sue you for slander."

"Maybe I can't prove you or Bo killed her," I admitted. "I'm fairly sure it was either Bo or Shaloub. But in the meantime, Bo's crooked business deals are starting to come unraveled. I know what's going on out at L'Arrondissement. That's why Bo had those thugs attack me, to try and scare me off. I know he paid off Shaloub and those other council members to get his property annexed into Kensington Park. Bribing an elected official is a federal offense, and I intend to see he goes to jail for it."

Tears glittered in her eyes, but none fell. "Tell me something," she whispered. "What is any of this to you? I just told you, Bo's not a murderer, he's a businessman. He doesn't sell drugs. He's not a slumlord, he doesn't make poisoned baby food. He doesn't hurt anybody. Why don't you leave us alone?"

"I tried to leave you alone," I told her softly. "Remember? You got me into this thing. So I'm in. And I'm not getting out of it until I find out who killed Kristee."

27

AN UNFAMILIAR GUNMETAL-GRAY Mercedes was parked at the curb when I got home. We don't get a lot of new Mercedeses in Candler Park, so I walked out to look at it. It had a car phone antenna on the trunk, an alarm sticker on the front windshield, and a front plate that said KENSINGTON PARK, WHERE EVERYBODY IS SOMEBODY.

I had a feeling I knew which somebody was visiting the Garritys this overcast spring Saturday.

He was sitting in the living room, glancing nervously at his reflection in the front window. He wore spotless white jeans, a navy blue knit sweater, and white deck shoes, like he intended to spend the day yachting on Lake Lanier instead of slumming in Candler Park. He'd let his thick black hair grow longer since the last time I'd seen him, and I thought he was showing a lot less gray around the temples, too. There was an enormous gold watch on his wrist, and a gold medallion shone among the curling mass of black chest hair visible above the sweater's V-neck. I wondered idly who was the patron saint of corrupt politicians. He was very tan, even for Eddie Shaloub. Must have been all that golf he was playing at his new country club.

He stood up quickly as I entered the room. "Callahan," he said warmly, putting an arm around my neck and drawing me close to him. He reeked of some kind of musk cologne. I managed to sidestep his embrace, but it wasn't exactly a subtle move.

"OK," he said, folding his arms across his chest. "You're right. This isn't a social call. So why pretend?"

"How'd you get in here?" I asked, looking around for any sign of Edna.

"Your mother let me in. You know, I don't think she likes me. She didn't even offer me a glass of iced tea."

"You're right," I said, seating myself in a wing chair near the fireplace. "She doesn't like you. Neither do I. I especially don't like your having your buddies on the force harassing me."

He seated himself, uninvited, on the sofa across from me. "Oh. Is that what they're doing? Trying to enforce city ordinances prohibiting illegal businesses in a residential neighborhood and keeping unlicensed vehicles off the city's streets?"

"It's harassment," I said hotly. "I want it stopped."

"Suppose you stop harassing me," Shaloub said evenly. "Dick Bohannon called me today, asking me all kinds of questions about my relationship with Bo Beemish and did I know this dead girl, Kristee Ewbanks." He laughed abruptly. "Even he doesn't even really believe all this shit you're handing him. Nobody does."

"But he called, didn't he?"

His face darkened under his Palm Beach tan. "You and I have known each other a long time, Callahan. You were special to me at one time. That's why I can't believe you've been going around making all these wild-ass accusations about me. I don't appreciate this shit. In fact, I've talked to an attorney, and he says if you keep up these malicious statements I can sue you for slander."

"Lots of people want to sue me for slander today," I said lightly. "But why bother hiring an attorney? Why don't you just have your skinhead friends kick the daylights out of me again, like they did last night?"

"You're crazy," he sputtered. "I don't know what you're talking about."

"I think you do," I said. "But let's be specific here. Which of my wild accusations do you object to? Is it the one where I've accused you of selling your vote to Bo Beemish and betraying your public trust? Or are we talking about my accusing you of being involved in some kind of illegal land use at L'Arrondissement? Or are we talking about my suggestion that you could be involved in the murder of Kristee Ewbanks?"

"You know damned well that's all a lot of bullshit," Shaloub said. "You don't honestly believe I did any of that."

"You know, the old Eddie Shaloub, the one I used to know when he was a cop, probably wouldn't have gotten involved in any of this shit. He was a hustler, sure, but not a criminal. But this new Eddie, he drives a Mercedes, rubs elbows with the country club set, has people beat up and shot at. The new Eddie has a lot more to lose. So I intend to prove everything I've accused you of. In fact, I can already prove you're on Bo Beemish's gravy train."

He clucked his tongue. "I always thought you were such a clever girl, Callahan. We were clever together, weren't we? Now you disappoint me by coming up with this wild conspiracy theory involving murder, bribery, assault, and God knows what all. Tell me, when did you first notice these symptoms of acute paranoia?

"Never mind," he added quickly. "It doesn't matter. Bo Beemish's dealings with the city of Kensington Park have been perfectly legal and aboveboard. Mr. Beemish was disappointed that the shortsighted bureaucrats in Fulton County wouldn't allow him the highest and best use of his land. Our city needed to broaden its tax base and attract a high-quality mixed-use development like L'Arrondissement. It worked out well for everybody. Does that spell a conspiracy? Hardly."

"I'd say you and your mayor and that other councilman—what's his name? Strong?—got more out of this deal than the taxpayers will," I said. "Let's see. You get a prime lot at L'Arrondissement, a membership in Bo Beemish's country club, and a contract to sell him beepers. The mayor got a sweetheart deal to market the houses out there. I haven't figured out yet what Strong got, but I will."

Eddie leaned over and gave me a patronizing pat on the knee. "You ought to stick to cleaning houses and leave the detective work to the big boys, Callahan. You don't know shit about how business works in the real world. All my business dealings with WDB Enterprises and Bo Beemish are perfectly legal. There's nothing in our city charter to prohibit council members from earning an honest living."

"'Honest' is the operative word here," I said. "But what about murder? You got anything in your city charter making murder acceptable?"

His black eyes glittered dangerously. "You're nuts," he snapped. "Why would I murder that girl?"

"Kristee told my client, Ardith Cramer, that she'd gone away to Hilton Head Island with Beemish and a 'business associate.' She was already blackmailing Beemish over the vote buying. After that weekend—when, by the way, she told Ardith she slept with both men—Kristee told Ardith that she was going to put the squeeze on the other man too. I think you were on that trip, Eddie."

"Get real."

"And I think after Kristee threatened to expose the fact that you'd sold your vote, you either killed her yourself or helped Beemish do it."

"You think."

"If my theory is so ridiculous, why don't you tell me where you were last Sunday night? I'm sure Bohannon already asked you the same thing."

I heard a staticky noise then, followed by a high-pitched beep. It was coming from Shaloub's midsection. He reached down, hiked his sweater up an inch, and pressed a button on the top of the black case attached to his belt. He glanced down at the readout window, then at his watch, and rose quickly.

"Gotta run now," he said. "But sure, hell, I'll be happy to tell you where I was last Sunday night. I had a pizza delivered to the house around seven P.M., ate it, watched a movie I'd rented, made some business calls, and went to bed early. Alone. Oh, yeah. The pizza was from Domino's and the movie was *Lethal Weapon Two.* Hell of a flick. It's not a very elaborate alibi, but then, you can't prove any of it's not true."

I got up and flung the front door open, standing inside to let him pass.

"'Bye, Eddie," I said. "Come again when you can't stay longer."

After he'd gone, I wandered into the kitchen looking for something to eat. Edna was sitting at the table playing solitaire and half watching an old black-and-white movie on the portable television we keep in the kitchen.

"I take it you overheard my conversation with Shaloub?" I said, sitting down beside her with a plate of cheese and crackers and a glass of wine.

She kept her eyes on the cards, scanning for a likely play. "I heard some of it when I was on my way to the bathroom. Totally by accident, of course."

"Of course." I nibbled on a piece of the cheese. "Play that Jack of spades, why don't you?"

She shot me an annoyed look. "You know I hate it when you do that. You wanna play, get your own deck of cards." She played it on the Queen, though.

"What did you think?"

She played two more cards, sighed hugely, then turned over the remaining cards. "There's the three of hearts I was missing," she said.

She pushed the cards into a pile and began reshuffling.

"I think that man has the shiftiest eyes I've ever seen. And he lies like a rug. But how do we prove he's not lying? Your theory sounds farfetched even to me, and I'm on your side. No wonder the cops think you're crazy."

28

I'D SET THE ALARM CLOCK for seven A.M., but the rain woke me early. I propped myself up on a pile of pillows and watched it falling softly but steadily through my bedroom windows. Edna had paid a neighborhood teenager to mow the lawn on Saturday, and the smell of damp fresh-cut grass wafted in through my window. It was perfect sleeping weather, with the kind of rain that makes you want to burrow down deep among the pillows and quilts and sleep the morning away.

Good for lovemaking, for being kissed awake and caressed into consciousness. But my big carved walnut bed was empty, except for me. It had been a long time since I'd awakened every morning with the same familiar someone beside me.

Two years, to be exact. Two years since Matt, my lieutenant in the property crimes unit, had gotten the letter of acceptance to law school and moved up to Athens and the University of Georgia. We'd drifted apart before then, but the career change made things permanent.

A few months after that, Edna moved in. She'd sold the big house, the one we'd grown up in, and was at loose ends. She didn't want the hassle of a big house all to herself, but she wasn't ready to move to the retirement community my sister Maureen had thoughtfully picked out for her. I had a yard she could garden in, a spare bedroom and bath, and I could always use help with my house note.

Friends were incredulous. "Live with your mother? Why don't you just move to a convent?" My sisters and brothers had predicted disaster and dropped hints that Edna was just bailing me out from a lifetime of spinsterhood. But the arrangement had worked surprisingly well. Maybe because we were both fiercely independent, yet social enough to want somebody else around a lot of the time.

"Who else but a Garrity could stand to live with a Garrity?" I'd asked Edna.

It would have been nice to have someone special in my life again, but Edna wasn't preventing that. It's like my friend Paula says: All the good men are married or gay. Paula always says she wants to be reincarnated as a gay man in Atlanta. "They have tight little butts, fabulous houses, and they get all the cute guys," she says.

As I'd done every morning and night since discovering the lump, I ran my fingers over my right breast. Every morning I expected a change. Maybe the skin would glow red as a sign of the cancer, or the lump would be bigger or smaller or, yes, gone. But every morning it was there, a silent threat, my own time bomb. The bruises ached to the touch.

Tomorrow, I promised myself, if we got Ardith bailed out of jail and I made some progress on the case, I'd think seriously about scheduling the biopsy. What, I wondered, would Dick Drescher think of my bruises?

I glanced at the clock again. Quarter to seven. The rain hadn't let up any. I wondered if McAuliffe would stand me up. I decided to get dressed anyway, maybe get some breakfast at a drive-through on the way to L'Arrondissement.

By the time I got out of the shower I could smell coffee brewing. The kitchen was empty. Edna had apparently gotten up, started it, and gone back to bed. She knows how I hate morning.

I poured the coffee into a thermos bottle, grabbed an old rain slicker by the back door, and threw it on over my jeans and sweatshirt. My old hiking boots made loud clunking noises on the kitchen floor. I felt like a Girl Scout off for a day of hiking and camping.

Once I got on the highway I decided to skip breakfast and head straight for the country store where McAuliffe had promised to meet me. If I was too early I could always drink coffee and read the Sunday *Constitution*, which I'd picked up out of the driveway.

It was not yet eight, but the green Wagoneer was already parked at the store. I pulled alongside it and McAuliffe motioned for me to cut the engine and join him in his car. I jumped in the front seat, clutching my thermos and my newspaper.

"You're early," he said grudgingly. "I wouldn't have picked you for a morning person."

"I'm not," I admitted. "The rain woke me up and I couldn't get back to sleep."

"That hot?" he said, gesturing toward the thermos. I poured some into the empty Styrofoam cup he held out. We sat there sipping our coffee, watching the rain ease from steady drizzle to intermittent drip. The inside of his Jeep smelled like damp dog.

"Where's Rufus?"

"Left him at home asleep." He grinned. "Rufus hates morning."

"Sun's up," he said, peering skyward. "You still want to do this? It rained pretty hard. It'll be muddy as anything back in there."

I nodded stubbornly. "I'm sorry to drag you out in the rain. You know, I halfway expected you to stand me up."

"I halfway considered it."

"But you're not that kind of guy."

"Not usually," he agreed. "If we're gonna do it, let's go. At least we won't have to worry about company in this weather."

I moved the van around to the back of the store where it wouldn't be so conspicuous and made a dash back to the Jeep.

Seated beside him, I had time to give McAuliffe a closer inspection. His hair had probably been red once. Now the ginger color was mostly gray. He wore a neatly trimmed beard, and his face had the look of someone who'd spent a lot of time outdoors, but not on a chaise lounge. I glanced surreptitiously at his hands on the steering wheel. There was gray hair on their backs and on his arms beneath the rolled-up sleeves of his shirt. No wedding band and no telltale white band of skin. I put his age at over forty-five, a little too old for my taste normally, but just this once, I thought, further study might be in order.

"How's your case coming?" he asked, startling me out of my carbon-dating process.

"OK."

"Just OK?"

"I don't know," I said. "Even my own mother thinks I'm crazy to think we can get Ardith off. There's so much evidence against her: the fight in the motel room, the scratches on her hands, the skin under Kristee's fingernails. Then there's Rich's. The body was found in the fur vault, and Ardith had been there two days earlier applying for a job."

"You didn't tell me this was the murder where they found the body at Rich's," McAuliffe said. "I think I read about that in the newspaper."

"Yeah, the story was buried among the tire ads at the back of the paper. Rich's is the *Constitution*'s biggest advertiser. It wouldn't do to publicize what a swell place their fur vault is to store a corpse."

"Doesn't look nice," he agreed. "Why did you take the case?"

"Who knows. Maybe I was just pissed off that Bo Beemish was getting away with something. I hate his type. Maybe I just love hopeless causes."

"Here we are," he said.

In the three days since I'd last been there, the construction crews had made substantial progress in completing the stacked rock wall. There were new NO TRESPASSING signs, and it looked as though the workers had finished building the guard shack, although it was empty this morning.

"Bastard's too cheap to hire a guard," McAuliffe said.

The new road was awash in liquid red mud. Streams of it gushed past the shack, splashing the sides of the Jeep.

"That's illegal right here," McAuliffe said, pointing at the gushing rainwater. "He's supposed to have sediment fences and hay bales in place all through here, to prevent this runoff. See how it's headed straight for the river?"

"Yeah, but they wouldn't shoot at me to keep me from seeing that," I said. "And it was dry and sunny the day I was here."

McAuliffe cruised slowly down Lilah Lane, stopping now and then to roll down his window and peer out at the ongoing construction. Another street had been paved since my last trip, and two or three lots had SOLD signs on them.

"Look at that," I said excitedly, pointing to a pile of felled trees that had been bulldozed to the middle of one of the lots.

"Trees," McAuliffe said. "What about them?"

"That oak tree was standing the last time I was here," I said. The tree in question must have been ninety feet tall, which meant it could be 180 years old or more. Now it was lying on the ground, its roots sticking up obscenely in the air. "Isn't there a law against cutting a tree that old? I thought the county had a tree ordinance."

"Fulton has a tree ordinance," he agreed, "but it doesn't prohibit a developer from cutting down trees on his residential property."

He pulled the Jeep into the cul-de-sac I pointed out and parked, then reached behind the seat and brought out the khaki hat I'd seen him wearing before and jammed it on his head.

"You packing a rod?" he said offhandedly.

"You mean a gun? You've been reading too much Mickey Spillane, McAuliffe. I have a little twenty-two automatic, but it's at home, in the nightstand beside my bed."

"Just wondering."

The hiking boots had been a good idea. As soon as I got out of the Jeep my feet sank two or three inches into the mud. Walking slowly, sliding some of the way, we slogged our way through the muck toward the riverbank. In several spots we could see places in the bank where the rainwater had cut a ditch and the river was a red-brown swirl.

"I see what you mean about runoff."

"Show me where you were standing when Beemish's guys spotted you," he said.

I pointed the way down the bank, and we walked until we were beside the dump. "Right here," I said, kicking a Pabst Blue Ribbon can. "Those construction workers made a trash dump on one of the prettiest lots on the river. Why would they do that?"

He edged some trash with the toe of his boot. "It's a borrow pit," he said. "They've taken soil from here and put it someplace else on the property, then filled the hole with construction debris. But it's strange for them to have used such a choice riverfront lot. Usually they put the trash pit on the smallest, least desirable lot, figuring it'll be the last to sell. Just before the lots are all gone, they'll cover it with dirt, run a motor grader over it, throw some grass seed around, and it'll look good as new—until the trash starts to degrade and the ground settles and some poor guy finds the foundation of his million-dollar house has two-inch cracks in it."

McAuliffe stood up and circled the pit, kicking, bending, poking at the trash. I followed in his tracks, doing much the same thing.

"Wait a minute," I told him. "Over on the side there, I saw a strange rock. Like a piece of an old granite house foundation or something."

"Show me."

I waded across the trash pile, looking for something to remind me of what I'd seen. "Here it is," I said, spotting a glistening gray stone poking out of a nest of old Whopper boxes. I stooped over and pushed trash out of the way so he could get a look. He squatted down beside me. "I saw a number on a corner here, somewhere," I told him, scrabbling with my hands in the trash. "Like a date or something. It might have been 1923, I couldn't be sure. Right after I saw it is when the guy in the golf cart started gunning for me."

He pulled a pair of leather work gloves from beneath the windbreaker he was wearing and handed them to me. "Here. You'll cut yourself."

I picked and prodded until I'd cleared away enough trash to reveal a twelve-inch section of the rock. "There," I said finally, running a gloved fingertip over the carved date. "It's 1928."

McAuliffe studied the rock for a minute, then stood up. "Be right back. I want to get something out of the Jeep."

I stood in the trash pile, in the early morning chill, with the rain dripping down all around me, and felt the hairs on my neck stand up. There was something here.

McAuliffe was carrying a shovel and a rake when he came back. He handed me the rake. "See if you can clear the trash away from the rock while I dig around it," he said.

I wrinkled my nose against the stink of the rotting garbage but kept raking away. After ten minutes, McAuliffe stood back and rested his elbows on the handles of his shovel. "That's it," he said grimly. "That's what Bo Beemish doesn't want anybody to see."

Our digging had exposed a smooth round-topped tablet. A single lily bloom was carved on it and there was old writing, but we couldn't make out much of it, what with the crumbling rock and a coating of green-gray lichens and red mud.

"An old gravestone," I said. "What's it mean?"

"Where there's one old headstone like this, there are usually others," he said. "This is an old graveyard, probably been inactive for years."

"And?"

"And disturbing it is strictly against the law," he said patiently.

"Even though it's his land?"

"The land is his, but the graves belong to the heirs of the people buried here," McAuliffe said, sifting through the rest of the trash with the edge of his shovel. "I wonder how many other graves there are."

"Is this really that big a deal?" I asked.

"Oh, yeah. There are small graveyards like this all over Georgia. A lot of them aren't marked on any surveys. But once you discover one, you've got a big headache on your hands. Like in De Kalb County, when MARTA was putting in the east train line, they found an old graveyard with more than two hundred graves. It was a mess. They spent all kinds of money contacting the heirs and moving the bodies. Delayed the project by nine months."

"Is that what you're supposed to do?"

"Yeah. Contact the heirs, which can take forever, to get their permission to disinter the bodies. If you can't find any heirs, you get a court order. Then you've got to get a permit from the county health department to have the remains exhumed and relocated."

"Why didn't Beemish do any of that?"

"Mr. Beemish doesn't seem to think nit-picky regulations like those apply to him," McAuliffe said dryly.

"So he had his people bulldoze those graves into a pit and cover it with trash so no one would know they were there."

I looked down at the trash around my feet and felt squeamish. I stepped out of the pit and scraped my boots off on a rock, hoping McAuliffe wouldn't notice.

"You know," I told him, "some portion of this property belonged to an old lady named Inez Rainwater. Beemish had to buy her land in order to be contiguous with Kensington Park's city limits. I wonder if she knew anything about the graveyard."

He shrugged. "Would it matter if she did?"

"Maybe. At least Beemish couldn't claim his people bulldozed it without his knowledge. The city clerk told me Beemish paid Miss Inez eighty thousand dollars, more than twice what the property's worth. Maybe that's why he paid her so much, because she was selling off the family burial ground."

"Eighty thousand, did you say? Look around you, Garrity. This land is worth much more than that. But the county hasn't reappraised land up here in decades. You've got the former governor of the state living in a two-million-dollar mansion on the river not half a mile from here, and the house and the three acres it sits on are appraised at a hundred and two thousand."

I'd apparently hit a nerve. McAuliffe talked on and on about property values and millage rates and such, but by that time I'd tuned him out. I looked up at the sky out of boredom. The sun was trying to break through a plum-colored bank of clouds.

"Say, Mac," I said, "have you got someplace else you need to be this morning?"

"Why? You wanna dig up some of these stones and see if Jimmy Hoffa's out here?"

"No. I want to see if I can locate Miss Inez."

He muttered something about needing to do some yard work and feed Rufus, but he didn't head back to the Jeep.

We slogged through the muddy carpet of fallen pine needles for five minutes or more, dodging stray branches and looking for signs of civilization.

Through a clearing in the trees, I finally spotted a flash of turquoise. As we got closer we could see it was an ancient house trailer, one of the early ones with the rounded edges that made it look like a toaster on wheels. A strand of shiny Christmas tinsel was garlanded around the front door, and two orange kittens darted in and out from beneath the trailer's concrete block underpinnings. A rough wood picnic table stood beneath a tree in the clean-swept clearing that served as Miss Inez Rainwater's front yard. Around the edges of the clearing she'd scattered pots filled with red, blue, pink, and purple plastic flowers. In the center of the yard a concrete black-faced jockey boy held a ring to which was tethered a bawling baby goat.

Before we could get any closer, the door of the trailer swung open and a wizened old lady stepped out holding a painted porcelain pot.

She wore a black baseball cap, and her main garment appeared to be a yellowing cotton slip, which she'd topped with a threadbare man's plaid flannel bathrobe. Her stringlike legs were covered in some kind of thick black hose, and on her feet she wore a tattered pair of red high-topped sneakers. She was a tiny thing, not even five feet tall, and her face was a mass of wrinkles. But she wore no glasses and the buttonlike brown eyes were surprisingly clear.

"Miss Inez?" I said tentatively.

"Who's that?" she cried. "Waddya want?"

McAuliffe stood still a few feet behind me, but I approached her with my hand held out.

"Callahan Garrity, Miss Rainwater," I said. "I'm a private investigator."

She set the pot down quickly on the front stoop and disappeared back into the trailer. She came out again, holding a white business-size envelope, which she handed to me.

"This here's my social," she said. "You check it, Susie. It's not a penny more than it should be. I don't get no food stamps. The lady over to the post office told me I don't qualify."

I pressed the envelope back into her hands. "No, Miss Rainwater," I said. "My name's Callahan. I'm not from the government. And I'm not here about your social security check. I just wanted to ask you some questions about the land you sold Mr. Beemish."

She narrowed her eyes and glanced back at McAuliffe. "What'd you say Bubba's name was? Is he with the government?"

"He's a friend. Could we ask you a few questions?"

She looked at the jar on the front stoop. "Wasn't expecting no company," she said. "Just finished listening to the *Hour of Power* on the radio. I love that Robert Schuller fella. Looks like you caught me emptying my chamber pot."

So that's what the jug was.

"Oh, I'm so sorry," I told her hastily. "We didn't mean to intrude. Maybe we could just sit out here at the picnic table, since the rain stopped. See, it's starting to get a little sunny."

She squinted up at the weak yellow rays trying to break through the tops of the pine trees surrounding her clearing.

"I reckon," she said. "Y'all set. I'll be right back."

She grabbed the pot and hurried off through the undergrowth, surprisingly surefooted for an old lady who looked at least eighty.

The picnic bench was soaking wet, so we both took off our rain slickers and used them as cushions. McAuliffe had a silly sort of grin.

"What?" I said. "What's so funny?"

"I was just wondering if Beemish knows Miss Inez is emptying her chamber pot at L'Arrondissement. I was wondering how they explain her presence to potential home buyers."

Before we could discuss the matter, Miss Inez was back, popping into the trailer, then out again. She sat lightly at the table, in apparent disregard for the wet bench.

"What's that jackleg Beemish want now?" she said. "I done told that real estate lady he sent over here I can't move till the Idle Hours Comfort Care Home has a room ready and till I find a home for Katie."

She smiled indulgently at the baby goat, who was busy nibbling at some plastic poinsettias. "I told her all that, didn't I?"

"I don't know what you told her," I said pleasantly. "Has Mr. Beemish been pressuring you to move out of your trailer here?"

She snorted. "Has a cat got a climbing gear? Before I signed his pieces of paper it was 'Take your time, Miss Inez; you can stay as long as you like, Miss Inez; no hurry, Miss Inez.' Then, after I signed, quicker than you can say Billy-be-damned, seems like the next day his people were out here pesterin' me to get out. Cut off my lights and water last month. Said they were burying underground lines for the new houses. Huh! Inez Rainwater knows when she's being messed with. But like I told them, I can't leave till me and Katie got a place to go. And Idle Hours won't take no goats. So I'm a-staying. Got me a kerosene lantern to see by, a camp stove to cook on, and a chamber pot to piss in. Let's see 'em cut that off."

"Miss Inez," I said, "do you know anything about an old graveyard back in the woods? Right by the riverbank?"

Her wrenlike face flushed then, and she hopped up from the table. "Ain't gonna talk about it. No, ma'am. Inez Rainwater don't flap her gums."

McAuliffe reached out and touched her hand lightly. "Miss Inez, we found some old gravestones. We saw where they'd been bulldozed into a big trash pit and covered over. Do you know who was buried there?"

Her eyes got watery and she sat back down. "Rainwaters and McAdoos and Peepleses, my husband's folks. My folks are buried over at Flowery Branch. None of them Rainwaters was any real kin to me. All been dead and gone sixty years or more. Figgered it wouldn't hurt nothing."

"But wasn't your husband buried there?"

"Shoo-oot," she said, extending the word to two syllables. "James Rainwater wasn't fixing to be buried in no piny woods. He's buried in his World War One infantry uniform right there in the National Cemetery in Marietta. Been out there since 1972, something like that."

"Did you know Mr. Beemish was going to bulldoze the cemetery on your property?" I asked.

"Didn't say he did, didn't say he didn't," she said mysteriously. "Give Miss Inez cash money. Miss Inez done paid for her own funeral and a nice cherry-wood coffin and a room at the Idle Hours Comfort Care Home with cable television, forty-two channels. Miss Inez Rainwater don't owe nobody nothin'."

McAuliffe looked over at me and shrugged. "It sounds like

Beemish got permission to move the graves. If she really is the last Rainwater descendant, it might be legal. Well, partly legal. I doubt if the people who buy that lot will be told it's an old cemetery. And bulldozing isn't exactly disinterring. Come on," he said, half rising from the bench. "We better get out of here. Now that the rain's stopped, Beemish's people might decide to get in some overtime. And I don't particularly like getting shot at."

"Wait," I said. Miss Inez seemed unaware of our presence. A single tear rolled down her cheek, and she rubbed at it with the sleeve of her bathrobe. She seemed unaccountably sad about some long dead in-laws she'd never even known.

"Miss Inez," I said gently, "what about your son? The one who was killed in the logging truck accident? Was he buried with your husband? Or did Beemish bulldoze his grave too? Did he, Miss Inez?"

The old lady didn't bother to brush away the tears that streamed down her face. She sat, looking straight ahead, her hands clenched tightly on the table, crying silently. The goat, Katie, wandered over on its chain, put its soft gray head in her lap, and butted her playfully.

"He did, didn't he? Bo Beemish tore up your boy's grave right along with the others, didn't he?"

Without warning, she jumped up again from the table, so suddenly the goat bawled in surprise. The only sound in the clearing was the metallic bang of the aluminum trailer door slamming shut.

McAuliffe and I sat there, not knowing what to do. But after some hesitation, I followed her, opening the aluminum door slowly, letting my eyes grow accustomed to the sudden dark.

The inside of the trailer was cramped but clean and tidy. An old butt-sprung leather sofa and a coffee table took up one end of the room. Hanging in the place of honor was a sepia-tinted framed photograph of Franklin Delano Roosevelt. At the other end of the room there was a tiny kitchenette, with a green Coleman stove set on top of the counter. Aside from a narrow door that looked like it led to a bathroom, there was only one other room, a bedroom so small as to be closetlike.

I could see her from the doorway, sitting on the edge of a narrow bed that was neatly made up with a faded pink chenille bedspread. She held something wrapped in a tattered quilt in her lap.

"Miss Inez," I called. "May I come in?"

She nodded her head mutely. I scraped the mud from my boots and stepped inside, feeling like a giant in a parakeet's cage. I seemed to fill the room.

I looked down at her. Wrapped in the quilt, she was cradling a fairly new-looking headstone, with one corner chipped off. "Was that your son's?"

She ran a fingertip over the writing.

JAMES MALCOLM RAINWATER, JR.
beloved son of James and Inez
1954–1976

"Always called him Big Boy," she said. "Doctors told Miss Inez she'd never have no babies. Like Sarah in the Bible. I didn't, either, till I was forty-five. Jesus gave Miss Inez her Big Boy. Weighed twelve pounds, eight ounces. Walked when he was eight months old. Had the sweetest disposition you ever saw."

"I understand he was killed in a logging truck accident," I said. "You must have been heartbroken."

"Jesus needed Big Boy in heaven," she said simply. "He's gone to be with his daddy now."

The bedsprings sagged mightily when I sat down on the bed beside her. "Can you tell me what happened to his grave?"

"Those dirty dogs," she said. "Those dirty damned old lying dogs. Mr. Bo, he told me the Rainwaters would be moved, properlike. Said they'd put 'em in a back corner of the property, with a pretty little fence around it and a place for me and Big Boy to be together. I signed him a piece of paper sayin' it was all right. Then one morning early, before daylight, I heard a racket over in them woods. I got over there, and those dirty dogs had machines digging up the ground, breaking up headstones, piling trash and dirt on top of 'em."

She looked at me solemnly. "There were open caskets. I tell you it put me in mind of what the Bible says about Judgment Day. 'Lo, the Lord empties the land and lays it to waste; he turns it upside down, scattering its inhabitants.' Isaiah," she said wearily. "You know your Bible, Susie?"

"Not like I should," I admitted. I didn't bother to explain that most Catholics aren't big on Scripture quoting.

"I run over there hootin' and screechin' at 'em to stop, but they acted like I wasn't even there. The boss man told me to get out of that private property before they called the police. It was all I could do to get Big Boy's stone and drag it back here before they chopped it up and buried it with all the others."

"Oh, no," I whispered. "How awful. Did you call Beemish? You should get a lawyer, you know. There are laws against what he's done here. You could have him put in jail."

"Vengeance is mine, sayeth the Lord," she said, grinning wickedly. "Ain't nobody out here in Kensington Park fixing to put a rich man like Mr. Bo in jail just on crazy old Inez Rainwater's say-so. And Miss Inez, she ain't got no truck with no jackleg lawyers. Talk about it." She cackled. " 'Woe to the wicked man! All goes ill, with the work of his hands he will be repaid.' That's Isaiah too, Susie. Miss Inez done got the gold star at Mount Pleasant Baptist Church for Scripture reading."

She hugged the headstone tighter to her chest and looked up at me. "Susie, what'd you say Bubba's name out there in the yard was again?"

"It's McAuliffe," I told her. "Andrew McAuliffe."

"He your daddy or somethin'?"

I smiled and shook my head. "Mr. McAuliffe does work for the government, Miss Inez. And he tells me what Mr. Beemish is doing on this land is illegal. He's going to help me get Mr. Beemish to do right by you, Miss Inez. I promise."

She ran her fingers lovingly over the headstone. "That's all right, then. Want me a burial plot for me and Big Boy," she whispered. "Want what was promised me."

29

OUTSIDE McAULIFFE SAT at the picnic table tossing pieces of an apple in the air and watching the goat leap up to catch them. "Good girl, Katie. Get it, girl."

He looked a little embarrassed when I sat down beside him. "Had a piece of apple in my jacket pocket, and the damned thing wouldn't leave me alone till I gave her some."

"I didn't know goats could jump like that," I said.

"Oh, yeah. Goats are smart. My Uncle Omer kept goats for years. They'll outsmart a human every time." He tossed the last of the apple to Katie and stood up. "Let's get. You can tell me about Miss Inez later."

He walked so fast I had to trot to keep up with him, which left me too out of breath for any clever conversation. Back at the Jeep, he unlocked my door, but I was barely seated before he threw the car into reverse and began speeding away from the cul-de-sac.

"You really are in a hurry," I said. "Got a heavy date or something?"

He shot me a look. "I'm an employee of the Atlanta Regional Commission, not a private investigator. We're on private property out here, and I don't have any good explanation for why I'm with you. I'm just being cautious. Do you mind?"

"No, not at all."

McAuliffe wheeled into the parking lot of the country store where we'd left the van. It was still deserted, but an occasional car now whizzed by on the road in front of it. He parked in back beside the van and cut the Jeep's engine.

"What did the old lady have in that trailer? A bag of bones, a witches' cauldron? More goats?"

"She had her son's headstone, wrapped up in a quilt. Beemish promised her he'd move the cemetery to another lot in a remote corner of the property, even promised her she could be buried there with her son. Of course, as soon as he had title to the land, he sent his men in before daylight and started bulldozing. She barely managed to drag her son's headstone away before they plowed it under with the others."

"Can she prove any of that?"

"It doesn't matter. She's in her eighties, Mac. She's got no money for lawyers. She already spent the money from the land sale to pay for her own funeral and burial plot and the nursing home fees. She's not in any position to fight Beemish. Not in court, anyway."

"What do you mean?"

I laughed for the first time that morning. It felt good. "That's some gutsy old lady out there. One of the reasons Beemish is so keen on security is that there have been all kinds of vandalism at L'Arrondissement. Shaloub, who's head of the police committee, told me truck tires had been slashed, someone put sugar in the gas tank of a piece of heavy equipment, and the construction trailer was broken into and some expensive office equipment stolen. Miss Inez didn't exactly confess to doing any of that, but she did throw some Bible passages at me that suggested the Lord had directed her to retribution."

"Praise God," McAuliffe said, laughing with me.

"Amen to that, brother," I said. "You wanna know what else she said to me?"

"What?"

"She asked if you were my father."

He threw his head back and guffawed. "Not bloody likely, thank you very much."

"Well, just how old are you?" I asked.

He stopped laughing rather suddenly. "How old do you think?"

"Hmm," I said. I reached out and traced the laugh lines around his eyes. "Lemme see your hands," I ordered.

He thrust them out in front of me. The nails were square and cut short, the skin weathered and freckled. The hairs on the back of his hands were white. There were calluses on the palms.

"I do a lot of yardwork," he said defensively. "Play a little golf."

"What kind of music do you like?"

"Early rock and roll, some Motown . . . hey, no fair."

"You're forty-two," I said, deliberately underestimating. He was forty-six if he was a day.

"You're a crappy liar, you know that, Garrity? I'm forty-nine and I look it. So how old are you?"

"Guess."

"What kind of music do you like?"

"Early rock, some Motown, Carolina beach music to dance to," I said teasingly. "Give up?"

He reached out and ran a finger along my cheek, the one with the scrapes. I hadn't bothered with makeup that morning.

"Nice skin," he said offhandedly. "You're maybe, what, thirty-six?"

I slapped his hand away. "Thirty-two, damn you."

"Jesus," he said, looking stricken. "I really *could* be your father."

"Well, technically, I guess. Speaking of fathers," I said, trying to sound casual, "what about you? Any kids?"

"A daughter, Gillian. She's twenty, a junior at Auburn. She lives with her mother in Birmingham when she's not at school."

"You're divorced?"

"Yeah. It's been eight or ten years, I guess. Long enough that I forget sometimes I ever was married. My ex-wife got remarried right afterward. What about you?"

"My sister enjoys referring to me as the family spinster," I told him. "I've come close, but somehow I've never made it to the altar."

He lightly traced the bruise and the scrape on my face. "Where'd you pick up this little beauty?"

So I told him how I'd been stomped by a couple of skinheads at Little Five Points.

He listened, asked questions, commiserated, but he didn't seem horrified or shocked, and he didn't try to tell me I'd asked for trouble by walking home alone.

"You seem to be one of those people stuff happens to," he said. "You get shot at, beat up. Is your life always like this?"

"Not usually this violent," I said thoughtfully. "But yeah, I do seem to attract—uh, stuff. Maybe it's negative ions in my magnetic force field. I can't even wear a watch. It stops."

"What other kinds of things happen to you?"

"Name it. It happens."

"And you think it's caused by negative ions."

"It's just a theory. It's not for sure or anything. Although now I don't know."

"What? Has somebody got a contract out on you?"

"Actually . . . there's a chance I might have cancer."

"Cancer. That's scary."

I studied his face to try to see what he was thinking. "I don't know why I'm telling you this. I haven't told anybody, not even my mother. In fact, I think this is the first time I've even said the c-word. My doctor and I have been dancing around it, calling it a lump, or a mass, or suspicious tissue, like a Kleenex with a bad attitude."

"Where is this mass?"

I pointed my chin downward, toward my chest. "Right breast. It's just as well; that right one has always been a half a size larger than the one on the left."

"What are you going to do?"

"Rich, that's my doctor, wants to do a biopsy. There's a history of breast cancer in my family. He's been after me for weeks to get in to his office and discuss it, but I sort of hid out. He's supposed to call tomorrow and see about scheduling the procedure for this week at the Women's SurgiCenter."

"And will you do it?"

I rolled down my window and took a big gulp of the rain-washed air.

"The timing is difficult."

"How so?"

"I'm right in the middle of a murder investigation," I said. "My client gets out of jail tomorrow. Several of our best cleaning jobs canceled this week, thanks to Lilah Rose Beemish. And the cops, thanks to Eddie Shaloub, have given us a citation for operating a business in a residential neighborhood. I don't have time to get cut on this week."

"That's bullshit," McAuliffe said.

"Excuse me?"

"You know what I mean," he said. "You didn't ask my advice, but since you dragged me out here in the rain on a Sunday when I could have been home tying flies, I'll give it to you. Let your mother or somebody else run the cleaning business. Hire a lawyer to fight the citation thing. And let the public defender take care of getting your client out of jail and lining up evidence against Beemish. That's his job. Get your ass into that hospital and have the biopsy. Quit being such a wuss."

"A wuss. Who you calling a wuss, asshole?"

"You, Garrity," he said, leaning across me to open the Jeep door. He smelled clean, like some kind of green soap. "Go on, get out now. I don't have all day to sit here and shoot the shit with you. I got a dog to feed."

I gathered up my slicker, the thermos, and the newspaper. "Maybe you're right, McAuliffe. Thanks. I'll let you know what happens."

"You're welcome," he said. "Maybe I'll call you to let you know about my river review, and to see how the surgery thing went. Maybe we could have some dinner and listen to my Jackie Wilson records. You like Jackie Wilson?"

"'Your Love Keeps Lifting Me Higher and Higher,'" I said. "Great tune. I'd like that a lot."

30

EDNA BURST INTO THE KITCHEN humming. Something was definitely going on. First of all, she was wearing a flowered polyester dress with puffed sleeves that my sister-in-law had given her for Christmas. She also sported a string of pink plastic pop beads that had been a gift from one of my nephews. And she was wearing a pink flowered hat I'd never seen before, and a suitcase-size straw purse Ruby had brought back from her cruise to the Bahamas.

I glanced up at the calendar on the wall. "Trick or treat, Ma?"

She took off the hat and put it in a plastic bag on the counter, stepped out of her shoes, and unpopped the beads. She lit up a cigarette and took a deep drag. "God," she moaned, "that tastes good." She backed up to me. "Unzip me, will you, Jules? I've gotta get out of this rag before any of the neighbors see me."

A pink high heel in each hand, she padded down the hall, still humming, leaving me in the kitchen inhaling a cloud of cheap-smelling perfume. I could swear it was Evening in Paris.

She was back a minute later, barefooted, dressed in a cotton housecoat. She puttered around the kitchen, fixing herself a cup of coffee, all the time humming some weird tune I'd never heard before.

"What's that song, Ma?"

She sat at the table across from me, picked up the coffee cup, and inhaled deeply. She took a huge gulp, swishing it around in her mouth to taste the bouquet, then swallowing. "It's 'Love Lifted Me.' Inspiring, isn't it?"

The clothes, the hymn humming, all gave me an idea.

"Jesus, Mary, Joseph, and all the saints. I believe you've been to church this morning. What's the deal, Edna? You haven't been to mass since Dad died."

"I still haven't been to mass," she snapped. "I'll not step foot inside the door of Sacred Heart again until I go to a funeral for that old devil Joe O'Connor. When I think about him refusing to come to the hospital to give your father last rites, it still makes my blood boil. The old hypocrite!"

My father, Jack Garrity, had been president of the Men's Club at Sacred Heart, and head usher for years, until he and our pastor, old Father O'Connor, had gotten into a dispute over the christening of my nephew Devin. Devin's mother, Peggy, had been divorced before marrying my brother Kevin, and Father Joe said it wouldn't be proper to baptize her son, since she and Kevin hadn't been married in the church. Dad had been enraged, of course, and quit Sacred Heart in a huff. When he took a turn for the worse in the hospital, Edna had had to turn to the hospital chaplain, a young priest barely out of the seminary, to give Dad last rites. She'd never forgotten or forgiven the insult, and to tell the truth, neither had I.

"Well, if you didn't go to mass dressed up like a church lady, where did you go?" I asked. "I distinctly remember your saying you wouldn't wear that dress Peggy gave you to a dog fight."

"Extreme situations call for extreme measures," she said serenely. "I have been fellowshiping this morning at the Church of Jesus Christ of Latter-day Saints."

"You didn't!"

"Yes, ma'am, I did. Why else would I go out dressed like that?"

"No reason I can think of, unless there was a Mel Torme concert at the Fox."

"Funny," Edna said. "You're a very funny girl. See how hard I'm laughing? Ooh, stop, my sides are splitting."

"All right," I said. "I'm sorry. Now tell me, what was the Mormon church like? Do they handle snakes or anything? And did you meet anybody who knew Kristee or that Collier guy?"

"It was like a Kiwanis meeting, for crying out loud. And the church, it could have been a Holiday Inn conference room, that's how much it doesn't look like a church."

"It's a Protestant church, Ma," I said. "And I read somewhere that Mormons don't believe in churchy trappings. They think they're too earthly."

"I'll say they don't believe in churchy. They got no altar, no crucifix, no stations of the cross, no statues, not even a picture of Jesus, for crying out loud. I'm walking into the sanctuary, or whatever they call it, and I had to stop myself from genuflecting."

"Yeah, good thing. That might have caused some stares. So what was the service like?"

"It was just like your dad's Kiwanis meeting. They give you a program when you walk in. Then a guy they call Elder Something gets up and tells who's gonna talk. Next a couple of church sisters and a guy in a brown suit take turns talking about being a home teacher, that's the men, or a home visitor, that's the women. They sing a couple hymns. Then some pimply-faced teenage boys they call priests pass out communion."

"You didn't take it, did you?"

"Hell, yes. When in Salt Lake City, right? Besides, they bring it around to everybody. It would have looked funny if I'd refused. And all it was was torn-up pieces of Wonder Bread and little plastic cups of water."

"I guess Mormons wouldn't pass out wine like the Catholics do. Then what happened?" I asked.

"That was it." She shrugged. "The elder gets up at the end and makes some announcements, then some of them leave and some of them go to more meetings."

"Were you able to talk to anybody?"

She took a deep drag on the cigarette she was smoking, then lit another and set it carefully on the edge of her ashtray. "Wait a minute," she said. "Spending an hour and a half in a church that doesn't allow smoking or coffee drinking or booze has my nerves really on edge. We got any Bloody Mary makings in the house?"

"I'll look," I promised. "If Neva Jean didn't drink it, I think I saw a can of V-Eight in the pantry."

"Anyway," Edna continued, "I sort of hung around after the service, or whatever they call it, and chatted up some women who were waiting for their husbands to come out of a meeting."

I poked my head out of the pantry. "Did any of them know Kristee?"

"No," she said. "They were older, in their mid to late twenties, with kids. But since she was single, they said they probably wouldn't know her."

"What about Collier?" I asked, emerging triumphantly with the V-8.

"Him they knew. Put a lot of Tabasco in that, all right? And don't use too much celery salt or I'll swell up like a toad. One of the women I talked to said Collier was a dedicated saint. He leads one of the singles groups and he's a home teacher, sort of an up-and-comer. Apparently, the Mormon church has a distinct hierarchy for members. But another woman, Eileen was her name, acted like she thought Collier was sort of odd, almost too zealous."

"Zealous is the word for him," I said, setting two Bloody Marys on the table. "What else did you find out?"

She poked her pinkie finger in the drink and licked it. "Could stand a little more lemon juice," she said. "But it's drinkable." She took a sip and smacked her lips appreciatively.

"Oh, yeah," she said. "I saved the best for last. This Eileen woman said Collier is especially dedicated to his temple work. She explained that to me after I told her I was thinking of converting. See, Mormons think they have to convert everybody in the world to their way of thinking in order to achieve the highest level of heaven. Their heaven is kind of like a Hilton, with different floors for different levels of believers. If you sign up enough people, you get to stay in the concierge level."

"I already know about that," I reminded her, "so get on with it."

"Eileen said Collier's girlfriend died recently."

"Kristee."

"She didn't mention the name. But Collier is going to have her baptized in the Temple pretty soon, so—get this—he can have her sealed to him in marriage. They'll be married, even though she's dead."

"Holy shit," I said. "That's the kinkiest thing I've heard in a long time."

"Me too," Edna said. "Imagine what the wedding night would be like."

"For an old lady, you've got a pretty smutty mind, you know that, Edna?"

She blissfully sipped her Bloody Mary. "I prefer to think of myself as someone with an inquiring mind," she said. "And cut out that 'old lady' shit."

I tasted my drink, got up, went to the refrigerator, and fetched the lemon juice. I poured a dollop in Edna's drink and some in my own.

"You know, I figured this Collier guy was just sort of a harmless flake," I told Edna. "Maybe I should rethink that. But, hell, after all we know about Beemish and Shaloub, I still think with a little more evidence we can pin it on one of them. I mean, for Christ's sake, Whit Collier's an *accountant*. You ever hear of a homicidal CPA?"

She thought about that for a while. "No, but you remember

Sam Arnold, the CPA who lived across the street from us in Decatur? Married to Mary Pat, that cute little blonde? One time your
dad and I were at the Taco Bell down at the airport and he came
in there dressed up like a hooker. Had on a gold lamé strapless
cocktail dress, sling-back heels, a long black wig, and some of those
Lee Press-on Party Nails. Your dad like to died; he wanted to leave
before Sam saw us. But I walked up to him and said 'Sam Arnold,
what in God's name are you doing?'

"At first he acted like he didn't know me. But I stood right there
and faced him down. You know what he told me? He pulled me
aside and whispered that he was working undercover for the FBI."

"You're making this up."

She put her hand over her heart. "If I'm lying I'm dying."

"What happened?"

"What do you think happened? Mary Pat found out he'd been
wearing her best clothes to fast-food places all around the Perime-
ter. Broke the zipper on her black velvet Christian Dior sheath and
stretched her Charles Jourdan pumps all out of shape. She divorced
his ass in a New York second. So don't tell me about CPAs."

31

SUNDAY NIGHT, MY FRIEND Paula came over. We cooked steaks on the grill, made a bushel basket of popcorn, then had ourselves an Alfred Hitchcock double-header on the VCR, with *Notorious* and *North by Northwest*. It was after 1 A.M. when we got Cary Grant down off the face of Mount Rushmore, and by that time we had also killed most of a bottle of Wild Turkey, so I was exhausted.

But sometimes I do my best work in my sleep. In my dreams that night I went over and over the Ewbanks murder, making lists of all the leads we needed to pursue.

Monday by 8 A.M., I was up, dressed, and on the phone. I wasn't cheerful, mind you, but I was up and working. When Neva Jean, Jackie, Ruby, and the Easterbrook sisters straggled in around 9 A.M., I had the day's schedule all lined up.

"Jackie," I said, "get out of that House Mouse smock. You're going over to the Beemish house on West Paces Ferry."

"Are you nuts?" Edna said. "They fired us. You crashed Lilah's tea party and called her husband a murderer."

"I know, but when I was over there Saturday I noticed the place was a sty. Their live-in Jamaican girl doesn't know squat about cleaning. So Home Sweep Home, a wholly owned subsidiary of the House Mouse, called Lilah Rose this morning and informed her of our introductory offer of a twenty-five-dollar whole-house cleaning."

"When did we form a subsidiary?" Edna asked.

"This morning."

"You are nuts," Edna said. "We'll go broke at that price."

"This is strictly a one-shot deal," I promised. "Here's the setup, Jackie. Lilah Rose has a Junior League meeting this morning, and it's the babysitter's day off. She'll leave the key under a big urn by the door. Hit the major crud first: you know, vacuum in the living room and den and mop the kitchen real fast. Then you start the real work. I want you to look in every corner of that house for a file folder full of papers labeled L'Arrondissement, two-carat diamond earrings and some Georgian silver. That's the stuff with all the curlicues and crap on it. Check in the safe too; here's the combination."

"How'd you get that?" Edna said.

"Beemish told it to me," I said. "Kristee figured out the combination because it was the kids' birth dates.

"Now, Baby and Sister," I said loudly, "I've got a special job for you too." The Easterbrooks don't work every day, but they love it when we give them a new job. Makes them feel important.

"You're cleaning a townhouse that belongs to a man named Whit Collier," I told the sisters. Home Sweep Home is giving him a two-for-one cleaning deal. "It's over in Garden Hills. You're looking for the same things as Jackie: some fancy women's jewelry, some silver coins, and a file on L'Arrondissement." I spelled it out for them, and they dutifully wrote everything down.

"Mr. Collier will be home when you get there," I said. "So get right to work cleaning. As soon as he leaves, you can start searching. He'll be at work all day, so you should have plenty of time. You find any weird religious literature or anything out of the ordinary, you let me know, OK?"

"All right," said Baby. "But you ain't fixin' to have us work for no twenty-five dollars a day, are you? Sister and me, we made more than that doing day work. Twenty-five dollars don't pay the gas on our car."

"No, Baby," I said. "I'll make up the difference. You two go on over there and get started. And make sure you get a key so we can go back if we need to."

"Ruby, you do the Eshelmanns and the Browers, like always."

After the first gang of mouses left, Neva Jean slammed her Mountain Dew can down on the table with a vengeance.

"What about me?" she demanded. "I wanna help too."

"I've got plans for everybody," I promised.

Just then I heard a car door slam outside. "Good," I said. "That sounds like our new House Mouse."

There was a timid knock at the back door.

"Come on in," I sang out.

A week in jail had left Ardith Cramer looking like she'd been rode hard and put up wet. Her skin was a mess, and her hair, although at least clean, looked like it had been combed with a toothbrush. She wore a pink T-shirt, so new and loose you could see the folds from the store package on it, and a cheap pair of new blue jeans, along with the tennis shoes I'd bought her. She carried a paper sack full of her belongings.

"Sorry if I'm late," she said. "After the bond hearing, Dinesh stopped and got me some new things to wear. I'm gonna burn these clothes I wore to jail."

Neva Jean and Edna eyed Ardith with open curiosity. She stared down at her feet to avoid meeting their eyes.

"Ardith Cramer," I said, "meet Neva Jean. You already know Edna."

Neva Jean and Edna told her hello.

"Mrs. Garrity," Ardith said, "I'd—uh, like to apologize to you for the way I acted that time in the motel room. I was scared, and I was sick, and I guess I was pretty nasty. I'm sorry about that."

"It's all right, hon," Edna said. "You did act like a bitch, but now that I know the circumstances, I can understand why you did us that way. But what was wrong with you that you were sick?"

Ardith grimaced. "I had a terrible bladder infection. I've had them before, but this time it was awful."

"*You* had the bladder infection?" I said. "Edna found a pill bottle in your bathroom. I'm afraid she sort of searched it while she was in there. At the time, we were working for the Beemishes and thought it proved that Kristee was living there with you."

"So that's what happened to the pills," Ardith said. "They had to give me another prescription in jail." She laughed bitterly. "There is no way Kristee would have stayed in that dump of a motel. See, I didn't have any money to go to a doctor, but I knew what kind of medicine I'd taken for the infection before. Kristee got the name of Mrs. Beemish's doctor from a pill bottle in her medicine cabinet. She just called the drugstore on Pace's Ferry and told the pharmacist she was Dr. So-and-So's nurse and was calling in the prescription. Then when Kristee picked up the medicine, she just charged it to Mrs. Beemish's account."

"Ballsy," I said in admiration.

"Yeah," Ardith said, her eyes misting. "Kristee was always doing stuff like that. She had no fear."

"So," Edna said briskly, trying to change the subject before Ardith broke into tears. "You're going to come to work for us?"

Ardith looked at me questioningly. "That's what Callahan says. My lawyer told the judge this morning that I had a job here, which proved I had ties in the community and wouldn't jump bail."

"You do," I said. "Neva Jean here is going to take you on her jobs today. Monday mornings she cleans an eight-thousand-square-foot house in Druid Hills. Belongs to Ezra Zimmerman, the head of the psychology department at Emory University, and he's a total nut when it comes to bathrooms. He's got four, and he wants them all as sterile as a hospital operating room."

"Yeah," said Neva Jean, snapping her gum. "I hope you like the smell of Pine-Sol, honey, because we're gonna use about a gallon of it this morning."

"I can stand it," Ardith said. "Callahan, what about my room? Dinesh said you had something to tell me."

"I talked to that motel manager until I was blue in the face. The upshot of it is that with the arrest and the newspaper story about where you were living, and the cops searching the place, he doesn't want you back. He had the room cleaned and threw out all the stuff the cops hadn't already confiscated. But for right now we're going to have to find you another place to live."

She seemed unconcerned about her belongings. "Any place is fine," she said. "But I've got no money for an apartment deposit."

"We got that worked out, honey," Neva Jean said, taking Ardith by the arm. "There's an itty-bitty apartment up over Swanelle's body shop over here on De Kalb Avenue. It ain't much, just a bedroom with a curtained-off toilet, sink, and shower stall and a hot plate for a kitchen. But Swanelle says you can stay there till you get back on your feet. How's seventy-five dollars a month sound?"

"Neva Jean," I said. "I thought you were gonna talk him into giving it to her for free."

"Callahan, honey, you know how cheap Swanelle is," Neva Jean said plaintively. "The word 'free' ain't in his vocabulary. Why, I had to turn myself inside out to get him to agree to seventy-five dollars. We're talking sex on demand for two, three months."

"Spare us the details," I told her. "She'll pay fifty dollars a month, tops. Now y'all get going before Dr. Zimmerman starts calling here to chew my butt. And call in before you go on to your afternoon jobs. I may have something else for you to do."

When the last car had pulled out of the driveway, Edna gave me that look. "You sure you know what you're doing, putting Ardith to work for the House Mouse? What if she decides to help herself to some of Zimmerman's expensive doodads?"

"She won't," I said lightly. "Neva Jean will be watching her like a hawk."

"We'll see, Little Miss Social Worker. Now what have you got planned for me to do?"

I flipped through my notebook, looking for the list I'd made for her. When the phone rang, I literally snatched it out of her hand. "House Mouse."

"Callahan," a voice said, "this is Rita in Dr. Drescher's office. He'd like to talk to you."

Rich came on the phone quickly. "Is Edna there?"

"Right here," I said warily. "Why?"

"Because if you don't agree to come in at seven A.M. tomorrow, I'm coming over there right now with a set of your X-rays. I'll show them to her, then we'll hog-tie you ourselves and take you to the hospital."

"That won't be necessary. I thought you said any time this week," I said grumpily. "It's only Monday. Call me back Wednesday."

"Can't," he said. "I showed your films to Lonette Jefferson, the breast specialist I told you about. She thinks we may need to do a lumpectomy, and she's agreed to consult. Tomorrow's the only day she has free for the next month."

"No way," I said. "I've got tomorrow booked already. I'll pencil you in for later in the week."

"This is no joking matter, Callahan. We're lucky to be able to get Dr. Jefferson. I'm going to put Rita back on the line now, and she'll give you your instructions. See you tomorrow, sweetheart. Don't forget to bring your hooters."

Rita came back on and told me to be at the Women's Surgi-Center at 7 A.M. Tuesday and not to eat or drink anything after midnight. "Oh, and can you bring someone with you to drive you home? You'll probably still be woozy from the sedative we're going to give you."

"I'll take care of it," I said, and hung up.

"What was that about?" Edna asked. "Can't what wait?"

"Oh—uh, that was the podiatrist's office," I said, trying to think fast. Luckily I'd had two cups of coffee, so the old cerebrum was in gear. "I'm going to have that darned corn on my left little toe removed, and he says tomorrow is the only time he can do it. He's going to a medical convention in Puerto Rico on Wednesday."

"Ain't that the way?" she said. "You know why doctors and lawyers never have conventions in places like Pahokee, Florida, or International Falls, Minnesota? It's all just a big scam so they can take a vacation and write it off on their taxes."

32

TO CHANGE THE SUBJECT, I handed Edna the list of calls we needed to make. "Do we know anybody who works in the business office at Rich's?"

She closed her eyes and thought about it. "Bunny Levine. Remember her from the beauty shop? Always got a pedicure and a bikini wax? I think Bunny's daughter Heidi works at Rich's someplace. She got married a couple of years ago, though, and I don't know what her name is now."

"I remember Heidi from college at Georgia," I said. "She was in my sociology class. Call Rich's and ask for Heidi Levine. She was a real ball-buster. I bet she kept her maiden name."

"Then what?"

"Find out if any of these people ever worked at Rich's," I said, handing her the list. "If they did work there, find out where and when."

"And what are you going to be doing?"

"I'll use the house phone. I know Lilah lied about going to Beaufort that Sunday. Now I want to check and see if I can't find a leak in Bo's alibi."

First I tried calling every air charter business in the Atlanta yellow pages. But it was next to useless trying to pry information from the efficient secretaries and receptionists who answered the phones. "Our clients demand discretion," one secretary told me. "If you want our flight records, you'll have to get a court order."

Exasperated, I went back in the kitchen, where Edna was working on the books. "Say, Ma, what's the name of that travel agency you and Agnes used the last time you went to Las Vegas?"

"Golden Age Globetrotters," she said. "You can't believe the package they got us at Caesar's Palace. Prime rib dinner for two ninety-five, tickets to see Siegfried and Roy, and a bus trip to the Hoover Dam."

Marcy, the friendly travel adviser at Golden Age, told me that, yes, there was a small airport on Hilton Head Island, serviced by a commuter airline called Air Palmetto. They had a Sunday night flight leaving Hilton Head at 10:30 P.M., but it went to Charlotte, North Carolina, before heading for Atlanta, where it arrived at around 1 A.M.

"And what time does the flight return to Hilton Head?" I asked, crossing my fingers tightly.

"That'd be two A.M., going back through Charlotte and arriving in Hilton Head at four-thirty."

Lilah Rose had told Bohannon that she and Bo had gone to bed around 10 P.M. Saturday and that she had fallen asleep reading. But Beemish could have left the condo and taken either a charter or the Air Palmetto commuter flight to Atlanta. He could have rented a car at the airport, driven home, strangled Kristee, then hopped a flight back to South Carolina and still have been in bed in time to kiss Lilah Rose good morning. Unless Lilah was lying and covering up for her cheating husband or herself.

I wondered whether Bohannon had already discovered the hole in Lilah's story. Despite her petty, grasping ways, I still found it hard to believe Lilah Rose Beemish was a murderer. On the other hand, though, if it meant protecting her husband and kids, not to mention her home and social position, Lilah Rose could be capable of anything.

As for Shaloub, he'd made no pretense of having a good alibi. He'd gone to bed early that night, he'd said—alone.

I tried to call Dinesh to ask him about getting a court order for the flight records for Air Palmetto and the most likely air charter services, but the secretary in the PD's office said he'd gone to lunch and after that he was due over at the jail.

Oh, yeah, lunch. In the kitchen, Edna's head was half buried in the refrigerator. She was setting covered dishes and unidentified aluminum-foil-wrapped objects on the counter and talking to herself. Other items she was slam-dunking into the kitchen trash can. "Disgusting. This has got to go," she muttered.

"What's for lunch, Ma?" I said.

Her head popped up over the door. She was wearing yellow rubber gloves, and she had a plastic clothespin on her nose. "Leftovers," she said, in a weird nasal voice. "I can't squeeze another thing in this icebox until I clean it out. We've got pot roast, some string beans, some macaroni and cheese, squash casserole, a little bit of coleslaw, and half a deep-dish apple pie. I'm gonna heat it all up, and we'll pretend we're at Morrison's Cafeteria."

The front doorbell rang just then. We were both surprised, because the only people who ever come to our front door are strangers and salesmen.

"Go see who it is," Edna said. "And if it's the goddamn Mormons again, set the dog on 'em."

"We don't have a dog," I reminded her as I headed for the hallway.

"We'll get one," she hollered. "A rabid pit bull."

It wasn't the Mormons, though. It was a tall guy with spiked blond hair. He wore a pair of brief red nylon running shorts and an oversized Pittsburgh Pirates baseball jersey, with the name *Clemente* written in cursive script over his breast.

"Bucky," I said, waving him inside. "You're just in time for lunch."

He sniffed the air expectantly. "What're we having?"

"It's an Edna Mae Garrity smorgasbord," I said. "All you can eat and the price is right—absolutely free."

I could tell Edna didn't recognize our lunch guest. "Ma, remember Bucky Deaver? You talked to him on the phone the other night."

Her face brightened, and she rushed over and gave him a big hug and kiss. "Of course I remember this rascal," she said, laying it on thick. "I just didn't recognize him without his ponytail."

"Ponytail?" he said blankly. "When did I have a ponytail?"

"Remember, when you were working that Jamaican drug case and went undercover? Edna is always after me to let my hair grow out like yours was back then."

"Takes a lot more time to take care of, though," he said seriously. "That's why I got mine cut."

In the meantime, Edna was pushing Bucky over to the table, pulling out his chair, and pouring him a tall glass of tea. "You still dating that girl who works at Georgia Power?" she asked sweetly. "The one with the eyes that were kind of googly-like?"

Bucky had his mouth full of squash casserole, so all he could do was shake his head no.

"Edna thinks I need a steady gentleman caller, Bucky," I said. "I believe she's under the impression that you are from the Deaver family who owns the Toot 'n' Tote convenience store."

He swallowed quickly and wiped away a stray piece of cracker-crumb topping from his upper lip. "Oh, no, Mrs. Garrity. I'm no kin to those Deavers. I'm from the Waycross Deavers. My cousin Fay-Anne used to cashier at the Toot 'n' Tote over in Ocilla, but the rest of my people mostly work in my granddaddy's tire recapping business. He's the recap king of southwest Ware County."

"I knew that," Edna lied. "How are your mama and daddy and them, Bucky?"

"Fine, ma'am, just fine," Bucky said. "You reckon I could have a smidge more of those butter beans?"

Watching Bucky inhale Edna's leftovers sort of put me off my own feed, so I sat there and watched his knife and fork action. The boy could flat put away groceries.

He was polishing off a piece of apple pie when I realized he hadn't told us why he'd come.

"Oh, yeah, Callahan," he said, setting down his fork with a sigh of ecstasy. "I came by to give you some news I think you're going to enjoy."

"Yeah?" I said, helping myself to just an eensy sliver of pie.

"You remember Tommy Manetti, the FBI guy who worked the missing-and-murdered case with us?"

"Short guy with bushy eyebrows? Sharp dresser?"

"That's him. I saw him at the pistol range this morning, and we got to talking about what he's doing these days. They've got him working on a special public servant corruption unit."

"How interesting."

"He let it slip that they're working on a case up in north Fulton County."

"Kensington Park," I said excitedly. "Yes! The feds are working Kensington Park!"

Bucky glanced over at Edna. "Uh, is it all right to talk about this in front of your mama?"

Edna looked hurt. She got up abruptly and started clearing the table.

"It's all right, Bucky. Edna's been helping me investigate. Come sit back down, Edna."

"I absolutely did not tell you any of this," Bucky started out. "Understood?"

Both of us flashed him our Girl Scout oath.

"It seems some developer, whose name I can't mention, approached a person on the Kensington Park City Council over a year ago, to suggest that he might make a sizable campaign contribution if the councilman would look favorably upon his request to have his property annexed into the city."

"Beemish," Edna and I said in unison.

"I didn't say that," Bucky said. "The councilman, some guy who manages a K-mart or something, thought the offer was odd. He'd only spent eight hundred dollars on his last campaign. So he called his sister-in-law, who happens to be in her last year of law school, to ask what he should do. The sister-in-law called in the FBI."

"That's got to be Edwin Strong," I told Edna. "He manages the Wal-Mart."

"Since then, the guy has been cooperating with the FBI, voting in a bloc with two other council members who've been backing the development. He wore a wire to all his meetings with the developer and the other two council members, but the developer was real cautious. He never mentioned money or favors or anything not kosher for all those months. Tommy said the feds were ready to dump the whole investigation. Then, Sunday night a week ago, the shit hits the fan. Another council member, who's also been on the developer's gravy train, calls, like at ten o'clock at night. Says the developer wants to meet all three of them at the De Kalb-Peachtree Airport, at like one-thirty A.M. The K-mart guy calls Tommy, they put his wire on, and everybody meets out at De Kalb-Peachtree. The developer's flown in all the way from South Carolina. He's scared. A woman, he says, the family nanny, has stolen his file on the Kensington Park project. It's got names and amounts and dates. She's blackmailing him, demanding a hundred thousand dollars in exchange for keeping quiet about what she knows about the developer's payoffs to the council members."

"A hundred thousand," I said. "Wow. I knew Kristee was blackmailing Beemish and Shaloub, but I didn't know she wanted that much. I figured she was just nickel-and-diming them."

"I didn't say those names," Bucky protested. "Mrs. Garrity, did you hear me say any names?"

"What names?" Edna said.

"So they sit in this big gray Mercedes parked right at the edge of the runway. The developer lays out the whole thing, how he's given these people money, done 'em business favors, and how they are gonna have to help pay the blackmail money. Then the three council members get to arguing about who's done what for who and who got paid more and who should kick in some money."

"Tell me they got it all on tape," I said fervently.

"Most of it. The K-mart guy was so nervous he kept jiggling the wires. And a couple times planes landed and drowned out the conversation. But Tommy said they've got enough."

"Enough to indict Beemish for murder?"

"Not the feds," Bucky said. "Murder's not a federal offense. They're gonna kick that part of the investigation over to the Atlanta cops, eventually."

"Eventually," I said glumly.

"The good news is they've called a federal grand jury in to investigate," Bucky said. "That make you happy?"

"I'm happy," I said, sliding the last hunk of pie onto Bucky's plate. "If Beemish flew back here for that meeting, depending on what time he flew in, he could have taken a quick spin over to the house and strangled Kristee. He could have stashed the body somewhere, even in the trunk of his car; then he could have run it over to Rich's first thing Monday after he got back to town."

"That reminds me," Edna said. "Heidi Levine is married to a doctor. She's got two beautiful children and she's vice president of merchandising at Rich's. She was only too happy to look your names up for me. Bo Beemish worked as a menswear buyer downtown for a year after he got out of Tech, before he went back and got his MBA. Eddie Shaloub worked there and at the Lenox store for four years, off and on, moonlighting as a security guard. Even Lilah Rose worked at Rich's; she sold perfume there for a month one summer. Whit Collier worked there summers during college, in the cash office."

"Just about everybody my age worked at Rich's at one time or another as a kid," I reminded my mother. "It was like McDonald's is now. Plus you got a discount."

"Say, Callahan," Bucky said. "You know, speaking of discounts, your girls really did a great job cleaning my place last week. It hasn't been that clean since the last time my mama came up from Waycross. I was wondering—uh, do you have a special law enforcement rate?"

"I sense a shakedown here, Edna," I said. "What do you think?"

She picked up her bifocals, reached for the appointment book, and scanned it at length. "I can let you have Ruby on Wednesday afternoons," she said. "Let's see, with the professional discount, that'll run you—oh, forty bucks a week."

Bucky's face fell. "That much?"

"Did I mention she'll do your laundry and iron your shirts?"

"All right!" Bucky said, giving me the high five. "Clean underwear every week. Righteous."

33

"WILONA?" EDNA SAID, drawing the name out lovingly. "Edna Garrity. Remember, from Women for Better Government? How in the world are you?"

She rushed ahead with her spiel.

"I feel so stupid for having to bother you about such a picky little thing, but I was wondering, on that Jell-O salad, is it all right to substitute a can of crushed pineapple for the fruit cocktail?"

Edna listened intently as Wilona filled her in on Jell-O variations. Suddenly she shrieked.

"What? Oh, I'm so sorry to have caught you at a time like this. . . . Oh, no! Oh, dear Lord, they didn't. You say they came right in without knocking? That many of them?"

The conversation continued in a like vein for another five minutes. When Edna hung up the phone she looked deeply saddened.

"Wilona says you can use pineapple, but if you do, she likes to add a cup of miniature marshmallows for texture."

"Anything else?"

"She did mention in passing that five FBI agents burst into the city clerk's office this morning with subpoenas for all the council meeting minutes for the past two years, plus all the files on the L'Arrondissement project."

"Really?" I said. "How very interesting."

"Poor Wilona was too upset to chat for long. Those awful FBI men! Can you imagine? They have nigger agents—her words, not mine. They interviewed her for two solid hours, asking questions about Mr. Beemish and Mr. Shaloub and the mayor, Mrs. Over-meier. Wilona was really distraught. And on top of that, right after the agents leave the office she gets a phone call from the Ali Baba Shrine Temple. They've canceled their appearance in the Kensington Park Founder's Day Parade."

"Why?"

"Seems their go-cart unit was in the line of march in the St. Patrick's Day parade down in Savannah, and the Grand Potentate was zipping in and out among the clown's legs when all of a sudden he suffered a massive coronary, right in the middle of a compli-cated double-figure-eight maneuver. The potentate's go-cart went out of control and ran over the drill team from St. Ignatius Paro-chial School."

"Anybody hurt?"

"The drum major, Boo-Boo the clown, and Sister Mary Per-petua."

"Wow," I said. "Some tragedy."

"I should say. Now the Ali Baba Temple has temporarily moth-balled the go-carts and Wilona is out her lead parade unit. She said she was so upset she drank a whole bottle of Maalox."

"Poor dear," I said, getting up from the table and grabbing the keys to the van.

"Where are you lighting out for? I thought there were some more calls you wanted to make."

"There are," I said. "But I'm going to run over to the cop shop and see if I can get anything out of Bohannon on whether or not they're going to consider Beemish and Shaloub as murder suspects now the feds are investigating them."

I had to circle the block twice to find a space in the tiny lot at the police department. Out of patience, I finally docked the van in a slot marked OFFICIAL POLICE VEHICLES ONLY. Quickly I scrawled a note indicating I was working undercover, signed Bucky Deaver's name to it, and tucked it under the windshield wiper.

It was obviously a slow day for homicides. Bohannon was leaning at a precarious angle in his chair, his feet up on his desk, when I walked into the office. The leg of his polyester pants rode up enough to reveal the .32 caliber revolver he wore in an ankle holster. The air-conditioning in the homicide office wasn't quite up to the job of cooling the place, so Bohannon had his jacket off and his tie loosened. I could see perspiration rings on the tan short-sleeved shirt he wore.

He couldn't see how I looked because he had his face buried in the box scores.

"Hot on the trail of another fiendish killer, I see," I said, as I sat down next to the desk.

Bohannon didn't bother to lower his newspaper. "What do you want, Garrity? I'm pretty busy right now."

"Just wanted to see if the feds are going to let you take a peek at all those files they seized out in Kensington Park this morning. Plus, I was wondering if you'd checked out how long Beemish was in town when he flew in here last Sunday night from Hilton Head for his little business meeting with the civic leaders of Kensington Park.

"Or if you've found out where Lilah Rose really was that Sunday. I called the restaurant she said she ate at that day. They've been closed for a month."

Bohannon threw the sports page down on his desk. "How the fuck do you know about all this? Goddamn feds can't keep their mouths shut about nothing. What are you doing, sleeping with Tommy Manetti?"

"Give it a rest, Bohannon. I heard about some of it from the city clerk in Kensington Park. She was right peeved about having all her files seized and being interrogated for two hours. The rest you can attribute to heads-up investigative work. Something you should try sometime."

"Big talk, Garrity. But I'm not telling you shit about an ongoing investigation." He crossed his arms over the mound of his stomach. "Now why don't you run along and chase dust bunnies instead of bad guys?"

I propped my own feet up on Bohannon's desk. "You gonna tell me you're not looking at Beemish and Shaloub as viable suspects in the Ewbanks murder now that the feds are in on this? Ardith Cramer didn't do it, you know."

"Bullshit." He snorted. "That Pakistani PD of hers has copies of our reports. You know what's in them. If I was him, I'd be worrying about pleaing her out instead of trying to pin the murder on somebody else. The DA doesn't give a shit about this case. One dyke killed another dyke. Big fucking deal."

"The DA's going to give a shit when he sees that the cops deliberately ignored two other much stronger suspects," I said. "One a former cop—that looks bad—the other a corrupt developer, both of whom are the subject of a federal grand jury investigation on vote buying. Wait until the newspapers get ahold of that story, Bohannon. You'll be back directing traffic and working security over at the Omni for Wrestlemania."

His face flushed pink, reminding me of raw hamburger meat. "We know all about the grand jury investigation. We even know where Lilah Rose Beemish was that Sunday afternoon." A slimy leer crossed his face. "Apparently what's sauce for the goose is sauce for the gander. Just between you and me, your friend Mrs. Beemish left the kids with a sitter and spent most of that Sunday afternoon and evening in a hot tub with a twenty-six-year-old tennis pro. Guess he was helping her with her foreplay, eh?" Bohannon chuckled happily to himself. "And yeah, for your information, we're looking at Shaloub and Beemish's relationship with the dead girl. So they both banged her. So what? That don't let your client off the hook. You satisfied, Garrity? Any other questions you want us to ask?"

I slid my foot off his desk, accidentally knocking a pile of reports onto the floor. "Oops, sorry." I paused at the door, though, to enjoy the sight of Bohannon's big brown behind stuck up in the air while he retrieved the scattered papers. "Oh, Bohannon," I said. "You are aware, aren't you, that Shaloub and both Beemishes used to work at Rich's years ago? Of course you know that. I know how thorough you big smart homicide guys are."

Driving home, I went over the pros and cons of the cops' case against Ardith. Lilah Rose had an alibi after all. It wasn't one that would do her marriage much good, but it definitely ruled her out as a murder suspect. Bohannon had a point, much as I hated to admit it. The cops had evidence that made it look like Ardith and Kristee had argued violently that night: the screaming coming from the room, the scratches on Ardith's hands, and Ardith's skin under Kristee's nails. Plus all the evidence showed that the two had set up the nanny scam in order to burglarize wealthy families. The worst strike against Ardith, though, was Ardith herself.

At her best she was sullen and uncooperative, with a giant chip on her shoulder. The DA would play that up, making it look like Ardith was some hardened pervert who'd seduced this poor innocent girl from South Carolina, then duped her into unwittingly participating in the nanny scam.

I wondered if we could get her off if the case went to trial. Idly, I wondered about myself. Wondered how Ardith would fare if I wasn't around to goad the cops into considering Beemish and Shaloub as suspects. All day long, I'd managed to push aside any thoughts about what was going to happen to me the next day. Unbidden, all the repressed fears now seeped into my consciousness. What if the lump was cancerous? What if they decided to do a mastectomy while I was on the table? Suppose they couldn't get it all? Could I run a business and cope with cancer? Shoot a gun? Make love to a man?

I heard a tapping on the window of the van. It was Edna. I'd been so absorbed in my worries and fears that I'd pulled into the driveway at home and shut off the engine and was just sitting there, staring off into space.

"I thought that was you," she said. "What are you doing, sitting here like a zombie?"

"Thinking," I said, heading for the back door.

"Well, you'd better get in the house," she said. "There's a long-distance phone call from Utah for you. Says her name is Patti Jo something. She's calling collect. Only reason I accepted was I thought it might have something to do with our case."

I dashed into the kitchen and picked up the phone. "Patti Jo? Patti Jo Nemeyer?"

"Yes, ma'am," a young girl's voice said. "I'm sorry to be so long returning your call. But after I left Atlanta I went touring around California with two other girls. I just got back home last night and got your message. My mother said this has something to do with Kristee Ewbanks?"

"I'm afraid it does," I said slowly, searching for a way to tell her the news. "I'm sorry to tell you that Kristee is dead. She was murdered a week ago. I'm a private investigator, working on behalf of Ardith Cramer, the woman who got Kristee her job here in Atlanta. Ardith has been charged with the murder, but I think she's innocent."

"Oh, my goodness," Patti Jo breathed. "My heavens. How awful." There was a silence.

"Hello, are you still there?"

"I'm here," Patti Jo said. "I was just saying a little prayer. You know, for Kristee."

"That's sweet. I'm sorry to be so blunt about this, Patti Jo, but I was wondering how close a friend you were to Kristee."

"Not very close at all," Patti Jo said. "I took her to some singles activities, when she first got to Atlanta, and got her to go to church with me once or twice. But after that I got the feeling she was avoiding me."

"Did she ever discuss her relationship with Mr. Beemish with you? Or talk about any other men she was interested in?"

"I know she liked men a lot." The girl giggled. "It's not very nice of me to say, but Kristee was man-crazy. She moved right in on the cutest guy in our singles group during the very first activity she went to."

"Would that be Whit Collier?"

"Yes," she said quickly. "I guess you already know all about Whit. If your client didn't kill Kristee, do you think Whit might have?"

"I've met Whit," I said cautiously. "What makes you think he could have killed Kristee?"

"Oh, I don't really," she said. "But considering where he's from and all—well, it's silly, but you hear things."

"I don't understand what you're getting at, Patti Jo. Is there something unusual about where Whit Collier is from?"

She lowered her voice. "I don't want my mom to hear me. She thinks I don't know about this kind of stuff. You mean you never heard of Beechy Creek, Arizona? I thought everybody knew about it, after the movie and all."

"No," I said, trying not to lose my temper. "What about Beechy Creek?"

"They still practice polygamy there," she whispered. "I know a lot of Gentiles think all LDS are polygamists, but the church officially banned the practice a long time ago, back in the 1890s. But the people in Beechy Creek still do it. Most of them have been excommunicated from the mainstream LDS church. They're like some offshoot or something. They use the Book of Mormon and the D and C, but they're very fundamentalist, totally weird. Their leader, they call him their patriarch, is this old guy they call Uncle Something. I can't remember what. Just about everybody in town is related to him. A few years ago, Uncle Something wanted to have this young girl sealed to him, like for his fourteenth or fifteenth wife. But the girl's father wouldn't let her, and this man killed the father and the girl in some kind of ritual thing. Are you sure you didn't see the movie? *Blood Atonement*, it was called."

I'd never seen any movie about Mormons that I could recall, unless it was that old Gary Cooper film *Friendly Persuasion*. No, wait, that was about the Quakers, I think.

"Patti Jo," I said. "Do you mean that Whit Collier was a polygamist or a member of this weird sect? He seemed pretty normal when I met him."

"I know," she agreed. "He never talked like a polygamist or anything, and he did go to our LDS ward. So he must have had a temple recommend from his bishop back in Arizona. But I had kind of a creepy feeling about him, even though he was so cute and all. You'd think a young guy like that would have some other interests. You know, sports or something like that. But Whit was always at church. Every Sunday, all day. He was a home teacher and he led the singles group and was in everything. I don't know what Kristee saw in him. He was too serious for me. And she was a real live wire, you know?"

Patti Jo lowered her voice even more, so that I could just barely hear.

"She told me she was going to get Whit to have sex with her. She even set a deadline. She said she'd get him in bed by their third date, and if she didn't she'd drop him."

Before I could ask any more questions, I heard a woman's voice in the background, calling Patti Jo. "I have to go now," she said. "My mom needs to use the phone. Good luck."

34

AS I HUNG UP THE PHONE, a car roared up the driveway, followed by three long blasts of the horn. "Neva Jean, get your butt out here," a man's voice called.

I could feel my temples starting to pound. "Just what I need now," I said. "Swanelle McComb. Mama, go out there and tell him we don't expect Neva Jean back for another half hour. Tell him we'll give her a ride home. Get rid of him."

It was too late. He swaggered into the kitchen, slamming the screen door behind him. "How y'all?" he said casually, flopping down on a chair. "Neva Jean back yet?"

Swanelle McComb thought he was God's gift to white-trash women. And in a way, maybe he was. I always thought of him as James Dean with pellagra. His hair was jet black and greased into a sort of pompadour with elaborate mutton-chop sideburns reminiscent of Elvis Presley in his *Viva Las Vegas* days. His eyes were light blue and his lips were full, sensual, if you like that look. I didn't, personally.

"Neva Jean won't be back for another thirty minutes or so, Swanelle," I said. "You go on home. We'll give her a ride."

"I'll wait," he said, glancing meaningfully at the refrigerator. "Y'all got a beer for a man dying of thirst?"

Edna started to get up to get him one. "Sorry," I told him, stopping her short. "We're out."

"What was that you started to tell me about the phone call?" Edna said.

"Oh, yeah. Patti Jo said the town Whit Collier comes from, Beechy Creek, is a hotbed of fundamentalism. They've got polygamists, and some guy named Uncle Something has a cult, and one of the cult members killed another one and—"

"Uncle Nehemiah," Swanelle said. "Dude had about two dozen wives and forty dirtball kids. One of the Carradine boys played him in the movie. David Carradine, I think it was, the dude who did the kung-fu movies."

"You saw *Blood Atonement?*"

I don't know why I was so amazed. Swanelle and Neva Jean devour bad movies like most people do peanuts. They've probably seen every Grade B drive-in movie ever made, at least once.

"Yeah, like I said, David Carradine was in it, so I figured it was gonna be an action flick. Me and Neva Jean seen it over at the Starlight Drive-In a couple summers ago. Turns out it was some kind of true-crime-type deal, but hey, there was some heavy shit in that flick."

"Patti Jo was telling me about the movie," I told Edna. "But she couldn't remember much more about it, other than the title."

"Man, this Uncle Nehemiah, he was into some radical religious stuff," Swanelle said, enjoying being the center of attention. "See, he wants to marry this fifteen-year-old chick. I think Audrey Landers played the chick. She spends the whole movie walking around in a torn halter top and hot pants. But her old man goes 'no way,' and he takes her up to the mountains and hides her from Uncle Nehemiah. Actually, he wants to get it on with her himself, 'cause he's really only her stepfather. So Uncle Nehemiah and his sons get guns and knives, and they hunt Audrey Landers and her old man down. But they catch 'em in the sack, so Uncle Nehemiah goes batshit and decides they have to die because they got it on and it's like incest, almost."

Edna by this time was drumming her fingers on the tabletop and anxiously eyeing the clock, hoping Neva Jean would arrive soon to deliver us from Swanelle McComb, White Trash Film Critic.

"So they beat up the father and choke Audrey Landers, but just before the two of them die, they drag 'em outside in the snow. Audrey, like, is only wearing these red bikini panties. Talk about bodacious tits. And they cut Audrey and her old man with a knife, and they let the blood run out on the ground. See, that's why the flick's called *Blood Atonement*, because this Uncle Nehemiah guy thinks the only way Audrey Landers can get to heaven is for her blood to mix with the dirt."

"Wait a minute," I said.

Swanelle looked startled. "Well, maybe it was Judy Landers instead of Audrey. I get them mixed up."

"Did you say they cut the girl, even though she's almost dead from strangulation?"

"Yeah," he said enthusiastically. "And Audrey—or Judy—man, she's groaning and wiggling around in the snow, and the blood's all over the place. Man, it was really something."

"And the movie's called *Blood Atonement?* You're sure?"

"Hell, yes, I'm sure. Swanelle McComb knows his movies," he said hotly. "Especially movies that got David Carradine in 'em. He's my main man."

"What's so important about this movie, Jules?" Edna wanted to know. "Is it supposed to be true?"

"Patti Jo said it was based on a true murder that happened in this fundamentalist sect in Beechy Creek, Arizona. That's the same place Whit Collier's from. And Kristee had a cut on her finger that Ardith said wasn't there when she left the motel. I don't know. It's sort of far out."

"I told you that CPA was a homicidal maniac," Edna said. "Just like Sam Arnold who lived next door. It's always those quiet accountant types. One minute they're figuring depreciation on your Chrysler; the next thing you know they snap, just like that. And the neighbors are on the eleven o'clock news telling the reporter, 'He kept to himself. We were shocked when he went over to the mall and blew all those people away with an Uzi. We didn't even know he had an Uzi.'"

"Calm down, Edna," I said. "The Easterbrooks should be back any minute. I still think Collier's just a harmless religious nut. Beemish is the one, you wait and see. The rest of it is all circumstances. Hell, if Swanelle and Neva Jean saw *Blood Atonement*, maybe Beemish did too. Maybe he set it up to look like some kind of crazy Mormon ritual killing. Beemish is smart enough to pull it off, you've got to admit."

We heard loud voices outside, quarreling. "I told you I can't stomach that Mexican food," Baby was yelling. "Last time I stayed up all night with the gas. It's my turn to decide, and I say we go to Mary Mac's Tearoom."

Baby and Sister didn't stop quarreling after they came into the kitchen, Baby guiding Sister by the arm, Sister trying to yank away from her.

"Selfish hussy," Sister hissed.

"I heard that," Baby said. "You better watch your step, missy, or you can stay at home tomorrow while I go off to wrasslin' with somebody else."

"Sit down, girls, and I'll get you a Coke," Edna promised. "Did you find anything suspicious in that Mormon's townhouse?"

"Never seen a bachelor's place so clean. Neat as a pin, that boy is," Baby marveled. "And Bibles? That boy has a Bible in ever' room. Met him when we got there. Sweet little blond-headed boy."

"This fool stood there and swapped Scripture verses with the man for thirty minutes," Sister griped. "We like to never have got rid of him."

"But did you find anything? That's what I'd like to know," Edna hollered. "Remember, you were supposed to look for the jewelry and papers and stuff?"

"I'll say we found something suspicious," Sister said. "Right there in the kitchen. Stuck way up under a stack of potholders."

"What?" Edna said. "The jewelry?"

"Can of Chock Full o' Nuts," Sister said triumphantly. "Coffee! And him a Mormon. I knowed he was up to something with all that sweet-tongued Scripture talk."

"A can of lousy coffee?" Edna said. "That's it? You spent the whole day there and all you found was coffee? Did you look everywhere?"

"This one here mostly looked at the TV," Baby said. "Sat and watched *All My Children* and *General Hospital* too."

The sound of the kitchen door slamming stopped the argument. Jackie dropped a plastic caddy full of cleaning supplies on the floor and sank wearily into the nearest chair. "Callahan," she panted, "you got any iced tea in the fridge?"

I poured her a tall glass and handed it over. She smiled her thanks and drank deeply. Tall and reed slender, with skin the color of milk chocolate, Jackie is one of those women who manages to look cool and elegant in the midst of any disaster. But today she looked like she'd been through hell. The bright turquoise scarf she wore wrapped around her head had started to come undone, her smock was soiled, and her usually spotless white jeans and tennis shoes were covered with stains of every description.

"Tough day, huh?" Edna inquired.

Jackie shut her eyes and leaned her head back. "You don't know how tough. Those Beemishes live like pigs."

"But did you find anything?" I asked gently.

She sipped the tea slowly. "Nothing that could help Ardith. I couldn't get the safe open. They must have changed the combination."

"Shit," I muttered. "Beemish must be hiding something in that safe."

My thoughts were interrupted by another bang of the back door. Neva Jean, Ardith, and Ruby came dragging in. Ruby and Ardith flung themselves onto the chairs, and Neva Jean snuggled in Swanelle's lap.

He whispered something in her ear, and she giggled but got up.

"Gotta go," she explained, heading for the door. "Bowling night. McComb Auto Body versus Buddy's Minit-Lube. It's a grudge match, you might say. Buddy hired away Swanelle's paint-and-trim man, and we think he's fixin' to start diversifying into body work. Swanelle's out for blood."

We waved them out the door. "Well, Ardith," I said. "How was your first day as a House Mouse? Did you work your fingers to the bone?"

Ardith pushed a strand of hair out of her face. She looked exhausted. There were dark circles under her eyes, and her shoulders were in a permanent slump.

"It's a job," she said. "I think I've got the hang of dusting and vacuuming. Look, can somebody give me a ride to this apartment I'm staying in? I'm beat."

"We're going that way," Sister said. "Baby," she hollered, "we're going to give the new girl a ride. She's staying over to De Kalb Avenue."

Baby struggled to her feet, digging in her smock pocket for her car keys. "Come on, then," she said. "I need to get some food in me and take my water pills. My feet are so swole up I don't know what to do."

Ardith stared intently at Baby for the first time. "Where'd you get that shirt?" she whispered.

"What?" Baby said. "You say your feet hurt too?"

"That shirt," Ardith said loudly, pointing at what Baby was wearing underneath her unbuttoned smock. "That's the shirt Kristee was wearing last Sunday night."

Baby looked down at her chest. She was always showing up in

someone else's cast-off finery, stopping at curbside trash heaps to rescue some outlandish hat or pair of shoes or blouse. This afternoon she was wearing a pink sweatshirt with cut-off sleeves. SKI PARK CITY, it said. I didn't recall seeing her in the shirt this morning.

"I tole her not to take that thing, didn't I?" Sister said. "She come out of the garage wearing it. Said she found it in a barrel of trash. Tole her it was stealing. She said no, it's trash. Sinful to throw away good clothes."

"Baby," I said, grasping her arm and leading her back to the chair she'd been sitting in. "Sit down and tell us where you got that sweatshirt."

The old woman hung her head in shame. "Sister's right. 'Thou shalt not covet thy neighbor's goods,' the good book says. I was looking in the garage for some cleaning rags, and I seen a big old barrel of papers and trash and such. Reached down in there and come up with something pink. Always did favor pink. Dug way down in there till I got it out."

"What about the other stuff in the barrel? Did you take anything else?"

"No, child. Tell the truth I was too ashamed. They was some typed papers, and some other clothes and stuff, and a big old pile of newspapers and such. Nothin' else pink."

"That's Kristee's sweatshirt," Ardith repeated dully. "She cut off the sleeves because she said they were too long."

Edna gave me a triumphant smile. "Told you it was him."

"Collier told me he saw Kristee on Sunday night," I said. "Maybe she loaned it to him then."

"She was wearing it when she came to the motel," Ardith insisted. "That and a pair of designer blue jeans she said she'd ripped off from Mrs. Beemish's closet."

"Baby," I said sweetly, "how about letting me have that sweatshirt?"

"All right," she said. "I'm right ashamed of taking it. Will you get it back to that nice boy?"

I promised. She slipped the sweatshirt off over her head, revealing a Day-Glo orange "Springsteen Tour '88" T-shirt.

"Kinda warm in this stuff anyway," she said, peeling off the T-shirt to reveal a starched aqua blouse with a pert Peter Pan collar. She saw my look questioning the layers. "I'm bad to take cold," she said.

"Can we go now?" Ardith said, leaning against the doorjamb.

I'd assumed she'd want a full report of the progress we'd made on the case, or at least want to know more about Whit Collier, but I was wrong. She had detached herself from the whole situation.

"See you tomorrow," she said.

"No," I said quickly. "I've got a doctor's appointment tomorrow. I'll talk to you Wednesday morning. Jackie promised to pick you up on her way in, so be ready by eight A.M."

After the last of our mice had left the house, Edna crossed her arms expectantly. "Now what?"

"It probably means nothing," I said. "Maybe Collier and Kristee got together after she left the motel. Maybe she went over to his place and they hopped in the sack together. A good Mormon boy like Collier's not going to admit to fleshly pleasures. There are lots of possibilities."

"Like maybe he killed her in some crazy Mormon voodoo ritual," Edna said. "What's our next move?"

"First off, we're going to keep you away from Swanelle Mc-Comb," I told her. "I can't believe he's got you thinking some grade B drive-in movie is real-life stuff."

"I said what's our next move?"

"OK, OK." I sighed. "Where's that church bulletin you brought back from the Mormon church? Didn't it have a listing of activities for the week?"

35

THE CHURCH BULLETIN SAID the singles group would have a putt-putt golf outing Monday night, led by group president Whit Collier.

I called his house around 7 P.M., and when he answered, I hung up. Thirty minutes later I called and let it ring fifteen times. He was gone.

For breaking and entering, I like to dress simple. Blue jeans, dark T-shirt, sneakers, and a blue bandanna over my hair. Edna was nowhere to be found when I came out of the bedroom dressed for my expedition.

I should have known. She was sitting in the front seat of the van, wearing her own cat burglar outfit: dark brown polyester slacks, dark brown shirt, orthopedic brown walking shoes.

"Get out," I said, yanking the car door open. "You're staying home."

"Try and make me," she said, poking out her lower lip and clutching her purse tightly to her chest.

"Look, Ma," I said. "I told you at the beginning, I was going to do the detecting and you were going to do the paper work. Remember?"

"I'm going," she said, staring straight ahead. "You can stand there and argue with me and waste valuable time when we could be tossing Collier's place, or you can get in and drive. Which is it going to be?"

I drove. You don't argue with Edna Mae Garrity when she gets that lower lip stuck out.

"Give me the address again," I ordered, as we pulled out of the driveway.

She pulled her palm-sized spiral-bound notebook out of her purse and scanned the top page. "Twenty-seven seventy-two Peachtree Promenade Way."

I groaned. Half the streets in Atlanta are named Peachtree, and once you get on the Peachtree maze, there's no getting off.

"Don't worry," Edna said. "I know a shortcut."

Famous last words. Edna always knows a shortcut.

"When we get past Peachtree Battle, we're going to take a right, just past the florist's shop where Kevin used to work."

Fifteen minutes later we'd gone a mile past Peachtree Battle and doubled back twice looking for the florist's shop. "Mama," I said suspiciously, "didn't Kevin work at that florist when he was in high school?"

"Yeah," she said. "So?"

"Kevin's thirty-six years old," I pointed out. "It's been twenty years. When was the last time you saw the place?"

"I don't know," she said crankily. "I quit coming over here to Buckhead once the rents got up so high. I could swear that thing was here a couple years ago. . . . Turn right here," she said suddenly. I made a hard right, went over the curb and onto the sidewalk, then back onto the roadway. A loud blast of a horn let me know the driver behind us hadn't appreciated my move.

"You better let me drive," Edna said. "You'll get us killed before we can find the place." I shot her a look and she shut up.

After another two blocks she spotted a street called Peachtree Park. "Left here," she said. "Peachtree Promenade is off here some-where, I'm sure of it."

We found Peachtree Overlook, Peachtree Summit, and Peachtree Ridge, but no Peachtree Promenade Way. Dark clouds scudded ominously across the sky overhead, and I could hear thunder in the distance. It was nearly 8 P.M.

"I thought you knew the way," I fussed.

"Me?" Edna said. "You're the hotshot police detective. I thought you knew every back street in Atlanta."

"Not too many cuttings or shootings in this zip code," I said. "And all these Peachtrees are starting to make me dizzy."

"Have I mentioned I need to pee?" Edna said offhandedly. "Turn here at Peachtree Prospect," she said. "I'll bet Promenade is up the street."

Peachtree Promenade, as it turned out, was the entry street of a vast English Tudor-style condominium complex. The main artery had numerous cross streets running off it, each with a name on the Peachtree variation.

"Goddamn," Edna said, crossing her legs. "How do these people find their way out of here to go to work every day?"

"I don't know," I said. We'd been in the car for forty-five minutes, and I was getting nervous. It still looked like rain. Who knew how long Collier would be putt-putting? My own bladder was starting to feel full too.

"There it is," she said, pointing to a street sign written in nearly unreadable Gothic lettering. Peachtree Promenade Way was actually a short cul-de-sac, with ten two-story townhouses perched on top of full garages.

"What kind of car did the sisters say Collier drives?"

"Some kind of red Japanese compact was all Baby could tell," Edna said. "There's twenty-seven seventy-two right here." The garage doors on the ground floor were closed, but the light was on and we could see the car was gone. I pulled the van into a row of empty spaces marked "visitors."

"You willing to stay here?" I asked Edna. She had her teeth gritted now. "Get me inside that condo," she said. "I've got to pee."

"Have you got the key?"

She reached in her purse and pulled out a bronze key on a piece of string with one of our House Mouse address tags.

I tossed Edna a smock and got one for myself out of the back of the van. "Put it on. If anybody asks questions, we're here to clean house."

The complex was quiet. We could see the blue flicker of television sets behind curtained windows, and most of the parking spaces were occupied.

We walked briskly to the front steps of the parlor level. I unlocked the door quickly and we stepped inside. The small foyer had a wood floor, but the rest of the condo was a sea of off-white carpet. The tang of Pine-Sol rose up pleasantly and assaulted our noses. Edna and I exchanged glances. We always want our clients satisfied, even if they were potentially homicidal.

The house was spotless, as the sisters had promised, and furnished all in whites and off-whites and chrome.

I looked around for Edna. I heard a toilet flush in the downstairs bathroom, then water running.

She stepped out and shut the light off behind her.

"Let's get busy," I said. "Those clouds out there looked stormy. If it starts to rain, Collier might decide to come home for a rousing game of Parcheesi or something."

We found the stairs to the garage in the kitchen. Edna reached in her purse and brought out a lethal-looking black flashlight. She snapped the garage light off and the flash light on. The room was pitch black without the overhead light. Edna played her flashlight over it.

The garage was as neat as the rest of the house. A blue racing bicycle hung from hooks in the ceiling, and a tool bench on the back wall was trimmed with wrenches and pliers and hammers, each hanging from its own hook.

Beside the tool bench stood a tall cardboard barrel, the kind professional movers use to pack dishes.

"That's the barrel where Baby found the shirt," I whispered. "Hold the light on it so I can look inside."

The barrel was too tall to peer into and too fragile looking for a healthy-built girl like me to crawl into, so I tilted it on its side and laid it on the floor.

Some of the contents spilled out: greasy rags, used motor oil cans, old aluminum cans, and a big stack of old newspapers. Farther down there were wadded up cleaner's bags and back copies of the same magazines I'd seen upstairs. At the very bottom of the barrel I saw a torn black plastic garbage bag. I hauled it out and away from the other trash.

"What's in it?" Edna said, kneeling beside me and pointing the light on the bag. I could see papers, and what looked like a pair of women's jeans, a bra, panties, and a handbag. "Bingo," I said.

But I could also see the play of headlights shining into the garage.

"Jesus, Mary, Joseph, and all the saints," Edna said, crossing herself before shutting off the flashlight. "He's back."

"Hide," I hissed. But the only sanctuary in the nearly empty garage was beneath the tool bench. Hastily I shoved everything back in the trash can and set it back where it had been. Edna squeezed herself under the bench.

We could hear an engine idling directly outside the garage door and voices, a man's and at least one woman's. The woman was laughing.

"Doggone," I heard Collier's voice say. "This darned garage door opener is on the fritz again. The door is sticking." The lights moved as he started to back up the car.

I ran to the door and tried to yank it open. Collier was right, it was stuck. "Come on," I told Edna. "We'll never get out with this door stuck. We'll have to bluff our way out the front."

We raced up the back stairs, shutting the door to the stairs behind us. "Just keep your mouth shut and agree with me," I told Edna. "Act normal."

The two of us stepped leisurely out the front door, pretending not to notice the three people coming up the walkway behind us. I made a show of locking the door, and we turned to face Collier.

"Can I help you?" he said. He was wearing a pink polo shirt and neatly pressed khaki pants with Docksiders. His face was flushed. Two young women were with him, dressed in shorts and T-shirts and tennis shoes. There was a red Celica in the driveway.

"Oh, hello," I said, deliberately affecting a high-pitched Southern accent. It came out badly, something like Prissy in *Gone With the Wind*. "We're with Home Sweep Home. Our girls, the Easterbrook sisters, cleaned your condo today, and when they got back to the office they noticed they'd left some keys at your place."

Edna nodded vigorously and jingled her house keys.

Collier and the young women stared at us as though they'd caught us burgling the place, which they had.

"Mrs. Magillicuddy and I were nearby tonight giving an estimate, so we told the ladies we'd drop by and pick up the keys for them. They gave us the key, just in case, so we let ourselves in. Was that all right?"

Collier's eyes narrowed. He stared at me thoughtfully for a moment, then shrugged. I couldn't tell if he recognized me from our previous meeting.

"I'd have preferred that you wait until I was home," he said, not bothering to hide the annoyance in his voice. "No harm done though, I suppose." He held out his hand. "May I have my key back, please?"

I dropped it into his outstretched palm. "Thank you. So sorry about the mix-up. We'll be calling you about our next special," I said.

As we walked down the steps I fought the urge to break into a run.

"Just walk slowly," I said to Edna through clenched teeth. "Nice and easy. I don't think he suspects anything."

We could feel Collier's eyes on our backs as we got into the van. After I started the engine, I glanced in the rearview mirror. He stood there by the doorway, staring straight at our bright pink van—the one that said House Mouse on the side, not Home Sweep Home.

That's when I remembered having given him my business card during our meeting in his office.

"He knows who we are. He must have recognized me."

"Told you so," Edna said. "What are we going to do about it?"

"Time to call the cops, I guess." I dreaded the idea of trying to convince Bohannon that Collier, the Mormon do-gooder, was involved in Kristee's murder, especially after I'd insisted it was Beemish and Shaloub.

"Won't do any good," Edna said. "Collier's probably loading that trash in his car right now, taking it to some dumpster to get rid of it. Time the cops get there, the barrel will be gone and he'll be sitting there drinking milk and cookies."

"You're probably right. But there's nothing else we can do. I'll call Bohannon as soon as we get home. Maybe if he sees Kristee's sweatshirt he'll be more inclined to believe us. Especially if that desk clerk tells him it's what she was wearing the night he saw her.

"You know," I said thoughtfully, "the only clothes I saw in the bag in the trash barrel were some Guess jeans, a pair of shoes, a bra, and panties. Sounds like what Ardith said Kristee was wearing when she went to the motel. I wonder what Collier did with all Kristee's other clothes. Not to mention the Beemishes' silver and coins and the other stuff that never has turned up."

"Let Bohannon and the other cops find out," Edna said. "I'm not going back to that condo again. The way that boy looked at us made my skin crawl."

But Bohannon wasn't at the cop shop. I called his home number, but there was no answer. Finally, I got Bucky Deaver at home.

I told him why I needed to find Bohannon. "No good," he said. "Bohannon and two other guys from homicide left this morning for Savannah for a two-day case management seminar. Some deal, huh? Savannah, the beach, all that seafood."

"Where's he staying? I've got to talk to him tonight. If the cops don't get to Collier in a hurry, he'll get rid of that barrel."

Bucky gave me the name of the hotel. I called the Savannah Inn and Country Club. "No answer in Lieutenant Bohannon's room," the operator said. I left him a message to call me when he got in, but I didn't have much hope that he would. Give a cop an out-of-town trip and he does what everybody else does; he parties.

Edna got a new bottle of Wild Turkey out from under the cupboard and poured us both a stiff drink. "We never did eat dinner," she said, slapping a bag of chips and a bowl of dip on the table. "This'll have to do."

"If I don't hear from Bohannon tonight, I'll get Dinesh to do something tomorrow morning," I said, licking a smidgen of dip from my pinkie. "Maybe I'll go see Bohannon's commander, Major Foster. He knows me from when I was a patrol officer. Maybe he could get a warrant to search Collier's house."

"What about your surgery?" Edna said. "You're supposed to be at the hospital at seven A.M., aren't you?"

I waved off her concerns. "I'll postpone it," I said lightly. "Those corns aren't going anywhere."

Edna took a sip of her drink and lit up a cigarette. "Rich Drescher called me today," she said slowly. "He told me about the lump. Told me you'd probably pull some stunt like trying to get out of having the biopsy."

"Asshole," I muttered. "Whatever happened to patient confidentiality?"

Edna put her hand on my wrist and squeezed hard. "This murder case can wait," she said. "Kristee Ewbanks isn't getting any dealer. Ardith's out of jail. It can wait a week or so, if need be. You're going to that hospital tomorrow if I have to tie you up and carry you there myself, Julia. I lost my mother to cancer, lost a breast of my own. I'm not gonna lose you too. If Collier's the one, the cops'll get him. Right now you've got more important things to worry about."

36

I CALLED SAVANNAH three more times that night, trying to reach Bohannon. In between calls I typed a case report, stating that one of our employees had found a shirt belonging to Kristee Ewbanks at the home of Whit Collier and that we had reason to believe more evidence connecting Collier to her murder could be found in a trash barrel in Collier's garage.

At 1 A.M., red-eyed and too tired to care any more, I handed Edna the report. She was in the den, curled up on my dad's beat-up old recliner, watching a Susan Hayward movie on Channel 17. She did that when she couldn't sleep. Sometimes I'd get up in the morning and find her there, curled up in that chair, out cold, with the remote control in her hand and the television still going.

"Take this down to the cop shop in the morning and ask for Major Foster," I told her. "Pull your tough old lady act. Tell him you're not leaving until he promises to get a search warrant for Collier's place."

Edna had begged me to let her take me to the SurgiCenter and stay during the surgery, but I managed to stick to my plan.

"I told you already, Paula's going to drop me off. I'll call you when I come out of surgery, and you can come pick me up. If it's good news, we'll go to Mary Mac's for chicken and dressing to celebrate."

She sniffed. "My chicken and dressing's just as good as theirs. *When* the news is good, we'll go to Coach and Six for prime rib. My treat."

After all the nights I'd stayed awake worrying about the lump, that night I slept like a baby. Six o'clock came too early.

Paula didn't say much when she pulled up in front of the hospital. "Let me come in with you?" she said tentatively.

I shook my head no and got out of the car. I was relieved she hadn't insisted.

"See you tonight," she said, and pulled away from the curb.

I took an instant dislike to the Women's SurgiCenter. Maybe it was the state I was in. I was hungry, jittery, and head-achy from the lack of food and, most important, coffee. My skin felt itchy and I couldn't concentrate.

The surroundings didn't help. The SurgiCenter had been decorated during an era a couple years earlier when designers theorized that certain colors had different effects on people. They had apparently decided that mauve and gray would make women feel better about having their pelvic cavities roto-rootered or having large portions of their breasts removed.

Everything was mauve: the carpet, the sofa, even the coffee table. There were plastic ferns scattered about the room. For reading material I could choose between a pamphlet extolling reconstructive breast surgery or a brochure listing the kinds of hormone therapy available to women who'd had a hysterectomy.

Fortunately, the woman at the reception desk had so many questions about my insurance and what it would or wouldn't cover that I didn't have time for any light reading.

Once the papers were filled out, a slim young man dressed in a mauve uniform arrived with a wheelchair. "I don't need that," I told him. "It's my breast they're operating on, not my knees."

Apparently he wasn't a morning person either, because he didn't crack a smile. "I'm going to take you up to pre-op now," he said. "They'll get you ready for the doctor."

We rode up one flight in the elevator and got off at a floor marked PRE-OPERATIVE WAITING ROOM.

The aide took me to a small room, gray with mauve accents. He showed me a mauve plissé gown that had been laid across the foot of the bed. It reminded me of the jammies I'd had as a little girl. The thought was slightly comforting. "Put that on, please, and go in the bathroom and empty your bladder."

I did as I was told, and when I came out, the aide was gone. I climbed into bed and pulled the thin sheet up to my chin.

The Muzak in the room was playing something familiar. It was "Yesterday" by the Beatles. I was humming along softly when a large black woman in a white nurse's uniform pushed through the doors with a stainless steel cart full of bottles and hospital doodads.

"Miss Garrity?" she asked, checking the plastic bracelet on my wrist. "I'm Sharon," she said, pronouncing it Sha-*ron*. "I'll be your pre-op nurse today." Somehow, in my caffeine-deprived state, that amused me. I expected her to hand me a chalkboard menu of surgery options. *And our special of the day is a biopsy with green peppercorn sauce.*

Instead she flicked the sheet off, looking disinterestedly at my flabby white body, ill concealed by the scanty hospital gown.

"Them panties got to come off," she announced.

"I'll just leave them on, if it's all right with you," I said.

She didn't flinch. "Can't wear no panties to surgery," Sharon said. "We got rules. Them panties got to come off."

I'd worn new ones too, to make a good impression and all, just like Edna'd taught my sister and me. Reluctantly I slid them off and tucked them into my purse, which she took and promised to deliver with my clothing to my post-op room.

After the offending garment had been removed, Sharon started swabbing the back of my wrist with a bright orange solution. She brought out a huge syringe then, so I decided it was time to rest my eyes. I felt a sharp sting, then the sensation of something being taped to my hand. When I opened my eyes an IV was in place, its long thin tube leading from the needle to a plastic bag suspended from a pole by the bed.

"That's intravenous Valium," Sharon told me. "I'll come back in about ten minutes to see if it's making you relaxed enough for surgery."

Relax? I said to myself. How can I relax when I haven't had any coffee?

I shut my eyes and concentrated on trying to feel the Valium trickling into my bloodstream.

There was another familiar tune playing on the Muzak, but somehow I couldn't place it. I hummed along until the title and artist came to me. My God, I'd gotten middle-aged overnight. One minute I was smoking dope with the girls in the Tri Delt house at Georgia, listening to rock music; the next thing you know I was in a hospital room in Atlanta, with no panties on, listening to Jethro Tull on Muzak. Yes, that's what it was, "Living in the Past" on Muzak. I could only hope the members of Jethro Tull had all overdosed years ago so they'd be spared the pain.

Sharon bustled back in. I could hear her pantyhose-enclosed thighs rubbing together under the starched layers of her uniform.

"Ready to go?" she said briskly, checking the IV bag. I looked up at her groggily. "Did you hear Jethro Tull playing on the Muzak just now? Or is the Valium making me hallucinate?"

She shook her head. "Girlfriend, I ain't studyin' no Jethro Tull mess. Now let's get going up to surgery."

She brought a gurney in from the hallway and helped me onto it. "Why can't I walk?" I said weakly.

Sharon shot me a grin, exposing a gold front tooth. It made her look a little less efficient, which helped. "It's like the underwear, girlfriend. It's a rule."

I guess the Valium must have kicked in for real about then. I nodded off in the elevator and didn't wake up again until I was in the operating room. It was a white-tiled room, with banks of bright lights surrounding me. Rich Drescher looked down at me. A surgical mask covered the lower half of his face, but his eyes seemed to be smiling. "Callahan," he said, nodding to a petite black woman standing next to him. "This is Dr. Jefferson. Best boob doctor in the city." I think she winked at me.

"Let's do it," Rich said.

I closed my eyes and fell down an elevator shaft to nowhere.

As I was falling, I kept hearing the melody of a Jethro Tull song: funny. I couldn't remember the words.

Then someone was tapping me lightly on the shoulder. I opened one eye slowly. "Callahan, Callahan," the voice whispered. "Are you with us? Wake up, Callahan." I didn't, though. I went back to sleep.

The next time I woke up, yet another nurse was calling my name. Only she wasn't whispering. "Callahan," she yelled. "Time to wake up. Come on now, Callahan, talk to me."

It was my first grade teacher, Miss Halsey. Only this Miss Halsey was younger and taller, with a frizzy yellow perm and an unfortunate amount of hair on her upper lip.

This time I managed to stay awake. "What happened?" I asked. "Did they get it all?"

Miss Halsey pushed a damp strand of hair off my forehead. "Dr. Drescher left instructions to tell you, and I quote: 'You now have a matched set.'"

I looked down at my chest. The gown had slipped enough that I could see a large piece of gauze taped across my breast. "That's nice," I said. "What time is it? Do I go home now?"

Miss Halsey frowned a little. "Not yet, I'm afraid. You had an allergic reaction to the Valium and your breathing got a little irregular. We've given you something to counteract it, but Dr. Drescher wants to keep you here overnight for observation."

"No way," I whined. "He promised me day surgery. I've got to go home. My insurance won't pay for staying overnight."

I tried to sit upright, but she easily pushed me back down. The room tilted in an alarming fashion. "No, dear," she said. "Dr. Drescher was very insistent. You're going to stay here. He said he'd check on you later this evening and talk to you then about the tissue culture."

"This evening?" I repeated. "What time is it? I thought I'd be home by noon."

"It's six o'clock. They'll bring you a little Jell-O or applesauce in a few minutes. Won't that be nice?"

Miss Halsey left then, left me alone in a strange hospital room with no underwear, no insurance coverage, and a big Band-Aid on my boob.

"I'm fucked," I said to no one in particular. I wanted to cry. Instead I remembered Edna. I'd promised to call her as soon as I was out of surgery. That should have been hours ago. I couldn't believe she hadn't stormed the place by now.

Miss Halsey popped her head in the door just then. "By the way, a young man has been calling the nurses' station for you all afternoon. At first he wouldn't leave a message. He called back about an hour ago, though. He said to tell you Mr. Collier called, and he said not to worry, because your mother is with him. He said he'd call again later."

I felt my blood freeze. Collier. He had Edna! Then I relaxed a second. Edna was the one who was convinced Collier was a wacked-out murderer. She'd never get within a city block of him.

There was a telephone on the nightstand beside my bed. I sat up and reached for it. The room tilted again, violently. I clenched my teeth and dialed the house. No answer. I left a message on the machine, explaining why I was still at the hospital and asking her to call right away.

While I waited for the room to stop sliding back and forth like a child's teeter-totter, I had another idea. I leaned as far over as I dared and looked at the nightstand. There was a door under the drawer. I pulled it open and there was my purse and a plastic bag full of my clothes. I leaned even farther and nearly fell out of bed. Grasping the handrail on the side of the bed, I managed to fish the purse out and put it on my lap. This wasn't going to be nearly as easy as I'd anticipated.

I found the remote beeper for the answering machine, dialed our number, and beeped the thing into the receiver.

The machine had a string of messages, mostly clients with requests or questions. A woman's voice came on and said, "Fuck you, Callahan Garrity. Fuck you. Fuck you." It sounded like the refined tones of Lilah Rose Beemish.

"Back at ya," I said to the receiver.

The next message wasn't from a House Mouse client. "This is Whit Collier," a man's voice said. My breathing stopped for a minute. Before he could leave a message though, Edna picked up the phone. "Hello, don't hang up, I'm here," her voice said. "House Mouse, how can I help you?"

"Mrs. Garrity?" Collier said politely. "This is Whit Collier. Remember, we met last night after you and your daughter broke into my house? I found something in the garage, in a trash barrel, that I think you might have been looking for." I heard Edna gasp. "I wondered if you and your daughter would come over and get it. I called earlier and one of your girls told me your daughter is in the hospital. I hope it's nothing serious. I've called several times there, but they say she's unable to come to the phone. I thought you and I could have a quiet chat at my place. Say around three o'clock?"

Edna was strangely quiet. "I'm sorry," I heard her say, her voice halting. "I've got an appointment this afternoon, I couldn't possibly meet you today. Perhaps tomorrow, when Callahan's home." She hung up quickly.

"Call the cops, Edna," I said into the phone. There were more messages, but none as sinister as Collier's. Bohannon had called, to say that he was having a nice time in Savannah and wasn't really interested in talking to me.

Where the hell was Edna? I remembered it was Tuesday, the day of Edna's standing hair appointment at Frank's Salon de Beauté.

I called and demanded to talk to Frank. "Callahan," he said. "Tell that no-good mother of yours that if she stands me up again, she can just go to that fast-food hair place in the mall from now on."

"Didn't she show up at all, Frank?" I said. "Did she call or anything?"

"No," he said, "and I'm frosting Minna Mitchell's hair now, so I haven't tried to call her to ask what came up."

"I'm afraid I know what came up," I said. "If you hear from her, tell her to call me at the hospital right away."

I called the house again. Still no answer. Paula wasn't home, either.

I called the Atlanta Police Department and asked to speak to Major Foster. "He's gone for the day," his secretary said. "They've all gone over to the Holiday Inn for an FBI briefing on this white collar bribery deal. They won't be back until tomorrow morning."

Out of desperation I called Neva Jean. She picked up on the first ring. "Don't ask why and don't argue with me," I said. "Have you seen Edna today?"

"Not since this morning, I haven't. She gave us our assignments, and I left. I called in around two and talked to her. She said she was going to her hair appointment after that."

"She never made it," I said. "I think that crazy Mormon must have kidnapped her. Now listen, this is important." I reeled off a list of instructions for her; then after I hung up the phone I called the nurse and asked for some pain medication. She left a white paper cup full of tiny yellow pills. "Only take one at a time," she said. "We're understaffed tonight, so I can't be coming in here giving them to you like I normally would. One every four hours, you hear?"

I heard.

37

"YOU SURE THIS IS ALLOWED?" Neva Jean said, glancing anxiously at the door of my room. I took three of the painkillers the nurse had left me in a little paper cup. I guess the Valium was wearing off, because my chest hurt like hell. I was sick to my stomach, too, but a couple of trips to the bathroom had fixed that.

"Mellow out, Neva Jean. Now help me get my clothes on. I'm still sort of dizzy from the medication they gave me. We've got to go find Edna."

I'd called Collier's house at least half a dozen times, but no one answered. After I called Neva Jean, I'd called every place I could think of that Edna could be. Even my sister's house. No one had seen or heard from her since around 3 P.M. I had a sick feeling in the pit of my stomach, a feeling that had nothing to do with the surgery I'd just had.

With her white House Mouse smock, white slacks, and white waitress shoes, Neva Jean looked almost like a nurse's aide. Almost. She helped me tie my shoes, and when I got off the bed and nearly slid to the floor, she gave me a hand up. I hadn't realized how rubbery my legs would feel. Or how badly my breast would hurt where they'd removed the lump.

With Neva Jean beside me, I walked unsteadily through the hospital's front doors and out to the van. "You'll have to drive. Those pain pills have got me a little tiddly."

I settled myself in the passenger seat and fastened the seat belt as tight as it would go. I'd just had a brush with cancer, and I wasn't taking any chances. Neva Jean gunned the engine. "Let's head the bastard off at the pass," she said. "Where to?"

Where to, indeed? I didn't have any idea where to look for Collier.

I gave Neva Jean directions to get to Collier's townhouse. I remember leaving the hospital parking lot, and telling her about the left-turn signal not working, and then I sort of dozed off.

When I came to again, we were parked in front of the townhouse. "Glad you woke up," Neva Jean said. "We been driving around in circles in this damn Peachtree maze for thirty minutes. I was about to get out and call us a cab." The garage bay in front of us was empty. "If this is the right place, it looks like nobody's home," she said.

I fumbled in the glove box. "Did you get my twenty-two out of my nightstand like I told you?"

She nodded yes.

"How about the bullets? In the empty bran flakes box at the back of the pantry?"

She nodded yes again. "I don't know what good that little old peashooter will do you. I still think you should have let me bring Swanelle's thirty-ought-six. He lets me use it when we shoot rats out at the county dump. You oughta see what that baby does to those bad boys. When I get done the only thing left is the squeak and the tail."

I found the twenty-two, checked to see that it was loaded, and jammed it in the waistband of my jeans. "Wait right here," I told her. "I don't think he's home, but if he is, I'm just going right up to the front door and draw down on him. If something goes wrong, you lay on the horn there. Start honking and screaming and don't stop till you see blue lights on top of a white sedan."

I lurched up the steps of the condo, holding tight to the hand rail. My breast didn't hurt anymore, but my feet were suddenly detached from the rest of me, making any kind of a real frontal assault pretty much a joke. I rang the doorbell and put my hands behind my back, with the pistol cocked in my right hand. No answer.

Since the windows were all on the second floor and I couldn't reach them, I decided to give up on the condo. I put the safety back on and put the pistol back in my jeans.

Neva Jean had slumped so far down in the front seat all I could see of her was the dark roots on the top of her head. "We'll try the office," I told her as I got back in the van. "His secretary said he called in sick today. The office should be closed by now. Maybe he took Edna there."

Traffic was still fairly heavy, even though it was by now after 7 P.M. I dozed lightly, waking up a time or two when Neva Jean blasted the horn or hung her head out the window to holler at somebody to get the lead out.

The parking lot at the accounting office was empty. I walked around the building, peeping in windows. The foyer light was on, casting some light into the ground-floor rooms, but there was no movement inside.

In the van, I tried hard to concentrate. Where would Collier have taken Edna? And why? I felt groggy and lightheaded and guilty. Where the hell had that wing nut taken my mother?

"Let's cruise through the parking lot of the LDS church on Ponce de Leon," I suggested. "I doubt he'd take her there, but right now I'm fresh out of ideas."

The parking lot of the church was filling up fast with carloads of fresh-faced children and their parents. The lot was a beehive of activity, people talking in knots and others coming in and out of the building with covered casserole dishes. It looked like potluck supper night. But I didn't see a red Celica.

"I don't know anything about this guy, Neva Jean," I said quietly. "I don't know where he goes, what he likes to do, what sets him off. I don't even know why he might have killed Kristee. I have no idea where he might have taken Edna. He could be out at the river or over at Piedmont Park or the zoo at Grant Park—hell, they could be anywhere. Think, Neva Jean, where would they be?"

She squeezed her eyes shut tight and wrinkled her forehead, her lips drawn into a clownlike grimace. Thinking was clearly an alien process for her. "I don't know, Callahan," she wailed. "This is giving me the creeps. Let's call the cops before he puts your mama in cold storage like he did that other girl."

"What was that last part you just said?"

Neva Jean looked startled that she'd had an idea. "I said I hope he don't put your mama in cold storage like he did that other girl. Fur coat or no fur coat."

Something finally registered in my Demerol-drugged mind. "Rich's," I said. "That's the only place I can think of that he might be. Let's go there."

"Which one?"

"Downtown. The big store. That's where they have the fur vault."

The pain pills had me in their hold now. We drove west on Marietta Street, right into a soft springtime drizzle. The neon lights on the buildings seemed to shimmer in the rain, and the streets looked like patent leather. On Marietta, the median strip had been planted with dogwood trees. Here the shiny dark gray pavement was snowy with the fallen white petals of dogwood blossoms.

It was full dark now, and only a few souls were out on the streets.

Neva Jean swung the van hard left onto Forsyth Street, then left again on Alabama. She pulled to the curb directly under the old Rich's clock tower that had been a meeting spot for generations of Atlantans. Instead of numerals, the clock said SHOP RICH'S. MARTA buses lined the other side of the street, right in front of the Five Points train station that's the heart of the city's transit system.

The mannequins in the windows were all dressed in white linen. They wore white gloves, big elaborately flowered hats, and haughty expressions. *With All the Frills Upon It* the window backdrop said in bright green script.

"Look, Callahan, hats are back this year," Neva Jean said. "Ain't those something? But the store's closed. Let's go back to your house and call the cops."

I rubbed at my eyes. "Closed? No, as far as Collier's concerned, the store's not closed. He used to work here. He knows how to get in if he wants to. Drive around the block," I went on, "and when you get on Forsyth again, turn right and head for the viaducts."

She shook her head but did as I said.

"Now turn left again."

The turn plunged us into the city's underbelly. Massive rust-stained concrete pilings formed tall arches, the viaducts supporting the city streets above us. The cobblestone pavement was uneven and pocked with pools of rainwater. Steam rose from dozens of manhole covers.

"This is creepy, Callahan," Neva Jean whimpered. "I wanna go home."

"Your window is rolled up, isn't it? And your door locked? I don't like it either, Neva Jean, but I think this is how Collier got Kristee into the store."

The van inched slowly down the street, with Neva Jean sniveling the whole way about swamp monsters and mutant rats who lived under the viaducts. To our left we could see the railroad tracks that led into and out of this subterranean part of Atlanta. To our right, the back of the store loomed large and gray. Tractor trailer trucks nestled against the loading docks, their tails stuck up under pull-down doors on the dock. Cars were parked here and there along the way, but there was no sign of Collier's red Celica—until we reached the last loading bay. He'd pulled the car all the way into the bay, right beside a trailer that dwarfed the little compact.

"That's it," I said, pointing. "Pull on past, and around the corner, and park."

She did as I told her and rolled to a stop. "Don't get out," she begged me. "You don't know what these religious nuts are like. You didn't see *Blood Atonement*, did you?"

I shook my head impatiently. It didn't clear the cobwebs. I needed a nap. "Quiet, Neva Jean," I hissed. "Listen now. I'm gonna try to creep back there real quiet like. You stay in the van and keep the door locked. If you hear me holler, or a gun go off, lay on the horn like I told you before. People are working inside the store tonight, I think, so if they hear enough noise outside, they should come running. After you honk the horn, drive over to the MARTA station and get a cop; there are always bunches of 'em over there. But remember, until you hear something, stay in the van and keep the door locked. Understand?"

I checked my waistband to see that the .22 was still wedged tightly. It was. I got out of the van and watched Neva Jean lean over and lock the door.

My heart was pounding as I crept around the corner, keeping almost to a duck walk. I came up behind the Celica and peeped in. It was empty, but the contents of Edna's big straw purse were spilled out on the floorboard in front. My heart sank.

"Christ," I muttered. I was dizzy and weak as a kitten. Where could they be? If they were already in the store, it was hopeless. The loading dock in front of me was bathed in darkness. I crept closer, up the steep steps, to see a tiny pool of light spilling from under the closed bay door. They weren't on this dock.

I stood up and moved around the corner to the next bay. Three trailers were pulled up to the dock. It was dark here too. I inched around the end of the first trailer and peered into the blackness.

Nothing. No sound, no motion. On my knees now, I crawled around the side, conscious of kneeling in an oily, evil-smelling puddle. The cobblestones cut into the knees of my jeans, and my head swam every time I moved too fast.

Then I heard it: a gasp, and a small, terrified cry. It was coming from the next bay over. Lying flat on my belly now, I pulled myself along on the ground, wincing as my chest made contact with the pavement. Finally I reached the end of the trailer and could see where the cries were coming from.

Collier, dressed in a white zip-front jumpsuit, was on the loading dock, half dragging, half carrying Edna, who was resisting with all her might, toward a large metal merchandise hamper that stood on the dock.

"No, please," she said in a tiny voice I could hardly recognize. "Please, please don't do this. Please."

He pulled her roughly upright, and for the first time I saw the hunting knife in his hand. The blade gleamed in the semidarkness. He held it up to my mother's neck and gently nicked her earlobe. She cried out, but he made no effort to quiet her. I could see the blood dripping onto her white blouse.

"Let me go, please," she cried. "I won't tell."

I heard more cries now, but they weren't coming from Edna. It was Collier; he was crying—sobbing, really. "It's the only way," he sobbed. "You'll be in a better place, where your wicked earthly ways will be forgiven." He took the knife blade and held it to her throat. I pulled the .22 from my waistband and prepared to rush the dock.

But Edna had other plans. She dropped to the ground, clutching her chest, rolling herself into a tight ball. "My heart!" she gasped. She started to choke and cough. "Heart . . . heart attack." She rolled back and forth, gasping and crying and clutching her heart. Collier stood there transfixed, staring down at the victim who was dying before he could guarantee her salvation.

"Get up," he shouted hoarsely. "Get up, or I'll kill you." He gave her a brutal kick to the side, and Edna screamed and rolled onto her side, clutching her chest and gasping for air. "Heart attack," she cried. "I'm having a heart attack!"

It was the best chance I'd have. I made for the dock, my heart pumping a mile a minute, my hands extended in front of me, the .22 pointed at Collier. He was so busy kicking Edna and witnessing the spectacle of her heart attack that he didn't see me approaching until I was on the dock and only a few feet away.

"Leave her alone!" I shrieked, pointing the .22 directly at his heart.

Shock registered on his face. Edna groaned loudly and tried to roll out of harm's way, which is when I stepped on her. She screamed, and I went down in a heap on top of her. Collier reached down and wrenched the gun out of my hands.

"Harlots!" he shouted at us. "Unclean vile contaminated filth! I know who you are. I know your sins. You make a mockery of our Heavenly Mother."

Edna and I clung tightly to each other, there on the filthy floor of the loading dock. Her face was greenish white, and her breathing really seemed labored. I thought she might die of her heart attack before Collier could shoot or stab us both to death.

He was ranting and raving for real now, calling us Semites, unclean prostitutes who defiled God's holy places. He kicked Edna again, then jerked me upright, shoving the gun in his own waistband and brandishing the knife before my eyes. "I will pluck out the eye that offends thee," he shouted. "Your blood will atone for your sins. I am the avenging angel Moroni, brought forth to clean these defiled places." He took the knife and nicked the skin under my chin. I felt a sharp sting and a warm trickle of blood. I screamed until I thought my lungs would burst.

"Quiet," he thundered. "We'll pray now, before you and the other harlot—"

But he never finished his sentence. From behind and above his head I saw a shining silver wand come down in a crushing blow on Collier's head. He swayed for a moment, and the wand struck again, then again. The pretty blond hair turned bright red on one side, and he finally crumpled to the ground.

I think I sat down rather suddenly myself at that point, in a heap beside Edna, who had stopped groaning and gasping and seemed to be recovering quickly from her coronary.

"Y'all all right?" Neva Jean said anxiously. "Lord, I thought that boy was gonna do a Veg-O-Matic on the two of you, right here at Rich's Department Store."

I looked at the long silver wand she was brandishing. "What the hell is that?" I said groggily.

Neva Jean's laugh echoed weirdly in the empty loading dock. "You are out of it, Callahan. This here's nothing but the business end of that big old vacuum cleaner you had in the back of the van."

She looked admiringly at the pipe, which was flecked with tiny drops of blood. "You can have your Hoovers and your Eurekas and all them fancy machines. Give me an Electrolux three and a half horsepower any old day. Those babies can flat suck."

Epilogue

——

YOU GONNA FISH or sunbathe?" McAuliffe wanted to know.

We were in his battered red rowboat, out in the middle of Lake Burton, on a Wednesday in May that was so beautiful it felt illicit.

"Can't I do both?" I said. Mac was fly-fishing, for bass, I guess. I was mostly soaking up the rays, stretched out in my new bathing suit on the plank seat in the back of the boat. We were both enjoying a rare midweek day away from work.

We'd left Rufus back at the car. "No room in the boat for a dog and a woman," Mac had said. He got a tennis ball out of the Jeep and gave it to Rufus to play with. I guess I was lucky he didn't give me the ball and take Rufus in the boat.

I propped my head up on my bent elbow and turned to watch his leisurely casts into the deep green lake water.

"Something on your mind?" he asked casually.

"I can't stop thinking about Ardith Cramer," I admitted. "You know she left town without ever seeing Demetrius? He's seventeen years old, Mac, nearly an adult. And she'll never know him. And she doesn't care."

"What makes you think she doesn't care? Just because she doesn't carry his picture around in her billfold? Maybe she cares desperately and can't articulate it. Maybe she feels guilty about abandoning him. Don't be so hard on her."

"I'm not," I said stubbornly. "I hate to say it, but I think Ardith is one of those women who are totally without maternal instincts."

"Is that bad?"

"Not if you don't have a child to raise, I guess." I'd been seeing Andrew McAuliffe steadily for a month now, and he never failed to surprise me with the matter-of-fact way he looked at life. He didn't get all emotional about things, the way I tend to.

"How did Ardith get the money to leave town?" he asked. "I thought she was broke."

I felt myself color a little. "She had a paycheck coming from the work she did for the House Mouse. And I—uh, gave her the rest of Wendell Driggers's money."

"You're a soft touch, Julia Callahan Garrity."

I kicked his leg lightly with my bare foot. He caught it, squeezed my toes, and let go.

"Have you heard anything more about Whit Collier?"

"He's still down in Milledgeville, being evaluated by the state's shrinks. I hear they've got a whole team of 'em looking inside his twisted little mind. His lawyer called me two days ago, to ask some questions about the kinds of things he said when he kidnapped Edna and when he was trying to dispatch both of us to an early grave. The lawyer wouldn't tell me much, but I gather they plan to plead him guilty but insane. He did belong to that crazy cult in Arizona, you know. Collier's folks are mainstream Mormon, fairly wealthy from what his lawyer said. When they found out a couple years ago that he'd gotten involved in this Uncle Nehemiah thing, they arranged for him to get this job with the accounting firm in Decatur. He joined the LDS church here and was fine, but I guess the followers back in Beechy Creek started sending him books and tapes and stuff. The lawyer claims that when Collier met up with Kristee, he thought he'd found the girl of his dreams. Then, when he discovered what she was really up to, he came unglued."

"Does anybody know exactly what happened?"

"Only according to Collier. Bucky Deaver sneaked me a copy of the statement he made to the police when they arrested him, before the lawyers got there and shut him up. Collier told the cops he went to the Beemishes that Sunday night to ask Kristee to marry him. The front door was unlocked, so he went in the house to look for her. He says he found her in the Beemishes' master bedroom, standing stark naked in the closet, trying on Lilah's fur coats. She had packed up her things and taken a stack of stuff: jewelry, silver, the papers from the safe. Kristee laid out the whole scam for him right then and there, how she'd slept with Beemish and Shaloub and was blackmailing both of them, how she and Ardith had dreamed up the Mormon nanny scam, and how they were planning to cash in their chips and head for the Cayman Islands.

"He told the cops he had to kill Kristee in order to guarantee her salvation. He strangled her with his hands, then dragged her down the back staircase out the garage to the garden. That's where he cut her on the finger, so that her blood could mix with the soil as atonement for her sins. Blood atonement, as it were.

"Once the deed was done, Collier pulled his car into the garage, loaded Kristee in the trunk with her suitcases and the Beemishes' stuff, and took off. He says he drove around for hours, trying to think what to do. The furs finally gave him an idea. He'd worked at Rich's, remember, so he knew they'd be open late stocking the store for the big doorbuster sale. While he was driving around, he told the cops he passed a church-run thrift shop. He couldn't remember the name of it, just that it was in a run-down part of town, somewhere near a big housing project. Collier said God told him to donate the Beemishes' ill-gotten goods and Kristee's worldly belongings to someone doing the Lord's work; he pulled around to the back of the thrift shop, saw a donation bin, and heaved the stuff in."

McAuliffe laughed appreciatively. "Did the cops ever track down the lucky recipients?"

"The Bountiful Jesus Outreach Mission Thrift Shop on Techwood still had some of Kristee's clothes on the racks," I said. "But the shop manager said an antique dealer who stops by regularly looking for vintage clothing snapped up all the Georgian silver and the coins and jewelry the day after she put them on the shelf. The manager said she didn't know the dealer's name, but he paid in cash, like he always did. Seventy-five dollars. Praise Jesus.

"Collier told the cops he felt a white glow surround him after his good work. So he went home and got a good night's sleep in anticipation of the next morning's work. Then early in the morning he put on that cute little white coverall he was wearing when he tried to do us in. Hours before the store was due to open, he drove around to the loading dock and wheeled a merchandise hamper off the dock and around to the trunk of his car. It only took a moment to stuff Kristee and the furs inside. After that, he simply pushed the hamper through one of the loading bays and wheeled it up to the fur vault. No problem. As their security chief told me, they stop people from taking stuff *out* of the store, not people bringing stuff in. If Lilah hadn't started to wonder whether her furs had been put in storage, there's no telling how long that body might have stayed in there."

"Did Rich's announcing they're gonna close the downtown store have anything to do with the unfortunate discovery of that body?" Mac asked.

"Well, it couldn't have helped the perception in people's minds that downtown Atlanta is full of crime and criminals," I admitted. "But hell, that store's been going downhill for years. 'Course the closing broke Edna's heart. She and her cronies used to go there all the time for the chicken salad plate and fashion shows in the Magnolia Room."

"You think Collier really thought he'd get away with killing that girl and hiding the body?"

I shrugged. "He told the cops he planned all along to commit suicide, but first he had to complete his temple work, having Kristee baptized and then sealed to him in marriage."

"Spooky," Mac said.

"Yeah. I bet they never bring him to trial. And as long as they keep him locked up, that's fine with me."

"How's your mother feel about that?"

"You know Edna. She'd like to pull the switch herself. She claims she nearly *did* have a coronary when he grabbed her as she was leaving the house for her hair appointment. She claims he's putting on the crazy act to get away with it."

"Speaking of being locked up, when does Beemish go away?"

I took off the straw sun hat I was wearing and fanned my face with it. It was starting to get fairly hot out there on the water.

"I read in the *Constitution* that they're sending him down to that country-club federal prison camp at Eglin Air Force Base in Florida, for twelve to fifteen months."

"He got a sweet deal for ratting on Shaloub, didn't he?"

I propped myself up on my elbow again, the better to tan the back of my legs. "Yeah, but look what else happened to Beemish. His creditors took back the land at L'Arrondissement, he lost all his equity in it, and he paid a two-million-dollar fine. He's been publicly humiliated. Best of all, I heard from one of the sorority sisters that Lilah Rose was asked to step down as chairman of the Garden of Eden Ball. Sissy Alewine says she heard Lilah Rose is going to court to fight Big Mama, that's Bo's mother, for control of WDB Enterprises. That's one court fight I'd like to watch."

"Well, the courts can't do Lilah Rose any worse than they did Eddie Shaloub," Mac observed. "Eight years in a maximum security joint like Marion, Illinois, seems kind of harsh, if you ask me, considering the sentence Beemish got."

"Beemish wasn't an elected official," I retorted. "And he didn't pay those thugs to beat the shit out of me. Shaloub did."

"Are we harboring a personal grudge?" Mac asked teasingly.

"Yes, we are. Hey, did I tell you I got a call from Miss Inez?"

McAuliffe got a funny look on his face, as though he'd swallowed one of his fancy feathered flies. "Really?" he said innocently.

"Yeah. She finally got her room at the Idle Hours Comfort Care Home. They won't let her dip snuff, and she says they have cherry Jell-O three meals a day, but otherwise she loves it."

"That so?"

"Uh huh. She also said my friend Bubba came out to her trailer a couple weeks ago and told her he had a home for Katie, her goat. You know anything about that?"

Now it was Mac's turn to blush, under his tan. "It's no big thing. My brother's got a little farm in Conyers. He keeps some pigs and a cow, even got a mule. His kids were thrilled to add a goat to the collection."

I prodded him again with my toes. "You're a soft touch, McAuliffe."

He pulled his fishing hat down over his eyes. "Lean over this way a little bit more and do that again," he said. "The sight of you in that bathing suit of yours is a whole lot easier to look at than the rear end of Rufus."

© 2006 by Deborah Feingold

About the Author

MARY KAY ANDREWS is the *New York Times* bestselling author of nine novels, including *The Fixer Upper, Deep Dish, Blue Christmas, Savannah Breeze, Hissy Fit, Little Bitty Lies,* and *Savannah Blues*. A former journalist for the *Atlanta Journal-Constitution*, she lives in Atlanta, Georgia.

www.marykayandrews.com

BOOKS BY
Mary Kay Andrews

Inquisitive Atlanta cleaning lady—and former cop turned part-time P.I.—Callahan Garrity is on a course for adventure as she investigates mischief and murders in this original and witty mystery series by Mary Kay Andrews.

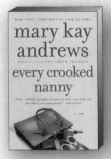

Every Crooked Nanny

Homemade Sin

To Live And Die In Dixie

Happy Never After

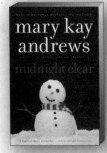

Midnight Clear

Strange Brew

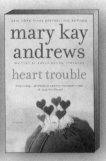

Heart Trouble

Irish Eyes

**Mary Kay Andrews Titles Are Available
in Paperback and eBook
Wherever Books Are Sold**

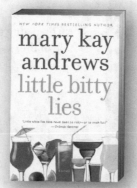

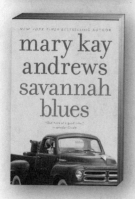

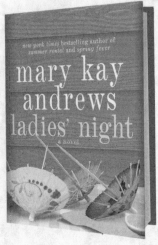